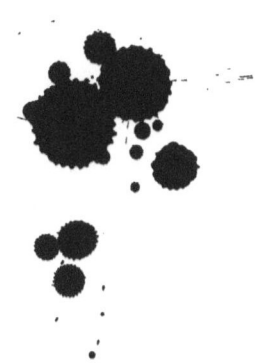

# SAAMAANTHAA

THE WOLFSHADOW TRILOGY | BOOK 1

FOR MY BOYS, WITHOUT A DOUBT.

# THE WOLFSHADOW TRILOGY

*Saamaanthaa*

*The Happening*

*Norm*

# OTHER WOLFSHADOW BOOKS

*Lupinia:*

*The Selected Poems*

*of Polly Drinkwater, 2007–2015*

## OTHER NOVELS

*Chosen*

*Suckage*

## NOVELLAS

*Relict*

*Summerville*

*The Day of the Nightfish*

THE WOLFSHADOW TRILOGY 1

# SAMANTHA

ADT NEAL

N*P

NOSETOUCH PRESS

CHICAGO | PITTSBURGH

Saamaanthaa
© 2011 by D.T. Neal
All Rights Reserved.

ISBN-13: 978-1-944286-00-2

Published by Nosetouch Press
Chicago, Illinois

www.dtneal.com | www.nosetouchpress.com

For more information, contact Nosetouch Press:
info@nosetouchpress.com

Cataloging-in-Publication Data
Names: Neal, D.T., author.
Title: Saamaanthaa
Description: Chicago, IL : Nosetouch Press [2011]
Identifiers: ISBN: 9781944286002 (paperback)
Subjects: LCSH: Horror—Fiction. | Paranormal—Fiction.
GSAFD: Horror fiction. | BISAC: FICTION / Horror.

Cover & interior design by Christine M. Scott
www.clevercrow.com

It's my stage. Everybody's eyes are on me. My thing. BacchUS is packed, 70 people, dressed like sheep. A sea of white, milling about, their own interpretations, watching me. A dozen in wool sweaters, dresses. A few in furry sheep suits. Sheeple. More than a few came in white, and still more are wearing knitted white woolen scarves. One guy stands there in black wool, with a "SHEEP" placard around his neck. A black sheep.

I'm dressed as Bo-Peep, zazzed up a little with industrial chic, wearing a black vinyl dress that pops out in a triangular shape, making me look like a groupie for Klaus Nomi. White thigh-high stockings, black lace-up platform boots (20-hole boots, a bitch to lace up, but so worth it), tight baby blue bodice, white bonnet, and a long, white shepherd's crook. I'm wearing fake eyelashes, and in the background, a projector shows news clippings while I speak:

### Coyote Loose in City: Mauls Woman's Dog in Lincoln Park–Authorities Investigate

"Little Blow-Peep has lost her sheep,
And doesn't know where to find them;
Leave them alone, And they'll come home,
Wagging their tails behind them."

Pictures flash, dead dog atop a car hood, in black and white, blood running down the otherwise pristine ragtop like chocolate sauce on a sundae. The old movies, isn't that what they used? Like chocolate sauce for blood?

"Little Blow-Peep fell fast asleep,
And dreamt she heard them bleating;
But when she awoke, she found it a joke,
For they were still a-fleeting."

## Man Attacked in Gold Coast by
## Unknown Assailant Dressed as "Furry"

Police sketch of malevolent fur-wearing attacker, wearing a helmet. The thing looks ghastly: big mouth, long claws, long ears, big eyes. The eyes are particularly dreadful, staring out at this canine mask of a face.

"Then up she took her little crook,
Determined for to find them;
She found them indeed, but it made her heart bleed,
For they'd left their tails behind them."

## Stray Wolf Chases Tourists Downtown–
## Lincoln Park Zoo Says None Got Out

Blurry photograph of something chasing a car. Lupine, jaws agape, running on all fours. Eyes like lantern lights. Even though blurry, there's a hint of something in them. Intelligence.

"It happened one day, as Blow-Peep did stray
Into a meadow hard by,
There she espied their tails side by side,
All hung on a tree to dry."

## Three Local Women Found Dead in
## Grisly Gold Coast Condominium Scene

Photograph of a friend of a friend's place. I know that place. Blood everywhere, but in black and white. It was soooooooooo much better in person.

Cameras rolling. Camcorders, webcams, cellphones. Video. Streaming. Rhymes with "screaming." Yes. While everybody in the audience is a participant, in a way, some are confederates, others are marks. Victims.

That's the point of it, isn't it? I take my crook and I hook the Black Sheep. Just perfect. Self-conscious, short-haired, he smiles, looks around, tries to act like he's cool with this, like he's in on the joke, that he's part of the performance. I can tell which ones are his friends, body language, scents.

But he's not in on the joke. I know, because I'm in on the joke. I'm the motherfucking punch line. I reel him in and speak softly in his face. He smiles, confident, cocksure. He reminds me of my dead friends.

Bye bye, Black Sheep.

I smile back at him, and then I split my skin.

# PART 1

"SOCIETY TAMES THE
WOLF INTO A DOG.
AND MAN IS THE
MOST DOMESTICATED
ANIMAL OF ALL."

— FRIEDRICH
NIETZSCHE

# 1. THURSDAY EVENING: 25 OCTOBER, 2007

"Samantha?" Polly said. "Hello in there?"

"Sorry," I said. "Just daydreaming."

We were in Fizzle, in Wicker Park, busy chilling in the milling, maddening crowd of hipsters and scenesters.

"Yeah," she said, smiling widely, her red lips bright against her pale face. Reagan walked over to us, hugging herself.

"Lee's STILL going on about live performance as the crucible of the Rock Magisterium, and why, exactly, this matters," she said. "Good lord, the energy that man expends on his nonsense. Save me from pop culture."

"Pop culture is an oxymoron," Polly said. "Pop culture is an infection."

Reagan looked conservatively fetching in a Burberry skirt and a maroon turtleneck sweater, black hose and loafers. She got another chardonnay, perched opposite of Polly, putting little me in the middle.

"What's the cure?" I asked.

"Art, of course," Polly said. "Bringing fine art to the masses."

"Lee says 'the masses are asses,'" I said.

We all felt Lee hated to be counted among the human race, saw himself as something of a demigod, exiled to a life among the mortals, the hoi polloi.

"The masses will drown us," Polly said. "They dilute culture into camp, art into kitsch, kitsch into lowbrow, lowbrow into no-brow."

Reagan scoffed. "Kitsch" was a four-letter word in our ranks.

"Art must be utterly without compromise," Reagan said. "For the greatest impact."

"Art must be the chrome cleaner for the trailer hitch of society," I said, prompting Polly to snort wine and Reagan to eye me slyly.

"I think young Samantha's having a bit of sport with us, Polly," she said. "But truly, Samantha, we are an evolutionary vanguard. We swim upstream, fight the currents, the dreadful lethargy of postmodernity."

Another four-letter word for Reagan: "postmodern." Her cheeks flushed at the outrage of it, and her wine slurred in her glass.

"We are the point of the spear," she said.

"The canaries in the coal mine?" I asked.

The other two didn't like that image so much, but their self-seriousness made me want to laugh at them. I loved them, sure, but they could be really silly at times.

"We're at war," Polly said. "At war with the mundane, the boring, the mediocre, the dreary, the unimaginative, the ignorant—these are our artless enemies, and our art is our weapon."

Polly was into her wine, and she got feisty when she'd had a few. Feisty and flirty-horny, depending on the length of the evening.

"Pop culture is the disease. And we are the cure," Reagan said.

That made me laugh. "We're the artful antibiotics to society's syphilis?"

"Something like that," Polly said, wrinkling her pointy little nose.

"But not enough people see our work for it to make a difference," I said, glancing at Lee, Sheldon, Willa, and Gabe continuing their discussion at their table. Clay was circulating, chatting up some women. "Our work doesn't do anybody any good if nobody sees it."

"That is the eternal tradeoff," Polly said. "Accessibility versus integrity—the purity of your vision contrasted with the expectations of the audience. Impact gets diluted if you water down content for wider acceptance. Let me be inaccessible, my message pure."

I wondered what Polly's message was, beyond "Look. At. Me."

"The artist should create only for herself," Reagan said. "Or for other artists. That's the only way to keep on top of her game. To create for the audience is to pander, which, to extend Samantha's analogy, is like a placebo, instead of the actual medicine needed."

"Sugar pills might be sweet going down," Polly said, "but they do nobody any good. We don't want to be sugar pills, Sam."

"Right," I said. "We need wider exposure. No offense to Clay, but BacchUS is so small. Nobody goes there but us. That gallery is more about him than about anything else."

I think they recruited me into their ranks as a way of bringing in fresh blood, new ideas. Maybe they didn't value my ideas, but at least I was into action, versus just hunkering down in the BacchUS bunker.

"What do you suggest, Sam?" Reagan asked.

"Something insurrectionary," I said. "Something out there. How about an Artmobile? A traveling museum?"

Polly laughed. "What, like a school bus?"

"Sure," I said. "We could take out most of the seats, put stuff on display inside it. A roving gallery and performance space."

Reagan laughed. "How sinfully lowbrow!"

"I don't think anybody can drive a bus," Polly said. "We'd probably need permits."

"Yeah, but the exposure would be good," I said. "And the imagery of the school bus, I like that—like you're talking about schooling people, basically, and this would make it, you know, explicit."

"I doubt the others would go for it," Polly said, glancing at the others.

"Well, they're all lame," I said. Reagan laughed.

"It's too hippie-ish," Polly said. "Electric Kool-Aid, Merry Pranksters in a Magic Bus. Lee would never go for it."

Always with Lee, ringmaster in our little one-ring circus. And Polly, who I was sure wouldn't go for something as gauche as a rolling gallery, but unwilling to go out on a limb and say that flat out.

"It would be a carnival on wheels," I said. "We could make it magical."

Reagan patted my arm. "Keep thinking, Samantha. We value your contributions."

"Mmm," I said. They were always talking insurrection and artistic revolution, but nobody ever DID anything.

"Forget bricks-and-mortar, Sam," Polly said. "We should just create a virtual gallery. That would be far easier. Widest reach, lowest cost."

Reagan didn't like that. "It's so sterile, clinical. It's not the same as sharing a room with a painting or a poet. Attending a reading or a showing requires more volition than the click of a mouse."

I laughed, having shared enough rooms with poets to know how that felt. I couldn't imagine them saying the lines into a webcam, like that working at all.

"What's funny?" Polly asked.

"You're talking about being at the point of the spear, right? So, that means getting out there," I said. "Any way you can. Being seen, being ostentatious. But you guys all look like norms—classy, yeah, but totally middle-to-upper middle class. Bourgeois."

Another four-letter word. Polly and Reagan actually gazed at me open-mouthed, incredulous.

"Sam," Polly said. "We're not bourgeois! We're avant-garde."

"Mmmultimedia is where it's at. You guys are all embracing fine art, but are stuck in classical modes of expression. It's like somebody today mastering the blues—it becomes a technical exercise, versus, you know, something groundbreaking. Like where do you go from where you're at?"

"You mean what's our oeuvre?" Polly asked. "We all have our areas of expertise and excellence, Sam. I'm not sure what you're driving at. I've lost you."

It drove me bananas how Polly would say she lost me, putting herself in the mental driver's seat, even though she was the one who was confused. Most people would say "You've lost me," but her ego prevented her from admitting that, so she lost you, not the other way around. Grrr.

"I'm saying that by confining yourselves to old media, you're being technicians, not artists," I said. "Craftspeople and artisans."

I wanted to call them dilettantes, but that would just make them mad. Another four-letter word in their dyslexicon.

"There's always new ground to be covered, Samantha," Reagan said. "Even with old media. New approaches, materials, techniques."

"But nobody in our group is doing it," I said. "Your work is competently New Realist, laced with Expressionism. But New Realism is, what, 40 years old, now? It's not new, anymore. No offense."

"None taken," Reagan said.

"Oh, don't listen to her, Reagan," Polly said. "We're talking about somebody who once wore a tinfoil bikini."

She was talking about "Funicellist," a piece I did at the lakeshore last year, where I channeled Annette Funicello with a borrowed cello, did a performance on the beach. My folks had made me learn an instrument in middle school and high school, so I'd picked cello, because it was inconvenient and costly. I could actually play. Anyway, that was one of the pieces that I'd posted on the Net, me wearing a bouffant wig and playing "Pipeline" by The Chantays on cello in a bikini I'd fashioned out of aluminum foil, before running into the lake, disappearing from view with a splash.

My friend Martin had filmed it, so it looked good on camera, although in person, it kind of didn't work so well, judging from how the others received it. Lee had suggested that I do it in a green wig, so I'd look like an alien babe from the old Star Trek show. He'd sent me a picture of her, and I didn't think that would've worked at all. It was always ironic to me how Lee, who always bragged about not having a television, would always reference old shows from the 50s, 60s, and 70s—he HAD watched television at some point in his life, just not for a long time. It was such a point of pride for him, you'd think not watching television actually meant something, like he'd discovered something new, cured a disease.

"You think I should try new modes of expression?" Reagan asked.

"Sure," I said. "Just see what happens."

"Painting isn't performance art," Polly said.

"It could be," I said.

Reagan nodded. "Curious perspective, Samantha. Although I can only paint how I paint, what feels right, what inspires me."

"But maybe what feels right can change, in time."

Polly laughed. "Tastes change, but style endures. This is art, not fashion."

"All the more reason to hit hard as you can," I said. "Art isn't something you put on in the morning, like makeup, Polly; you have to live it."

I didn't know what else to say, so I drank my beer, while Polly pouted. She was her own muse—she was always talking about muses, but I think it always came back to herself. It made me want to do a piece wearing a bodysuit covered in mirrors, and then to put myself in a mirrored coffin, with lights above and below, or some way of offering illumination. Maybe Christmas lights. Watch myself vanish in a sarcophagus of mirrors. If everything was reflecting everything else, then there'd be no ME. Nothing inside. God, if only I had the money for the projects in my head. Or access to a junkyard.

"Speaking of makeup," Polly said, setting her emptied wineglass on the counter. "I need to put on my lipstick again. See you in a bit, girls."

She strutted off, leaving Reagan and me at the bar. I glanced at Lee, who appeared to be arguing with Willa. It was just a heated discussion. I wished that I could read lips, so I could see what they were talking about. Probably whether forming a cover band that covered tunes nobody actually knew could be considered a cover band at all, or whether they could pass off as original.

"I like your thoughts," Reagan said. "We need more of that, Samantha."

"I had an idea, watching Polly," I said. "A mirrored coffin, or a small room, and an occupant with a mirrored suit, and lighting at the top and bottom. Somewhere, but indirect, I think, ambient."

"Nice," Reagan said. "The occupant might be invisible."

"Maybe I'll make a model version of it," I said. "Something small, see how it looks."

"Also nice," Reagan said. "What would you call it?"

"How about 'Narcissa?'" I asked.

Reagan smiled. "I think it was 'Narcissus' who had that eponymous affliction," Reagan said. "A lad, not a lass."

"Yes, but I had a girl in mind," I said. "Artistic license."

"Touché," Reagan said, raising her glass to me, taking a drink. "You're trying to give Plato a run for his money, you know, with your poet-bashing these days."

"I just don't see why they should be our social catbirds," I said. "They hardly produce anything. We're busy busting our asses, and they just, you know, talk."

Reagan graced me with a long-suffering smile, like the sorceress addressing her uncomprehending apprentice.

"It's all they have," she said. "Words are all poets have got."

"You're more merciful than me, Reagan," I said, and got another beer, and she got another wine. "Should we rejoin the others? Looks like Lee's running out of breath."

Lee sauntered up. "What are words for, when no one listens anymore?"

"Missing Persons," I said. Lee sometimes liked to drop lyrics our way, a bit of a pop culture quiz. He was always quizzing everybody.

"Let me buy you another beer, Sam," he said. "Are we boring you ladies?"

"Not at all," Reagan said. "We just needed a breath of fresh air; you were sucking up all of the air in the room."

"And I suppose you don't think The Who are the greatest Rock band of all time?" Lee asked.

"I wouldn't know," Reagan said. "I adore Mahler and Wagner."

"Ah, yes," Lee said. "Classical to a fault. But they are. The Who, I mean. Do you want to know why?"

Reagan treated Lee to a patronizing smile. "I have a feeling you're about to tell me, Lee."

At this point, the others had followed Lee's lead, had drifted around us at the bar, enfolding us in a hipster semi-circle, and Lee, seeing his audience, cleared his throat and commenced, as if he hadn't already been arguing this before.

"My doubting friends, The Who is the greatest Rock band that ever was, or ever will be," Lee said. This was like a throw of the hipster gauntlet.

"Beg to differ," Sheldon said. "Rolling Stones, hello?"

Nobody would say the Beatles; they were Pop, and only people who didn't rock would have called them a Rock band. Maybe when they were the Silver Beatles, maybe then they were a Rock-n-Roll band, but a Rock band, another matter, entirely.

"The Who? Fuck them," Clay said. "Loudest band, yeah, but best? Explain."

This was such a boys' debate; the rest of us just drank our drinks and kept our heads down, although I paid attention, just because I liked music, and wanted to see where Lee was planning to go with it.

"The Who are such a GUY band," Willa said, rolling her eyes. She liked to play with the boys, liked to pretend she was the only girl in our group, like the rest of us weren't there, since we were all prettier than she was, even if we probably weren't smarter.

"True," Lee said. "But let me get to that later. They are the best Rock band for a variety of reasons: First, they played better live than any band—that's not even a debating point. Like all bands aspire to play as well live as the Who did. In fact, the Who sounded better live than most bands do in studio. That alone earns them that honorific, but it doesn't stop there."

Lee held up another finger, his middle finger. "Second, they were a leaderless band—that's the key to their glory. Pete Townshend wrote most of the songs, but Roger Daltrey tried to be their leader early on, tried to make them an R&B cover band, and the others rebelled, and so what you ended up was four guys all trying, in their own way, to upstage each other three. A war of all against all, right onstage."

"How does that make them any good?" Sheldon asked. "Sounds like a recipe for disaster."

"Because they were at each other's throats early on, the savagery of their approach came out in the music," Lee said. "Pure power, raw energy. Daltrey's leather lungs versus Moon's manic drumming versus Townshend's rhythmic windmilling versus Entwistle's percussive, melodic bass, all of them fighting each other for supremacy onstage, becoming this animal Rock monstrosity that took you in its jaws and shook you until you were drained and spent. And that brings me to my next point."

The image of the animal monster onstage stuck with me, this Rock monster Lee had conjured up in The Who.

"Third, they did everything wrong—at least in the sense that they broke all of the rules for what a band should be, and who a band should be, how they should behave."

"The Who's who," Polly said, laughing, returning to the fold, lipsticked and ravishing, her grin a slash of bright red, like maraschino cherries.

"I wish they'd make Who Cares, a retrospective compilation," Clay said.

Lee didn't like being interrupted, waved Clay away like a wizard banishing evil spirits. "What I'm saying is they went at it differently than other bands: Townshend couldn't match Crapton or Beck or Page as a straight-up iconic British guitar god. Most players would have given up, but Townshend came up with another angle of attack: rhythm-as-lead. Townshend came up with his signature style of play that completely changed the role of the guitarist in a band. And because he was busy doing that, Entwistle was called upon to pick up the lion's share of the melody with his fucking bass. So, you have a rhythmic guitarist matched with a melodic bassist, and then, you throw in a drummer who didn't play drums right—Moon had his own unique style of drumming, completely at odds with everything sane drummers should do: Moon wouldn't keep the beat, but instead, treated his drums as a lead instrument, filling Who songs with waves of percussion, like storms of sound, angular fills that rose and fell like ocean waves. And just so he could be heard over all the noise, Daltrey came up with his scream-singing. I mean, he could carry a tune, but nobody would say his singing was a delicate thing."

"Crapton?" Clay said. "You mean Clapton."

"I mean Crapton," Lee said. "I'm not a fan of his. Bluesman, my ass."

Lee took a drink of his wine, clearly enjoying that we were all paying attention to him. This was always his element, monologue-in-lieu-of-conversation, him holding the stage, the rest of us his rapt audience, some pop cultural Socrates he was, schooling us.

"So, they're all doing it wrong," he said. "They're breaking all the rules. Nobody's doing what they're supposed to be doing—but it works, and it works fucking well. And what's more, they, and especially Pete—crank up the volume, so the attack is made still more savage, like a fist in the face. They could have played it straight, but they went for the brutality of volume. The noise is incredible, unrelenting, impossible to ignore. And because they're a singles band, they're forced to go out and earn their bones, night after night, onstage—they perfect their performance chops on endless live circuits, honing their edge, learning right away what works and doesn't, because they're getting feedback from the audience as they go. They become masters of the stage, the world's greatest live Rock band. Power Pop personified. And I'm not even throwing in their auto-destructive antics, the smashing of guitars and drums, the demolition of hotels, the violence of their shows, which is what the norms fixate on when they think of The Who, playing loud and breaking instruments. They're more than that—any decent Rock band, any band worth the name 'Rock band' has studied The Who. Any band that wants to be top-notch should emulate The Who from about 1966–73: that's the textbook course in Perfect Rock Band 101."

"That's your opinion," Clay said.

"No," Lee said. "That is fact. The Who are, without question, the all-time greatest Rock band that ever was. I'd put Led Zeppelin as second to them. Of course, they were a unique monster—there was Townshend, Daltrey, Entwistle, and Moon, and there was the Who—that was the fifth member of the band, a gestalt organism that far exceeded the individual parts, and when fed live audiences, when put onstage, they killed, again and again and again."

"Like Voltron," Sheldon said.

"Not like goddamned Voltron," Lee said. "The Who could destroy Voltron with a single power chord."

My hands sweated, Lee's imagery, the killing, the feeding, the audiences, densely packed and deafened. It was evocative, persuasive in the way Lee could hold a moment in his hand, purely through his oration, his dulcet tones. A poet born, his voice was his instrument, his words, his music. He was persuasive. It made me want to listen to some Who albums. On vinyl, of course.

"I disagree," Sheldon said. "There are plenty of better bands out there."

"No," Lee said. "They're all wannabes. The Who are the gold standard of Rock excellence. Everything people THINK they know about Rock, the ones who don't know their Rock—well, it's all wrong. Everybody who GETS Rock understands The Who, venerates The Who, worships The Who."

"Rock? The Stones—" Sheldon said, but Lee cut him off.

"The Who made the Stones their bitches in 1968," Lee said. "The Rock'n'Roll Circus, their movie, intended to showcase the Stones, where they invited these other bands to open for them. They fucked up, invited The Who—Number One Rule in '60s Rock: NEVER follow The Who. The Who owned it, completely out-performed every other band on that movie, and so shell-shocked Jagger and Richards that: 1) they wouldn't release that movie for ~25 years, and 2) they cancelled plans for a tour with the Who. Owned. Now, The Stones are good for people who want to feel cool about rocking, they're a cool band to like: the bad boy thing, all of that; they're a cult of personality, not unlike the New York Dolls, who took a page or two from The Stones. But if you are a true connoisseur of Rock, are deadly-serious about rocking, of kicking absolutely everybody's ass onstage, then The Who are who you MUST turn to. You must learn from them, study them, live them, love them."

He paused, drank some more wine, clearly satisfied with himself, while the rest of us fidgeted. Lee looked at each of us in turn, with amusement in his eyes.

"Sounds like you put a lot of thought into this," Willa said, sneering into her wine glass.

"They never had as good an album as the Beatles," Polly said.

"Fuck the Beatles," Lee said. "And fuck albums. The Who sound was simply too big to capture on tape. It was too wild, too powerful. Only by actually being there could you possibly experience it. The Mods knew; it was the ultimate scene. The tape record only hints at the power, and even then, it's amazing."

"That's just it," Clay said. "You weren't there, man. You're talking out of your ass, as usual."

"You'd almost think he'd been in a band," Sheldon said. "Or that he knew shit about music."

"True," Lee said. "But I am an inductive Rock autodidact, and I tell you, my words are true. They're demonstrable. If you took three new bands, had them model their style after The Beatles, The Stones, and The Who, I guarantee that the first two bands would suck ass, and the third band would rock. The first two would sound like pale imitations, but the third band would rock, and they would rock like gods, because you can't really sound like The Who; but you can take their approach, their sonic attack, and make it your own."

"It's Lee's Rock Laboratory," Polly said. "Mad scientician of Rock!"

"Rock Apostle," Sheldon said. "I disbelieve. But serious, what about Led Zeppelin?"

"Zeppelin are great," Lee said. "But I've yet to hear any live clip of Zep that comes close to The Who live. Page was a session man, a production wizard—a guitar god, for sure. Their studio albums are better, I'll concede that, but that was the problem; their live stuff never sounded as good as their studio work. Keith Moon actually named Led Zeppelin, as a joke. And I'm sure that Zeppelin tried in their way to out-Who The Who, out-Beatles The Beatles, and out-Stones The Stones. The Who actually sounded better live."

"Didn't Jimmy Page play guitar on some Who singles?" Clay asked.

"Page played on everybody's stuff before he went out on his own," Lee said. "But he wasn't onstage with The Who when they were kicking everybody in the teeth."

"What about that cool using-a-violin-bow-with-the-guitar thing?" Sheldon said.

"The Creation did it first," Lee said. "Eddie Phillips did it, although everybody thinks it was Page, just because more people saw Zeppelin, and because people are stupid."

Lee could go on all night with his Rock scholarship, so I slipped out of the dilettante mosh with a turn and got the bartender's eye. Polly edged close to me.

"Guess he forgot his Ritalin tonight," she said, ordered another glass of red wine. I got another beer, felt like a lesbian. I couldn't help that I liked beer.

"So, how's, you know, Tristan?" I asked, trying to sound casual about her never-there husband, the Company Man™ who was always using frequent flier miles to circumnavigate the globe, making the world safe for free enterprise, and comfortable for Polly.

"Great," Polly said. "I want to make a poem out of him."

"Why haven't you?"

Polly gave me a wicked little candy apple-red pin-up grin. "We've been way too busy. I barely have time to think. I have some idea in my head."

How would Tristan would take something like that? I could just see him sitting, listening to Polly throw poetry at him. Would he even be touched? I imagined Polly in a red velvet minidress, Tristan shirt-less, close-cropped and gym-fit, and her quoting her poem to him…

Company Man
Jet-set martinet
My stratospheric swain!
Reckless ambition
And market-led contrition
Let me open up my veins…

"What's funny?" Polly asked, looking into my eyes, like she'd find the answer there.

Reagan touched my elbow, smiled, glanced at her watch. "This has all been so enlightening, to be sure. I'll probably just say my goodbyes; Gretta's likely home by now. She had midterms."

"Alright," I said, when I got my beer, getting ready to turn and face Lee's words again. "Let's reenter the fray."

Lee didn't miss a beat as we turned back around. He looked up at me, insouciant as ever.

"Right, Sam?" he said.

"Right about what?" I asked, foolishly.

"Right about now," Lee said. "We should go someplace else."

"Yeah," I said. "Totally. This place blows."

Lee was satisfied, we left Fizzle, headed to Vertigo.

Vertigo was a dead place, full of norms—sheeple and zombies. I knew it the last time we were there, the way Lee held his PBR in his hand, the lazy cant of the bottle; I knew it was finished: Lee was already bored.

We called ourselves "Horrorshow"—a phonetic expression of Russian "khorosho," for "good." Lee had remembered it from *A Clockwork Orange*, had liked it, thought it signified on many levels—we were good, we were cultural, we liked Russian writers, we were revolution-aries, we were subversives. We were the Horrorshow, an art collective. Plus, it looked great on handbills that advertised our happenings.

Not that I didn't agree with Lee's assessment of Vertigo. There was a point of no return for anything, and the key was jumping ship before you got there. It was like surfing, or what I imagined surfing would be, like riding one wave to its inevitable conclusion, before paddling out and finding another. Such a mundane analogy, one I'd only share with the inside of my head, or maybe on my blog, but never with my friends.

My friends were my everything: my Reagan, my Polly, my Lee, my Sheldon, my Clay, my Gabe, my Willa. Well, not Willa. Willa was more enemy than friend, and she inflicted herself on us because of her long association with Lee, going back to their graduate school days. All roads led to Lee, or that's how I saw it, and I know that's how he saw it.

I'm not going to go into an extended biography of everybody, because you didn't know them, and they're all mostly dead, now, anyway, so who cares who they were? What matters is who I am, or who I was, anyway.

What matters—WHO matters, is me. I'm Samantha Hain. My friends call me Sam; Lee would call me "Samhain," which would have Willa sniping about him mispronouncing "Samhain." Willa would never call me Sam because we were never friends; she'd call me Samantha. I knew she was doing it to be snotty, to get on my nerves.

At 28, I'm supposed to be above such reindeer games, but nobody in our group ever was. We were artists. Or we THOUGHT we were artists—I didn't realize that back then. I think I'm the only true artist of the bunch; the rest of them were pretenders. Maybe not Reagan. She had something, a bit of a shine to her.

Here's what I think: artists are monsters, which is why so few people are actually artists, and why so many only pretend to be. Only norms think monsters are bad; you can almost hear the sheeple bleating about it, like afraid that there's a monster coming to get them, that they've got to drive the monster away with pitchforks and torches. Fuck them and their microwaved meals and their living room living, and their pedestrian, strip mall, outlet store ways. Let them cower in their televisionary caves, and let the monsters roam wild in the streets. That's the way it should be. Leave artful things to artists, monstrous things to monsters, and leave sheepish things to sheeple, who fret in our hulking shadows. But I'm getting way ahead of myself.

Back in the day, we all saw ourselves as this elite group, the Horrorshow. Lee Smathers was a published poet, who had taken his handful of publishing credits as an excuse to do nothing ever since. He was blonde-haired and black-hearted, given to a brooding baritone and a dapper style that called to mind a lapsed socialist: olive-drab chinos and sweater vests, running slender poet's fingers through his mane of hipster hair. Lee cared nothing about everything, and it showed in the upraised brow and his affected lack of affect.

And so, it was us at Vertigo, in a contemptuous circle, our backs to the other patrons, our own exclusive club, pretending Chicago was Paris; itself, a statement, a performance, a final kiss-off orchestrated by Lee. We would discuss weighty matters, and the patrons would know that giants sat among them.

Sheldon Carter led the attack. Sheldon was the visual artist and resident Joyce scholar. He had a bit of a 50s Jackson Pollock vibe to him, wore Buddy Holly glasses and velvet blazers, took pages from Joyce and glued them to matte boards splashed with paint, called it art and was fond of vintage electronics and vacuum tubes, but would squint in irritation if he was termed a "buff" or a "hobbyist." Sheldon chain-smoked, and made each cigarette seem like a worldly burden that would've cracked the shoulders of Atlas. He mastered a restive, pacing stride, and was losing his hair. His wit was preternaturally quick, his voice was perennially steady, yet his nerves were perpetually frayed.

"I think all the brave Frenchmen died at Waterloo," he said. "The seeds of their disgrace in World War II were sown at Waterloo, as natural selection saw the depletion of French valor in Napoleon's campaigns."

Sheldon was always staking out odd positions, digging himself in and being, at least in his mind, inflammatory and intellectual. The more whacked-out his stance, the more he'd dig in. He was a staunch advocate of intellectual trench warfare.

Clay Potts had his own approach. Clay was our resident alpha male-in-training, with a leathern face and studied metrosexual styling; he made his way through professional women, a kind of hipster gigolo, fond of fat pinstripes and designer jeans and champagne breakfasts and tantric foot massages—he considered the women he graced with his presence to be his patrons, in the finest of Renaissance traditions. His art was commerce, a keen understanding of the gallery business, at least in his own mind. He rented his own gallery, where he would feature the works of Mr. Carter and Ms. Whitehouse, and would host poetry readings by Ms. Drinkwater and Ms. Powers and

Ms. Whitehouse. He'd host wine-tasting parties at his gallery, because he had a Dionysian relationship with the spirit. He even called his gallery BacchUS, in the god's honor.

"That's retarded," Clay said.

"No," Sheldon said. "I call it sociological selection. The sociological tendencies of a given group are played out that way. For example, the most ideologically-committed Nazis were probably the likeliest to die for the cause, thereby taking themselves out of the gene pool."

"Preposterous," Clay said.

Reagan Whitehouse took her turn. Reagan was my best friend among the Horrorshow. Though a Classicist at heart, Modernist to the bone, Reagan was our resident Epicurean, all appetites and Amazonian curves. While Polly and Willa competed for the anorexic honorific of skinniest chick, Reagan was more Valkyrie than vixen, broad-hipped and -shouldered, with matronly thighs that called to mind a blonde Wonder Woman. Pint-sized pixie that I was, I was definitely not in the game of alpha female, but could easily see Reagan assuming that position, if only through her statuesque bearing that would've made Pygmalion proud, to say nothing of her wit and intelligence, which were, along with her unfailing grace, her deadliest weapons. And yet, I could easily imagine young Reagan playing field hockey in a navy blue pleated skirt, throwing shoulders, knocking her opponents flat.

Reagan offset her heroic dimensions with stately infusions of preppy plaid and ballet slippers and Mahler, whom she worshipped, along with James Joyce. Reagan came from Old Money along the East Coast, which gave her some cred in our ranks. She was our resident blonde cultural maven, with writing, poetry, and painting as her three areas of specialty. Lee called her a dilettante, but it was precisely that cultural trifecta which gave her prominence in our group. That, and she cooked, which was a useful craft. She played hipster den mother to us all, bringing us sustenance at odd times, different arcane recipes she'd dredged up from somewhere; nothing she cooked was ever simple, or easy.

"I would think you'd need some data to back that up, Sheldon," Reagan said.

"The Shakers," Lee said. "Weren't they so virulently anti-sex that they became extinct?"

"Nearly extinct," Clay said. "I think there are still Shakers out there."

"But not original ones," Lee said. "I mean, they couldn't have kids. I think there are only four actual Shakers left in the world today."

I didn't know Shakers from Quakers, just kept quiet when they were going on like this.

Gabe Burns tried his own line of attack. Gabe saw himself as an undiscovered literary legend, though what he'd written could only be called dismal by those privy to it (he hadn't let me read his work, but people who had had talked, in furtive grimaces and painful winces). He dressed like the professor he wasn't, with dark brown corduroy as his favored fabric and hue, and to his credit, he was the first of the boys to sport a beard—a Satanic chin beard, which gave him points for being ahead of the curve, I suppose, though his nasally, lazily-affected West Coast drawl and lethargic manner required him to express only scorn for trend-whoring. He looked like an agnostic Trotskyite, perhaps recently converted to neoconservatism, already plotting the overthrow of another hapless Third World government.

"I don't know, I think Shel may be onto something," Gabe said. "The ideas you hold must influence the way you live, and if you live. The more virulent an idea, the less likely it is to continue. If I advocated a philosophy where I killed everybody I didn't like, well, either I'd end up a menace to society, and would be locked away and/or executed; or else I'd run into somebody else who was tougher and they'd kill me. Either way, I'm out of the gene pool."

"Kill or be killed," Clay said. "That's what you're saying."

"More like kill AND be killed," Gabe said. "The categorical imperative rules from the shadows."

Lee scoffed. "You Kant be serious."

I had heard Lee say that enough times to know what he was really saying.

"What about 'Live and Let Live?'" Reagan asked. "Isn't that a better axiom to live by?"

"Certainly," Gabe said. "It has demonstrative survival value. Like the Christmas Truce of 1914, during World War I."

"'Kill or be Killed' is a death sentence," I said, immediately regretting saying it, because they all paused and looked at me like I was an idiot. Then Reagan laughed, like I'd made a joke. But I'd been serious. I wasn't punning!

"Funny, Samantha," she said.

Willa Powers was next. Willa was a poet, but her specialty was the dissection of language—she was the empress of olive drab, had managed to corner the market on every shade and permutation of muted colors she could find, from rust red to mustard yellow and ash grey, and wore terribly clunky buckled shoes that only accentuated her matchstick legs. Willa had a cat she loved, named it James, and doted on the thing, in the cryptlike apartment she and the dark tabby shared. Willa did nothing to adorn her dwelling, seemed to think decoration was, I don't know, a nod to the material world, a blow to transcendence. Willa was an ascetic, I think, trading in worldly pleasures with her own self-denial, measuring the passing of her days with the notches of her belt, drawing it in ever tighter. Willa loved Lee, though to admit to that would be something she'd die before doing, though we all knew she adored him. As if to punish herself (and Lee) for the hold he had over her, she tried to be combative with him whenever she could, to challenge him as a way of defining herself.

"I don't think it's funny," Willa said. "I think it's stupid. The ideas you hold determine how you live, and whether you live. It's why cannibalism isn't widespread."

"Not yet," Lee said.

"A society of cannibals is an impossibility, because the nature of cannibalism undermines the social nature of humanity. People are sheep, and can't tolerate something as willfully antisocial as cannibalism."

"Exactly," Sheldon said. "It proves my point—sociological selection."

"Unless there was an in-group and an out-group," Gabe said. "What if there was a selected group that could be predated upon? Then you could have a society of cannibals; they just wouldn't eat each other."

"Exocannibalism," Lee said. "That's what you're talking about."

"Ewww," I said.

"Adds a whole new meaning to 'eating out,' don't you think?" Gabe said. They laughed, except Willa, who rolled her eyes and shrugged. She hated quips and puns.

"This plays into a master morality and a slave morality," Clay said. He was always, always trying to bring Nietzsche into it. Always. That was his area of self-professed expertise. But Reagan cut him off at the knees.

"The masters can't eat the slaves," Reagan said. "In so doing, they undermine their own society. The masters in a master moralistic world are more dependent on their slaves than if they did things themselves. Masters need the slaves; slaves don't need the masters."

"Tautology already?" Lee asked, yawning into his hand.

"I'm saying that a master morality requires the subjugation of another people for it to even exist," Reagan said. "Take away the slaves, and you have no masters."

"Slaves are those who allow themselves to be enslaved," Clay said. "Who permit themselves to be mastered."

This is how it always went with our group. It always went like this.

"Now he's about to blame the Holocaust on the Jews," Willa said.

"I didn't say that," Clay said. "But the religious beliefs of the majority of the victims of the Holocaust did play a part in their deaths. The Judeo-Christian ethic is, by definition, a slave morality—it elevates suffering into a virtue, favors meekness and submission."

"Well, duh," Willa said. "They were Jews, for God's sake. They knew suffering."

"Yes," Clay said. "But the majority of the victims were practicing, orthodox Jews."

"More obvious targets," Lee said. "They stood out more."

"I'm saying their belief is what got them killed," Clay said. "Their faith, it had them more focused on the afterlife than this life. Of course this life was about suffering, pain, and death. If you believe death is your ticket to Paradise, why bother living at all? Why fight the inevitability of suffering, pain, and strife in this life?"

"Emancipatory metanarratives," Gabe said, shaking his head. I didn't even know what the hell that was, but from the smug look on his face, Gabe sure did. He stroked his beard, looked every bit the part of the professor who'd gladly sleep with his students.

They were really rolling, these friends of mine. I often wondered what they could achieve if they actually put their brains to work on something other than intellectual posturing.

"I don't think we're supposed to talk about this," I said.

"Oooh, yeah," Lee said, making a mock afraid face. "Too much for you, Sam?"

"I just don't think we should," I said.

"It precisely validates my point," Sheldon said. "The belief system determines life or death, one's evolutionary chances."

"What, that the French became cowards because the Napoleonic Wars sacrificed their most valorous numbers in battle?" Lee said.

"That assumes that they hadn't had children, that they were killed before they could breed."

Reagan spoke up: "Couldn't you also argue that the Jews that survived the Holocaust were correspondingly the most ruthless, dangerous, and opportunistic? I mean, couldn't you invert your master/slave morality, Clay, and say that survival is itself the measure of mastery of one's environment? Are all victims created equal? Seems like in the moral abyss of the concentration camp, being peaceful, benevolent, compassionate, and generous would almost guarantee your demise."

Sheldon steepled his fingers, reflective. I didn't even want to think about concentration camps, but with our group, any protestation would almost guarantee me to be a norm, a weakling, a mundane. So, I kept mum.

"If the Nazis were a selection factor on Jews," Gabe said. "Then, by Sheldon's yardstick, the Jews who survived were the fittest of the Jews—either physically the hardiest, or socially the most cunning, enterprising, intelligent, and/or ruthless. Perhaps all of the above."

Sheldon held up his hands. "I'm just saying, human nature is at least in part socially derived—we like to think we've somehow beaten evolution, but have we really? Maybe our social evolution is part of the overall process. In fact, I'm sure of it."

It was Polly's turn. She nursed her glass of red wine, her ever-present elixir.

Polly Drinkwater was another poet, though I'd consider her a poetess, because she wore her poetry on the cupid's bow of her lips, in her impeccable fashions, her ludicrous runway walk and 1920s looks—she looked like a flapper, with this cutesy-cute little curlicued brunette hairdo and her big eyes and her scarves and her endless, mincing ways. Polly flirted with most of the men, but had the most fondness for Sheldon, who she had deemed a worthy among worthies, given his artful pretensions and Beatnik stylings. Which was odd to me that she would hold such views at all, because she was married. This was something not lost on the rest of us, although we never saw Mr. Tristan Drinkwater, who traveled more than he sat still. His success is what freed up Polly to practice poetry, when she wasn't slumming it at a law office. She was the most prolific among the poets, writing early and writing often, and telling us about her latest work whether we asked her or not. She mostly self-published.

"Can we talk about something else?" Polly asked. "This is too grim and unbeautiful."

"Not at all," Gabe said. "I like it."

"Sheldon, it sounds like you're just projecting a stereotype, buttressed by fallacy," Reagan said.

"It's not fallacious," Sheldon said. "Just as the art a culture makes is reflective of the culture's priorities, so are the decisions a culture makes reflective of its people's evolutionary success or failure. For example, America leads the First World in infant mortality."

"Dead babies," Lee said, humming the melody from the Alice Cooper tune of the same name. Willa smiled, although I highly doubted she ever listened to Alice Cooper.

"So?" Clay said.

"Well," Sheldon said. "That's, what, 28,000 or so children snuffed out each year, never given a chance to live."

"People die all the time," Gabe said. "More people die on the roads every year."

"Also reflective of cultural norms," Sheldon said. "One could infer from our high infant mortality rate that the well-being of children isn't a terribly high priority among American people. Or at least the government. The culture that values its young thrives, while the culture that does not, well, it dies. And as for those traffic fatalities— well, they are themselves a selection factor."

"The Darwin Awards," I said, remembering those things that would recount really stupid things people had done. It was like I hadn't even said anything. Like I was a ghost. It drove me bananas.

"Nobody here has any children," Polly said, unconsciously smoothing her already-smooth tummy.

"Precisely," Sheldon said. "What does that say about us? About our society?"

I drank my beer, trying to follow all of this. I was the mascot of the gathering, the dancer, performance artist and textile artisan, prone to sewing and styling and construction, the artful fashionista, short and limber, broad-hipped but petite, a trifle bow-legged—though I think that's from my Hungarian ancestry, men born to horse and saddle, to riding down peasants on the steppes, and raping them. I kept my hair pixie-short, colored it fiery red, and my laughter came easy and often, even at my own expense. Lee liked me, or liked making fun of me, so he suffered me to stay in their company, and the others simply followed his lead.

"I think you're saying we're all evolutionary failures, then?" I asked, which had everybody laughing—with me, at me, whatever. Although none of us had precisely succeeded at anything, we had no doubt of our inherent superiority.

"Strictly speaking, along purely Darwinian lines, yes," Sheldon said. "Evolutionary failures, but it's the fault of our government's failure to invest in the future of its people. America is slitting its throat as surely as the French did, just by its failure to live up to its professed ethics."

"Don't get me started on ethics," Lee said. "Please. Let's not be vulgar, here."

"We should all be donating sperm and eggs, then?" Clay said. "Is that what you're fucking saying?"

"We're all evolutionary dead ends, unless we have kids," Sheldon said. "The culture that values its future must value its future. Children are the future, and in a culture that doesn't value them, there IS no future."

Reagan shook her head, but didn't speak. I wondered what she thought about being an evolutionary dead end.

"Our art is our legacy," Polly said. "It's what we leave for future generations to enjoy."

"There is no future," Willa said. "And America's dreaming."

"No future, no future, no future for you," I said, humming the Sex Pistols tune. Somehow, that was gauche, where Lee's Alice Cooper rendering was clever, as they just sort of looked at me. Especially Willa.

"What?" I asked. Willa scoffed.

"We're all doomed," Polly said. "Doomed! That is the central lesson of humanism. The vital core. Search and destroy, search and destroy. Life, liberty, and the pursuit of happiness gives way to death, tyranny, and fleeing from unhappiness."

"'The urge to destroy is also a creative urge,'" Clay said. "Bakunin."

"Strike Two," Lee said, looking at his watch. "Fuck Vertigo; I'm bored. Let's fly."

# 2. THURSDAY NIGHT

We left Vertigo behind, and settled on a place called Flinch, a new club that was down the street, and held some promise, judging from the spray of neon that graced its entry, to the reasonable number of people waiting in line for it. Lee knew somebody who let us in the back, so we bypassed the lines and got right in, didn't have to pay a cover charge or anything. By now, everybody was getting pretty tipsy from the booze. It was like a progressive drinking party.

My head was reeling from all the jibber-jabber at Vertigo. To be tongue-tied in the Horrorshow was the kiss of death. You always had to have a comeback, a witty retort, something to bring to the table.

Flinch was loud, playing a rabid kind of electronica that I didn't mind, reminded me of Industrial, but Willa clearly didn't like it, was sulking and complaining to whoever would listen, so I took a liking to the place. Nobody else in our group would dance to this music, except for Polly, and she only danced to get attention, whereas I danced because I liked to, so we hit the dance floor at Flinch, while the others managed to find a table.

The inside of the place was like a cartoon explosion, with jagged angles and three levels, like a basement dance pit, then a main floor bar and lounge, then an upstairs with booths. There was room at the far center of the main floor for a deejay or a band, both of whom were sheathed in light. Tonight it was a band on the lighted stage, who called themselves Brutal Truth.

They were a four-piece, with a frontwoman with cotton-candy hair, bright pink, and she looked Asian, sang her lyrics with a harpy's wailing, while the band pounded out a staggering rhythm, and she fingered a keyboard thing the color of Pepto-Bismol, hung around her neck.

There was nothing detectably ironic about the place, which meant that Lee would tire of it almost immediately, though for the moment it was okay. Everything was for the moment with the Horrorshow.

Polly and I went down into the underlit pit to dance, while the others took a spot near the railing on the main level, to better survey the multitudes.

"Who's Bakunin?" I asked Polly, figuring she'd know.

"He's dead," she said. "He's nobody."

She had to know who he was; she knew about Bolsheviks. She was wearing a red dress with a black scarf, and black heels.

"No, really," I said. "I've heard of Bukharin, but not Bakunin."

Polly took my hand, led me to a spot on the dancefloor, thick black bracelets clacking at her wrists, her nails perfectly done. Red, of course. I was proud some part of my brain had even remembered Bukharin, that I could drop his name, though I'd never read a word of him.

We started dancing in our spot, underlit, fey and fetching, keenly aware of the others watching from their perch above.

"He was just an anarchist," Polly said. "No one of consequence. He couldn't even write a proper book, wrote pamphlets."

Polly wrote pamphlets, too, but called them chapbooks. She self-published reams of her poetry by way of them, called it DIY, turning the sow's ear of self-publishing into the silk purse of a stack of chapbooks available online.

I nodded, watching Polly sensuously sway. For a married woman, she conducted herself like a single lady. I didn't think I was ever going to marry, but it would be cool to be the kind of wife who could regularly go out dancing and clubbing without a care in the world. I danced because I loved dancing; Polly danced because she wanted to demonstrate that she would.

And she could. In no time at all, we were laughing and swaying in the intimidating press of party people, the lights beneath our feet coloring lightsaber blue, and ecstasy orange, and C.H.U.D. green, and both of us were laughing.

Really, Polly's body was the better of the anorexics, because she dressed herself so perfectly, with her dresses or her ideally-fitted jeans accentuated with her studded belts. She had elfin curves to her, something neither Willa nor Reagan could claim, since Willa was like a pair of chopsticks, and Reagan was a rolling pin. But Polly was lithe, and knew how to move, how to sinuously slide about. And yet there was a charming self-consciousness to her, too, how she'd bring a bangled wrist up to push back a stray curling lock from her eyes, tuck it behind her ear, her bulging eyes full of mirth, her smile a vision of lipsticked laughter.

Most of the other dancers loomed above me; I never felt shorter than when I was in the press of a crowd on a dancefloor. I hated being so small, but was grateful that I was fit. Some short girls blew wide, while I was lean and wiry-curvy, thanks to endless hours of nightclub dancing and pathologically private pursuit of Pilates. It made me look perhaps a little like a little boy, I supposed, with my short hair artfully tousled, and my stovepipe jeans and my pointy gilt shoes and my ironic t-shirt and my shirt and vest atop it, and my loose necktie, my own bracelets accessorizing my look nicely, a touch of sugar and spice to go with my overall look.

Polly and I looked like a couple, and I liked that. A lipstick lesbian and her pixie-cut Peter Pandemic partner. We knew we were the queens of the dancefloor, knew the others were watching with alternating amusement and scorn, and the other dancers gave us a little space. Nobody even cut in, so perfectly coupled were we, and I felt a boozy warmth in my chest as I moved along with Polly. Whatever she felt was behind her mask of a smile, her white teeth flashing past her red lips like paparazzi flashbulbs.

All at once our song ended, and the singer for Brutal Truth yelped something I couldn't hear, and then the tempo shifted, and another of their songs started up, something not so danceable. Our endless moment had ended.

"Do you want to get something to drink?" she asked. "There's a bar over there."

She nodded in the direction of the smallish bar on this floor.

"Sure," I said, and hopped off the dancefloor and made my way there. It was nice to be out of the eyeshot of Lee and the others, who hung like vultures on the balcony. Dancing was unforgivable in our circle, in that it required activity, reciprocity, and engagement; to dance was to risk looking foolish, and what's more, it meant being moved by music. The level of ironic detachment demanded by our group precluded dancing. I did it because I enjoyed it; Polly did it perhaps as a gesture of defiance to Lee's languid dominance of our group.

The bar was a slender half-circle being tended by a pretty young goth girl with a pierced lip and a fishnet dress. She looked barely old enough to drink, let alone able to tend bar. I felt every one of my 28 years looking at her. I ordered a light beer, while Polly got herself an amaretto sour. The bartender babe served them up without comment or complaint. For the moment, Polly and I were content to lounge at the bar with our drinks, scan the crowd.

"We're not long for this place," Polly said. "I think I heard Lee yawn over the sound of the syncopation."

"I know," I said. "But I like it. Maybe we could just go, you and me."

She patronized me with a smile that was becomingly vague. She was so terribly girly, it charmed me.

"Sure, we'll see how it goes," she said, glancing at her watch. "What do you think of this band?"

"I like the singer's hair," I said. "It takes real work to get that color; I don't think she's wearing a wig."

Polly squinted in the direction of the singer, as if she could tell from this distance. Polly was nearsighted, but never wore glasses, didn't want to fuss with contacts.

"Oh, it has to be a wig, don't you think? Nobody can have hair like that. She'd have to bleach it white, then add the color. She'd have no hair left."

I shrugged, unsure. Polly's cell phone chirped in her little handbag, and she fished it out, her face glowing light blue as she read the message on it. She texted something back to him.

"They're leaving," she said. "Lee's bored, says they're splitting. Are we done?"

I hated the idea of just being jerked on a short leash by Lee's whims, shook my head.

"I'm just getting started; we just got our drinks, for god's sake."

Polly nodded. She understood, texted something back to whoever it was who was on the other end of the line. Lee didn't use a cell phone, was the only one of us who didn't own one, so that was even more annoying, like how the uncoolest, lamest, most obstinate of our ranks called the tune and we all were expected to go along with it. He ruled through force of will, and a childish determination to get his way.

Then she snapped shut her phone and perched elegantly against the bar, sipping her cocktail and surveying the crowd, which was mostly half-lit, gyrating bodies and ample shimmying shadows. I'd have felt alone if I'd been alone, but being together with Polly made it somehow better.

"I don't know why people follow Lee," I said. "Why does he rule the roost?"

"He's the squeaky wheel," Polly said. "Hey, do you want to hear my new poem? I'm going to read it at Clay's."

I looked around. In the noise of the place, it was hardly an ideal setting for one of Polly's poems, but I wasn't about to interrupt her. I liked what glimpses I got of her process. Each poet had their own way about them, their own approach. They were like competing magicians, each jealously eyeing the others, covetous of their craft, guarding their beats and rhymes like misers. The poets thought they were the best writers, had disdain for other wordsmiths, the lesser artisans, in their eyes. Never mind that nobody but poets paid attention to their words, anymore. They were literally preaching to the choir.

As the dancer, the fashionista, the performance artist, I realized that Polly's poetry reading with me wasn't so much a sign of trust or esteem, but rather, was some reinforcement that I was her inferior, that there was no risk in showing me her work, no fear of the caustic criticism of a worthy peer. I felt that even in the dark of Flinch.

Polly gave her sour a ladylike sip, and then said her words, like they were an incantation:

*My interiority emulously beckons—*
*suffering silence:*
*the lost mornings and ever-afters*
*between bated breaths*
*as I wait for the blithering kraken's kiss,*
*suckerlike saucers*
*slide against my tender flesh—*
*what slender sacrifice am I?*

She paused, sipped her drink again, her wide-set green eyes judging my reaction. I didn't know what to say. Interiority? Who said things like that? Emulously? Another mysterious, magical poet-word. "Blithering" felt made up. I felt stupid for not knowing these words, but was afraid to ask. I'd look them up later. Maybe on my phone, when she wasn't looking.

"It's great," I said. "Amazing. Like a long haiku."

"Haiku? Oh, please," she said. Polly smiled, showed her teeth again, like she knew all along that it was great, but that it was nice hearing it, anyway.

"Is that the whole thing?" I asked.

"Oh, that's only one stanza," she said. "It's called *Happily Never After*."

"Great title," I said. She accepted my praise with her characteristic knowing grace. Of course it was great. She knew it was great, only a fool would doubt its greatness, and her greatness, as well. I was just sharp enough to see the incarnation of her awesomeness, like Igor in the lab with Dr. Frankenstein.

"It's about a princess lost to darkness," Polly said. "She bargains for her life, pleads with a demon of the deep for her deliverance."

"Sounds serious," I said.

"Oh, it is," she said. "I want to get some slides to run with it, pictures of krakens, those old woodcuts, sea monsters and such. I'm going to make a chapbook of it, have the pictures make it seem, I dunno, mythical. Epic. I don't usually do epic, but the piece just moved me. I know someone who makes her own paper; I might use that, just give it the right texture, at least for the original. I'll have somebody print up the rest."

"Ambitious," I said. All I'd been doing was audiotaping myself walking through the city, capturing sounds, like a sonic collage, spending time with the tape, making them run together into this aural pastiche. It was all going to be background, like a soundtrack for a performance piece I was planning. I called it "Aural Fixation," although the piece wasn't fully together, yet.

A dark young man came to the bar, almost between Polly and me. He had dark hair, a Greek look to him, tanned, handsome, an almost endearingly careworn look on his face.

"Sorry," he said. "Can I get a beer?"

The bartender girl nodded, once he told her he wanted a Red Stripe, and, to my surprise, they had that down in the little bar. Polly looked him up and down, self-consciously tossed aside a lick of her dark hair, away from her pale face.

"Red Stripe," I said.

"Thanks," the man said. He wore a green t-shirt and a worn bomber jacket and jeans. His hair was thick and long, just to his shoulders, and his eyebrows were full. He looked like he belonged on a pedestal. He held the chubby bottle in a hand, turned from the bar.

"Red Stripe," I said again, and he noticed me that time. The bartender girl put two bottles next to my hand, looked at me expectantly. "Oh, no, thanks."

She took them away, gave me an irritated look.

"Hi," Polly said, extending her slender hand. "I'm Penny Lane."

"Yeah?" the man said, shaking her hand. "And I'm Arnold Layne. Maybe we're related?"

The man smiled, and his white teeth shined in the dark, against the tan of his face. Polly laughed, tucked the stray lock of hair behind her ear again.

"Oh, I think I'd know if I was related to you, Mr. Layne," she said. "I haven't seen you at any of our family reunions."

"I've been busy," he said. "Traveling."

"I'm Samantha," I said, clearing my throat. He turned and looked at me like he'd just seen me for the first time.

"Hi," he said.

"Pink Floyd," I said. "You're named after that Syd Barrett song."

"You know Syd?" he said.

"We all know Syd," Polly said, not wanting to have the attention taken from her. She didn't know Syd Barrett from Sid Vicious.

"He's dead," I said.

"Well, I didn't do it," the man said, holding up his hands. Polly laughed into her hand, high and lilting, carried right over the noise of Brutal Truth.

"Look, you ladies want to hang out?"

"Isn't that what we're doing?" I asked, catching Polly's eye from over the barrel chest of Mr. Arnold Layne. I felt ridiculously tiny next to him, and with Polly perched on the footrail of the bar, she added still a few more inches to her willowy frame.

"Oh, I mean, you know, like hanging out at my place?" he asked.

"Oooh," Polly said. "That's tempting, but I'm going to have to pass."

Her round face and high cheekbones registered well in the club lighting, her expression one of genuine regret. I was kind of surprised that she'd pass.

"That's too bad, Ms. Lane," he said. He was a handsome guy, with that longish, curly black hair and a big nose and a unibrow that kept trying to form over his sad, striking blue eyes. I wanted to trim those eyebrows, take a pair of tweezers to them.

"What's your real name?" I asked.

"Ansel," he said.

"Ansel Adams?" Polly asked.

"No," the man said. "Ansel Rupino."

Polly cocked her eye, gave me a meaningful look. Italian.

"Is that Italian?"

"Yes," he said, drinking his beer. "Half."

"What's the other half?" I asked.

"German," he said. "My ancestors were fascists."

Polly liked that, the political reference. "Really? So, are you a refugee?"

"Something like that. Argentina was all filled up," Ansel said. Though he was lean, he was broad-chested and muscular. Even the way he held his beer, that chubby little Red Stripe bottle, he looked strong enough to break it in his hands. "I'm an artist."

Polly liked that even more. "Really? What medium?"

"Painting," he said. "I'm a painter."

I liked that, too. We didn't have a proper painter in our ranks. I mean, Reagan and Sheldon thought they were painters, but somehow I could see Ansel was the real deal.

"I was hoping I could paint the two of you," he said. "I have a studio that's literally around the block from this place."

"For real?" Polly asked, leaning into him, eyes ablaze. I thought it was funny, how she was willing to pass on him before, but she finds out he's a painter, and she's all over him.

"Yeah," he said. "I haven't sold anything, though. But for me, it's the painting that's the fun part. I have some at the Atomic Café, on the walls."

"I know that place," I said. "You work there?"

"Nah," he said. "I'm friends with the owner."

Polly didn't want to hear about that, though. She wanted to hear about paintings. Usually guys in bars would talk about how they worked for the CIA or were soccer players, that kind of thing. Ansel looked like he could be either. He looked like he could have been a spy, had this brooding European way about him that was exciting. Maybe he was in Mossad.

"So, you paint," Polly said. "What kind of things do you paint? Portraits?"

"Sometimes," Ansel said. "I saw you two dancing, and thought it would be great if you could model for me. Like you two dancing."

"Sure," I said, just blurting it out. It sounded cool. He sounded cool. And I'd upped the ante on Polly, because I'd already committed to it, so she was roped in to either go along, or know that I had trumped her, so she swiftly worked to regain her edge.

"That'd be great," she said. "Take us to your studio, Painter Man."

# 3. EARLY FRIDAY MORNING: 26 OCTOBER

Ansel's place really was just around the block, part of a building with lofts. He'd explained that it had once been an office building of some sort, and then it had been gut-rehabbed and made it into studios. They'd turned the roof into this great green-topped deck, put all these plants and trees up there, as well as a wooden deck. He showed us that first, so we could see the great view of the city, twinkling in the distance, while where we were, it was pretty quiet, except for the periodic cackle-staggers of street drunks and partiers, and the bass thump of music now and then.

"Wow, what an amazing building," Polly said. "They did a great job on this roof."

"Yeah, it's pretty cool," he said. "Sometimes I come up here and I can forget that I'm even in the city, like if I lay on my back amid the plants."

"It's alright," I said, not wanting to appear as impressed as Polly was. "Where's your flat?"

His place was on the second floor, and faced east. We took the freight elevator to it, this great big elevator for a three-story rehabbed industrial building. Ansel explained that the owners had kept the freight elevators since mostly artists were in residence in the building, and it made carting materials up and down easier, less damage to the place, and that it was always helpful during Around the Coyote.

"Do you participate in that?" Polly asked.

"Sure," Ansel said. "Now and then."

Sheldon and Reagan always did, although nobody ever bought their stuff except for us. I always thought Sheldon's paintings looked like ass, but never told him that. Not like it would've mattered, anyway, because my opinion meant jack to him. Reagan's were well done, but they weren't particularly exciting. It was a faustian kind of enterprise—Sheldon thought he was great, but he sucked; Reagan was more modest, and her work was technically solid, but lacked something, a real vision. She should have been illustrating catalogs.

The hallway to his unit was industrial-spare, but it was actually a pretty nice building. Clearly he was the point of the gentrification spear in this particular neighborhood. Usually, the urban pioneers would get the great places in the shabby buildings in the crappy neighborhoods, while the second-wavers and latecomers would end up shoehorned in rotten little places that catered to the wannabes. Timing was everything, and though Ansel's building was bland on the outside and inside, the space held promise.

When he keyed in, flicked on the lights, we were richly rewarded. His place was huge. I was terrible at estimating square footage, but his loft had to be about four times the size of my own studio, easily. It went on and on.

He had a platform bed on one side, dark wood with a thick, creamy-white mattress atop it, and a huge kitchen, and a recessed tile shower wrapped in glass in a cavernous bathroom, with wardrobes near the bed, towering blocks of dark wood, and skylights overhead. On the far side was a cage, where he said he locked up his best pieces before he sold them. The cage was empty right now, he said, because he had sold a whole collection of paintings.

"Some cage," Polly said, testing the bars with her hands. "You have a problem with thieves around here?"

"Art thieves?" Ansel said. "Sure. They rappel down through my skylight. I figure this way, they have to work for anything of mine they try to steal. Over my dead body, of course."

"My sympathies for anybody trying to mess with you," I said. Ansel looked like he could break a stack of cat burglars over his knee.

There were canvases everywhere, framed ones piled up against the wall, finished ones mounted on the white walls (he only had exposed brick on the wall where the windows were). Fresh canvases piled up on some work tables that we could see as we went further into the place, and then his paint shelves, where he had tons of cans, tubes, bottles, and pots of paint. And endless brushes, all shapes and sizes, most of them spattered with old paint on the handles.

The place was incredible, so I had to swallow my amazement, lest I look like a norm. To have such a workspace was a dream of mine. I coveted his space.

"Pretty sharp," I said. "What's the heating bill on a place like this?"

"I dunno," he said. "My family owns the building."

All of his talk about the owners before; he had been playing with us.

"Rent-free," Polly said, and I could only be envious.

He came from money. It was clear as a dinner bell. He went to the kitchen, dug out a bottle of red wine. "You want some?"

Polly and I nodded, walking around as he dug out a corkscrew. Polly's heels clacked on the floor as we went about the place.

"Wine before beer, never fear," she said.

"Beer before wine, you'll be fine," I said. It was a joke I sometimes made, like coming up with other ways of mangling those old adages.

"Liquor before beer, my dear," she said.

"Beer before liquor gets you on Flickr," I said, poking my tongue at her.

"You'll have to hold my hair if I puke," she said. Her hair was so short, only her stray bang could come near her mouth. I glanced up, saw the track lighting, the exposed beams. Ansel's place was awesome. I wanted to move right in, put a sewing machine on one of his tables, and bring my shoe tree and hang it from one of the rafters, use it to climb up there, build a tent city.

The paintings were pretty good, I thought. Boldly colorful, passionate, honestly Expressionistic. There were portraits of women all around the place.

"His conquests," Polly said, nodding at them. "Better than notches on a bedpost, I suppose."

We looked around, and there was a profusion of them. Redheads, blondes, brunettes, whites, blacks, Asians. Women, women, women. But all of them were exceptionally rendered, bold brushstrokes evident on the canvas. A sure hand. A steady, manly hand.

Ansel came over, holding out two big goblets of red wine in those man-hands of his. We took them, and Polly tucked a hand beneath her elbow as she held the wine, legs akimbo, pulling her skirt tight against her slender frame.

"Do you just paint women, Ansel?" she asked.

"No," he said. "I just like women, is all."

"Is it your Hall of Fame?" she asked, sipping her wine. I drank some of it, too, not wanting to stand there like a tool. Polly really was good. I knew, because I was good, but she'd always beat me to the punch. "Your tally of your conquests?"

Ansel just smiled, gestured to some of the paintings that leaned against the wall. Other pieces, bold and abstract, or mundane scenes shot through with vibrant, unnatural colors that were odd to our eyes.

"These are ones I'd put up for sale," he said, of the unhung paintings. He nodded to the portraits on the wall. "Not those; those are mine."

I was drawn to the castaways, the oddly-colored ones.

"Your color choices are wild," I said. "This cityscape looks psychedelic."

He seemed pleased by that, held up the piece for us to look at a bit. It really was a striking piece; neither Sheldon nor Reagan painted anything as interesting as this. They were all about portraits of James Joyce, Sheldon's pieces of paper ripped from books and stuck to matte boards, perhaps with a splash of paint across them. Even though Ansel had done something as mundane as a cityscape, his use of color and the texture of his brushstrokes made Chicago look alien and exotic.

"It's really nice," Polly said. "Although I can't help but notice that the colors of the portraits are a lot more conventional."

"I paint what I see," Ansel said, setting down the painting. "Why don't you two come over here?"

He gestured to an overlit area that was screened by sheets, where there was a stool. He moved the stool out of the way, gestured for us to go in the center. Polly trotted over, and I followed on her high heels.

Ansel reached for a remote and turned on some music somewhere. I couldn't see the speakers. It was dance music, up-tempo, chugging bass. He turned off the other lights in the apartment, so that where we were was the only source of light.

Polly giggled into her wineglass, took a sloppy sip. It was good wine.

Then he emerged from behind a sheet with a camera in hand.

"Now, pose," he said. "Like you were dancing at Flinch."

Polly laughed. "Strike a pose?"

She froze in this iconic posture in the lights, deadpanning through my laughter. The wine made me laugh harder, made everything funnier. Polly took my glass and set it down with hers, on the stool. It was like our wineglasses were already partners on their own little stage. I smiled at that, and Polly came back, her eyes on me. She was buzzed, obviously, or she'd never have been game for it.

But I considered myself a pretty great dancer; I wasn't trained officially, but I knew my way around a dancefloor. I began to pose with

Polly, eyes only on her, while Ansel circled around us like Austin Fucking Powers, snapping shots with his digital camera.

It didn't take more than a few moments for us to practically forget that he was even there, as we posed with each other, meeting halfway, hip to hip, leg to leg, foot to foot, beat to beat, breaking against each other in natural rhythm like waves, me blushing, though on my naturally tan skin, it wasn't so apparent, while Polly's own pale cheeks flushed pink as she held her arms out against me, around me, in this intricate imitation of a club dance we performed for Ansel's camera, which clicked and flashed to a beat of its own, Ansel's eyes flashing as he photographed us. He was as turned on as we were, or as I was; I couldn't tell if Polly was really as into it, or whether she was just playing along.

Pose. Pose. Pose. Pose. Pose. A couple of poseurs, we were. Posing.

Seeing her like this, the intimacy of the setting, I could study the roundness of her face, her dimples and high cheekbones softened by the curves of her flesh, and her wide-set eyes, and even the breadth of her straight nose, her wide mouth, skin like dusty chalk. Her lean body, with a succulent shapeliness to it that I seldom fully appreciated—skinny was skinny, but some skinny was more appealing that other skinny—she was New York-skinny, of course, since everything about Polly was run through with Gotham. She had style and sinuous grace, and as she writhed against me, eyes only for me, I felt my heart pound in my chest. On an instinct, I reached out for her, grabbing her arms, bringing her in, while Ansel's camera stared.

Though I was smaller than she was, I was stronger, and for a second I held her, and her eyes were inches from mine, her breath on my cheeks, and without a thought of the consequences, I kissed her.

She tasted like melon, her lips were soft and wonderful, and in the kissing was a communion, and she yielded to it, if only for a moment, touching my own face with her hands, running slender fingers through my pixie hair, while Ansel's camera winked.

Only a pose.

We parted, laughing, embarrassed. None of the others had ever done anything like that, we were sure. Too uptight, too lame. We had inspired an artist, posed for one. We were cool. We were muses. We were amused.

"Lip gloss," I said to Polly, who shrugged with a grin, spun on her heel and fetched us our wine.

"Sweet," Ansel said. "That was great. It's how you two were on the dance floor, what caught my attention to begin with. You're not lovers, then?"

"No," Polly said, looking at me over her wineglass. "We're artists. Friends."

"Ah," he said. "Of course."

But it felt presumptuous to say that, in a way. I mean, we were artists, but Ansel was like a real artist. There was a difference, and it was clear as could be to me.

"She's a poet," I said. "I'm a dancer; well, a performance artist... multimedia."

"Poetry is art; art is poetry," Polly said. Ansel turned off the music, came back and looked through the log of pictures on his camera.

"One medium among many," he said. "These are great. I'm tempted just to use them as they are, versus painting them. Usually, I'll take pictures and paint from them, but these are good on their own."

"Let's see," I said, but he waved me off.

"Not yet," he said. It was weird to be a subject, to become the property of someone else. In the art that I inflicted upon the world, I was my own property, my own subject. I'd never sat for another person's pleasure. But in Ansel's camera part of me resided. I was reminded of the Indians fearing that cameras would steal their souls. Rightly or wrongly, I could sympathize.

"Hope you have release papers handy," I said.

Polly scolded me with a click of her tongue. "I trust you'll make us look beautiful, Ansel."

Ansel looked up from his camera, smiled. My, what big teeth he had.

"That work has already been done. I might blow these up really big, have them printed on Lexan or aluminum. Like four plaques. That would be awesome. I doubt I could improve the purity of your forms with a paintbrush. I would only profane you."

"Thanks?" I said. "I've never been sacred before."

"Profanity *is* sacred to me," Polly said.

I could tell that Polly was genuinely turned on, wasn't just playing. The way she looked at Ansel, eyes focused on him. Not me, though. As ever, I was the also-ran, the consolation prize. That made me kittenish.

"Won't Tristan be worried?" I asked, tracing a circle on the lip of the goblet with an outstretched index finger. Tristan, the one who paid for her lovely dresses and jewelry and everything in between.

"Oh, he's out of town," Polly said. "I think it'll be okay."

Ansel smiled at both of us, his teeth so beautiful and almost blue-white. "I've got a sofa and some chairs on the other side of this divider, if you'd like to sit down."

"Sure," I said, walking around the corner, not waiting for Polly. I took a seat on the buttery-smooth brown leather sofa, while Polly clacked her way to a matching chair, sat on it, crossed her legs fetchingly.

Ansel came last, sat down on the sofa, an arm's length away from me.

"So, who's Tristan?" he asked. I wanted to blurt out that he was her husband, but I waited, just to see what Polly would say.

"My husband," she said, after giving me a glance.

"That's too bad," he said.

It bugged me, being second fiddle in the lineup. What was I supposed to do, call a cab? I was fucking available.

"Well, I'm not married," I said. "I'm not with anybody."

That came out so stupidly, everybody laughed. Even I laughed, and it broke the weird vibe that Polly's adulterous ambitions had created. Still, I didn't know why Ansel found Polly more attractive. I was fun, I was perky, I was pretty. It was irritating that somebody like Polly would immediately take center stage, just because.

I couldn't really put my finger on why.

"Well, we should probably be going," Polly said, glancing at her watch.

"So soon?" Ansel said. "That's too bad."

"We?" I said. "I'm wide awake."

He smiled at me, nodded. "I'm a night owl, myself."

Polly whipped out her cell phone and dialed up a cab, gave the address of Flinch. "Are you coming, Samantha?"

I shook my head.

Polly got up, thanked Ansel for the wine and asked to let her know how the pictures came out. She gave him one of her business cards, jotted her cell phone on the back of it, clicked shut her little silver card case with an authoritative snap, tucked it into her little bag, along with her phone.

"You know, you don't have to go," Ansel said, getting up as well. "You can stay all night, if you like."

"No," Polly said. "Probably not the best idea, however tempting it might be."

Again, she looked at me like I was the killjoy, even though she was the one with the husband, not me. I didn't want to be a flirt buffer for her. I liked being able to flaunt my singleness in front of her, like confronting her with her own shallow morality. It was kind of a little bit of performance art. She liked to run with our group like she was one of us, but as the only one besides Reagan attached to anybody; she didn't really belong. Not for real. There was a limitation in being in a relationship, of course—she had to be places, do things, couldn't just be there for herself, or for her art. Poseur.

I mean, Tristan gave her a very wide leash, but it was still a leash. Me, I was free as could be. I could go anywhere I wanted, anytime, without a thought of the consequences. And I liked that I flaunted that in her face just then. I'd probably pay for it in the coming weeks, like Polly freezing me out, but then again, maybe she'd not say anything about tonight, because in doing so, she'd make herself look pretty slutty.

Lee would have had a field day with it, and we both knew that.

"Well, do you want me to wait with you?" he asked.

"No, that's alright," she said. "It's just a block. I might not even have to wait for the cab I called; there's usually a bunch."

She extended her hand, shook Ansel's. I stayed seated on the sofa. Boys were supposed to get up, not girls, right?

"Bye, Sam," Polly said.

"Bye," I said, as Ansel showed her to the door.

Triumph, I thought, taking a big sip of wine, enough to make my belly warm and my eyes glaze. It felt good—and even though I was friends with Polly, it felt good to thwart her a little. I realized it was really my ego that had compelled me to do it.

That was worth it, in my eyes. Polly could hardly call me out on it and bang Ansel, anyway—either she was intending to cheat on Tristan, or else she was too chicken to call me on it. Neither spot put her in a good position; either way, I kind of won. So, I'd pay for it socially, but it would likely just be between Polly and me.

Ansel came back with the bottle of wine, set it down on an end table that was next to the chair Polly had vacated. He sat down in it, leaned forward. Ansel was dazzling to the eye.

"So, now what?"

He was making it tough for me, which was kind of pissing me off. Was I really that repugnant? He should've been throwing himself at me. Then I thought maybe he was playing some kind of head game with me.

"I thought she'd never leave," I said. My head was spinning from the wine, and I drank some more, all the same, when he'd refilled my glass. The room was spinning, I felt like a bobblehead doll.

"Too bad," he said. "I was thinking of something, you know, a trifle exotic."

I laughed, wondering what Polly would've done if he'd suggested a three-way. My laugh came out as a snort, which only made me laugh harder. Polly wasn't a square, but I doubted she'd be willing or able to do something like that. Polly sometimes did unusual things just to spite herself. Like she would shoot pointless documentaries about ephemeral things with great gravity, do dissertations on the politics of paperweights, study the mating rituals of centipedes, the sociology of wallet contents, any number of things. But it was an affected eccentricity she cultivated, a self-conscious worldliness that, to me, was the death of the truly bohemian.

In fact, if I'd called her a bohemian, I'm sure Polly would've coyly demurred, even though she'd have been very satisfied with that label.

"She'd never have been down with that," I said, although it's too bad I'd jumped the gun; had Ansel suggested it, it would've been funny to see Polly try to worm her way out of it. The floor was seesawing, and I realized it was just me turning my head this way and that, pitching it like a ship lost on a stormy sea.

"I don't know," he said. "People can surprise you."

"Not me," I said. "Not her."

He laughed, and took the goblet from my hand, because I was waving the thing around like a scepter in the hands of a mad princess. His hand was hairy.

Watching him set it down so carefully made me snort with laughter again, and then Ansel scooped me up in his arms, and I let him, my head lolling. He was terribly strong, and I felt so tiny as he hoisted me up. His fingers pressed hard into me, dimpling my skin.

"Let's get you to bed," he said, and I curled my head in against his cheek, which was rough and unshaven, his stubble prickly against my forehead.

He walked me across his loft to his bed, and set me down. I was hammered, and couldn't stop snorting with laughter, embarrassing myself. Ansel grabbed one of my legs and pried off one of my gilt shoes, the toes comically pointy to my drunken eyes. I had such a collection of shoes, it was awesome. I babbled about it to him, and he just smiled, took off the other shoe, then went to work on my jeans.

It was easier said than done, because my jeans were tight, they were Rich & Skinny, and he had to peel them from me like I was a banana. That image stuck in my head, and I was laughing all the more, while Ansel tugged them off me.

He climbed the bed, loomed overhead.

"Now we're ready," he said, wiping drool from his lips, showing me his perfect teeth.

# 4. FRIDAY

I woke up with a gasp to the sound of traffic and trains, my head throbbing, my mouth dry. Sunlight streamed into the loft, and for a second I had no idea where I was, who I was, what I was doing. I only realized that I was naked and in a bed other than mine.

Ansel was next to me, motionless.

My head was spinning. I couldn't remember anything after we'd gone to bed, although from the ache of my body, I knew the night had been pretty wild. I'd passed out. I hadn't done that since college. It was embarrassing.

I sat up, looked around for my clothes. As I was glancing around, I saw that there was blood on the bed, a lot of it smeared all over, gone to maroon, dried.

"What the fuck?" I knew it wasn't me; I'd been on the Pill. But there was blood all over the bed, on the sheets and, on me.

I jumped out of the bed and yelped in pain—I had gashes across my ribs, like a half dozen brushstrokes on either side of me, and as I looked at those, whimpering, I felt a sting on my shoulder, like on my back.

Absurdly, I spun around like a dog chasing its tail, trying to look at my shoulder. There was a big splotch of blood there, and a chunk taken out of me.

"Jesus fucking Christ," I said. "Ansel! Wake the fuck up."

I was seriously freaking out at that point, sweating all over, covered in dried blood. Ansel didn't move. Had I killed him?

"Ansel!" I yelled. "Ansel!"

Without waiting for him to wake up, I ran over to his bathroom, where a big mirror hung. I had to see what I looked like.

There was blood on my face, smears of it, and the marks on my ribs, and all over my shoulder. I had blood on my hands. What the hell had I done?

I turned and looked at my shoulder in the mirror. There was a gouge taken out of me. The wound was raw and hadn't really scabbed over.

"What the fuck?" I asked my reflection. "Ansel!"

He appeared in the reflection, muzzy-headed, his mouth bloody. I became acutely aware that he was blocking my passage from the bathroom.

"Jesus Motherfucking H. Christ, Ansel," I said. "What the hell happened?"

Ansel wasn't hardly fazed by it, was still bleary. "Yeah, you were pretty wild last night."

"You fucking bit me?" I said, connecting two and two, remembering it made four, not three. "You crazy fucker, you actually bit me. Not just a bite-bite, either, but a motherfucking bite."

"Whoa," Ansel said. "Yeah, sorry about that."

"Sorry?" I said. "You ate my goddamned tattoo, you psycho."

And he had. I'd had this beautiful pink octopus tattoo on my shoulder, something I'd gotten in college, really well done, something Lee had endlessly ridiculed, saying only norms got tattooed anymore, that it was a veritable badge of normalcy. My first tat.

But it was gone. The bite had obliterated it.

"Are you a fucking cannibal, or what?" I asked, looking for something sharp to stab Ansel with. He held up his arms, defensively. There was dried blood, my blood, on his hands.

"Look, you were a hellcat," he said. "You were all over me. Don't you remember?"

"I was wasted," I said.

"We just fucked," he said. "And fucked and fucked. I got carried away, alright? Just take a shower, get cleaned up, you'll see, it's not as bad as it looks. When I was a kid, I'd sometimes get nosebleeds at night, and I'd wake up with blood all over the place. It always looks worse than you think."

I flexed my shoulder, which hurt. It actually burned.

"I can't believe you bit me that hard," I said. "You know how many germs are in a person's mouth?"

Ansel shrugged. "A lot?"

"Yeah," I said. "Like it's worse than a dog bite."

"All the more reason to get showered," he said. "Look, I'm totally sorry about that. I was a little high last night, you know? You can't go out like that, anyway."

"I should call the cops," I said. "Is this like felonious sexual assault, or something?"

I wasn't up on law so much, but it seemed like it could be. Ansel's face looked concerned at the mention of the police, and I pressed my advantage.

"You fucking owe me an apology, a tetanus shot, a doctor's visit, and a tattoo," I said.

"I'm sorry, Samantha," he said, and he looked it, truly. He looked apologetically handsome. Despite myself, I felt attraction for him, sick as it was, stirring in me. There was just something elementally pure about him, despite my blood on his face and hands.

"Are you a kink?" I asked, feeling like a norm for even asking that. Part of me felt bad about bringing it on myself by being drunk to begin with. It made me almost wish Polly was there in bed with us, that maybe she'd have been a barrier, that maybe things wouldn't have gotten so out of control.

"No," he said. "Look, I don't know what happened. It was dark, you were writhing under me, and I thought it was just a nibble, I swear."

I looked it over again. It was a gouge the size of a tennis ball, right out of my back. I couldn't even believe it, how bad it looked. My skin was smooth and flawless, like coffee with a ton of cream in it. Now I was scarred. I liked sleeveless stuff in the summer, too, and could just imagine people seeing this massive oval scar on my back, staring at me, wondering. They'd think it was cancer.

In fact, as I looked it over, I wasn't even sure if it wasn't a couple of bites. I mean, it was a big fucking bite. I looked at Ansel, who was totally shamed, or looked that way. For sure, if he'd wanted to kill me, he totally could have. I took some solace in that, I guess.

Still, it was fucked up.

"How many bites did you take out of me, man?" I asked.

"I don't know," Ansel said. "I was really fucked up."

"You didn't seem that bad," I said.

"Oh, you know how it is, like you don't know when something's gonna kick in," he said.

"Mmm," I said. The freakout had mostly passed, since it appeared that Ansel wasn't about to kill me, whatever else the hell he had in mind the night before. It was amazing what I could talk myself into, but I'd done that plenty of times before. "You owe me breakfast, too. Something fucking nice."

"How about the Signature Room?" he asked.

"How about the Drake?" I said. "I mean, if you're going to treat me to fucking brunch."

He ventured the most cautious of smiles, almost gentle. Ansel felt sincere, and I was nothing if not a great judge of character.

"Where would you like to go?" he asked.

"Someplace expensive," I said. "Someplace that serves vegetarian."

"Okay," he said. "How about Green Elephant?"

"Meh," I said. "Too trendy. How about Moogatoo?"

"Okay," he said. "Moogatoo's it is."

I was almost charmed by his addition of the "s" to the end of Moogatoo, which specialized in top-shelf Ivory Coast cuisine, including killer vegetarian food. In Chicago, people were always adding an "s" to something that didn't have one.

"Alright," I said. "Now, I'm going to get cleaned up. You're going to stay outside of the bathroom while I do this, right? No coming at me with butcher knives?"

"Promise," he said.

"And I'm going to need some first aid," I said. "Like gauze and some antiseptic and some medical tape. You got that?"

He nodded, and I felt really fucking cool, like I'd handled myself and the whole situation really well, and Ansel was left kind of holding the bag. I felt like I had hand in the relationship, and we didn't even have a relationship, yet. He owed me a stack of solids with the whole biting thing.

"Look," I said. "Does this building have any open units? I could really use a studio. Something rent-free, like."

Ansel smirked. "What, is this extortion, then?"

"You fucking bit me," I said. "It's the least you can do. I mean, are you a junkie? Do you have AIDS? Herpes? Anything I need to worry about?"

His face was almost hurt by my sharp little tongue, and I felt kind of satisfied, kind of powerful. He was in boxers, I was naked; he was about six feet tall, I was barely 5'3", and yet I felt like an amazon standing there.

He sighed. "We'll talk it up over breakfast, howsabout?"

I closed the door in his face and rooted around in his bathroom, seeing what he had in there. His medicine cabinet was full of drugs. Ketamine, Benzodiazepine, Midazolam. Serious stuff, maybe. I knew what Ketamine was, but not the other two. I took out the bottles and checked them out, opened them, sniffed them, put them back. I thought about sneaking them out with me, but didn't want to give him an excuse to go berserk on me.

So, instead, I went about taking a shower, using his nice white washcloths and towels. The shower felt great everywhere except where I'd been bitten and clawed. Where the water hit that, it stung like fuck, and I had to blink back tears as I quickly rinsed off the wounds, carefully patted them with washcloths.

The dried blood came off with a little scrubbing, and he had great soap, fragrant and firm, smelling of oatmeal and just good stuff, quality soap. But as a painter, he probably needed good stuff to get paint off him.

The shower was wonderful, a big broad head that was probably bigger than my own head, and I was squeaky clean when I got out of the shower, and then took to toweling off, being really careful not to hurt my wounds more than they already were. The one on my back looked hideous, got gross when the water had been added to it, like it remembered it was a wound again and wanted to bleed.

"Ansel," I said through the door. "You have the bandages?"

He said he did. I opened the door and he was sitting on a stool in the kitchen alcove, with a big medical kit on the countertop. He'd washed his face and hands. They were clean. He was wearing some nice black jeans and a grey v-neck cashmere sweater over a crisp white t-shirt. He had on some shiny black Kenneth Cole loafers with a silver buckle on them. The sheets were off the bed.

"You have to help me," I said.

"Oh, I know," he said. "No problem."

"Don't fucking stab me when my back is turned, right?" I asked.

"Yeah," he said. "No stabbing. I'll use Safety Scissors, howsabout?"

I kept my nose up, held onto a fiendish pout. If nothing else, it would be an interesting story, assuming I survived.

He held up some Bactine. "This has an anesthetic in it, so it'll hurt at first, but it should go numb."

"Hit me," I said, and he spritzed my back, and I yelped, again biting back on tears. I wouldn't cry in front of him.

Then he took a couple of thick squares of gauze and gently put it to my back. That hurt, too. The whole thing burned and stung.

"You'll need to see a doctor," he said. "Just to play it safe."

"Yeah," I said. "But breakfast, first."

"Sure," he said, and then he taped the gauze to my back. He dressed the wound pretty well, and I said as much. "I was a Boy Scout as a kid. We learned that kind of stuff, when Scoutmasters weren't busy raping us."

The mention of rape made me stiffen, even as a quip. Had I been raped? That was a curious question, like how much of a violation did a rape make? Having a bite taken out of me without my consent sure as hell felt like a violation, and since it was during sex, it surely qualified. That kind of skeeved me out, made me uneasy again.

I stepped away from him, turned, flexed my arm. It still hurt to move it. I grabbed the Bactine and sprayed the gashes on my ribs.

"What the fuck were these all about?" I asked.

"I just grabbed you really hard, and broke the skin," He said. "I clipped my nails, see?"

He held up his hairy hands, showing off his pristine nails.

"What were you on, PCP?" I asked. "Do people still do that shit?"

"Yeah," he said. "It was some stuff from the Ukraine. A friend said it was great for sex."

"Animal sex, maybe," I said.

I put band-aids on all of the gashes. There were eight in all, on either side of my ribs. It didn't take a forensic pathologist to put who was where. He'd pinned me on my hands and knees and dogfucked me, holding onto my ribs and digging into me and taking a bite out of me, probably when he came. At least kitty felt alright.

"Hey, did I at least enjoy myself?" I asked. "I'd better have, to make up for all of this."

"Yeah," he said. "You were great. You came and went like you owned the place."

"Small but mighty," I said. "That's me. People underestimate short girls, but we just have to be that much better at absolutely everything we do."

I walked over to my clothes and put them on, while Ansel hung back, looking pensive and worried, like maybe wondering if he needed to call his lawyers or something. I could just imagine a rich boy like him with some lawyers on retainer.

With my clothes on, the towels thrown aside, I felt more in control. When I had my shoes on, it was like I was in full armor. Sure, I hurt, but I felt more like myself again. Maybe better, in a way. I'd been tested, and I'd emerged triumphant.

"So, we ready for breakfast?" I asked. "What time is it?"

"Ten," he said.

"Brunch, then," I said. "How about a cab?"

"Fine," he said.

"Great," I said. "I'm famished."

We walked out together, and I felt glad to have the open sky overhead, out of the confines of his loft, which had seemed so roomy the night before, but the morning after, seemed way too tight.

# 5. FRIDAY

Moogatoo didn't do a brunch buffet. They just served good food, and you ate it. The place oozed with neo-colonial imperialist ambiance, with old wood and actual plants growing in pots, and African art on the walls, like heads and stuff that looked like ivory.

Even though the place was expensive, I had something simple: plantain pancakes with mashed cassava on the side, and a big glass of pomegranate juice, while Ansel had a plateful of sliced goat and yams, with a cherry chutney sauce that smelled good, even though the sight of the roast goat meat made me kind of queasy. The portions were obscenely big.

"Look," Ansel said. "I owe you big time for being so cool about this."

"Yeah, you do," I said. "Tell me you don't do that with every girl you bring up there."

"No," he said, looking thoughtful as he savored his goat. "I haven't done that for a long time."

"Oh, so you're a repeat offender," I said.

I wanted to like Ansel. Ansel was cool. Weird, but fucking cool.

"No, I meant had sex," he said. "It's been awhile."

I laughed, despite myself. "For real?"

It seemed impossible. Ansel was hot. Like dark, Southern European hot. Like get-any-woman-he-wanted hot.

"Yeah," he said. "I got tired of how complicated everything gets. I just try to focus on my painting."

"Mmm," I said. "Sexual tension as muse, eh? I get that."

I didn't have any sexual tension, aside from that funny vibe with Polly the night before. I shoveled that stray thought away with another forkful of pancake.

"That's it," he said. "Painting's easier than people."

"But you're painting people," I said.

"Sometimes," he said, looking distracted. I glanced around, but saw only a few other patrons in the shadows. The potted plants and little trees caught the light curiously. Moogatoo was usually a dinner place, was better-suited for late-night outings, but the owners were cool about being open early to accommodate Morning-After people like us. The Walk of Shame was easier on a full stomach.

"I'm just saying," I said. "So, what about that free apartment? I could really use a studio."

"No way," he said. "For what?"

"For art," I said. "Of course."

"What do you have in mind?" he asked.

I told him about my performance art, mixing dance and props and fashion and music and other things. He sighed, and I could see he wasn't too into that.

"Performance art is, you know, messy," he said. "How many times can you see somebody naked in a see-through raincoat throwing raw meat at white walls?"

"I've never done that," I said, kind of hurt that he'd even suggest something like that. "Performance art is really tough; it's a little of everything. We're like the superheroes of the art world."

"Is that it?" Ansel asked, smirking.

"What?" I said.

"Nothing," he said. "You're cute."

That made me mad. Of course I was cute; it was an obvious quality I possessed, and that Ansel would go for the obvious in me bugged me. There was a lot more to me than that. I was spunky, too.

"Did I taste good?" I asked. I wanted to throw that back in his face, lest he get too comfortable. "What does 'cute' taste like?"

"Like veal," he said. "Milk-fed."

"I'm an ovo-lacto vegetarian," I said. "Herbivores invariably taste better."

"That's for sure," he said, shoveling more of the goat in his mouth. I watched him chew and I carved a Pac-Man into my pancakes, a slender wedge that I progressively widened. I turned my plate into performance art: *Cute girl eating plantain pancakes.* I wondered if I could get an audience to watch me do that. I knew where I could: on-line. You could do anything, could *be* anything online. I already had a half-dozen recorded performances I posted online, but I wasn't about to share those with Ansel. Part of me hoped he'd be taken enough with me to check them out, and the other part hoped he'd not do that, because then maybe he really was a psycho, and I needed to be away from him. The mix of yearning and danger was inflammatory. I wanted him to stalk me.

"So, were your ancestors really fascists?" I asked, one of the last things I fully remembered him saying from the night before.

He nodded.

"German-Italian?" I said. "A combustible pairing."

Ansel smiled. "My grandparents were the fascists. Grandmother was Italian, Grandfather was in the *SS*. World War II."

"Intense," I said. "Was your Grandfather a Nazi?"

"Yes," Ansel said. "But almost everybody was one in Germany back then, or at least pretended to be."

History was dead people doing dead-people things, ghosts rattling chains in the attic. History was death. I liked that notion, thought I'd get a tattoo of that on my arm.

"German-Italian," I said. "I'm like Heinz 57. I don't know what I am."

"You look exotic," he said.

"Is that good or bad?"

"Good," he said. "Exotic women are beautiful."

"Awww," I said, sipping some pomegranate juice. "Here I thought I was just cute."

"Why did you cook your hair with that dye?" he asked.

My hair was an altogether boring shade of brown, like the color of dirty sand. Color was a requirement.

"You don't like red?" I asked. I'd picked out a vivid shade of red, specifically because it looked good with my brown eyes. It was European red, like what Austrian women used.

"It's striking," he said. "But you should let your true colors show."

"What are you, a stylist?" I asked, laughing, cutting another piece of pancake and popping it in my mouth.

"Women are so cruel to their hair," he said. "Dyes and bleaches and so forth. One girl I dated, she'd colored her hair so much, it was brittle, like straw. Half of it fell out and she had to wear a wig."

"Sounds like a real winner," I said. "Was she a prostitute?"

"No," he said, laughing. "You just say the first thing that comes to mind, don't you?"

I nodded, smiled wolfishly at him.

"I think I have ancestors who were Magyars."

"Really?" he said. I nodded. I liked the idea of being descended from barbarian tribes, so I ran with that. Lee claimed I had bow legs because my ancestors were descended from the Huns, and the Huns with straight legs couldn't ride their horses as well, and were extinguished from the Hunnish line.

"Yep," I said. "Don't mess with barbarians."

"Yeah," Ansel said, swirling some goat in the cherry chutney. It looked like fresh blood against the meat. "So, are we good?"

"What, am I boring you?" I asked.

"No," he said. "Not at all."

"Because we'll be good if the doctor gives me a clean bill of health," I said. Ansel nodded, drank down some water.

"I'm not sick," he said, more to himself than me. It was weird. I couldn't wait to blog about it, but then I was wondering what, if anything, I should say. The whole situation made me feel pretty weird, whereas if I wrote about what actually happened, people might freak out and wonder what was going on, and I'd hear lots of advice I didn't need. Context was everything, and my instincts told me that Ansel was alright; maybe a little weird around the seams, but mostly okay.

It was weird to be a kind of spectator to myself, to talk to Ansel and at the same time wonder how I'd present this to the world, to my fans, when I wrote about it. Describing him would be easy. The rest, not so easy. I wasn't sure if any of the others read my blog, even knew it existed. I didn't make it too easy, but I supposed somebody suitably committed or obsessive could find it and connect the dots.

Polly had her own blog, *Polytician*, where she talked about everything she experienced. I wondered how she'd frame last night. I reminded myself to check on that once I was done with Ansel.

It took me a minute to realize that he'd been talking while I was drifting off, and I could see him waiting there for me to say something.

"Mmm," I said.

Ansel smiled, again more to himself than at me. "Now I think maybe *I'm* boring *you*."

My cell phone chirped, and I fished it out of my pocket, checked it out. It was Reagan. I popped open the phone, texted her:

*Im alive; Im w boi; ask Polly bout it*

She wrote back:

*wot hapnd? U guys jst disappeared. She sed U met som dud.*

"Sorry, Ansel," I said. "Friends, checking up on me."

My fingers flew on my phone. Of course, it was easier just to pick up, but I didn't want to be one of those people jawing on the phone at a restaurant.

*yyssw, Hs nAmz Ansel. He's pritE kewl. Hes an Rtst! 4 real! Hes totally :-$$$.*

Ansel smiled into his plate, ate his goat, shook his head.

*I knO, I hErd.*

"I don't see how people can use those things," he said. "My fingers are too big."

"You don't have a cell?"

*wer havN breakfast.*

He shook his head.

"I don't want to be reached," he said.

*Pollys :-|| @ U.*

Polly was pissed. I knew she would be.

*L%k, I gota go. SBTA!*

Reagan was always looking after everybody. Den mother, she was.

*U shud caL her, str8 it out.*

Sigh.

Ansel waved the waitress over, had her bring us some doggy bags.

*wiL do; Im supa BY rght nw. TLK 2 U l8r.*

I snapped the phone shut, but not before checking my messages. There was one from Polly, one from my mom, one from Clay. The waitress dropped off the doggy bags, and Ansel shoveled the rest of his roast goat into it.

"Are we leaving?" I asked. I wasn't planning to take my pancakes with me on the road.

"Somebody might want this," Ansel said.

"What, are you all filled up on me?" I asked, poking at the pureed cassava with a fork, taking a tentative taste.

Ansel shrugged.

"Hey, can I have one of those business cards you gave Polly last night?" I asked.

"Back at my apartment," he said. "Sorry."

That bugged me, just a little, made me think again that I was still second fiddle to Polly. "Say, would you have chewed up Polly?"

Ansel finished filling his doggy bag, tucked the Styrofoam box in the plastic bag that had a smiley face on it, printed in orange.

"I don't know," he said. "Probably. I really lost it last night."

I dug out my phone again, held it up, like a challenge.

"What's your number?" I asked.

"555-9653," he said. I added him to my log, dialed him up. The phone rang, and I heard Ansel's bored voice pop up on his voicemail.

"Hi, this is Ansel Rupino," he said. "I'm not here right now, but please leave your name and number after the beep, and I'll get back to you."

It beeped, and I left him a message, looking across the table at him challengingly as I did so. "Hi, Ansel, it's me. Just checking to see if you're there. I'll call you after the doctor's visit, let you know how that goes. Bye!"

I hung up. He smiled.

"Alright, Samantha," he said. "Give me a call, let me know how it goes."

He got up and left me alone with my pancakes and cassava, and I was kind of glad. I dug out my phone and played my messages.

# 6. SATURDAY, 27 OCTOBER

Of course, I went online and blogged about everything that had happened, putting my own spin on it, just in case Polly was reading my blog:

> Met Adonis last night, at Flinch, new club that was swimming with scenesters, so we bugged out of there really quickly. Anyway, I went there with Polygon as my wingwoman, and we danced and then ran into Adonis. He was gorgeous, quite literally tall, dark, and handsome. It was funny, I was thinking that at the time, like how he could be a Greek god, for real. Although he's not Greek; he's German and Italian, has this really cool Old World/Old Money vibe to him.
>
> Anyway, Polygon and I were dancing, and he noticed, and it turns out that he's a working artist, and he wanted to photograph us! We were like, "Uh, okay." and agreed to check out his flat, which was not too far from there.
>
> So, he has this great place, a real artist's loft, full of paintings, and it's kind of wild, because you can see he comes from Old Money. I know this because I've got friends who're Old Money, and they have that way, like this casual, unassuming vibe about them, where they're like all normal-seeming, but they're really not. Like they try to fit in, but you can just tell.
>
> His place was great, and he wants us to pose the way we were dancing at Flinch, so we agreed, after having a lot of wine (really good stuff, I don't know

wines, would have to check on my sommelier friend about that), we started dancing, and he took pictures, said he loved them, would make prints of them.

By then, it was getting late, and it was clear he was getting into us, so then Polygon and I were going to thumb wrestle over who would get to sleep with him, and I pulled some social jujitsu on Poly, and she had to leave, so it was just me and Adonis.

And we talked, and drank, and then had mind-blowing sex. It was amazing, like us on his emperor-sized bed (the thing was huge), and we just went at it all night. He was really sexy and tender and it was just way cool. So, when he found out I was an artist, too, he wanted to see my work, but I told him I was mostly a performance artist, like he'd have to come to a show or something, but he was into that.

Amazingly, he was pretty shy, despite being such a great guy. Like the next day, he was a perfect gentleman, and treated me to breakfast--brunch, really, because we slept in (grin), and we went to Moogatoo, which has great vegetarian food, and we just hung out and talked awhile, and it was great.

I'm hopeful that we'll see each other again.

Zipstrip, one of my fans, was online, of course, and commented almost immediately after posting.

*Zipstrip: Sounds hot.*
*Samhain78: Hey, Zip!*
*Zipstrip: Hi. More details! Spill!*
*Samhain78: Not yet. Have to go do stuff.*
*Zipstrip: K.*

I paused, nibbling on a fingernail. Okay, so the entry was mostly bullshit, but I wasn't about to tell the truth. It would be too weird and embarrassing. This read lame, but I knew if Polly read it, she'd at least not have the satisfaction of being glad she had chickened out. Zipstrip was my favorite commentator, fan, cyberfriend—the words weren't really there for what she was, exactly, since I'd never met her. Maybe she wasn't even a she, though I think she was.

On a whim, I checked out *Polytician*, just to see what, if anything she said.

> Christ, S can be such a bitch. The whole night was a wash. Though she's right: I AM married. That's really what it comes down to. I've always been faithful to T, but I'm just a flirt, too. That's part of who I am, as much as everything else. Flirting is fun. And that's all it really was, just a flirtation, and now I feel like I can't even do that. I have no doubt that A would've hopped right into bed with me; you could tell he wanted me.
>
> Me, not her.
>
> I couldn't believe how close I'd come, how much I'd been tempted by him. He was strong and sensitive and passionate. He's everything T isn't. I'll admit I was a little drunk, and I'm sure that didn't help matters, but there was just some chemistry between us. It was really strong, like musk.
>
> But nothing happened, so there's nothing to confess. That's an enormous relief. T's still out of town, who knows what he's doing, or who. No, that's not fair. I shouldn't project my own iniquities on him.
>
> I was the near wrongdoer here, not him.
>
> Thank heavens for small favors, eh? S's tirelessly whorish instincts accidentally got me out of a jam. I know that wasn't her intention, but that was the result of it. And for that, I suppose, I'm grateful.

"Tirelessly whorish?" I said aloud, biting my lip in annoyance. Polly's plaintively snarky soul-searching—Catholic guilt without the faith to go with it. I shrugged, thought about leaving a comment, but I didn't know if Polly knew that I knew about her blog. Some people were okay with others seeing their blogs; I mean they were out there, right? But other people were really furtive about their blogs, and were more comfortable with strangers reading about their lives, than friends and family.

I clicked off of her blog and logged back into mine. Of course, Taliesinner, my cyber-stalker, had left a comment, too. It seemed like he never slept.

*Taliesinner: Was his thing huge, too? (snerk)*

For a second, I didn't know what the creep was talking about, then I reread my post, and realized it was what passed for wit with the man.

*Samhain78: You said a mouthful there, Tal.*

I wanted to scratch off the gauze on my back, caught myself almost doing it, stopped myself. When it started healing, whenever that was, it would itch like crazy. I couldn't imagine not scratching it raw. On a whim, I blogged a little more.

> Adonis bit off my tattoo; my octopus tattoo, the one I photographed in the mirror. He actually bit it off me. But we were so into each other, I didn't even care. It's not like there's an ink shortage or something.

I thought that might be just bizarre enough to really catch my fans' attention, get them wondering. Had to put some raw meat out there for the fans from time to time. Plus, it was just too weird not to include.

There wasn't much more to say, so I went surfing on the Web, tried Googling "Ansel Rupino," just to see what would turn up. Nothing. There wasn't anything on him.

Well, that sucked. I tried searching for his name a variety of ways, but nothing turned up. Guess he wasn't that much of a working artist.

So, I googled myself, checked out the comments on some of my YouTube clips. They were the usual blend of lewd and stupid. I'd even salted them with some comments of my own, under an alias:

*Jasmint178: I think the artist's work speaks of unrequited expectations in an unfamiliar world. She hurts, and in hurting, finds both peace and salvation.*

That prompted some tart replies from other YouTubers, and I didn't bother to read those. Instead, I watched my performance, evaluated it, thought I could do better. I'd done a piece where a girl turned herself into a printing press, inked herself in a manifesto that she slapped onto heavy paper with her body. I liked the way the words smeared in places, how my body made it alternately more clear in places and distorted in others.

The words I'd used for my manifesto were just freewriting, something I'd plucked out of the confines of my mind:

*Empty battles and sunlit occupations find me wanting; I am a child of the night, a bringer of breathless woe, arbiter of the arbitrary, keeper of conditional affirmations and legendary legerdemain, the spritely [BLUR] wallower, the plucked wallflower, vestal valkyrie, sundered maiden and apothecaries' [SMUDGE] working wild and wanton with decimated doctrine and*

I paused the clip, stopped myself in mid-writhe. It was two years ago. I looked like a baby when I'd done "Womanifesto." Touching my hand to my forehead, I thought I was feeling a little feverish. Maybe that son of a bitch had infected me, after all. I dialed up Polly, just to see what she'd say. She let her voicemail get it, or wasn't around.

"Hi, this is Polly. Leave your name and number, I'll call you back."

"Hi, Polly, it's Samantha. Hope everything's alright after last night," I said, hesitating. I wanted to kind of tell her off a little. "Call me when you get the chance."

I hung up.

What I wanted to say was something like "You weren't really going to put the moves on Ansel, were you? Don't you think Tristan would mind? Where do you get off?"

But, of course, I didn't want to bury the hatchet between her wide-set eyes, so I had to play nice. That image disturbed me. Where the hell had I come up with that?

I took some Motrin, tried to feel better.

Then I waited for Polly to call me back. She didn't. I blogged some more.

> Had a weird dream last night. My teeth all fell out, lots of blood. And I got fangs, instead. Then I woke up and thought someone was watching me. Wasn't you, was it, Taliesinner?

I smirked as I wrote this. Calling him out would annoy Taliesinner, I was sure. Maeve69 was online, IM'd me when she'd read my post.

> *Maeve69: Fangs in dreams can symbolize feeling threatened, or a fear of somebody intruding on you, compromising your integrity, or even attacking you on some level. Teeth always symbolize health issues, general well-being, being able to express yourself, handle your own life.*
> *Samhain78: Thanks for the dream analysis, Maeve. It was messed-up, for sure. What does losing my teeth mean, though? Like losing my health?*
> *Maeve69: Usually, it's a sign of fear of aging.*
> *Samhain78: Gotcha.*

I thought that made sense. I was feeling old at 28, remembered my mom saying that women lived longer than men, but suffered more.

# 7. SUNDAY: 28 OCTOBER

Work for me was at Nonpareil, an art supply store, where I was a cashier. Just something to pay the bills, and to give me a hefty discount on art supplies, even though, as a performance artist, I relied more on myself than on materials, it was useful, anyway, both for props for myself, and also to be a kind of art supply dealer for Sheldon and Reagan. They'd have me buy stuff at discount for them. That deal alone guaranteed me a seat at the Horrorshow table. Even some of the poets had some use for me in that regard, if they wanted good calligraphy pens, or choice paper to print their stuff upon.

The uniform at Nonpareil was a black short-sleeved shirt and a white pocketed smock, giving us a kind of workmanlike look. We could wear what bottoms we liked, and I usually favored designer jeans and one of my many hundreds of pairs of shoes. Today it was some cardinal red Adidas Sambas.

Because it was Sunday, it was pretty busy, just students and befuddled artso wannabes. I was lucky in having Saturday off, but I was in good with the manager, Lance Garvick, who was in his mid-30s, and was pretty mellow about hours, overall. He looked kind of like Philip Seymour Hoffman. He liked having artists and hipsters as his cashiers, thought it offered some kind of cachet to the place, like said right off the bat that Nonpareil wasn't for norms, tourists, poseurs, or whatever.

My coworkers were usually Dean, Darryl, and Simone. Darryl was a tall black guy who always dressed sharp in primary colors, who shaved his head and had gold earrings that made him look like a pirate, while Dean looked like he would be more comfortable in a morgue, with jet black hair artfully and perennially tousled, and black eyeliner, and jeans that were tighter than mine. He always wore mangy black Chuck Taylors, both toes of which were repaired via duct tape. I told him he should just get new shoes, but he wouldn't hear of it. He played bass in Twystyd Krystyn, his gothic neo-emo band.

Simone was Assistant Manager. She was tall, with brown hair cut in a hipster shag with bangs across the front and long strands to either side of her face. Her eyes were deep-set and dusty green, and she had tattoos on her arms, and was fond of wearing big Tex-Mex belt buckles. I was certain she was screwing Lance—there was just that overfamiliarity, that presumption of intimacy between them. Made me want to retch.

I liked Nonpareil, which was like a warehouse as much as it was an art store, with every art supply you could possibly want or need, and towering shelves and dark back corners you could lose yourself within.

"Wow," Simone said when I came in. "You look like crap."

"Huh?" I said. Dean looked over from his register, where he was busy dropping a giant white pastel carelessly into a customer's bag, this old Trotskyite guy I nicknamed Johnny Dubrovnik, who showed up regularly for his pastels, usually whites, pinks, reds, and yellows, his favorite proletarian hues, I guess.

I didn't think I looked that bad. Tired, yeah, headache, sure. But bad? Come on. Simone was just being a cunt.

"You have rings around your eyes, Sam," she said. "Look in a mirror."

I went to the small mirror we had on a pole outside Lance's office, checked myself out. Yeah, I suppose I had a little raccoon eye action going. It hadn't been so noticeable at home, where the lighting was better. Nonpareil didn't have the best light, just fluorescents overhead. Everybody looked like ass under fluorescents.

Without hesitation, I clocked myself in and went back to the employee lounge, this tiny room in the back, put on some more makeup to cover up the rings around my eyes. I wasn't feeling so hot, I'll admit. Putting my stuff in my locker, I went to work.

"It was way busy yesterday," Dean said. "You missed it."

"I had Saturday off, hello?" I said.

"Oh, I know," Dean said. "I'm just saying you missed it."

"Sheldon was in here," Simone said. "He was looking for you."

"Fine," I said. "Who's working today, besides me?"

"I'm here until seven," Simone said. "Deano's done in like five minutes. You're closing."

"Alone?" I asked. Nonpareil was open until nine.

"Looks like it," Simone said. "I wouldn't worry; it should be dead tonight."

I was okay with it, I supposed, although it was spooky working Nonpareil alone at night. After what had gone on with Ansel, I supposed I was more than a little on edge.

"Lance is out?" I asked.

Simone nodded.

"Great," I said. I was senior to Simone. Not like I was a careerist or anything, but it still bugged me that somebody junior to me was somehow my boss. That she'd been made assistant manager on the strength of fucking Lance was more salt in the wound.

"Can you handle it tonight, then?" Simone asked. I nodded.

Dean clocked out and threw off his smock. "I'm gigging tonight, Princesss. Wish me luck."

He sauntered out, his smock over his shoulder like it was a matador's cape, and I slumped at my register. I really was feeling like shit, a hint of a fever, and sweating, too. Had my Ansel-wounds gotten infected? I'd put some antibacterial ointment on them, figured that was enough, at least until I got a doctor's visit squared away. It was hard to make an appointment, like with work and all. I'd set one for after work tomorrow.

I'd set my phone to vibrate, instead of ringing, because Lance and Simone would get annoyed if anybody but them took phone calls during the day. It buzzed while she had gone into the manager's office, so I checked it out.

It was Sheldon, texting me.

*whr d feck wer u? I nEd canvas & matte borDz.*

Sigh. I quickly texted a reply. It was so nice and quiet.

*Im hEr untl 9, doucheface.*

I hit send and glanced around. Nobody was in the store except for Simone and me. It was already getting dark outside, since I'd come in at four, and in the fall, the light gave out quickly.

*Ill cum by @ 8.*

Fine, fine. I was surprised Sheldon hadn't tried his reptilian charm on Simone, tried to snag himself a 20% discount on a few wags of his bushy eyebrows.

*fiN, fiN.*

I cut him off before he could lay out my marching orders, like what he wanted. Let him shop around, find what he could. Frankly, I was thinking I needed to work out some kind of commission deal or something on the supplies, although Simone and Lance and the others thought I was some kind of super-artist, always buying up shitloads of stuff. Lance hardly cared, so long as the cash registers rang.

Simone came back out after awhile, gave me another appraising, disapproving look. "You're sweating."

I touched my forehead. Yeah, I felt bad, like fever and chills at the same time. Hot and cold. I wasn't going to take off sick, especially since I was expected to close.

"I'm fine," I said.

"You don't look fine," she said. "Are you doing junk?"

"Yeah, right," I said. "I hate needles."

"Snorting it?" she asked.

"No," I said. "You always think everything's tied to drugs."

"Everything is," Simone said, watching me. "What did you do this weekend?"

"Drugs." I managed a smile. I wasn't feeling nauseous or anything. "Just got together with some friends."

"Maybe you need some new friends."

Simone was always full of useful advice. She was a total norm. Her hipster affectation was just that. She looked like a NYC hipster, which tipped her hand as far as Chicago was concerned. It was all so very complicated, like now there were even particular looks for hipsters, like hipster subcultures.

There were the classic 90s irony-worshipping hipsters, who had the thrift store look down pat, were fond of sweaters and Malcolm X or granny glasses or big clunky frames and odd collections and worship of vinyl LPs and Motown and R&B and obscurity. There were plenty of them still around, and I would wonder if they were doing it because they were really totally not hipsters, and were simply embracing an indie rocker look that they thought would properly signify, or if they were perhaps ironically embracing a willfully retro hipster look.

And then there were the NY hipster wannabes, who would ape the Williamsburg look, like the tousled bedhead or off-center shags, the ironic t-shirts and stovepipe jeans, the studded belts, the trucker caps, the cowboy shirts and big belt buckles and endless affectations. Like were *they* more authentic than the retro hipsters?

This didn't even factor in the rockabillies, the guys aping a blue jeans-and-leather jacket look, the workboots and pompadours, and their girls with their scarves and serious bangs and saddle-fucking-shoes and roller derby-worship. Or the Mods, or the Goths, or Emo kids, or any of the thousand other niches out there.

Since all of the looks were uniform within their own subcultures, and there was some incestuous trendswapping among them, they all seemed like norms to me, conformists. Sheeple, looking for their flock. Even if their herd was a bunch of freaks, it was still a herd. A subcultural herd was still a herd. I wanted a pack, not a herd.

And to make it more complicated, not a single one of them would ever cop to being a hipster. Like, if I said to Simone, "You're such a hipster"—it would be immediate war between us. She would vehemently deny it, even though she totally was. And, of course, I wasn't a fucking hipster. It was like it was part of the Code of the Hipster. The hipster was the enemy of the authentic person, and the enemy of the artist, only because they masqueraded as both.

So, Simone, working at Nonpareil could only be seen ironically by me.

"New friends? Thanks, I'll get right on that, Simone."

She glanced at her lime-green Swatch. "Alright, well I'm out of here. Don't forget to lock everything up when you're done. And could you sweep? It's been getting dusty. We got some new acrylics you can stock if it gets slower. They're in the back."

I nodded. It was worth it just to be there alone. I really was feeling like ass. I went to the manager's office and dug out some Motrin, took some. I was aching behind my eyes.

With Simone gone, I had control of the music, so I put on some electronica and piped it through the store speakers, then went back to the stockroom, put the boxes of acrylic paints on one of our store carts, and walked it out through the lonely aisles.

I took out my utility knife, which I kept in my smock, and carefully cut open the box. Sometimes Dean or Darryl would be careless when they opened some paints and would cut open a tube or three, making a mess. I was always careful, adjusting the blade to a mere eighth of an inch.

My phone rang, and I picked it up. It was Ansel.

"Hey," he said.

"Hi," I said. "I'm surprised to hear from you."

"Look," he said. "Are you feeling alright?"

I touched my sweating forehead with the back of my hand. "Fine, why do you ask?"

"Just wondering," he said. "Did you make that doctor's appointment?"

I was kind of flattered that he even called me back at all. It hadn't even been three days.

"Yeah," I lied. "Tomorrow, after work."

"Let me know how it goes," he said.

"Sure," I said. "You want to get together Friday?"

He paused on the line. "Sure. We can go to dinner somewhere. How about Disraeli's?"

Disraeli's was a steakhouse. I thought that was an odd choice, me being a vegetarian and all; what the hell would I eat there? Why would Ansel even suggest it? Then again, if he wanted a follow-up date, then maybe that was alright.

"Great!" I said, then caught myself a little. "Yeah, I mean, that's cool. Should we just meet there or what?"

"That's fine," he said. "How about eight?"

"Sure," I said. "You still owe me a tattoo."

"I know," Ansel said. "We can handle that later."

Sheldon sauntered through the automatic doors, wearing a black velvet jacket and some baby puke-brown corduroy trousers. He grabbed a shopping cart and tooled into the place, giving me a nod as he went by.

"Alright," he said. "You know how to get there?"

"Sure," I said, watching Sheldon disappear around a corner. Disraeli's was in the meaty heart of the Viagra Triangle, where the old guys took their young girlfriends and mistresses out on dates. It would at least be somewhat fancy, like a real date place, versus something more casual.

Sheldon appeared around a corner, basket rolling along, canvases piled up in it. He gave me another nod, disappeared down another aisle.

"So, we're good?" Ansel asked.

"Sure," I said. "I'll see you at Disraeli's, like eightish."

"Great," he said, hanging up. I snapped shut my phone, pocketed it.

I was feeling wild. Really fired up, out of breath. I imagined Ansel and me fucking right there in the store, like him coming in and hoisting me on the countertop, my legs clamped around him, and our regulars and shoppers just going by with their carts, watching.

"Who was that?" Sheldon asked, appearing down Aisle 4. There were ten aisles in Nonpareil.

"Ansel," I said, short of breath. Christ, I was fired up. I wanted to fuck Ansel. Bad.

"THE Ansel?" he said. "Ansel Rupino, right? I know that guy. He's a painter."

"Yeah?" I asked. Sheldon nodded. "He sucks, but he paints. Once in a blue moon he'll put one of his pieces up for sale. He's rich. Really, he should just start his own gallery."

I felt itchy all over, tingly, like I had yellowjackets squirming under my skin. How feverish *was* I?

"You okay?" he asked. "You're flushed."

"Fine," I said. "Fan-fucking-tastic."

I actually braced myself against the counter, felt shivers pass through me, gritted my teeth. The store felt like it was burning up. I was sheened in sweat, gasping.

Sheldon just sneered. "Whatever you're on, give me two. Put it on my tab."

He went down Aisle 5, and I dropped to a crouch, feeling like I could faint.

Then I went into the manager's office, cranked up the in-store music, turned off the lights in the office, tore off my smock and took off my shirt, was scratching myself all over. Every nerve, every pore felt like I'd bathed in napalm and lanolin.

I rolled around on the floor, moaning, gritting my teeth. I bonked my head on the corner of Lance's desk, looked up at the whiteboard he had on his wall, where he kept a schedule of who was working that week. Darryl opened tomorrow. The store opened at 10:00.

*Tomorrow was Monday.*

*Tomorrow was Monday.*

My brain latched onto that, as I was heaving and writhing on the ground, shirtless. I threw off my shoes and yanked off my jeans and crouched there in the manager's office, in the dark, nearly naked, praying Lance didn't show up, no customers were coming in, hearing me yelping.

I screamed, but I don't think Sheldon heard me over the noise of the music.

It was Aphex Twin.

It was "Ventolin."

My cell phone rang from the pocket of my jeans, while I scrabbled across the floor, cracked my head again against Lance's desk, snarling, saw my arms sprout hair, felt the stretching of my bones, an orgasmic agony that had me howling.

*My phone is ringing. Ventolin. Darryl opens tomorrow. Tomorrow is Monday. I am Samantha.*

My brain began working in a rhythm to the musical beats, absurdly, insanely, as I whimpered and wailed, watched my bra snap and my panties stretch ever-tighter against my hips until they tore.

*My phone is ringing. Ventolin. Darryl opens tomorrow. Tomorrow is Monday. I am Samantha. I am Samantha.*

Christ, it hurt worse than anything, the wound on my shoulder like a sunburst, the snapping of bones, like the chicken bones Grandma would toss into a stewpot, over a low flame, bubbling, the skin and fat slipping off the bones, the water turning to broth. Enough heat, gentle flame, bubbling water, turned to broth, drawing meat from bone, flesh and fat slip free from the bone. Grandma humming, fat, withered fingers dropping herbs into the pot, a recitation, an incantation.

*The water becomes the broth. My phone is ringing. Ventolin. Darryl opens tomorrow. Tomorrow is Monday. I am Samantha. Sheldon's in the store.*

*Sheldon's in the store.*

*Sheldon's in Aisle 4.*

*No. Wait.*

*Sheldon's in Aisle 8.*

*Best not wait a minute more.*

I was there, mute inside my body, coiled flesh and sinew, muscled, lean and limber like I'd never been before.

*Sheldon's in the store.*

I called to him, my voice not my own, a howl, a demonic thing, a monstrous thing.

Ventolin. I drank in the air of the store, tasted the smells, the solvents, the paints, the canvases, the wood, the charcoals, the pastels, the linoleum, the rafters, the rats, and Sheldon. I could smell him. Aisle 9.

Aisle 9.

I ran out of the manager's office and into the store, stumbling across a cart as I went, landing on the ground with a grunt. The cart skidded away from me, went clear across the store, knocked over some little tiny artbooks Lance had for tourists. They flew free like giant confetti.

"You need a strobelight," Sheldon yelled from Aisle 9. He hadn't rounded the bend, had just seen me dart past. "We could rave this place up."

I was back on my feet in a second. Then I could see that my feet had claws on them. My toes ended in fucking claws. I looked at my hands and saw that my nice manicure had become claws, too. Big, long, curving claws.

*Aisle 9. Title 9. Ventolin. My phone stopped ringing. Darryl opens tomorrow. Tomorrow is Monday. I am Samantha. Sheldon's in the store.*

*Sheldon's in the store, but only for a minute more.*

I charged down the aisle toward him, saw his face go from his characteristic sneer to shock and then fear, as I bounded for him, smashing into his cart, snarling, knocking him back, right off his feet, his Elvis Costello glasses flying clear off his face, flat on his back, the cart beneath my feet, making me stumble, the cart tipping, canvas ripping, me flipping.

"Holy motherfucking shit," Sheldon said, the poet-painter, lost words, muted tongue. He turned and ran down the aisle, toward the back door, with me hot on his heels.

Without more than a snarl, I was on him, catching his throat between my teeth, champing, snapping, cutting off his scream in one quick movement, and his nicotine blood was in my mouth. Furious at the smoky stink of him, the bitter taste, I bit down hard on his strangled gasps, and his head came right off, tumbled away, while I tore at him in rage, while his body pumped blood on the ground, sprayed it in my face.

Christ, I was all over him, ripping the shit out of him, wanting to devour him, taking bites, but finding the taste all wrong, not what I remembered, and it just pissed me off all the more.

I don't know how long I tore at him, but I didn't stop until Sheldon didn't look like Sheldon, anymore, and it was just him and me, me crouched in his blood, sniffing it, hating the smell of him. He smelled bad.

I howled in the shadows of Nonpareil, loud and long, and somehow spent, satisfied. And yet frustrated. The itching, the ache, the yearning, the burning, all past.

And then the thing that had claimed me went away, creaked and cracked and fur faded, replaced by my own shivering flesh, and I was just a naked little woman in a pool of blood in a store in the heart of the city, near the savaged remains of a friend.

I couldn't believe it.

I realized I was shuddering from the rush of the kill. I just laid my head against the floor, a baptism of blood, and then got back to my feet. Christ.

Not knowing what else to do, I went back to the office for my clothes, praying that no customers had come in while all of that had gone on.

Then I went to the employee restroom and looked at myself in the mirror. I was covered in blood, like on my hands and my face and across my chest. The blood soaked through my clothes.

I grabbed paper towels and ran hot water in the sink and soaped myself up and cleaned off. It was almost reflexive, like me being dirty, wanting to be clean.

"I'm sorry, Shel," I said, wiping blood from my face with the back of my hand. I kept going until I was clean. Until my hands and face were clean. I was shaking.

I had to call the police. I had to do something. What, exactly, I didn't know. That I'd turned into a monster and had murdered Sheldon?

My reflection looked back at me.

"Fucking no imagination, Sam," I said to myself in the mirror. Without even moving my lips, I said it. "Try harder. Do better."

I touched my lips with my fingers. Had I just said that?

"You want to get locked up? Is that what you want?" I asked myself.

My reflection just looked me up and down. She'd slicked her hair back, this other me. Looked freshly-scrubbed and feral, like she'd been drinking dewdrops and rolling around in the grass, bathing in Buckingham Fountain, hit by the ice-cold spray that geysered up from its antiquated fixtures.

"Look," I said. "I just killed Sheldon."

"You didn't," she said. "I did. Your hands are clean."

I looked at my hands, saw they were clean. Maybe not under the fingernails. My reflection held up her hands, and they were covered in blood. Blood dripped down her arms. She looked at me challengingly, then reached out and touched the mirror, putting a bloody pawprint on the inside of the mirror. Sheldon's blood ran down from the print, already thickening, the red darkening.

My own hands were clean. I could see this. I was losing my fucking mind.

"You go to the cops, you go away," she said, licking her fingers. "Christ, I think we did Sheldon a favor, Sam. He was already dying. Cancer. Can't you taste it?"

My stomach heaved, and I leaned back against the employee lockers.

"I can help you, Sam," she said, this Mirror-Me. "Let me help you with this."

"Fuck," I said. "What's wrong with me?"

"Are you fucking kidding me?"

She licked each finger, just took her time with it, slowly, sensuously. She was savoring Sheldon's blood, sick as he was. Because she knew the sickness wouldn't touch her, or that the sickness inside her was worse than anything Sheldon had.

"Look," she said. "You have two choices: sink or swim. You know how to swim, right?"

She playfully worked her gooey hands at me, like she was doggy-paddling.

"You know how animals know how to swim? All they're doing is walking through the water. That's all. They just walk through the water, move their legs like it's the same as land. That's the secret. People forgot how to swim because they forgot that they were animals. They have to learn how to walk again, how to swim. We're born in water, Sam. We just forget who and what we are, we get stupid. You can swim through blood, too. Sure, thicker than water, right? But you just move your arms and legs, get them moving, and you'll get moving, too. I need you to get moving, Sam. Can you do that for me?"

My arms and legs felt like lead. My head throbbed. But I didn't feel sick, not like I was before. Not like when I'd been behind the counter.

"Get a fucking mop, get a bucket, get to work," she said. "You always did have a lousy work ethic, Sam. Clean up in Aisle 9. Come on, Sam. Move. Sink or swim, Sweetie. Fight or flight. Live or die."

Sink or swim.

I didn't know what she was talking about, or perhaps didn't want to think about it. She was asking me to do something I knew was wrong. I looked at the mirror, at the bloody pawprint on the inside of the glass. I'd never be able to get that off. She looked at me mockingly, safe inside the confines of the mirror. She was safe. She was in there. I was out here, in the cold.

"Poor baby," she said. "Look, don't fuck this up. Opportunity is knocking, here."

She playfully rapped the mirror with her outstretched knuckle, held her fist there, glanced to it. "Don't leave me hanging."

I held out my own fist and bumped hers, feeling like a marionette. The mirror was cold against my knuckle. Touching my reflection, I felt better, like a circuit had been formed. She smiled soothingly at me in the mirror.

"Clean up in Aisle 9," she cooed. "Simone wanted the place all scrubbed, right? This way everybody's happy."

"What about Sheldon?" I asked.

"Euthanasia," she said. "He was dying from the inside out, already. You just saved him from years of chemo, from going fucking bald, from losing whatever money he had. You just gave him peace. He's at peace, Sam. You could taste it, the sickness. That's what we do. We cull the weak and the sick, let the species thrive."

"Eww," I said.

"Humanity's been on a dead end for a long, long time," she said. "It's our own fault. We stopped evolving. We got around the food pyramid, started building real pyramids, instead, and it's been downhill ever since. Now you've got a way out. You're part of the solution, now, not part of the problem."

I ran some hot water into the mop bucket and poured Mr. Clean into it, the astringent scent of it making me wrinkle my nose.

"Go get'em, Killer," she said. "You know where I'll be."

She tapped her forehead with a bloody fingertip, winked at me. Crazy bitch.

Then I walked the mop over to Aisle 9.

"Clean up in Aisle 9," I said, and went to work. I noticed one of the canvases that Sheldon was going to buy was splashed with his blood. Like this sideways, catty-cornered spray of the stuff, still red, but slowly trending darker. It looked beautiful, dynamic. On a whim, I set that aside, and went to work cleaning up the rest of my dead friend. I don't remember the rest of the night, lost as I was in the metronomic sway of the mop.

# PART 2

"A CORPSE
IS MEAT GONE BAD.
WELL AND WHAT'S CHEESE?
CORPSE OF MILK."

—JAMES JOYCE

# 1. MONDAY: 29 OCTOBER

I woke up at home, not even really remembering how I got there. I was in a stupor after what had happened. I didn't even remember for sure what I'd done. Something with mopping. Cleaning something up. Sheldon. Cleaning him up.

I got the shower going, wanting to wash the city grit off me, the stink of the place. As I was changing, I saw that I had some hair on my belly, just a little strip between my belly button and crotch.

"What the hell?"

I looked at it, ran a finger across it. I usually had a belly button ring down there, a gold ring for luck, which I brushed with my finger as I traced the pattern. But I'd lost it at Nonpareil, when I'd become that thing. It was a thin red-brown line that widened as it reached my crotch, connecting it. The hairs were thick, but soft to the touch. Like fur.

"A fucking happy trail??" I said aloud. "What the fuck?"

I thought pregnant women sometimes got something like that, some hormonal weirdness. I found myself humming "Happy Trails" as I examined it. I went to my bathroom vanity mirror and stood on the toilet and checked it out under the unforgiving half-dozen lights that topped the mirror. My Hollywood lights, I liked to think of them as.

In the light, the reddish cast to the hair was unmistakable, like an arrow pointing to my crotch. Without a moment's hesitation, I fished out a washcloth and some Veet, and went to work on that happy trail, and in no time, turned my flat tummy back to its golden expanse of taut, hairless flesh that looked so summer-sumptuous in a bikini.

I rubbed my shoulder, where Ansel had bitten me. The skin was firm to the touch of my fingers; the wound was gone. As I did so, I noticed my forearm was a little hairier, kind of the way the happy trail had been.

I wasn't very hairy, so something like the reddish hairs on my forearms stood out to me. I ran my fingers over it. The hairs were thick, but soft. Just a peppering of them along my forearm. I looked at my other arm, and it had the same thing.

"Christ," I said. I went back to the mirror and held out my arms, looked at them, checked my armpits. The pits were mercifully clear.

I fished out the Veet again and the soap and water and washed my forearms, then put the stuff on, mindful of the stink of it, the chemical burn, and when the time came, I took the hair off. It wasn't so bad that somebody would just notice it straightaway, would point their fingers and call me Cousin It. But I knew the hairs were new, that they didn't belong there.

I didn't stop until it was gone, until my arms were smooth. I actually thought they were too smooth, now. Fall was upon me, though, like long-sleeve time. It was like when I'd not shave my thighs in wintertime, because usually people weren't seeing me naked that time of year, anyway. At least nobody sober.

But what bothered me was the principle of the thing. It was like a follicular insurrection on my body. Maybe something with hormones. I didn't approve of it. I looked at myself in the mirror, really scrutinized myself, looked for anything out of place. My eyebrows looked the same; they were always pretty full—I left them that way, didn't pluck them down or anything, just a little shaping of them, as required. My upper lip was pristine, and my temples looked alright. Just my arms and on my belly. Weird.

I stepped in the shower and got cleaned off, started my day. I thought maybe I had dreamed that whole thing last night, since no way did I turn into some fucking monster and kill Sheldon at the store. NFW. I had tripped out or something. Hallucinated because I was feverish.

Looking in the mirror, I was stunned to see that my hair had lost its color: the beautiful, atomic bombshell red I'd gotten done was gone. It was back to its native, natural, dusty, rusty brown. Red dye never lasted long, but I'd just gotten it done a couple of weeks before, and now it was like I'd never done it. I pawed at my hair in wonder, trying to find a trace of the color. Turning this way and that, I saw that the tattoos on my back were gone, too.

"What the hell?" I said to my reflection. I rang up Ansel on my cell phone, got his fucking voicemail, left a message.

"Ansel? Sam. My hair's not red anymore. And my tattoos are all gone. What the fuck is up with that? Call me, wouldja?"

I hung up, got dressed. What the fuck, man? My tattooes were an integral part of who I was; they were intimate parts of my identity, for all to see. And now they were gone.

In addition to my poor, lost, pink octopus, I had tattoos across my shoulders, a delicate scripted text that said "I am one" in Sanskrit. Between the points of my shoulder blades was a spade, a motif that was repeated at the base of my back, the point of the spade pointing to my neck up top, and my buttocks down below. I had a butterfly across my lower back, too. All gone.

It was like I'd lost some friends. My skin was back to its ordinary, drab self. Except with more hair. Like me, only hairier. What the fuck?

Going outside, I was at least feeling better after being sick the past couple of days. I don't know what I had, what was wrong with me, but whatever it was, it had passed. Although I found I was more sensitive to light and noise and smells than I was before I got sick. The city just got irritatingly noisy, everything sawed at my nerves, like the bleating of car horns and the gritty grind of buses, the rush of dirty city air in my face as they passed. Everything was getting on my nerves. It was cloudy, even, but I would wear my shades, anyway, just wanting to tune everything out.

I put my headphones on, which I usually jacked into my MP3 player when I was going around the city. They were special ones that would cut off outside noise, and were great for really hearing the music, but instead of playing music, I just wore them and sealed off the city around me and walked around only hearing my own breathing, and everything else muffled and far away. It was nice.

Polly finally called me back, and I was glad to hear from her, in a way. I was getting a latte at Starbucks, and my phone rang, and there she was. I was wearing shades, trying to shield my eyes from the annoying city lights. Even the smell of the coffee was kind of getting to me a little, like too much, making my head ache.

"Hi," Polly said. "So, how'd it go with Ansel?"

"Pretty wild," I said. "He's, you know, wild."

"Yeah," Polly said. "Anything else?"

"Why?"

"Just wondering," she said. That made me paranoid, made me wonder if maybe she'd gotten together with Ansel at some point, on the sly. Had he called her? Had they talked? Had he said something?

"You didn't hook up with him, did you?" I asked.

"We talked," she said. "Yeah."

That made my heart sink, made my stomach churn. "For real? Did you call him or did he call you?"

"He called me," Polly said. "Wild, eh? Yeah, he's pretty wild."

I mean, we weren't in a relationship or anything, but I felt territorial I leaned on brownstone wall and nursed my latte, thought about Sheldon, or what was left of him. Oh, Christ, what had I done? I took refuge in the mundane.

"So, uh, did you guys, you know?" I asked.

"Yeah," she said. "I know, I'm terrible. Tristan would cry if he knew."

"Yeah," I said. "You know, I was trying to protect you from all of that."

"Saint Samantha," Polly said, with more than a splash of sarcasm in her words. "Trying to save me from myself."

"He and I are going out Friday," I said.

"Funny," Polly said. "We're going out Saturday."

I couldn't believe he was still chasing after Polly. I mean, yeah, she was cute and stylish-sexy and was a total, shameless flirt, but still, I had my own charms. I was cute, too, and spunky, and perky, full of life. And I was, apparently, a monster.

Still, part of me wondered if he'd attacked her the way he'd attacked me. But it wasn't something I could just come out and say. I scratched my back where my wound was, only to find that nothing was there. The skin was smooth. There was no bite. I pawed around back there, finding nothing. It had healed. What in the hell?

"So, what'd you think of him?" I asked, straining to reach my back, to find it.

"Hot," Polly said. "Sexy. Gentle, too."

"Gentle?" I said. "Not kinky?"

"Kinky?" Polly said, laughing. Her laugh was cruel, on the phone, on the receiving end of it. "He was a perfect gentleman."

That annoyed me, too, like why'd he cut loose on me, and then been all nice to Polly? Wasn't I worth respectful treatment, too? Or perhaps he'd learned from his mistake with me and then played it extra-nice with Polly?

My mind was racing, I was trying to figure out what the hell I'd say to Ansel when I saw him again. I wasn't going to call him and bitch about it; I'd wait until we were together, face to face, so he couldn't dodge.

"I guess I wore him out," I said. "He only had plain vanilla left for you."

"I don't know," Polly said. "He was pretty wild, like you said."

I really wanted to make further inquiries, but held off. The only reason Polly was even saying this was because she knew it would piss me off, I was sure. That's what friends were for.

"Where are you going Saturday?" I asked.

"Epiphany," Polly said, and then I really was pissed. That was a serious avant-garde restaurant, a new place with a five-star chef who made stuff like dark chocolate-covered bacon and insane *sous vide* creations. He'd treat *her* to Epiphany, and *I* got Disraeli's? Wow.

I was of a mind to cancel on the outing with Ansel, but then I thought I had to go through with it, just to put the pressure on him, just to roast and spit him. What did I care about chocolate-covered bacon, anyway? I didn't eat bacon. I ate Sheldon.

I took a calculating, punitive sip of my latte, wanted to spit it out. It tasted like hell.

"Why? Where are you guys going?"

Of course, maybe she already knew. It made me sweat, made me paranoid. Not knowing where else to turn, I turned to the truth.

"Disraeli's," I said.

Polly was quiet on the line, for a second. "I've never been there. It's supposed to be nice."

"Mmm," I said. I couldn't believe he was taking Polly to Epiphany, and more specifically, that she was going. I wanted to rat her out in the worst way, give Tristan a call and tell him to see his wife with another man at Epiphany.

"Although you know it's a steakhouse, right?"

"Yeah," I said. "I'll get by."

Polly had no problem eating meat, no ethical problems with it, whatsoever. That was Polly's breezy amorality, a veneer of civility that covered what, exactly? I don't know. She was pragmatic and ruthless to a fault, but candied herself with courtesy, and most people didn't even notice. But I did.

"Does it bother you that we're both apparently, you know, with Ansel?" I asked. Polly laughed again, high and lilting.

"I'm just enjoying myself," she said. "I'm not 'with' him."

"When did you guys go out?" I asked.

"Sunday," she said. "We met for brunch. He called and said he hoped Saturday wasn't too awkward, and then we just took off. He's really great, like it's so easy to talk to him."

"Yeah, he's a peach," I said, throwing my latte in the trash. The thought of it made me sick. The thought of him getting along with Polly made me want to puke. But, of course, he'd been into her the moment we'd met.

"Anyway," Polly said. "I didn't want you thinking I was mad about the other night, because I'm fine."

Of course she was fine. The whole reason she called was to up-jump me, to show me that Ansel liked her better than me. Pure Pollytics.

"Great," I said. "Because everybody was saying you were pretty upset about the other night."

"Really?" Polly said, an edge to her voice.

"Yeah," I said, enjoying that this didn't sit well with her. "People kept telling me you were pissed, so I'm glad that you're not."

"Oh, well," Polly said. "People exaggerate. You know, it's like an endless game of Telephone."

I smiled. Yeah, Polly, that's what it was.

"I don't know," I said. "But I'm glad you seem to have gotten over it."

It bugged me how flippant she was about her adultery, like she was changing her stockings. And it bugged me that it bugged me, like wasn't I above norm morality? Seriously. Look at what I'd fucking done! I'd murdered one of my frenemies. I guess I felt bad for Tristan, who was busy hopping the globe to pay for Polly, and there she was screwing around on him with Ansel.

I mean, Tristan was a total norm, Joe Business. He liked how buttoned-down and sleek Polly was. Plenty of guys fell for that. She oozed this pert sophistication, like she'd be the girl who'd perch on the edge of a piano at a jazz bar, and everybody would think it was perfect, like she belonged there.

Maybe wife-as-accessory was what Tristan liked. I didn't know. Still, that she was so casual about it bugged me.

"Yes," Polly said. "No worries. Friends?"

I gritted my teeth.

"Friends."

"Great!" she said. "You'll have to tell me how it goes on Friday. Oh, and Clay's having a showing of Sheldon's latest stuff on Halloween, if you're going."

"Yeah, I know about it," I said. I planned on showing up. That made my stomach turn a bit. Sheldon wouldn't be showing at his showing. I imagined he'd take grim satisfaction in the value of his shitty art perhaps going up with his disappearance.

"He and Reagan are both featuring new pieces," Polly said. "And Willa's doing a reading. She never does readings, so that'll be a special treat."

"See you Wednesday," I said. Trick-or-treat.

"Great," she said, and we hung up. Part of me felt like I should just cancel on Ansel and let him and Polly have their little tryst, but that also felt like giving up on my part, like somehow I couldn't compete with Polly or something, or that I wasn't her equal, or whatever. And that set my teeth on edge, made me want to spit, it pissed me off so much. And I thought that let Ansel off a little too light, too. I mean, he owed me some contrition. He owed me a tattoo. He owed me an explanation for what he'd done to me. I wasn't exactly sure what he owed me beyond that, but I had to know why he roughed me up and apparently gave Polly a free pass. What was his problem? Had his ketamine prescription run out or something? Psycho.

I shouldn't have been as put out by it as I was. I needed to get control of myself, but at the same time, I was raging, actually pacing a little, back and forth, thinking it over, while the latte I'd pitched in the trash sat, forlorn and abandoned, a ghost of steam emerging from its little plastic blowhole.

A putrid bum in a raincoat with a crazy-man beard shuffled by the can, saw the latte, picked it up, smiled, his oily near-black hands contrasting with the creamy white of the cup. He had a sunburned, peeling face, and a black stocking cap on his head. His maniac eyes flicked to me as he brought the drink to his lips and swilled it. I could hear his drinking, and the smell of him was intolerable.

"I saw you drop it," he said. "Half a block away, I saw you. What's wrong with it? Poison?"

"No," I said. "I didn't want it."

"Poison?" he asked again. "You trying to poison me?"

"No," I said. "I'm feeling sick."

"They got rat poison everywhere," he said. "In the black boxes. It'll make you bleed on the inside. Stomach. Nose. Toes."

"Enjoy it," I said, turning on my heel, stomping down the sidewalk, away from the man, away from Ansel and Polly and everything in between. Just me walking, something to clear my head.

# 2. THURSDAY NIGHT

I sat on the examination table, half-naked, while Dr. Resnick looked me over, read my file.

"What happened?" he asked.

"I got bit," I said.

"Where?"

"On my shoulder, but it's gone, now," I said. "Healed up."

Resnick smiled, putting a stethoscope to my chest, listening to my heart pummel out a beat. I watched him with a coy half-grin that was probably more wanton than he'd expected from a new patient. Usually they were reserved when they first came in, until trust had been established. I was feeling bold and brash, hoping nothing would be wrong with me.

"Bitten, eh?"

"Yup."

He asked me to breathe in and out for him, and I obliged.

"Bitten by what?"

"Not what, but who," I said. When he looked up, I added, looking down the end of my nose at him. "A guy friend."

Resnick nodded, running the stethoscope across my back, checking my lungs, which seemed to be fine.

"When?" he asked.

"Uh, over the weekend," I said.

"Which day?" he asked.

"Thursday night, or early Friday morning," I said, embarrassed that I couldn't exactly remember. The wound had been awful. It shouldn't have healed so quickly.

Dr. Resnick's smile withered on his lips. "That was nearly a week ago, Ms. Hain. You should have gone to the emergency room immediately."

That kind of took me off-guard. "I cleaned it."

"Nonetheless," he said, looking at my bare back. "You don't just let something like that slide. Human bites are worse than dog bites. You can get tetanus, syphilis, hepatitis, herpes, AIDS, any number of things from a human bite."

Only there was nothing there to see. "There's nothing here."

"There was," I said. "It healed. I'm fine."

"Where was it?" he asked. I gestured, and he poked and prodded my shoulder, looking it over.

"I feel okay," I said.

"I wish you'd come in sooner," he said. "As it is, I'm going to have to put you on some antibiotics, just to be safe. Have you felt any fever, any chills? Anything unusual?"

I thought about how I'd felt earlier in the week, like when I'd been sweating and flushed. "Well, yeah, but I figured—"

He cut me off. "When?"

"Sunday," I said. "And Monday. Look, I called to make an appointment, didn't I? I put Bactine on it, for god's sake, after washing it off."

"Bactine," Dr. Resnick said, like he was swearing.

"What was I supposed to do?" I said, raising my voice. "I didn't think it merited a trip to the emergency room. I mean, people with real problems go there, like missing arms and broken faces. You see there's not even a scar. I'm fine."

"A human bite is a serious problem," he said. "How did it happen?"

He was in full clinician mode, then, actually writing down what I said, which made me feel really self-conscious.

"It was during sex," I said. "He scratched me, too. Here."

I showed him my ribs, but there was nothing there, either. He probably thought I was out of my fucking mind.

"Were you fighting?" he asked.

"We were fucking," I said, feeling a little defensive. "Look, it just kind of escalated."

"Does this happen often?" he asked. "Routinely?"

"First time," I said. "I don't go for this kind of thing normally."

I was really uncomfortable, sitting there half-naked, while he was interrogating me. Who did he think he was, judging me? I thought of mopping up Sheldon in Aisle 9.

"Look, I was drunk," I said. "I don't remember everything. I don't even remember how it happened."

"Were you on drugs?" he asked, pen in hand, pausing, waiting for my answer. It felt like the whole fucking AMA was staring me down as he waited.

"No," I said. "But he was."

"What drugs?" he asked.

"I don't know for sure," I said. "He said he was on some killer Slavic PCP from the Ukraine, or something. I saw drugs in his medicine cabinet."

"What kind?" he asked.

I tried to remember the drugs. "Benzodi…ketamine…midala…."

"Ketamine, Benzodiazepine, and Midazolam?" Dr. Resnick said. I nodded. "Those are serious psychoactive drugs. Any of them, or perhaps a combination, could have caused him to act out. Some people get violent under the influence of them. Does he have a history of mental illness?"

"How should I know?" I said. "I only met him Thursday night."

Dr. Resnick glowered at my medical file, then looked up at me. "So, you incurred a human bite during unprotected sex with a stranger you just met."

Now I flushed, pissed off. "You make it sound so tawdry, Doctor. I don't know if the sex was unprotected or not."

"That, by definition, qualifies as unprotected sex," he said. "I'm just going to assume that he was high, you were drunk, possibly high, and there weren't any adequate precautions taken. The absence of a bite mark makes me wonder if you were hallucinating."

"I'm on birth control," I said. "I wasn't on acid. I didn't hallucinate him biting me."

"But there's no trace of a mark," he said.

"There was," I said. "I heal quickly."

"Birth control is the least of your worries right now, Ms. Hain," Dr. Resnick said. "I'm putting you on a 10-day course of amoxicillin, three times a day. And be sure to take the entire course. You're not allergic to penicillin, are you?"

I shook my head.

"Well, that's one point in your favor," he said, heaving a sigh. "I'm going to need to draw some blood, and do some tests on it, just to be sure. I'll have a nurse come in to do that. We're going to run tests and give you a call if there's anything unusual. Was this alleged bite consensual?"

"Mmm," I said. "I hadn't planned on it, no."

"Are you planning on pressing charges?" he asked.

"No," I said. "It was an accident, that's all. Look, why would he be on those kinds of drugs? If he even was. He was drinking, too."

Dr. Resnick shook his head. "Alcohol dramatically increases the risks for adverse reactions to those drugs. I wonder who prescribed them to him. They're pretty habit-forming; they're not drugs you can just simply quit. Your friend must be in therapy, although I can't imagine anybody giving him all three of those drugs, or for what. Not for somebody who's out and about in everyday society. You see those sometimes in institutions."

I didn't know where he'd gotten them, or whether he was on them all the time, or what. I didn't know much about Ansel at all, really. Dr. Resnick's bugging out made me feel even worse.

"The important thing right now is you, Samantha," he said. "How are you feeling?"

"I'm okay, Dr. Resnick," I said. "You freaked me out."

He didn't break into a smile, just stayed serious. It was really bugging me. "You *should* be freaked out. This is high-risk behavior you're engaging in. Have you ever been tested for STDs?"

"Christ," I said. "No. He attacked me."

"We'll run a broad array of tests on you, Ms. Hain," he said. "Get you straightened out. Do you want the number of a rape crisis and trauma center?"

"What?" I said. "I said I'm okay."

"You just said he attacked you," he said.

"Yeah, but, you know, I handled it."

He wrote me out the antibiotic prescription, told me to take them, just to be on the safe side.

"I'm writing you a prescription for Xanax," he said. "Something to help you cope with potential anxiety."

"I'm not anxious," I said, anxiously.

The way he said it, like he was talking down to me, really fired me up.

"If you have another of those episodes," he said.

"It wasn't an episode, Doctor," I said. "He actually bit me. It healed."

I thought of crawling around on all fours in Nonpareil, hunting down Sheldon. I could smell him a mile away, that cigarette stink of him.

"Alright, Dr. Resnick," I said. "Can I put my clothes on, now?"

"Yes," he said, jotting notes into my medical file. With the generally high-risk behaviors, I bet he figured I was at high risk of infection, although I'd reported no previous STDs and no history of intravenous drug use. "Set up another appointment after the antibiotics run out. I want to have a follow-up on you, assuming your blood tests come up clean. If your condition changes in any way, please don't hesitate to call."

"I don't have a condition, Doctor," I said. "I'm fine."

"Be that as it may," he said. "You call if anything changes."

"Fine, I will," I said, grabbing my wad of clothes as Resnick was leaving. I couldn't keep the annoyance out of my tone.

"A nurse'll be in here to draw blood," he said. "So leave an arm free."

"Okay," I said, buttoning up, waiting for the nurse.

I was pissed at him for scaring me and lecturing me. I was an adult, didn't need him giving me crap. It was an accident. I was balancing responsibilities. It really didn't occur to me to go to the emergency room. And, yeah, I shouldn't have gotten so drunk I didn't know what I was doing, or what was being done to me.

I thought maybe I *had* hallucinated the whole Sheldon thing. Maybe I was feverish or something. Maybe none of that had happened. I remembered Lee lecturing us on that. What was it, a fugue? Yeah, that's what he'd called it. Maybe Sheldon was okay. That made all kinds of sense. I'd lost my shit at Nonpareil.

I mean, my reflection was talking to me, for fuck's sake. That doesn't really happen to anybody.

The nurse came in, a young, pretty Latina, who went about drawing two vials of blood from me. She was quick, and did it mostly painlessly and silently, wearing latex gloves, making me feel like a fucking biohazard. My blood filled up the tubes really quickly, and she capped them and put the needles in the sharps disposal unit on the wall, put band-aids on the wounds, told me I was free to go, that I'd hear about the blood tests in about 48 hours.

I left the doctor's office feeling better, not because of the visit, but because the visit was over. I rubbed my arm where the nurse had drawn the blood. The blood tests would clear my head completely. I wanted that clean bill of health, I wanted to stick it to Dr. Resnick, to show him that everything was okay, that he spazzed out for no good reason.

Putting my headphones on, I tuned out the city as I went to get my prescriptions from the pharmacy. I was lucky that I had insurance at Nonpareil; the owners were old hippies, so they paid attention to things like coverage, although I still had to fork over a $10 co-pay with any doctor's visit. Like what was the point of paying if I had to pay on top of it? Seemed like a money grab. And my HMO would send me letters accusing me of having another insurance provider, and threatening not to pay my bill. I think they were just paid to do that, to find any excuse not to pay claims, so they could save money. And, of course, I had to pay $10 for my antibiotics and my Xanax, too. Sure, they cost a lot more than $10, but when I was already getting a chunk docked for health insurance, it annoyed me to have to pay on top of my payment for that, too. What a racket.

On impulse, I bought a couple more cans of Veet while I was at the drugstore, ignoring the raised eyebrow of the bearded clerk, who looked like he'd be more comfortable in a used record store. He probably recognized me as a fellow cool person, one of the tribe, wanted to hit on me.

He said something, but with my headphones on, I couldn't hear him.

"I can't hear you," I said, pointing to my phones.

"I said there's a special on Veet," he said. "Buy two, get one free."

He had raised his voice so I could hear it, and everybody in the store could hear it, I'm sure. I flushed.

"Thanks," I said.

"Do you want that third can?" he said.

"Sure," I said, now totally embarrassed, but I still didn't want to take off my headphones. I could imagine the other customers behind me, snickering or rolling their eyes.

I snatched up the bag and the receipt, and went back and got my third can. And sure enough, it was buy two, get one free. Cool beans.

I walked by his station, brandishing the can so he knew I was only taking one, not trying to clean the place out, and I walked out of there.

Curbside, I read the instructions for the antibiotics and pocketed them, then decided just to walk home. I pocketed the Xanax, figuring I'd sell them to some of the others. Work had been busy but boring, the way it always was. Simone had actually praised the mopping I'd done, said the place looked sharper than ever. The streetlights came on, and it was a little breezy. The fallen leaves smelled like cinnamon.

On a whim, I dug out my phone and dialed up Sheldon. I got his voicemail, his dry, melancholy voice the same as ever.

"Hey, Shel, it's Sam," I said. "Call me when you get a chance."

I know that might seem nuts, because you and I both know where Sheldon was, right? But at that moment, I just couldn't believe it. It was just too crazy. So I called. And part of me thought I could use the excuse, like not knowing that he was dead.

I thought about tracking down Ansel, brandishing my antibiotics and Veet, but I thought better of it. What a weirdo. God, to live rent-free. The new American Dream. No, sponging off your parents was the new American Dream. Unfortunately, my parents were not spongeworthy.

I went home and took my drugs and blogged a little, bitched about the thing with Polly and Ansel, using codenames, of course. Dinka-Doo was online, offered his own insights via Instant Messenging. As did Taliesinner, my ever-faithful cyberstalker.

> I don't get Adonis. If he's not interested in me, why's he jerking me around? Why's he taking me out one night and Polygon the next? Kinda pisses me off.

*DinkaDoo: Men are sluts.*
*Taliesinner: Takes one to know one.*

> I'm just confused and pissed off. Not used to being in this kind of situation, I guess.

I absently twiddled my belly button ring, touched the flesh below it, felt hair again. I actually jumped up with a squawk. It had grown back! Taliesinner and DinkaDoo kept at it while I was freaking.

*DinkaDoo: I'm not a slut.*
*Taliesinner: Then you're not a man.*
*DinkaDoo: I'm a man.*
*Taliesinner: Then you're a slut.*
*DinkaDoo: Your mom's a slut.*
*Taliesinner: I know, it's embarrassing.*

Pulling down my pants a bit, I looked at it. The happy trail was back.

"Oh, Christ," I said. I should have asked the doctor about it, but felt embarrassed about it. And the hair was back on my forearms.

That was definitely not something I was going to blog about. I went to take another shower, snagging one of my cans of Veet. I wasn't even thinking about chemical burns, or chapped skin; I just wanted the hair off me.

*Taliesinner: Samhain? You there?*
*DinkaDoo: Great, you scared her off.*
*Samhain78: BRB.*
*Taliesinner: You know "Samhain78" means "slow" in German.*
*DinkaDoo: You would know that.*

I hopped in the shower and turned on the water, made it hot, washed the city grit off my body with soap and scrubby, and took out the Veet and sprayed it on my arms and my happy trail, and waited. It had a little fake razor you used to take the hairs off.

When it was ready, I took the hairs off, rinsed off, toweled off, put on some sweats and a sweatshirt, and went back to my computer. Zipstrip had popped on, too.

> *Zipstrip: Did you guys scare her off?*
> *Samhain78: I'm here. Sorry, guys.*
> *Taliesinner: See? Told you I didn't kill her.*
> *DinkaDoo: Glad you're not dead, Samhain78.*
> *Samhain78: Me, too.*

I private IM'd Zipstrip:

> *Samhain78: Girl troubles, you know.*
> *Zipstrip: Like figuratively or literally?*
> *Samhain78: LOL. Had to get a bunch of Veet at the store.*
> *Zipstrip: I use Nair.*
> *Samhain78: Old school.*
> *Zipstrip: That's me!*

The boys kept going, as ever:

> *Taliesinner: I can't believe you'd think I would harm our lovely Samhain78.*
> *DinkaDoo: I can't believe YOU!*
> *Samhain78: Quiet, you two. I can't hear myself think with all of your nonstop pinging.*
> *Taliesinner: Feeling tired, irritable, Samhain? Is it that time again already?*
> *DinkaDoo: See? No class, Tally, no class.*

I kept the Zipstrip dialogue box open:

> *Samhain78: I really am hung up about Adonis.*
> *Zipstrip: You should not go out with him Friday. Just cancel.*
> *Samhain78: Why?*
> *Zipstrip: Cuz he's a creep, obviously.*
> *Samhain78: He's hot, though.*
> *Zipstrip: Still....*

*Samhain78: Yah, but I have to ask him stuff.*
*Zipstrip: Spill!*
*Samhain78: You'd think I was crazy. He bit me the other night.*
*Zipstrip: For real?*
*Samhain78: Yah. I think I might have some kind of infection.*
*Zipstrip: Ewww. What kind?*
*Samhain78: Not sure. I'm on amoxicillin, with a Xanax chaser.*
*Zipstrip: You should go to the hospital.*

I wanted to tell Zipstrip about the whole thing, the hair on the arms, the happy trail, Sheldon, all of that. It was funny, how these invisible people were, in many ways, more real to me than my real-world friends. Maybe it was because all I knew was what they said, and there was no other way of communicating with them, so all I had to hang on was their words. I couldn't explain it, but felt that someone like Zipstrip actually got me more than Reagan, or Polly, or Lee, or anybody.

I wondered if they played around online. I knew Lee did; he was a total whore for online things, whether secret file-sharing societies that swapped music on the sly, or geeky pop cultural message boards. Who *didn't* have a presence online, these days, except for old people and fundamentalists? Even everyday norms were online more and more, once they dumped their America Online accounts, at long last. AOL was the Antichrist. I couldn't believe people still used it. Internet with training wheels, like being in a fishbowl, and calling it the ocean.

*Samhain78: You're probably right. Still, I feel like I have to confront him.*
*Zipstrip: I wouldn't. I'd let him and Polygon have their fun. It'll blow up in their faces, and you'll have the last laugh on that one, for sure.*
*Samhain78: Yeah, that'd be sweet.*
*Taliesinner: Oh, they're probably private IMing.*

Then Taliesinner sent me a private IM:

*Taliesinner: Are you okay, kiddo? You haven't been on so much, lately.*

I hated when he called me "kiddo." It irked me.
*Samhain78: A-okay. Thanks. BRB.*

And then, to Zipstrip:

*Samhain78: If I ever turn up dead, it was Taliesinner, okay?*
*Zipstrip: How would I even know?*
*Samhain78: You'd know, because I'd be gone.*
*Zipstrip: Don't say that! Now I'll be paranoid, like you'll dump your account and then I'd be wondering if Taliesinner had gotten you!*
*Samhain78: Just kidding!*

I deleted the Taliesinner private IM box, which should have clued him that I didn't want private IM time with him. I went back to my blog. I didn't want to mention anything about sickness, because that'd prompt a flood of messages.

> I'm pretty tired, will probably just work on some knitting or something, watch television.

*Samhain78: Thanks for being there, Zip.*
*Zipstrip: (blush) For sure! Any time, Sam.*

If only Zip knew my name really was Sam. I thought about telling her. There probably wouldn't be any harm in it.

*Samhain78: You know, my name really is Sam. Samantha.*
*Zipstripß: Pretty. Mine's Zooey.*
*Samhain78: For real? Great name! Like the Salinger book.*
*Zipstrip: Thanks! Don't tell, though.*
*Samhain78: No way! You, too.*
*Zipstrip: Sämänthä. You should go like that—umlauts make everything rock; people would think you're Finnish. Add a few more a's and you'd have it. Like this: Säämäänthää.*

That made me laugh. And it made me think that Zipstrip...errr...Zooey, was smart. Because she was right about Finnish names. They loved the double-a umlaut combinations.

*Samhain78: That's awesome. I totally need to go by that name. Then people will think I'm this exotic Lapland performance artist. Awesome, Zip! Thank you!*
*Zipstrip: For sure!*
*Samhain78: I'm signing off, but thank you for cheering me up, seriously. We'll chat more soon, I promise.*

*Zipstrip: Great! TTYL!*

I signed off, didn't even bother saying goodbye to the boys. Säämäänthää.

That was awesome, made me think of a zombie moaning it, or a werewolf howling it to the moon.

# 3. WEDNESDAY: 31 OCTOBER—HALLOWEEN

At BacchUS, just inside the door, Clay had put a ton of candy corn in a bowl, on a little table with a purple cloth on it, and some black candles, and three bottles of absinthe, and a silver bowl full of sugar cubes, and some tongs for the cubes, and goblets.

Witchy Willa was last to arrive, of course. The track lights were burning low, showing off Sheldon's pieces, which looked like shit, as ever. I hated Sheldon's paintings. There were four of them, and four of Reagan's.

Sheldon's were *Apocrypha No. 5 (Grenadine Lantern)*, *Technofique*, *Apostrophilter*, and *Theramint Julep*. Reagan's were *Re-Joyce*, *Dublin Case Study*, *Lost Boy*, and *Chlorophylia*.

I actually kind of liked Reagan's *Chlorophylia*, because it was a monochromatic cityscape where everything was green, from a deep emerald, creamy jade, bold malachite, to a frosty mint, and she'd paid some attention to her brush technique, gave stuff texture. The trees looked like alien things.

*Lost Boy* was a portrait collage, where she'd rendered Kiefer Sutherland in his "Lost Boys" vampiric incarnation, in black, grey, red, and white. She must've spent many days carefully clipping the colored paper, what looked to be from magazines. The effect was that the nearer you got to it, the quicker the portrait dissipated, while if you got further from it, it showed up.

Was it kitschy? What was the point of it? Was Reagan trying to be experimental? Was she dipping her toes in Pop Art?

Fortunately, Lee asked.

"What did you have in mind with this?" he asked Reagan.

"Kind of a study of media manufacture," Reagan said. "Kiefer Sutherland played a Lost Boy, a vampiric youth, and this piece speaks to his transformation, assimilation, and preservation as a celluloid youth, forever young. But that Lost Boy is himself lost."

"Mmm," I said.

"Kitschy," Lee murmured, excusing himself to get another drink from Clay's trio of absinthes on a little table—two green, one orange. Clay and Gabe were having a spirited discussion about it, Gabe saying an orange absinthe wasn't authentic, and Clay arguing that absinthes, while most commonly available in the green hue, came in all colors and varieties. Lee offered up that absinthe was now legal in America, and that the ship had sailed on the beverage, and that they were absinthe hipsters, which made Clay and Gabe almost purple with indignation.

Of course, Lee just said "kitschy" to get to Reagan, who didn't tip her hand. She glided up to me, smile plastered on her face. "You're coming to my dinner party Sunday, aren't you, Samantha?"

"Oh, of course," I said. When Willa called me that, it was a smack in the face; when Reagan called me that, it was a testament to her mental delicacy, her gentlewomanly ways.

"Splendid," she said, drifting away. I wondered what drugs she took to get that glazed look in her eye. Something strong.

*Dublin Case Study* and *Re-Joyce* were more of her James Joyce pornography, and I hardly looked at them, could hardly stand to. I was sick to fucking death of James Joyce, of anything and everything associated with him. The ones who weren't busy singing his praises breathlessly were afraid to say anything against him, like if one admitted to not liking Joyce, one apparently hated the English language. Whereas I think Joyce was the Captain Beefheart of the literary world, with *Ulysses* as his *Trout Mask Replica*. Impenetrability was the new openness. And it wasn't even new, anymore.

Except for one, Sheldon's pieces were actually sculptures this go'round, which kind of broke the monotony of his usual approach to art. With *Apocrypha No. 5*, he'd taken a bottle of grenadine and somehow inserted a light into it, a small LED, and had rigged a mesh for it to hang from. The bottle looked like it held blood, or else just grenadine. It hung from an arm that looked to be made of corroded copper.

"The Picasso Patina," Gabe said, with greater smugness than usual, gesturing to his crotch. "Where the fuck is Sheldon, anyway? Who skips out on their own showing?"

"A bold artistic statement," Lee said. "Has anybody seen him?"

"I haven't," I said. "I tried calling him the other day, but I just got his voicemail."

"Nobody's seen him," Gabe said. "Fucking Sheldon."

*Technofique* was a film of sepia-toned celluloid, actually three sheets of varying hue, set about a centimeter apart, depicting a cityscape. It looked like he'd taken an original black and white photograph of... James Joyce...and his wife, Nora, appraising each other. Then he'd printed the pictures on the celluloid (beige, tan, brown, and black) and overlaid them, taking selective elements from them and reproducing them, which gave some depth to the images.

"Fuck Joyce," I said to Lee, who looked on without comment.

*Apostrophilter* was another bottle, but it looked to be made of solid glass, or else some kind of polycarbonate, and he'd put the name "Apostrophilter" on it in apostrophes, then set the thing on a shoebox-shaped shelf made of dark, stained wood. There was an old-time price tag attached to it that priced it at $.99.

"The price resonates with the name of the piece," Gabe said, doing finger quotes at "price."

"Oh, yeah," I said.

There was *Theramint Julep*, which was a still life of a Theramin with a mint julep perched upon it. I knew it was a Theramin because Lee pointed it out, quite impressed that Sheldon had incorporated a Theramin into one of his paintings. Lee then treated me to a dissertation on theramins, and their role in popular music, from the Beach Boys to Man or Astro-Man!?

The others chit-chatted about the artworks, while I paced around, feeling trapped, wishing somebody had done a proper Halloween party. Clay's gallery was small, but it felt more confined with the chairs and the people. Sheldon's absence was felt.

Clay was working the crowd, looking a little soused, cheeks red, touching the arms of the women, talking with big gestures, his blood-shot eyes looking about the room nervously. He was eager for the showing to be a success, kept calling Sheldon on the phone.

"I don't believe anything I see here," Lee said. "Frauds, one and all."

"Including yourself?" I asked.

"No," he said. "Of course not. But I don't create anything, so I can't be a fraud. All I do is criticize, which is invariably genuine."

Willa stalked in, carrying one of her black books. She placed all of her poems in black books, used a fountain pen. She was wearing an olive drab skirt, black hose, black loafers, a smoke-colored turtleneck, and a rust-colored tailored blazer.

"Where's Polly?" I asked. Lee shrugged.

"Where's Sheldon?" Reagan asked. I shrugged.

Willa went to the dais in the center of the room, cleared her throat, looked through her book of verse, one of a whole library she kept.

*"Almanac*

*The winter's kiss it lingers*
*Snow-flecked and abbreviated*
*On the whims of the endless ages*
*Where sullen silences contend*
*And elementary apprentices*
*Seek allotted wisdom*
*In drenchéd drams.*

*The autumn shade convinces me*
*Sad, lonely, lost prophetess*
*Of the error of my ways*
*In the candlelit shadow of a fortnight's*
*Dreaming, while spirituous sentinels*
*Rap on mullioned panes*
*And winsome folly ascertains.*

*The sultry summer fairy rings*
*Pass by beneath open sky in*
*Measured progression, and courtly clouds*
*Vie for the favor of Mother Nature*
*Though she would want only one*
*Kiss before her fleeting passage.*

*The sprightly spring cavorts and prances*
*Drunk on raindrops and pollen pudding*
*Here is where my heart resides*
*Not wanting, nor desiring, but gustily inspiring*
*This season of abundant lust*
*And craven hunger."*

She paused, and nobody was sure whether she was done or not. Then she stepped down, slumped like an unstrung marionette, and there was polite applause. I held my hands in my lap, pondering her words, and what, if anything, they even meant.

But I wasn't about to ask anybody what the hell it meant. Whether they even knew, I doubted anybody would say anything contrary. It was Willa's moment to milk.

Willa stepped back on the dais, for some more of her syllabic soma, drawn straight down from the Olympus of her ego.

*"Desideratum*

*One. Taking candy from a baby.*
*Two. Laundering lost keys.*
*Three. A charm!*
*Four. Bringing horses to water to drink.*
*Five. Saucing both goose and gander.*
*Six. Casting pearls before swine.*
*Seven. Catching water flowing from beneath a bridge.*
*Eight. Counting chickens before they've hatched.*
*Nine. Serving those who also wait.*
*Ten. Taking pocketfuls of wooden nickels."*

Again, there was applause from our attendees. I tried catching Lee's eyes, but he was studiously ignoring me, politely applauding, his face neutral, unreadable. Willa was panting, thin shoulders heaving with the effort of speaking to so many people at once.

I fished out my cell phone, texted Polly.

*whr d hell R u?*

Willa looked like she had another poem lined up, got herself some water, not absinthe, and sipped at it, while the others looked on.

*Im comin!*

*Willas spouting her crap-ass poetry. U R totally msN it.*

I looked up, and caught Willa's caustic, nearsighted gaze on me, for being so rude to be texting while she was sharing words with us.

*Whoops! Shes watchN me. gota go!*

I pocketed the phone, returned my attention to Willa, as much as I hated to.

"I hope I'm not boring you, Samantha," Willa said, prompting laughter from the others. "I used small words on this one, so I think you'll like it."

*"Little Grrl Lost*

*Breadcrumbed bustier and pampered digits*
*Ever-watchful is she upon mossy rampart*
*Yearning for her fickle Prince Charming's kiss*
*Our heroine pines forlornly in her tower*
*Taking consolation in all that she holds dear:*
*Clutching broken glass slipper tight*
*Hoping that her man will come for her tonight."*

There was more applause. It felt like Willa was mocking me in verse, with her bespectacled, nearsighted face looking at me as she read her poems from memory, holding the black book she hardly needed.

She stepped off the dais just as Polly came with Ansel, right into the wash of the applause for Willa among the gallery attendees, so their entrance was hardly noticed, except by me, who happened to see them.

Of course, Polly would masterfully time her entry that way, being able to miss Willa's whoration while at the same time turning up fashionably late, looking fetching in a snug little black dress and maroon Cole Haan patent leather heels and a putty-colored wool overcoat, her maroon lipstick framing her smile perfectly.

Ansel was in a white t-shirt with a bomber jacket and black jeans with loafers, looking around with singular insouciance, his black hair wild, tousled. Seeing him in the gallery with the others, I could only be struck by how manly he looked compared to the rest of them. Even Clay's gym-sculpted frame seemed somehow spare compared to the raw physicality of Ansel's presence. He caught my eye with an almost shy look. I must've been staring daggers, or trying to compose myself. I wondered how much the others knew about the whole situation.

Polly introduced Ansel to the others, making her rounds. Willa gave him a caustic "hello," while Clay offered a blankly intense handshake, crunching on a sugar cube, one of several he had in his hand, like beer nuts. Reagan smiled broadly, crisply extended her hand.

Gabe kept one hand in his pocket, the other around his glass of absinthe, gave Ansel a contemptuous nod of his head.

I walked up, having regained my cool.

"Hey," I said. "You missed Willa's performance."

"I know," Polly said, with a grin. "We didn't want to spoil our appetites. Where's Sheldon?"

"Nobody knows," I said. It was so easy to say this, you have no idea. Because there was no way I could precisely explain where Sheldon was.

Lee walked up to Ansel. "So, you're the guy who's stealing our women, right?"

Next to Ansel, Lee looked like a soda straw in a sweater vest. Ansel nodded distractedly.

"Yeah, that's me," he said.

"Well, New Guy," Lee said. "They're our women. It's our thing, see? You can't have them. We don't let norms into our inner circle."

Ansel shrugged. "Oh, I'm no norm."

"You look like a norm to me," Lee said. "If your name was Norm, in fact, I'd be totally unsurprised. Is it Norm? Norman? From Normal, Illinois?"

Polly was watching Lee make sport with some dismay, while I was curious to see what Ansel would do.

"That's pretty funny," Ansel said. "You're the poet, right? The published one? I mean, not self-published, but actually published?"

"That's right," Lee said. "A little rag called *The New Yorker.*"

Ansel actually scoffed. "Yeah, what a rag that is. I remember a friend joking that the way to get published in that magazine is, first you write a story, and then you take the ending off of it, and then you send it to *The New Yorker.*"

"I sent them a poem," Lee said.

"Oh, yeah, that's different," Ansel said, smirking. "It's too bad there isn't *The Chicagoan.* Doesn't it bug you, like having to worship a graven idol so far East?"

Lee just stared at him as if he was a bug. "What do you think we're doing, here? You're looking at a cultural consortium, here. We're artistic terrorists, trying to bring culture to the undeserving public at large. We're casting pearls before the swine."

Ansel squinted at the artworks along the wall. "Those are the pearls?"

Polly came up, caught Ansel's arm. "Hey, you two. Lee, is it possible for you *not* to be rude to a guest?"

Lee pursed his lips, looked Polly up and down appraisingly, cocked his head, gave Ansel a dismissive look down the end of his nose, then rolled his eyes at me and walked away. Hyperkinetic douchebag, our fearless Lee-der.

"Nice talking to you," Ansel said after him, then turned back to us. "What a dick. So, you guys really see yourselves as this artistic elite?"

Polly nodded. "Our goal is to embrace various media that communicate our own cultural aesthetic to the populace at large. We stand for the primacy of art in everyday life, see ourselves as a kind of battery for it, a form of cultural vaccination from mediocrity, the mundane, the prefabricated."

"But don't you have to be good at what you do?" Ansel said. "I mean, these pieces are uninspired. They're like what people who aren't artists think art should look like."

Polly skipped over them with a bat of her eyelashes. I actually agreed with Ansel, but held my tongue. I was just the performance artist; my opinion hardly counted in our ranks. I saw that Lee was slouched in a corner with Willa and Gabe, glancing our way.

"You really think so?" Polly said. "I don't agree, although my specialty is poetry, not the visual arts. Of course, you are a remarkable painter, so I respect your opinion."

"I'm just saying," Ansel said. "If you're setting yourselves up as some kind of cultural commissars, don't you have to, I don't know, have talent? Otherwise, it's more about you than about what you're creating."

I liked how Ansel would get fired up about art. You could see the flare of his nostrils, the blink of his eyes. He was passionate about it, and I respected that passion. I could smell it. Taste it.

Polly nodded. "Yes, although we feel that the artist is as important as the work he…or she…is creating. We are the wellspring of wonder."

"The artist is a conduit for the sublime," Ansel said. "You are what you create. And if you create shit, well, you are shit."

I laughed involuntarily at that, despite being peeved at Polly dragging Ansel to our thing, covered my laugh with the back of my hand.

Ansel said more: "Henry James said it well: 'We work in the dark—we do what we can—we give what we have. Our doubt is our passion, and our passion is our task. The rest is the madness of art.'"

"Oh, I like that," Polly said. "I love Henry James."

She way she stressed "love," this lilting thing, like an ornate fairytale carriage hitting a bump on a road, the way she laughed and touched his arm, oh my, was she laying it on thick.

"The madness of art," I said. "That is great."

I hated Henry James, found him incredibly hard to read. But hearing that quote, I wondered if I should give him another chance. I found it curious that Ansel read him, let alone quoted him.

Ansel smiled at me. "Oh, I've got a bunch of his in my head—'It is, I think, an indisputable fact that Americans are, as Americans, the most self-conscious people in the world, and the most addicted to the belief that the other nations of the earth are in a conspiracy to undervalue them.'—that's another one I keep in mind when seeing something like this BacchUS."

Polly laughed, and I just smiled. Clay looked pissed.

"'Art is what you can get away with,'" I said. "Warhol said that."

That was all I had to contribute. It was like I hadn't even said anything, although it inspired me. I had gotten away with something terrible. But was it art?

"One more," Ansel said. "'What was talent but the art of being completely whatever one happened to be?' That's one I live by."

"Quite the James scholar, you are," Polly said. "I'm very impressed. Do you like Proust?"

"I'm a painter, not a writer," Ansel said.

"I would quote him to you, in defense of our little enterprise," Polly said.

These dueling quotes transfixed me. I had no head for quotes, always wondered if people just took those words to heart, or rehearsed them. I could imagine Polly in a mirror, memorizing them, but as a poet, she had an ironclad memory.

"'Everything great in the world comes from neurotics. They alone have founded our religions and composed our masterpieces,'" Polly said.

"Who says religions are great?" Ansel said, shrugging.

"Well, I'm more enamored of the first part," she said. "It holds out promise for our little band of bohemians."

Gabe sauntered up, hands in his pockets, a cigarette tucked behind his ear, because Clay wouldn't let him smoke in his gallery.

"You don't like Sheldon's work?" he said to Ansel.

"No," Ansel said, flatly.

"I hear you quoting James, here, playing the art critic," Gabe said. "I've got a James for you: James Joyce. 'The artist, like the God of the

Creation, remains within or behind or beyond or above his handiwork, invisible, refined out of existence, indifferent, paring his fingernails.' What don't you like about his work?"

Almost on cue, Gabe took a hand out and inspected his nails, af-
fecting nonchalance as Ansel spoke.

"It's dreadful," Ansel said. "I mean, the artifice is adequate, I guess,
but the barrenness of your vision, it's really almost painful to look at.
What is he trying to say with 'Theramint Julep,' for god's sake?"

Gabe glanced over at it, then back at Ansel.

"What, you don't get it? Look, it's like explaining a joke to somebody who's not in on it," Gabe said. "You're not in on the joke, so,
yeah, the point's lost on you."

"Boys," Polly said. "Play nice."

But with Sheldon's work in his mouth, Ansel couldn't resist giving
it another shake of his head. God, I thought, if only I could bring that
kind of passion to the table.

"I don't mind 'Apostrophilter,'" Ansel said. "As mild conceptual
art, it works, although what it's saying about anything, I have no idea."

Gabe chuckled dryly, looked down at his weejuns. "Yeah? Is that it?"

"'Technofique' is just masturbation," Ansel said. "And the Grenadine piece is retarded. It looks like he got that out of a kit."

"God, I wish Sheldon was here to defend his piece," Gabe said.

Nobody in our group had ever said anything like that to anybody
else—not to their faces, anyway. I mean, I'd thought that plenty of
times, but had held my tongue, because I was afraid if I'd said anything, said what I was really thinking, they'd cast me out.

Gabe kept his cool, amazingly enough, held up his hand, cocked
his head, looked like the Beatnik he carried himself as. "Lee's got it
right: you're a norm, man. You don't get what we're doing, here."

"You don't get what you're doing," Ansel said, laughed in his face.
"You're doing *nothing;* that's exactly the problem."

Willa and Clay drifted over, sensing that one of their own was
under attack. Their faces were haunting in the track lighting, gaunt
and ghostlike. It occurred to me that this would have made a good
performance art piece, like a critic going to town in an art gallery, and
the artist going berserk, tearing the critic to bits in the gallery, like the
murder as her latest work, a pristine little white card identifying it, the
critic sprawled out on the floor, torn open, ribs cracked and broken,
the artist hunched over them, mouth red with dripping blood, blood

on arms and legs, blood spattered on the walls, the artist turning her head to the burning track lights and howling loud and long.

Christ, I'd broken into a sweat. What the hell kind of daydream was that? I clutched myself, suddenly cold. I watched Ansel holding his own against Willa, Gabe, and Clay, with Polly looking dreadfully uncomfortable, her cheeks flushed, and I couldn't even really hear them, just the blundering blur of words, while I heard, instead, my own breathing, the beat of my heart, this sense of dis-ease that haunted me.

Ansel glanced at me even as he was arguing with the others, a knowing, understanding glance. Yes, he came with Polly, yes, he was her date, but he got me.

He *got* me.

# 4. THURSDAY MORNING: 1 NOVEMBER

I woke up from a bunch of running dreams with a yelp, scratched my tousled hair. I'd dreamt that Ansel and I were running together, with Polly on our heels. Everything had been a blur, just us running and breathing, impossibly hot, the scent of wet ground and rotten leaves in my nose. The smell was pleasant, the chase almost erotic.

I was hung over, my head felt like it was packed with cotton. The rest of the gallery showing had gotten more bizarre, with Ansel and the others debating art and culture for the better part of an hour, before Polly got so uncomfortable that she asked Ansel to take her home. Then the others formed sullen circles and licked their wounds, cursed out Ansel as an imposter, a charlatan, a wannabe, a norm. The epithets were thrown aplenty, with ruminations about Polly's infidelity, how Tristan could possibly not realize his wife was cheating on him, while I spent the evening drinking and trying to get myself under control, since I was feeling out of sorts, more so than ever, while everybody was wondering where Sheldon was, everybody was calling him, and me as the only one who knew where he actually was, and I couldn't tell them he was in my stomach.

Opening the medicine cabinet, I took out a Flinstones multivitamin, a token from my childhood, a reassuring thing I took back in college, when somehow having water handy was too much to ask for, and a chewable vitamin was ideal. Looking at myself in the bathroom mirror, I cried out, dropped the bottle, spilling chewables on the bathroom tiles.

My right eye had turned blue.

"What the fuck?" I asked my reflection.

My left eye was brown, my right eye was blue as could be. Absurdly, I blinked it away, as if somehow that would dispel the oddness of my reflection. I leaned in close, turned my head side to side.

It turned my guts to ice, this oddity. This wasn't something like body hair, something I could hide away. This was something odd and immediately apparent.

I noticed that the happy trail and the forearm hair had come back, too, overnight. The fucking stuff grew back overnight. There was no way it could grow back so fast. I touched it, the little hairs in a line that went down to my crotch.

"Christ," I said. Obviously, the Veet wasn't cutting it. I needed something stronger. I needed wax. Or else to spring for professionals to take care of it, but it was embarrassing. I could just imagine me going in for that. I'm sure women did it all the time, but the fact that my previously near-pristine body was sullied by this insurrection was too much to bear.

But that was the least of my worries. My eyes were different colors. I couldn't even imagine calling Dr. Resnick with that. Maybe it was a reaction to the antibiotics or something. Yeah, that was possible, right?

As I said before, I could talk myself into anything. I wanted to sue the bastard, although I thought I should probably call him up, first, or his fucking office. But the prospect of being back on his examination table, with him lecturing me about safe sex and rape crisis centers, it was too much. And since I was due to check back with him in a few days, anyway, it seemed too much to call and schedule yet another visit.

And yet, he'd told me to report any changes or anything unusual, and I could just imagine his reaction if I waited a bunch of days before telling him about this. He'd think I was an idiot, or insane.

So, I called in sick at Nonpareil, leaving a message on Lance's voicemail. And then I called Dr. Resnick's office and told the answering service about it. The woman on the phone was polite enough, told me that Dr. Resnick would call me back.

I paced around, kept eyeing my reflection as I passed the bathroom, waiting for Dr. Resnick to call. It was around 7:00. Dr. Resnick was probably just kissing his trophy wife goodbye, hopping into his Jaguar in Kenilworth, ready for his morning commute into the city.

My phone rang, and it was Dr. Resnick. I guess the receptionist had paged him.

"Hi, Samantha," he said. "I'm glad you called. What you're experiencing is called 'heterochromia.' It's usually genetic, but sometimes it can be a reaction to a disease."

"To what disease?" I asked. "What is wrong with me?"

"Well, your blood tests came up clean," he said. "You have no known infections."

That should have been an immense relief. I should have felt fine, but instead, I was staring at my freaky-ass self in the mirror, this ice-blue eye gazing at me like an unfriendly stranger.

"What the fuck is wrong with me?" I asked. "Is it cancer?"

"No," he said. "I don't know, to be honest, but I doubt cancer causes anything like that. Why don't you come back in, and we'll do some more tests?"

"Is it the antibiotic?" I asked, my teeth set on edge.

"Again, I doubt it," he said. "Have you had any other reactions? Fever? Rash? Swelling?"

"Hair," I said, my eyes tearing up. I didn't care, anymore. "I've got this hair on my forearms and a strip that goes from below my belly-button to my crotch. That's new."

He was quiet, I could tell he was busy jotting it down.

"And it grows back fast," I said. "Really fast. I keep shaving it and, you know, Nairing it, and it keeps coming back. Like the next night, it's back."

"Okay," he said. "Do you have it now?"

"Yeah," I said.

"Well, don't remove it," he said. "We'll sample it when you come in, run some tests. Hirsutism is usually genetic, although there can be some environmental causes for it, too."

"But how could it grow back so fast?" I asked.

"I don't know," he said. "Can you come in around 10?"

"Yeah," I said. "I took a sick day."

Lance would be pissed, but fuck Lance. I had a problem, here.

"Good," he said. "And anything else? Please, try to think on that."

I did, and I didn't think anything else had happened to me. The eye distracted me so badly, I kept looking at it. I looked like a monster. If I got a unibrow, I'd hang myself.

"Nothing," I said.

"Okay," he said. "Come in at ten, then."

I hung up, snarled at myself in the mirror, on a whim. I snapped a picture of myself with my phone camera, checked it, snapped another one, trying to get it right.

"Don't be such a baby," She said to me. My reflection. "Wah wah." She said it in a mocking sing-song. "Look, I need to get out."

"I'm not crazy," I said. "I'm not having a conversation with you."

She smirked at me, that blue eye staring out at me.

"I need to get out," she said. "There's not enough drugs in the world to keep me locked up inside. God, you are such a letdown."

"What? What did I do?"

"Nothing," she said. "You've been a terrible disappointment. You haven't even put up your painting. Our work."

"What are you talking about?" I asked.

"I shlepped it all the way from Nonpareil, too, while you were curled up inside, sucking your thumb. You don't remember. It's in the hall closet."

"What is?" I asked.

She was impatient, folded her arms in front of her, cocked a hip. "Just go look."

I went to the hall closet, my hand on the doorknob. I was almost afraid to open it. Away from the mirror, she was silent, or at least was only in my head.

I opened the door, and sure enough, on the floor, leaning against the wall, was a solitary canvas. I picked it up with leaden limbs, turned it toward me. It was the untreated canvas with Sheldon's blood across the front of it, in a bold, dynamic diagonal splash. From when I'd bitten off his head. This spray of blood. The blood was now a maroon hue.

"That's right," she said.

Sheldon's last work, in a corner where I'd left it. The white canvas, half-splashed with browning blood. It was my work, he was my subject. I would make them all into works of art. Performance art. My art.

"Attagirl," she said. We looked at the painting together, studied it. The blood looked like violence. The whole painting spoke of it. It was obscenity, not art. It was a monument to Sheldon's murder.

My first painting.

I had a date with Ansel tomorrow. It was insane. There was no way I was going to cancel it. Not with Polly strutting about like she owned him. I was going to give him hell, and I was going to, I don't know, stick it to Polly.

But with the eye, Christ, it was bizarre. I mean, it looked cool, but the fundamental wrongness of it, the non-Samantha-ness of it, just freaked me out.

Ten o'clock. I had three hours. It was an act of willpower not to shave off that hair on my stomach, the stuff on my arms. All resentment I had for Dr. Resnick pretty much boiled away that morning, in my fear and desperation.

Unsure what else to do, I thought about blogging. But I didn't think I could just suddenly talk about what was wrong with me, not out of the blue like that. Then again, who cares? I could write whatever the hell I wanted to. On a whim, I just winged it. It was like performance art, in a way. That's how I consoled myself. It's just another performance, except that I'm not really performing at all. But my readers didn't know that.

> Out of the Blue
> I woke up this morning and found that my eye had turned blue. My right eye has gone to ice blue. There's no real explanation for it, and I'm going to see the doctor for it. I freaked out when I saw it, this eye, like a melting iceberg, like a glacier, staring at me. It happened overnight. Last night, I was at Orpheus's gallery, and Adonis showed up with Polygon, and I was really conflicted, not sure what I would do. My guts turned to ice, and I was embarrassed and jealous and humiliated.
> I kind of realize that I want them both. I mean, Adonis is like this ultimate dude, even though his personality kind of annoys me just a bit. There's just something wildly cool about him, this feral disregard of everything not him-related. But his presence is intoxicating.
> And Polygon, she's something else entirely, like boundless charm and yeah, she's superficial as hell, but at the same time, she's charmingly so. Her sense of style, her fashion taste, her lean body, they're total turn-ons.

When they turned up together last night, like a fucking couple (haha — yeah, they are a fucking couple, right?) I was jealous, but part of me wanted to be on Adonis's free arm.

I mean, the fucker's taking me to dinner tomorrow night, and Polygon the day after. I'm not telling you where, in case you're in the city and wanting to stalk me, but Adonis is dating us both. I feel like he likes Polygon maybe more than me, but why does he keep me along? I don't know.

But enough of that. My fucking right eye has turned blue. I'm looking like a fucking mutant, or a groupie for David Bowie. Talk about changes!

I was pretty pleased with that entry, with the therapeutic release of a confession. Without hesitation, I went to YouTube and got Bowie's "Changes" and played it, watched it, thought about linking it to my entry, but then thought that was just too obvious, almost a sentimental pairing, there. Better to just allude to Bowie in the "Changes" reference and leave it for my astute readers to pick up, if any of them would. It wasn't even an esoteric reference, but I was curious if anybody would take the ball and run with it. Zip was online, sent me comments almost immediately.

*Zipstrip: Wow. Intense. Picture? Spill!*
*Samhain78: It's bizarre.*
*Zipstrip: Don't let Marilyn Manson see you; he'll be in love.*
*Samhain78: Eww!*
*Zipstrip: Sorry! Yeah, get out the brain bleach! The eye rules.*
*Samhain78: Thx. I'm freaking about it.*

Looking at my entry, I waited to see if Taliesinner would say anything, but he didn't. I guess the perv was busy watching Catholic schoolgirls skip rope or something. I e-mailed Zooey one of my phonecam pictures.

*Zipstrip: Awesome. You're pretty, Sääm! I like the eyes.*
*Samhain78: Heh. "Sääm." I love that.*

On a whim, I went to *Polytician,* to see what, if anything, Polly wrote about the night before. She didn't disappoint me.

A is the most incredible man I've ever known. His every breath is packed with pathos, his eyes, full of untapped mourning and regret. I've found my true soulmate. He's going to paint me Saturday night. I'm terribly excited about it, because his strong, sensitive hands, which have already traveled upon me in all points of the compass, all directions--the prospect of those same hands, those gorgeous, soulful eyes, studying me, painting me. His brushes will capture me.

It's going to be a nude. I'm posing nude for him, and I'm so excited just thinking about it. It was his idea, too. He said he loved my body, wanted to immortalize it in brush and paint. So exciting! Better than anything T has ever given me, and he's given me a lot, but mundane things, not something like this. T is a businessman, not an artist. I'd never consider T to be my muse.

I know I should feel guilty, and I probably will, but at the moment, I'm intoxicated by him, and it doesn't matter.

S looked like she wanted to puke when she saw us. Poor thing. I feel terrible for her. I asked A about it, like why he was taking her out the night before our special night, and he said that he liked her, too. That they had something in common. When I asked him what, he shrugged, said it was hard to explain.

That made me a teensy bit jealous, but I didn't want to spoil the mood. I'm just thrilled that after this weekend, the next time she's at his place, she'll see a nude portrait of me hanging on his wall.

Do I sound too catty? I hope not.

Oh, and W did her poetry last night. Ghastly stuff, I'm sure. I showed up late, couldn't bear to hear her strident verse. The woman's most poetic act would be suicide.

That last line amused me, though my teeth were gritted, thinking about her special moment with Ansel this weekend. I looked at myself in the reflection of my monitor, could see the old me—my new blue eye wouldn't show in that reflection.

I was cute. That was the problem. Polly was pretty; I was cute. Damned cute, fucking cute, but cute, all the same. Cute stopped where Pretty began, and was across town from Sexy, Sultry, Stylish, and Beautiful. Polly was Pretty, Polly was Stylish. Reagan was Pretty. Willa was Plain.

Christ, I was so vain. But Cute had its own problems. Cute captivated, but it was hard to take Cute seriously. That was the problem. That was what always cost me in social gatherings. My lack of height, my petite little body, my pointy noise, my spunky giggle, my pixie hair. I was a big pile of Cute.

Fucking Cute. That was infuriating. Ever since I'd been a teen, I'd been able to make Cute work for me, but it also kept me in the Friend Zone, the accursed place, more often than not.

Well, that was going to change. I turned off my computer and went back to the bathroom to shower. Looking at that goddamned eye in the mirror, there was nothing fucking Cute about that. It was Weirdsville for me, from now on.

"I know how to keep him from painting Polly," she said to me, from the mirror, while I was running the water. "Just saying, I know."

"Shut up," I said. "Where are my freckles?"

"They went away when you changed your skin," she said.

"I didn't change my skin," I said. "I hallucinated."

"Suit yourself," she said. "Killer."

I got to Doctor Resnick's office a little early, making good time on the CTA (for once), and he was eager to see me. I'd been wearing my shades a little self-consciously, wrapped myself in a checkered scarf and a silver cropped parka, with pale denim designer jeans and snakeskin pointy booties. Okay, maybe I still looked fucking Cute, but I was feeling fierce.

Dr. Resnick had me go into one of his rooms, didn't keep me doctor-waiting, but instead had me take off my shades and my top, and he looked at my arms, and at the happy trail, and took his whatchamacallit and shined a light in my eyes.

"Amazing," he said. "If I hadn't seen you a couple of days ago, I'd not have believed it. You've been sticking to the antibiotic regimen, haven't you?"

"Yes," I said. "Like clockwork."

"Good," he said. "Because it's important to not cut that short, although I think what's afflicting you isn't bacterial, it's still best to stay the course on the medication."

"What is afflicting me?" I asked.

"I think it's some kind of virus," he said. "Although I'm really just speculating at this point. We'll need to draw more blood."

"A virus?" I asked. He nodded. "Possibly some kind of strange retrovirus."

"A retro-virus?" I asked, laughing a little nervously. I knew all about retro things, although I knew nothing about retro-viruses.

"It's a rogue virus that basically inserts itself into your DNA," he said. "We have them in our DNA. Last I read, the human genome is something like 8% retrovirus. What that means is that throughout our evolutionary history, viruses would manage to graft themselves onto our DNA, or little bits of themselves, and incorporate themselves into our makeup."

I nodded.

"The fact that you're suddenly experiencing these physical changes makes me think there's some kind of retrovirus at work in you," he said. "Something hitherto undiscovered, or at least not fully explored."

"What, should I patent myself or something?" I asked.

Dr. Resnick smiled. "They don't let people do that, yet. But I can see myself writing an article for *Nature* or *Science* or *The American Journal of Human Genetics* with something like this, if my suspicion is correct."

"Oh, great," I said. "You get a Nobel Prize, and what do I get?"

"Better, hopefully," he said. "You still haven't felt anything unusual?"

"Just sensitivity to light and noise, I suppose," I said. "And smell. Things have been getting to me a lot more than they used to."

He jotted that down. It did bug me, him thinking of me as a publishing credit, a notch on his careerist bedpost.

"We'll need to clip a sample of those hairs," he said.

"Look, what kind of treatment is there for this," I said. "That's what I'm concerned about, here."

"There might not be any," he said. "If some virus is changing your genome, there's probably nothing we can do."

I recoiled from him. "Then what's the point of taking a hair sample? How does that help me, exactly?"

"It'll at least help me diagnose what's happening to you," he said. "Get a sense of what we're dealing with, here."

It really did irritate me. I wanted him to help me and I could see him on fire with professional curiosity about me.

"And what's more," he said. "We have to figure out if you're contagious or not. We can do a cheek swab, a hair sample, get those examined."

"Contagious?" I asked.

"Yes," he said. "I'd love to get your boyfriend–"

"He's not my boyfriend," I said. "Just a friend."

"Yes, well, I'd love to get a sample from him, to see if he's the source of the retrovirus," he said. "The timing of it is pretty coincidental."

I could just imagine Ansel in there with Dr. Resnick. That would be a real treat. I couldn't wait to tell him about this whole deal. "Look, Fucko, you infected me with a retrovirus!" and he'd be like "Huh?"

"I doubt he'd want to come in," I said.

"What's his name?" Dr. Resnick asked.

"Ooh, I shouldn't tell you that," I said. "He'd not be too thrilled with me giving his name out."

"Yes, but if he's a carrier of some kind of contagious retrovirus, then the man qualifies as a biohazard," Dr. Resnick said. "We're talking public health, here. Homeland Security would be on it in a heartbeat."

Now I was getting a little worried. I had this image of Ansel and me at Gitmo, in pristine white examination rooms, with technicians and scientists and soldiers watching us behind plate glass, with electrodes wired to our bodies, giving blood samples every other day. Guinea people is what we'd be.

"Wow," I said.

"I mean," he said. "So far it seems fairly benign, but we can't be too careful with something like this. So, do I have your consent for a cheek swab and a hair sample?"

"Uhh," I said. "Okay. But if I end up shipped off to some government research lab, I'm going to be really, really pissed at you."

He smiled, did the swab himself, put it in a little vial. And he clipped some of the hairs from my forearms and from my tummy, carefully marked them.

"This helps you just fine," I said. "But all I know is that my eye's still blue."

"Are your boyfriend's eyes mismatched, too?" he asked.

"No," I said, and that made him wrinkle his brow as he jotted it down on my file. I noticed he hadn't sent any nurse in to do his dirty work for him, not with this, not with me.

"Curious," he said. "Well, we'll get those samples analyzed, see what we can learn from them."

I nodded. "Are we done, then?"

"Sure," he said. "We'll need to follow up still once your antibiotics have run their course, just to be on the safe side. And hopefully the gene testing will be back from the labs, then, and we'll have a better sense of what's going on."

"Okay," I said, getting dressed.

As I got out of there, another $10 lighter (fuck you very much, HMO) I thought about maybe getting some colored contacts, something to make my eyes uniform again, but, of course, I didn't have any spare money for something like that, and knew my insurance wouldn't cover something purely cosmetic; they barely covered anything I actually needed, let alone something I merely wanted.

So, instead, I thought about what I was going to wear for Disraeli's, and what I was going to say to Ansel. I mean, it had to have been him who infected me. I whipped out my phone, dialed him up. Got his voicemail.

"Hey, Ansel," I said. "It's Sam. Just wanted to say that I got the blood tests back from the doctor's, and everything's fine, except that, uh, Dr. Resnick said something about a retrovirus or something. You know anything about that? Call me."

I snapped shut my phone, hoped that would get his attention. I didn't want to just spring it on him, but felt like he should have some lead time, so he could get his bullshit straight. Having accomplished that, I decided to windowshop for some shoes, hoping nobody from Nonpareil happened to see me.

But I figured with my shades on, I was at least quasi-anonymous. As I walked around town, past innumerable boutiques, I saw a poster for Twystyd Krystyn in an alley, and smiled. I hoped that Dean's gig went well. I saw that Glandular Angst shared the bill with them, found that name resonated with me. Man, I felt that, for sure. Big-time glandular angst.

I passed by a Clucky's Chicken Shack, downwind of it, and found my stomach growling. The smell of grease and meat really hit me hard, so hard that I actually stopped on the street and looked at it, watched its chimneys spewing flavorful exhaust in the sky.

Almost on automatic, I jaywalked across the street and stood in front of there, salivating. The posters of the chicken, comically over-blown, as big as I was, like the surface of a planet, the extra-crispiness ripped by a fork, revealing tender, juicy white meat.

I hadn't had meat since I was 17, and yet I was drooling there on the sidewalk, staring in at the place.

"Wow," I said. "Fuck it."

Without a thought of the consequences, I went in and got myself a six-piece extra-crispy chicken meal, and sat by a window, devouring it.

It tasted so good, made me wonder why I'd stayed away from the stuff for so long. Everybody knew about vegetarians and even vegans backsliding; it was one of the risks of the lifestyle. Since it was just me alone, I felt like I could binge in peace, licking grease from my fingers, savoring every bite. I'd never backslid before, had prided myself on being steadfast in my vegetarian ways, but I ate every bite of that chicken, felt like it was First Communion all over again.

I wanted to buy a t-shirt from them, for god's sake. Bright yellow and orange, with the Clucky's chicken across it. I wanted to make out with their mascot. That's how good it was.

All too quickly, it was gone, and I was wiping off my hands, sniffing at the bones, swilling a soda, wishing I could vault over the counter and raid the whole store, eat every bite of chicken that they had.

While I was lusting for Clucky's chicken, part of me was mourning my fall from grace. I mean, I was proud I was a vegetarian, it had kept me lean and fit, and free of contaminants. I shopped organic when I could. There wasn't much I could defend about Clucky's, which was an institution in the city. Endless chickens slaughtered and fried for fat, greedy American consumers. Then again, I'd become a cannibal; what did eating chicken matter, when compared with that. But then, absurdly, what passed for a conscience in me spoke up, clarified that I hadn't really killed Sheldon to eat him, per se—rather, I had only killed Sheldon because he was there for killing. That I'd consumed some of him was almost incidental; what I'd really craved was slaughter.

As if that made a bit of difference, in the larger scheme of things.

My phone rang. It was Ansel.

"Hey, there," I said, wiping my lips on a napkin. The grease was intoxicating. Grease was hot fat. Fat was meat's slovenly cousin. Meat was my new passion.

"Hey," he said. "So, you're alright, eh?"

"I wouldn't say that," I said. "Kinda way far from alright. What the fuck did you give me, you shit?"

"It's complicated," he said. "Not really a thing to be talking about on the phone."

What *wasn't* complicated? It pissed me off, like how casual he was about it. But at least part of it was out in the open.

"So, you knew you had something contagious when we were, you know, doing it?" I said.

"Yeah," he said. "Look, I didn't think anything would happen. I just kind of lost control that night. I didn't plan anything. I hadn't fucked in a long time, because I was afraid of, you know, problems. It's nothing fatal, alright?"

I was so pissed off at him. "What did you give me? What?"

I wanted to tell him about the change in my eye color, but I thought I'd leave that little bit for him to see for himself.

"Who'd you say your doctor was?"

"Dr. Resnick," I said. "Abe Resnick."

"I'll make an appointment with him," Ansel said. "How about that?"

"Fine," I said. "Did you give it to Polly, too?"

"No," he said. "No. She read me a poem she wrote for me."

I could just imagine it, Polly wearing long, interlaced strings of pearls, naked, working her verse for Ansel...

*Natural man, I cannot find*
*The words to tame you*
*Or otherwise contain the*
*Savage clangor of your smile*
*Though in day or night*
*I find you in my thoughts and heart*
*And, wounded beast, I entreat, entice,*
*Trick, and tease with lustful lures*

*While you solemnize and play with caveman paints*
*Draw your lovely Venusian landscapes*
*On swanlike craning necks and lily-fresh flesh,*
*your Hun-like conquests on the broadest steppes*

*I wait for you, with bated, baited breath,*
*The huntress: your captor, conqueror, keeper*
*Redeemer.*
*Natural man.*

Then he'd whip out some amyl nitrate, huff on it, and bite the shit out of her.

"Yeah, right," I said. "I should call her, warn her about you, tell her you're infected with some fucking mystery herpes."

"Look," he said. "It's weird talking this out on the phone. Let's just get together at my place, okay?"

"No way," I said. "We're going to Disraeli's. You're not weaseling out of our date."

"I'm not planning on weaseling out of anything," Ansel said. "I just want to talk. To explain."

"Fine," I said. "After dinner. *Expensive* dinner."

# 5. FRIDAY NIGHT: 2 NOVEMBER

I put on some black knee boots with stiletto heels and wore a maroon knit dress, tied it off with a skinny grey patent leather belt. I spiked up my hair and put on some hoop earrings and some polished wooden bracelets that clacked when I moved them.

I didn't look fucking Cute; I looked fucking Hot.

Ansel sent me an e-mail, said we should just meet at Disraeli's (instead of him picking me up—See? Dick.), so I hopped a cab and went there, walked into the place like I owned it, my boots clacking out fuck-me Morse Code on the slate floor tiles.

The maitre d', an older man in a tuxedo, his white hair cropped short, his nose big, his eyes like raisins pushed into his face, smiled yellowly and asked if I had reservations. I told him I was meeting someone, and would like a spot at the bar.

Disraeli's was full of older men and lovely young women with too-long, too-blonde hair, too-big boobs and razorblade clavicles, and there I was in my maroon with my a-bomb hair. I felt out of place with the suits and the sleazebags and the trixies and long-faced boob-jobbed babes.

I ordered a Cosmopolitan from the portly bartender and nursed it, waiting for Ansel to turn up. The place had dark windows and mahogany counters and old brass, and the smell of steak hovered throughout it. It looked like the kind of place my dad would've liked.

A few guys made abortive passes at me at the bar, maybe thinking I was a prostitute. I was kind of feeling like one, in a way, waiting for goddamned Ansel and his answers.

He turned up a little later, looking freshly-scrubbed and sexy. Ansel had gone for an open-collared white shirt and a grey blazer with black slacks and ostrich loafers. He'd oiled up his curly hair a bit, and he smelled like Bay Rum. He looked, as ever, Euro-sharp and monied. I noticed several of the women at the bar checking him out, tracking him as he passed, until he stopped at me. Take that, bitches.

"You look great," he said, leaning in for a kiss. I dodged him with a turn of my head.

"Forget that," I said. "You're late."

"Sorry," he said. He went to the maitre de and told him he had a reservation under Rupino, and we were walked through the place, the dark maroon carpet that made me feel embarrassed, like I was the Disraeli's poster girl or something.

"You should've told me the place was fucking maroon," I said.

"Yeah," he said. "You blend right in."

"Perfect," I said. "You notice anything different about me?"

I stared at him, both eyes locked on his chiseled jaw. He squinted at me, staring. "You spiked up your hair."

"My eyes, Stupid," I said. "Look at my fucking eyes."

He looked. "Oh, yeah. Wow. Are you wearing contacts?"

"No," I said. "Your goddamned social disease did that to me, among other things."

Ansel looked around, but nobody had heard, or if they had, they pretended they hadn't. The waiter came up, a slim young man with a hint of a beard and tousled hair. He took an order for appetizers: a house salad for me, calamari for Ansel, and a bottle of merlot.

"Not so loud," Ansel said. "Look, don't lose it, here."

"What did you give me?" I asked.

He steepled his fingers, looked at me with those hangdog brown eyes, while the waiter uncorked the merlot for us.

"Not here," Ansel said. "Not now. Not like this. Let's just enjoy dinner, and then we'll go from there."

"Go where? Your place?"

He nodded. "I have to show you."

My salad showed up, and his calamari.

"You're going to kill me, right? Should I just call 911 right now?" I asked.

"Not a good idea," he said. "I'm not going to kill you, Sam. Christ. I like you."

I picked at my salad, when all I wanted was the calamari on his plate, but we are more than the sum of our appetites, I reminded myself. I don't know if anybody said that, but it felt like wisdom, and I clung to it by my fingernails.

"You've not been very, you know, up front with me," I said. "Like what's with dating both Polly and me? Kinda working it a little, don't you think?"

Ansel drank down some wine, shrugged, popped a fried O in his mouth. "I like you both, alright? Why shouldn't I have both?"

It irked me, made me feel like something he'd picked up on a shelf.

"You don't have me," I said. "You owe me. It's not the same thing."

He smiled, nodded. "You want some of these? Cuz you look like you want some."

"No," I said, though I did want them. I wanted to pour the whole plate in my face and gulp them down. I wanted to eat the whole plate of squid, lick it clean. Eat the plate. Eat Ansel's hand. The waiter showed up again, brandishing wrapped raw slabs of meat, asked us what we wanted. I was fucking drooling. I wanted to sink my teeth into the platter, and the waiter's wrist, besides.

Ansel ordered a filet mignon, medium rare. I bit my lip and ordered a porterhouse steak, also medium rare, as well as grilled vegetables and French onion soup.

"Thought you were vegetarian," Ansel said.

"I was," I said, glowering at him. I wondered if it was tied into it. Why not? Or maybe it was some kind of craving tied to hormones. I didn't know. "I ate my friend Sheldon the other day. You know, the guy whose art you hated?"

"You want me to explain it all to you? You'd run out the door and never come back."

That was a little much to bear. I looked around at the other patrons, the old squires and their little princesses, and Ansel and me. We didn't belong in a place like this. This was a place for norms, doing norm things.

"Give me a little credit," I said. "I've seen a lot of things"

He laughed, played with his wine glass.

"What, you've been to Lollapalooza? Smoked ditchweed at Burning Man? What have you done, what have you seen?" he asked. I liked the edge in his voice, the contempt. It was intoxicating, like a call to arms.

"I'm an artist," I said. "And, thanks to you, a murderer. And a cannibal."

"I've watched your work," he said. "Those clips on YouTube. That's not art; it's vanity. It's pretense. It's as bad as that shit in BacchUS."

"Vanity? What?"

Even amid our arguing, I was secretly pleased he'd actually taken the time to watch my performance clips, even if he didn't like them.

"Art is vanity," I said. "Art is pretense. Sheldon knew your work; he said you suck."

"Yeah, well *he* sucks," Ansel said. "How can you even hang with those people? I mean his stuff was pompous, uninspired. There wasn't a drop of heart in it. He's doing what he thinks art is supposed to be, without a drop of inspiration, or even talent. Everybody thinks they can write, that they can make art, but most people can't. Either they have no talent, or no vision, or no discipline, or nothing to say. Or some mix of those."

Our food arrived, and Ansel ordered another bottle of wine. We'd already cut through three quarters of our first as we sparred.

My steak smelled fabulous, and I sawed into it, popping bites into my mouth as I parried Ansel's attack. The Road to Heaven was paved with my saliva.

"So, what's my problem? How am I deficient in your eyes?" I asked. Sheldon was shelved for the moment, because I had to defend my art.

"No talent, no vision, nothing to say," he said. "You have discipline, but that's about it. Maybe it's just the wrong medium for you. I mean, performance art? Come on."

I was flushed, excited, angry, horny, hungry. I carved through my steak and vegetables with my knife and fork.

"I make happenings," I said. "I do things."

"It's a joke," he said. "Art endures. You're pimping sensation."

It was curious to see him passionate about something, better than the forlorn, aloof self he usually carried around in his back pocket. Then I thought about Polly.

"Is she a true poet?" I asked.

"No," he said. "She's a stylist, nothing more."

"All-seeing, all-knowing Ansel," I said. "Art critic. Maybe that's what you should be."

"I know what I am," he said. "That kind of clarity gives me perspective."

We ate in silence awhile, nothing but chewing and drinking, him savoring his bacon-wrapped filet, me decimating Planet Porterhouse and the mashed parsnip crescent moon on the side.

"Well, we can't all be you, Ansel," I said. He smiled into his plate, like at some private joke. My phone chirped, and I fished it from my clutch.

"It's Polly," I said. "Should I say 'hi' to her for you?"

He shrugged. "Your phone."

A few of the patrons glanced my way, and I stared them back into their own plates, before switching off my phone, tucking it back into my purse.

"You know, she told me she's modeling for you tomorrow," I said. "Weren't the photographs you took enough? Did you get those out on the Internet, yet, or what?"

"Not yet," Ansel said. "I told you, I'm printing them on aluminum sheets. I'm going to hang them in my place."

But I wasn't going to let him off that easily. "What about Polly? Why does she get a painting, and I get bitten?"

He laughed, his teeth red from the wine. "You want me to paint you, Sam? Look, where we're going tonight, a portrait's not even going to be close to cutting it for you, believe me. I'm painting Polly because, well, I want something to remember her by."

That gave me the willies. What the hell was he talking about? He could go from being broody to charming to passionate to irritating to creepy with each breath, each uttered word.

"Why, is she going someplace?" I asked.

"She's married," Ansel said. "We're having a fling, not something serious. She'll go her merry way, and I'll go mine. It's how it happens."

That made sense to me. "So, that's why you didn't tear her throat out, eh? Figured the husband might notice that?"

"Uh, yeah," Ansel said. "Not a mark on her, I'm proud to say. I'm a model of self-control, and believe me, that's not easy."

"Yeah, she's just so vivacious and exciting," I said. Christ, was I ever jealous. I was like his fuckbuddy, and Polly was in this special place, coyly perched on a pedestal. I hoped he painted her on a pedestal. That would have been great. Princess Polly Pedestal.

"She's not you, that's for sure," Ansel said, let that hang there, inscrutably ironic. Although I doubted I'd eat at Disraeli's again, it's not because it wasn't great. It kicked Moogatoo's ass; it just wasn't my kind of place. Way too normal.

Ansel ordered us a slice of dark chocolate chip cheesecake, once we'd finished our steaks. I was amazed to see that I'd cleaned my plate, and did, yeah, have room for dessert. The wine had made my cheeks hot, but I was okay, still had my feet under me.

The cheesecake came, had been drizzled with raspberry sauce, and he and I attacked it from both sides with forks. It was heavenly, the taste and texture of it, the raspberry tang and the bite of the chocolate and the thickness of the cheesecake. I was awash in sensation and alcohol and lust and determination to figure out what the hell was going on with Ansel, my magic monster man.

I shook it off, the stupid drunk-lust that was taking me, kept a little mantra in my head to center myself: *He infected me.* No amount of charm or passion could exorcise that demon, and it was like a bucket of ice water, brought me back to my senses.

"Why haven't you infected her?" I asked.

"I didn't bite her," Ansel said, drank down the rest of his wine. "That's how it's spread. I know that much."

My shoulder tingled in remembrance, in recognition.

"Ah, yes," I said. "The IT. The gorilla in the room."

"Not a gorilla," Ansel said. "The wolf."

"You're no wolf," I said. "You're a dog."

The waiter came, and we settled our tab, and I went to the ladies room to freshen my lipstick and to call Polly. I didn't want to talk to her, just e-mailed her, typing as quickly as I could.

*Ansel & I R goin bak 2 Hs plAc. Ill tenderize him 4 U. I'll try 2 Leav U som scraps.*

Then I went back out. I don't even know why I sent it. It was just impulse. Reflex. I figured if I suddenly disappeared, at least there'd be some kind of record of where I'd been. I won't say I was really scared. I was in a weirdly exhilarated place.

Ansel had driven there, took me to his car, which was a sleek sedan I didn't recognize. He opened the door for me, let me slide in, and the thing smelled delicious, the leather seats were soft and supple. I knew what Polly saw in Ansel, for sure. She had her price. Tristan drove a BMW.

"Is this some kind of Caddy?" I asked.

"Maybach," Ansel said. "It's a Maybach."

"It's gorgeous," I said.

"It's alright," he said, starting it up.

"How much does it cost?" I asked. We smoothly cruised out of downtown, headed west, across the river, back to our homeland.

"A lot," Ansel said. "You really want to know?"

"I want to know everything," I said.

"Oh, like 400 grand or so," he said, with a matter-of-factness that freaked me out. He was serious.

"Wow, you really are rich," I said. "Did your family have lots of looted Nazi gold when they fled to the States, or what?"

"Something like that. A lot of gold teeth. Bucketfuls." Ansel said. "My grandpa knew people in the rocket program, was friends with Von Braun, so he got beelined Stateside as part of the space program. Lots of Nazis got in that way, during Operation Paperclip. Any kraut with a sliderule, you know."

"Wow," I said. I didn't know who Von Braun was, but I knew shit about rockets, too. I was an artist, not a historian. "Operation Paperclip? Wow, that's a lame name."

Ansel smiled, nodded. "Yeah. He did some, uhh, you know, unorthodox kinds of things."

It was surreal. "Shouldn't you have a German name? Rupino's not German."

"Yeah," Ansel said. "That's an assumed name he picked up after he'd fled. Grandpa was SS, part of this terrorist group called *Werwolf*. He knew it was only a matter of time before even the US would start asking questions. So, we became proper, upstanding Italian-Americans. It's easier to blend in than you would guess. People see what they want to see."

"You said your grandma was Italian," I said. Ansel nodded.

"She was," he said. "Rupino was a made-up name. Grandma was Elnora Rubino, and Grandpa thought of flipping the 'b' and making it a 'p' and that was that. With the right paperwork, it was easy enough to disappear, to assume new identities. Grandfather knew ODESSA guys, and had friends in this country's secret police; he figured it was smarter to hide right under the noses of the government, versus slumming it in Latin America. He used to say the best place to hide a candle was in a candlestick."

"Nice," I said.

The intrigues were mysterious. I had never known anybody with a past like that. I wondered what Ansel's parents were like, how they made their money, but figured I'd find that out eventually.

We reached his building, and he parked his car in his own garage, and we went inside. My phone chirped, but I ignored it.

When we got into his place, I saw that everything looked about the same, except that he'd placed a stool under some lights, with his painting stuff. Where, I guess, he was going to paint Polly.

I tossed my clutch on his kitchen counter, sat on the stool.

"Alright, Ansel," I said. "What the fuck did you give me?"

"Okay, Sam," he said. "I'll show you. You want to know, and I'll show you. Show and Tell."

Ansel took off his jacket and shirt, set them on the counter, looked me over. Then he took off his pants, threw them on the other clothes, and walked over to the cage across the floor of his loft.

"I take a lot of drugs," he said. "I try to keep myself level. I'm sure you're getting it already, the mood swings, the irritations. Like a buzz, like static you can't quite tune out. Ringing in your ears."

He didn't even guess how far I'd gone. I thought of Sheldon, slamming to the floor, glasses flying.

He went to the cage and closed himself in there, locked it, tested the bars with his hands.

"I used to live in the country," he said. "Real pastoral, nobody for miles around. Wyoming. Nobody fucking there. But the problem with that is that there's nobody fucking there. And the people there have fucking guns."

His skin began to stretch, and he breathed heavily, and dropped into a crouch, his head against the bars. I could see where he was pressing his forehead into them, saw the dimpling of his flesh.

"It didn't help. You kill a rancher's goddamned cattle and they bitch to their Senator about it, call him up and then there's patrols. For a fucking cow. No, you stand out too much out there. The air's better, you've got room to run. But you stand out, too. There's not enough people, not enough of a flock."

His eyes flicked open, and they were red-orange, and his mouth became a snarl.

"Holy shit," I said, stepping off my stool. I started sweating.

"It doesn't work," he said. "The yokels find out quick, and It knows. It knows the difference between a cow and a man. It knows what It likes."

His skin darkened, and his mouth stretched tight, and he snarled. Where he had nails, his fingernails had turned into long, dark claws, and his arms lengthened, his body stretched, and he growled and groaned, eyes on me, voice changing as he spoke, from Ansel to something else.

"My fucking God," I said. My body knew this.

"It likes crowds and noise," Ansel said. "It annoys you when you look normal, but that's just because It wants to come out, thin the herd. It wants to come out and it wants to kill. Don't tell me you haven't felt It. I know you have. I'm sorry, Sam. Believe this: I'm sorry it happened. I slipped up. It wanted you."

The hands clenched the bars, gave them a shake. They didn't budge, thank god. I was off the stool, walking up to him, transfixed, stunned.

"Just a taste," Ansel said, snarling, straining. "I just wanted a little taste, for old time's sake. I had this cage put in here to keep me in if I was feeling...restless. You'll see that soon enough. On the bad nights, I just lock myself in here. The titanium bars are too narrow for It to get through. I know; It's tried. This place keeps me out of trouble. Timelock, 12 hours."

He roared at me, and I felt an explosion inside me that took me to my knees, while he watched me, his snout long, his ears longer, his body covered in hair, his eyes savage and sentient, flailing at the bars, reaching for me with clawed, roughly-callused hands. His fur was black and beautiful, his teeth bright and big and white. Long and curved.

I curled up on the floor, strained against my boots, yanked them off, crawled toward him, tearing off my dress, while he howled and snarled at me, and still he spoke, in this monstrous croak.

"It's not all bad," It said. "Beats being a norm, right?"

It snarled, what seemed like a laugh to my ears, while I writhed on the ground, saw red and watched my arms sprout fur, watched my nails slide themselves out of hiding, felt my teeth stretch as my mouth became a muzzle, felt the fur grow all over me, my smooth legs become hairy monstrosities.

"You fucking...bitch," It sneered, straining at the bars, magnificent and black, with blue eyes and bulging muscles.

It was like before, only more so. My arms grew strong and long, my back curled, I became something else. Smaller than Ansel, but larger than I normally was. I was reddish-brown.

"Dog," I said, my voice husky, the words alien on unfamiliar lips. I was drooling.

I sprang at the bars, and we met each other properly, Ansel and me.

# 6. SATURDAY MORNING: 3 NOVEMBER

I'd like to say I awoke on Saturday, but I never went to sleep. There was just some moment when I realized I wasn't her anymore, and I was just me again, naked on the floor of Ansel's apartment.

He was showering. I heard that, became aware of the sound before I realized what it was, where I was. I was right back where I started.

But different. There weren't even words for it. Ansel and I had fought and fucked against those bars all night long, clawing at each other, me teasing him, taunting him, him trying like hell to break free and get at me in earnest, snarling, cursing, raging. He'd caught me and held me fast in his less-than-loving, more-than-lusting arms.

Christ.

It was beyond anything I could describe, anything I could know, could relate to. It was incredible. I got to my feet, went to his fridge, snagged a beer, a Newcastle, drank it down. Ansel came out of the shower wrapped in a towel.

"Hey," I said.

"Hey," he said back.

"So, we're, like, werewolves?" I said. "I thought it was something serious."

He smirked. "Yeah, you know."

"This is the most awesome fucking thing ever," I said. "I mean, Christ, Ansel!"

It was like the coolest club I could ever belong to, the most amazing, most exclusive thing. There was nothing any of the others could do that would even touch this. It was like a baptism. Sure, it hurt, but it was an ecstatic kind of pain, something kind of sacred.

"Look," he said. "I fucked up. You can't go apeshit, now. The last thing I need is you flipping out and getting out there, butchering people. You want my advice? Get yourself a storage room someplace remote, lock yourself up on the full moon."

"There wasn't a full moon last night," I said.

"The change can happen whenever you like," Ansel said. "Day or night. Whenever. But the moon makes it harder to resist. I'm not going to teach you how to be a fucking werewolf, Sam. Just don't be stupid."

That hurt my feelings, pissed me off all over again.

"Well, who fucking taught you?" I asked.

"Mom and dad," he said. "Grandpa and Grandma."

"See? You had help," I said.

"It's not my job," Ansel said. "I didn't want to kill you, okay?"

"Chivalrous to the end," I said. "You're a real piece of work, you know that?"

"Polly's coming by at noon," he said. "You so need to be out of here by then."

He walked by me, went to his wardrobe, picked out some clothes. I stared at him, not sure what I would do, what I wanted to do.

"Don't worry about me," I said. "I'll be fine."

"I'm good," he said, putting on a t-shirt and some jeans. "No worries."

What a son of a bitch, I thought, grabbing my dress, slipping it on. Thank godless I'd taken it off before helter-skelter time. While I got dressed, he made himself some breakfast. Eggs and bacon. Three eggs, two strips.

"What did I do?" I asked.

"Nothing," he said. "It's not you, it's me, alright?"

I couldn't even believe he'd said that. But I had to know about the scene, had to know who else was out there.

"Fine, fine," I said. "Who else is in Chicago? I mean, are there lots?"

"No," he said. "There's one in DuPage—he works the Forest Preserves, mostly. One in Boys Town. One on the South Side, like near the state line. He's a trucker, though, so he's not around too often, thank god. He's kind of nuts. They all are. Stay away from them, if you're smart."

I could just imagine a werewolf trucker, mad butcher of the freeways, hunting hitchhikers. I wondered how many of them were in the whole country, but didn't bother with that. My concern was the here and now, in Chicago.

"So, five of us?" I asked. Ansel nodded. "Am I the only girl?"

"Sorry to drag you into this," he said. "Whoopsie."

"Mmm," I said. "Try not to eat Polly, at least?"

"No worries," he said. "Look, silver…you know…stay away from it."

I stared at him a moment, and he looked at me with something perhaps close to concern. It was hard to know, hard to read him.

"Yeah, any more useful tips you have for me, you have my number," I said, walking out, hoping I'd put enough sarcasm in my voice.

But I put the weirdness with him behind me as soon as the door closed, and, instead, decided to revel in my new condition. I took the elevator down, encountering a Goth couple just coming in, a skinny guy with a chubby corseted girlfriend, and I just smirked at them. Fucking norms. Sheeple.

Then it was me out on the street, not even minding the autumn chill to the air, jus savoring everything. I wasn't going to die. I was better than I was before. Reborn.

I caught a cab, had it take me home, just sat in the back, thinking about everything. I know it sounds sick, but I felt great peace of mind in the revelation of the night before.

Here I was, worried that Ansel had given me the venereal equivalent of Ebola, but instead, he'd made me the El Camino of monsters—a werewolf. How fucking cool was that?

I was a monster.

Wow. It felt good. It felt right. I had become Säämäänthää. I loved it, thought that's what my new screen name should be. I didn't have to care, anymore. I didn't have to be scared. I could go wherever I wanted to, whenever, without a worry in the world.

Not like I was scared, ever, but you know, in the city, you had to be careful if you were a girl. But now, wow, nobody could touch me. So I hadn't worked out all of the kinks in it, yet; I would. It was all just a matter of time and patience and discipline. I thought about what Ansel had said about me, like how I lacked talent and vision, but had discipline. I'd show him what discipline could bring to the table.

I was riding an endorphin high as I got to my apartment, just thinking of everything that had happened, how even Ansel's morning-after dickishness couldn't really rain on my parade. Sure, my apartment was tiny, felt like a cage. I could change that. There wasn't anything I couldn't do. That's how good I felt. I was like monster Mary Tyler Moore.

I took a shower, was amazed at how good that all felt. The water splashing on me, the steam, the sound of it. Every sense was fired up. It's like I didn't know what sensation was until that moment.

While the hot water soothed me, I just ran my hands over my restored body and marveled at it. Then, after scrubbing off, I put on a robe and savored its texture. I felt like every inch of me was more alive and aware than ever, like I hadn't even known what being alive was before. Like I hadn't even been living.

Going to the fridge, I looked for something to eat, sniffed around in there, found nothing to my liking, settled for a frozen pizza I threw in the oven, then I sat on my futon while the pizza cooked. Then, on a whim, I turned on my computer and logged on, my webcam staring blindly at me. I set the thing to record, stared at myself on my computer screen. I looked so small and pale onscreen; none of my true color turned up onscreen; it changed me as surely as the infection changed me.

"I'm Samantha Hain," I said to myself. Then I clicked on the camera, let it record me. "And I'm a werewolf. I call this piece 'Transformation.'"

Then I willed myself to change, wanting to see if I could do it myself. But how did you do something like that? The first time was a fluke, and the night before, it was something instinctive, just reacting to Ansel's own transformation, some chemical, neuronal two-step that took me from Alpha to Omega. But could I do it at will? Of course I could. It would come. It was like masturbation; you just did it, and the body took care of the rest. My body would know what to do.

The computer patiently recorded me staring at it, doing nothing, and I paused it, then deleted what I'd recorded. It wasn't a case of inspiration versus perspiration; this was something else. There was artifice in art; this was channeling something else, some other part of me I was unfamiliar with, or had lost acquaintance with at some point in my life, or in evolution, or something. To find the Beast within, to call it forth. It wasn't something volitional; I could feel it there beneath the surface of my skin, crawling around on all fours, scratching at me with her long claws.

Säämäänthää.

Having a name for her helped, made her an incantation, a curse, something I could latch my mind onto, something I could channel. A demon to invoke. But she wouldn't come. Maybe I was too much of a noob, couldn't just transform. Or maybe Säämäänthää was just being a bitch, trying to hide out in my heart.

"Come out, come out, wherever you are," I said, smelling the pizza cooking. In the movies, it seemed like somebody was always turning into a werewolf at the drop of a hat. You had a bad day, the fucking werewolf answered the door. Where was she? Maybe because it was daytime? Maybe she only came out at night.

But I thought that Ansel said I could transform any time. He'd said that, right? I admit that I was a little distracted when he was talking to me about it. I wanted to call him, but he was probably fucking Polly right now. Fucking her and fucking painting her, or vice versa.

I wanted to kick down the door and pounce on them. Säämäänthää wanted that bad. Then I found a trigger, something I could pull. I visualized Polly perched in her chair, draped in red velvet, something that would complement her marble-white skin, looking like a Gil Elvgren pinup girl, except naked, her long legs artfully turned and her black heels, long ones, five-inch stiletto fuck-me pumps, patent leather, just a hint of toe cleavage, her nipples erect because it was cool in his place, because Ansel had planned it, fucking Ansel. She's tipsy because he treated her to those big goblets of wine, and he's painting her. He's on his veterinary meds, keeping himself down, keeping his own Beast shackled up tight as he focuses on the brushstrokes and on the alabaster curves of her flesh, her smooth lines and walking-muscles, hypertrophied calves and razorlike shinbones, her lips parted, her red lipstick glossy, and she's laughing at whatever nonsense he's talking about to put her at ease. He's reveling in the sensation of his art, in the intoxicating scent of the paint, the soothing scrape of the brush against the canvas, in the sight of Polly giving herself to him, the sound of her laughter.

The trigger's pulled and I don't think Säämäänthää even knows who she's jealous of, she doesn't fucking care, and I feel my insides split and my skin begin to itch and the sweat pour out of me and my teeth ache, every bone begins to throb, and part of me keeps it together enough to record it, this time for real.

"I'm Samantha...this...is...'Transformation'," I manage to say, through gritted teeth, pushing against the desk with hands that want to be claws, and I glare into the webcam, the unblinking eye that doesn't judge me, doesn't care about me, is as blank as the eye of a shark, and I yelp and pitch forward, then back, falling out of my chair, hitting the ground.

152 | D.T. NEAL

My audience.

The hair boils out of my arms, and becomes fur, like blades of fur coming out of my flesh, not soft, curly dog fur, but like daggers, right through, and my fingers lengthen, the joints thicken, the nails curve, and I'm gripping the desk, scratching the wood laminate, the cheap shit sheathed in decorative I-don't-know, the color of sandstone, and yet I rend it, she rends it, with the flex of her fingers, her paws. Säämäänthää is here, I can feel her, she's me, but I keep thinking of her as another, it makes it easier. My face pulls snaredrum-tight, my teeth too big for my mouth, drool down my lips as my face tries to make room for itself, becoming a snout. Longer, my eyes seeming to sink into my face, burning, alive with sensation, every inch of flesh, rippling skin.

So much better. So much better than the night before. I was distracted the night before. Distracted by Ansel, and his beautiful, monstrous self. This is all for me, all for me, and I'm laughing amid the tears, the agony of the change. Christ, it hurts, but it's like tearing at a scab, or poking at a cavity with your tongue. It's a necessary agony, like childbirth, it's like how I imagined it being. I can smell the pizza cooking, hear the timer clicking out its beat, tick-tick-tick-tick like a goddamned bomb. The bomb is going off. The revolution is televised.

"FUCK!" I snarl, because I can see myself on the monitor, as I'm crouched on the floor, I can see myself staring with hellish eyes, full of malice, the face a ludicrous leer, something like a caricature of me, in a way, Samantha-as-wolf. The fur flies from me, my bones pop, my joints groan and creak, and all at once it's over, it felt like forever, but it's over, and she's there, we can hear the pizza cooking, can hear it bubbling in the oven, hear the hiss of the gas.

Säämäänthää doesn't want pizza. She wants flesh, wants me to knock down my door and bound down the hall, wants to find my neighbors. She knocks over the little coffee table I have in the living room, just flips back onto it and lands on it, breaking it, savors the sound of splintering wood. I realize that I'm not fully wolfen, but am, rather, some dreadful place between the two, hunched and lupine, but not a wolf. Not fully, not truly. The timer goes off, and I bound to it, snatch it in my hands, clumsy hands, now, only fit for slaughter, running, climbing, snatching. Good for plucking little lost lambs away from fat flocks, good for shearing flesh from bone and for digging out innards. I smash the timer.

Säämäänthää wants to run, not to flee, but to fight, to hunt. She wants to kill. She throws herself against the front door, and the door creaks against her shoulder, but does not break. I hold her back, force her back into the kitchen, on all fours, like a dog. She's slavering, she's fighting me, but I'm the monster; I'm her, she's me. I have to tell myself that, my mind wants to sleep, wants to hide and let her ride me across town on a limbic superhighway, wants me to hunt. I have to bring her to heel. Dogs have to be taught, or else they'll have the run of the house, have the run of you. You have to show them who is master. She bangs her head against the oven, brings talons against the handle of the oven, and I pull down on the door and the wash of heat makes us recoil. It feels like hell, but the pizza-smell draws a hand in, and I draw it out with the tips of my claws, because I know that it'll burn me, and if I'm burned, she'll rage and I'll lose control. The pizza tumbles out and falls to the kitchen floor, face up. I cackled at my good fortune.

Säämäänthää sniffs at the pizza, boiling hot, fresh from the oven. Cheese. I try to tell myself that the shades of grey I see are really vivid reds and molten yellows. The sauce is blood. The cheese is skin, the dough is flesh. She dips into it, snapping at it with her absurdly long teeth. Bites in and shakes her head this way and that, savagely, breaking that pizza's nonexistent neck. I'm in the driver's seat, but instinct is instinct, and there's nothing better than a good head shake.

Cheese and sauce spatter across the cabinets and onto my face, and the burn of it makes me snarl. It burns my face, burns my mouth, but I wolf it down, anyway. I eat it and pretend it's the flesh of nuns, of pregnant mothers, of Little Red Riding Hood, and in no time at all I've gobbled down the whole pizza, and am busy licking the floor clean, and the cabinets. I lap up every scrap I can find, and call it slaughter. Säämäänthää isn't fooled, but she tolerates the pain, savors the taste of the food, even if it's not what she truly wants.

We bound out of the kitchen, into the living room, panting, and catch ourselves on camera again, roar at the thing, bound closer, our muzzle covered with sauce that might as well be blood, and she wants to smash this counterfeit self, this little televised image, reaches out for it, but I hold her back.

"Just a dog," I say, our voice a marvelous mangling of human words, full of malice and freshly-decanted hatred. It's amazing, the rush of it, the raw sensation of it, the singing nerves.

"Just a fucking little bitch," I say to the camera, and I try to bring her to heel for real, take back myself, my soul, for the performance, regretting that I left that pizza-eating scene off-camera, because I'm sure it would have rocked. And then I pull it back, take Säämäänthää and put her in the kennel inside me.

"Not yet," she says.

She doesn't want to go back. She wants to stay, she wants to play. I can't believe how drowsy I am inside her, like drowning in endorphins and adrenaline, a mix of up and down and sideways and backwards, moods coming down like curtains on my consciousness. Was this what bipolar felt like? I had friends who claimed bipolarity, but this surely put them to shame, this urge.

"Not...yet," she snaps, and pulls me away from the camera. It's funny, she's the monster, but I'm the one out of control. Then she goes to the window of my apartment and dives through it, and we're tumbling to the ground in a hail of glass, where she lands on the hood of some norm's car, savoring the crunch of high-gloss paint and metal, and on the next bounce she takes me across the street, where we land in the grass, sniffing the air.

*No,* I'm saying. *Home.*

This is home, she says. Hush.

And from our crouch, she raises her head, tastes the air. There is prey about. The city is fucking full of prey.

*No,* I say. But we're running through the city, from shadow to shadow, and the feel of the cold grass against my feet is wonderful, the grip of earth and ground and the effortless propulsion as we hunt. I've never hunted, never understood the attraction of it, never thought it was fair, but Säämäänthää got it right from the start, knew just what she was doing, didn't need anybody to tell her what she was doing. Not Ansel, not me, not anybody.

We actually shot past a jogger, a middle-aged man in a jogging suit, and the man screamed as we went, but Säämäänthää didn't want him, had something else in mind. Over a wrought-iron fence and onto a lawn and then a blur as we ran across that and then vaulted over the other side of the fence and toward stone facades of condominiums, with their own postage-stamp yards. I was amazed at how quiet she could be, how secretive. Werewolves in movies were always making an ungodly racket, tearing everything up, but Säämäänthää had a scent, was stalking it, had a mind to bring it down, and was being so quiet, not wanting the prey to realize it was being hunted. Not yet.

Christ, let it be somebody's dog, I thought. Oh, god, please let it be a dog.

There was barking as we made our way along the sidewalk, past the condos, with a comforting row of parked SUVs on one side, and the tiny hedges of the condos on the other. It was like a tunnel, in a way, an almost perfect place for an ambush. We ran up the sidewalk, eating distance on all fours, in a bizarre lurching stagger-run that wasn't fully lupine, and certainly was many steps removed from truly human.

There were a couple of women walking their dogs. One was a little tiny thing, an ash-colored Pomeranian to my wolfish eyes, and the other was a great big mastiff. Of course, the dogs could tell I was there, hiding behind a phone pole, while the women had no idea what their pooches were barking at.

Säämäänthää watched them in the dark, while the dogs barked and strained against their leashes. The women scolded their pets, and then Säämäänthää howled, and the women froze, staring uncomprehendingly in the dark. Had they ever heard a wolf before? In the urban condominium canyon, my howl bounced off the walls, and made a couple of car alarms go off. I could see the women wondering what the hell they had heard, whether they had really heard it. The dogs kept barking.

"Don't go apeshit," I heard Ansel say in my head, remembering the night before. How was it possible *not* to go apeshit, I ask you? Säämäänthää began drooling, drew her teeth back, as the women backed away from us, trying to bring their dogs to heel. The mastiff broke free of its master and charged down the sidewalk at me.

"Winston, no!" the owner yelled. "Call 911!"

The dog ran snarling at me, brave, stupid Winston, and we were on it in a moment. He jumped right into my waiting arms, all 120 pounds of him, nicely muscled, and his owner wailed at the sight of me. I held him in my arms, his jaws snapping at me, and then I showed him what jaws were for, sank mine into his throat, snapped and tore it out, my eyes on the women as Winston went ragdoll-still in my grip, dog-blood spurting on my muzzle, where only pizza sauce had been before. Winston twitched and was still, and Säämäänthää watched the screaming women, Winston's blood spilling on the sidewalk, and entertained the prospect of charging down the sidewalk and tearing them to bits, especially their yapping little dog. Säämäänthää tucked Winston under her arm, wiped her muzzle with the back of her hand, held a finger out at the women, an accusatory claw, dripping blood.

"You're next," she said. She wanted them to know just what they saw, wanted them to see it, wanted them to fear it. Then she charged at them, and the women shrieked, and in a blur, despite my no-no-no-ing, Säämäänthää charged them, tongue hanging out, claws clacking on the sidewalk as she halved the distance between them before they could even react. They turned and ran, the other woman scooping up her little yapping Pomeranian and Säämäänthää going after them, heedless of a police siren wailing somewhere, getting nearer. The women were in running shoes, but it hardly mattered, though one of the women turned and pepper-sprayed me.

Säämäänthää hadn't been expecting that, the burn of the shit immediate and intense, driving me back. We dove through the bushes to try to clear the hateful burn from our face, from our nose, from our mouths, flailing through woodchips and hedge and lawn furniture, snarling, rubbing our eyes with our hands.

"Fuck," I snarled. "Enough."

It didn't do anything lasting. It wasn't a silver fucking bullet, but it still stung, and it fouled her nose, her ability to track a scent. Diving out of the mini-yard, onto the sidewalk, Säämäänthää shook off her injury, looked up and down for the women through watering eyes, saw nobody, just heard the police siren growing louder.

Wiping our nose with her paw, we ran back to Winston and recovered him and ran back down the street, into the shadows, as the police cruiser sailed down the street, shining a spotlight, arcing this way and that across the street.

Without further ado, Säämäänthää sank her teeth into Winston, and for the first fucking time in my life, I was eating dog, and was grateful for it. We ate him up, gobbled him down in hungry gulps. The dog tasted good. Winston had been a pampered pet, not too old, healthy, not sick. I ate him down and Säämäänthää tossed what was left of him onto the convertible top of somebody's car, the bloody carrion staining the white of the ragtop, the remnants dripping down the windows in long, ropy threads.

Then we raced back into my neighborhood, careful to not be seen. Not now. Säämäänthää was easier to control once she had a full stomach, and Winston had been a big fucking dog. I could only imagine what Sääm would do with a Newfoundland if she came across one.

We snuck back to my apartment building, and she went back to the car with the dented hood, hopped onto it, tested her footing, then used it to leap back into my unit. It was a feat of amazing grace, and yet it brought me no comfort, nor awe, as my stomach was filled with dogmeat. I wanted to puke.

"Are we done?" I asked the air around me, crawling back to the computer, to the webcam, dirty, bloody. I felt used, worse than a thousand bad dates, worse than the first time I'd fucked, when I was fifteen, and Bobby Lambert was clumsily snapping my panties with his thick fingers.

On my hands and knees she left me, let my flesh fold back into itself, reclaimed the fur and the fangs and let the bones regain their original shape, left me shivering and bloody on my floor—not my blood. I went to my computer and stopped the recording, lay on my back and felt the chill through my open window, felt the blood drying on my skin, the greasy dogmeat in my stomach, and Winston's fur in my teeth. I went to the toilet and puked, filled it with dogblood, dog-bones, dogmeat, flushed it down, prayed it would stay down, prayed the toilet wouldn't puke it back up. I flushed it until there was no trace of Winston, and then I took a shower. The rest could wait.

The whole world could wait.

# 7. SUNDAY MORNING: 4 NOVEMBER

I glanced at the papers online in the morning, wincing at the whine of the computer, saw a blurb about me, about us, about Sääm, about a big, wild coyote that had savaged a woman's dog, the remains of which were found on top of a car, and how Animal Control was out in force trying to find the animal before it harmed anyone else's pets. A coyote? I'd fucking talked to them, for god's sake. But, of course, the news wasn't going to report something like that. "Woman Attacked by Werewolf" would never appear on the pages of the *Chicago Tribune*.

I wondered if Sääm appeared at the copy editor's desk of the Tribune, dropped a head in their lap, kissed them on the lips—like whether that would be seen as newsworthy, or whether they would just quietly give that copy editor a retirement package or a reassignment. There's no way the newspaper would report it. There was just some news that wasn't fit to print, even if it was real. Better to sink heads in the sand and pretend nothing happened. Risk was not rewarded; it was punished. That's why real artists were the most avid of risk takers, with nothing to lose and everything to gain by diving into the abyss.

I was afraid to look at my video of the night before, like seeing how it would play out on the recording, whether it would do me justice, would do Sääm justice. I also debated whether to edit it or just let it play out without any revision. On one hand, playing it raw would fit with the natural aesthetic that was vital to a good performance, would make it seem more real. But I thought the long period where the webcam was just recording the empty room after I'd jumped out the window, that wasn't so good—too art house film. What's more, it might get me in trouble, if somebody actually connected the dots, like who owned the car I'd jumped on. But it did lend it some documentary authenticity. I thought I could run an unabridged and an abridged version, get maybe two different audiences with them.

Peeking out my broken window (I'd removed the broken shards of glass), I saw that the car was still there. The owner hadn't checked up on it, I guess. I didn't think somebody would immediately think "Crazy art chick dove out her window and landed on the hood of my car." From the vantage point of the street, they would probably think some drunk had danced on the hood of their car or something. I should have left a note, but no way could I afford to pay for fixing that, and there's no way I could have credibly explained it.

I went back to my computer, to my footage. Biting my lip, I played it, watched myself transform. The intimacy of it was really something, the dreadful beauty of it, a symphony of suffering. It brought tears to my eyes, stirred Sääm inside me, the memory of it, and how strange it was to see what I'd experienced that way. I decided I'd clip the part when she bounded through the window, the dead air. That kind of thing I might be tempted to play in a gallery, with people standing around watching the thing play nothing, but for YouTube, I wanted to keep it punchy, so I edited the clip to have me transform, running off-camera to devour the pizza, then to struggle in front of the camera, and then, with the edit, to return to human form.

It would appear to be a masterpiece of special effects that way, although there was the problem of the blood on the rug as I returned, but I decided to leave that unexplained, unexamined. It would be a mystery, and let my viewers decide for themselves that it meant.

I played the truncated clip, checked my edits, to minimize any jump cuts. It looked great. My own little horror movie. And the lack of production values added to it, I thought.

Horror film needed to look cheap, to have that documentary quality to it. That was why "Night of the Living Dead," "The Texas Chainsaw Massacre," and "The Blair Witch Project" worked as well as they did—they made it seem like you were voyeurs in something that had actually happened. My "Transformation" comfortably fit that mold, and I found it amusing, like reality masquerading as fiction. That added a cool little tingle to it, made me wonder how people would perceive it. I was tempted to add a soundtrack to it, a song or two, but then I thought that would diminish the quality of it. I wanted people to hear my screams and wails, hear me arguing with Sääm.

Holding my breath, I posted it, saved the Jesus freaks the trouble and flagged it as for viewers 18 and older, because I was nude in part of it. People were so lame about that; they were fine with violence; it was the sex they couldn't stand. Sheeple.

After posting it, I got ready for work in earnest, another dreary day. Lance had decided to show up, and Simone was there, and Dean, too. It was pretty busy, and I'd worn a long-sleeved grey shirt with three-quarter sleeves under my work shirt, to kind of cover up my forearms, even though I'd shaved them before getting ready for work. Who shaves their forearms? Me, I guess. Now.

I knew I'd made some progress with my performance art when Lance called me into his office in the afternoon. He'd gotten his hair bleached recently, had his surfer-boy laconic look to him he'd been cultivating for years.

"Hey, Sam," he said, running a hand through his artfully greasy hair. "I saw your video this morning. Fucking amazing."

I was surprised that he'd even looked it up.

"Really? You liked it?" I asked.

"Yeah," he said. "I got an e-mail from a bud, who told me I had to check it out. When I saw the link, I was like, 'Hey, that's Sam.' How'd you do it?"

I smiled. "I just did it."

"Radical," he said. "Seamless. What software did you use? I mean, I can't even see the cuts in it."

"What, you want to know my technique?" I asked. "Isn't that like asking a magician how they did a trick?"

Lance smiled, as oily-smooth as his hair. "Art isn't magic. This is going all over the place."

I was pleased that Lance, of all people, had seen it. If Lance was seeing it, then it meant it was getting around. Already! I loved the Internet.

"Did you look at any of my other stuff?" I asked. "I've got several on there."

"Yeah," Lance said. "The others, not so much, but that werewolf one, wow. You're one tripped-out little babe, aren't you?"

"What can I say? I'm just me," I said.

"Yeah, you are," he said. "Fuck me, yeah. I mean, it's fucking seamless. And it doesn't even look like you used CGI or anything."

My phone buzzed in my pocket, but I didn't reach for it, just savored Lance's admiration as he went on about it, played it, reacted to it. It was satisfying, seeing that reaction in him. Not like he was an art critic, or anybody at all, but still, it pleased me for him to see me doing something more significant than being his employee, like for him

162 | D.T. NEAL

to know that I actually did something cool, which put me light years ahead of Simone, who just fucked him. I mean, fucking only went so far. His eyes went up and down me, he licked his lips. I could actually hear him licking them, the smack of tongue against teeth, drinking saliva. I knew what that felt like.

"Weren't you afraid to, you know, take it off?"

"Nope," I said. "I used to model nude in college, for art classes. It hardly fazes me. I mean, only an ugly body is worthy of shame, right? And mine is tops."

"Christ, yeah," he said. "That video's going to be in my head all day."

"Is that all you got from it?" I asked. "Me furry and naked?"

"Well, you know," he said. "It's just wild that you did that."

He just let that hang there, like a lolling tongue, and I didn't say anything, just stood there, wondering what he'd say next. I could smell his lust, it was right there, in his pores, in the sweat. I could taste it. It was a weird feeling. Too much information.

"I should probably get back to work, eh?" I said.

"What's with the hair?" he asked.

"It's the new me," I said. "All-natural."

"Whoa," he said. "I liked your Kool-Aid Red. It was like your signature color."

"Yeah, well," I said. "That's done, I guess."

He laughed, looked me over again. "You can always decide to go red again, you know. Better red than dead."

"That's funny, Lance," I said, making my way to the door. "I think you've got it backwards."

"Hey, Sam, if you ever need anybody for your performances, you know, I'm available," he said.

I laughed. "I don't think you could take it, Lance, but thanks for offering."

I walked out of his office, just as Simone was heading toward it, her face set. The narrow corridor where the timeclock was meant we had to turn sideways to pass each other, and I could feel her looking down at me, while I could smell her worry and displeasure and her guerrilla perfume.

I'm sure she hated me being behind closed doors with Lance, and if she'd heard what Lance had said, she'd really be pissed. At me, of course, not at him. I just went back to my cashier's station and tucked my hands in my pockets, prepared to slouch through the rest of my afternoon, listened to Dean tell me about his gig, how it went down.

Once Simone had shut herself in Lance's office, I took out my cell phone. Ansel had left me a message. I looked around, checked if any customers were around, and played it back.

"Hey, Sam," he said. "Yeah, skinchanging's a bitch. Sorry about the tats and the dye job. I guess I should've mentioned that. I don't know why it does that, but something about the transformation does that. Takes you back to Square One. Anyway, uh, sorry."

He hung up. What a douche. I decided that any time something fucked up happened, I'd leave him a message, just to get on his nerves. I should have mentioned eating the fucking dog, but that was too embarrassing, I didn't want to go there. Just the memory of it alone made me sweat, and that Sääm seemed fond of the memory made me sweat more. That, and the fact that I hadn't puked all of Winston up, I was sure. I was running on dog.

"You are what you eat," I murmured.

"Huh?" Dean said.

"Nothing," I said, tucking my hands in my pockets again. I wondered how many people were clicking on my video clip, wondered how that was going, hoped it was making an impact. If nothing else, *Fangoria* would maybe want me to pose for them or something. That would rock; I could just imagine the spit-takes from the others on that, trying to decide on whether it was kitschy, campy, or ironic. Before my shift ended, on a whim, I bought a calendar from the tourist shelves, one of Japanese block prints, tucked it under my arm, where Winston had been tucked the night before, and got out of there.

From her position at her own register, Simone glared at me as I clocked out. "Lance really dug your video. I thought it was kind of lame."

"Yeah?" I said, folding my apron across my forearm, like I was a waitress somewhere. Simone was wearing red stovepipe jeans, had a horseshoe belt buckle, zebra print ballet flats.

"I mean, come on," Simone said. "A werewolf? Were you being ironic, or what?"

"I wasn't being anything except myself," I said. "You don't like werewolves?"

"They're so lame," she said. "1981 called, they want their monster back."

I smiled, showed my teeth, grin tight across my lips. "I forget, Simone. What is it you do, exactly? I mean, besides Lance?"

She just rolled her eyes. "That little video was just, I dunno, exploitation. Any girl can get attention rolling around naked on the floor. So you gave yourself some fangs and fur—is that supposed to signify or something? And what's with the eyes? So Marilyn Manson of you."

"Bowie, not Manson," I said.

She crossed her arms and cocked her head at me, what she thought was the very picture of bored defiance. But her smell told me that she was intimidated, resentful. That came out from under her hipster perfume, even.

"It's just a performance," I said. "Sorry you didn't like it, Simone. Lance loved it, though."

I turned my back on her and walked out, imagining her staring daggers into my back. I wondered if I should have posted the video on my blog, like whether that would've earned me more traffic. Though I didn't have the means to host video. That's what it always came down to: lack of means. I needed money.

My phone buzzed and I switched on the ringer, walked my way to the El as I talked. It was Polly.

"Hey, Sam," she said. "Ansel's amazing. He painted such a beautiful portrait last night."

"Yeah?" I said.

"Yes," she said. "He captured me on the canvas. It's fabulous, stylized. Really sexy. I was a little worried, but it came out great."

Sääm twitched under my skin at the memory of it, my daydream that spurred the transformation. Christ, if you only knew, Polly. One of you was my fucking monster's muse, and I think maybe it was you.

"That's awesome," I said. "I hope I'll get a chance to see it."

"I don't know," Polly said. "He said it was just for me."

"Did he give it to you?" I asked.

"Not exactly," she said, breathless. She was probably fast-walking somewhere. I could almost hear her heels clacking as she went, matriarchal Morse code. "He's going to get it matted and framed, once it's dried."

"Not the kind of thing Tristan would like, I bet," I said. I could just imagine Trist getting in a twist over that. No guy wants to be cuckolded through art.

"Yeah," Polly said. "It's so unfair. I mean, it's a gorgeous portrait. He's got the most amazing hands, doesn't he? I want to get it hung, but Tristan would have a fit. I'm thinking it should be shown at BacchUS."

That would work. It would fulfill Polly's own exhibitionism, while at the same time being someplace where Tristan would never turn up.

"Yeah, I bet Clay would love that," I said. "Though he's such a pimp; he wouldn't want the piece there if it wasn't up for sale."

"I know," she said.

The El thundered overheard, and I carded myself past the turnstile, past the ugly overhead lights, the dirty rotten wooden floor that made me think of the hold of a ship, and walked my way up the paint-and-rust latticework that called to mind walking through the skeleton of something, me-as-maggot. That image made me uncomfortable.

"Maybe you could give it to me," I said.

"Yeah, right," she said.

"I'm just saying, I could hang it on my wall, and you could come over and check it out any time you liked," I said. What the hell? Why not? Sometimes fortune favored the foolish, like how drunkards always seemed to walk away from car wrecks.

"It's not a terrible idea," she said. "I mean, I could just leave it at Ansel's, of course. That's the best place for it, but eventually Tristan's going to be wondering why I'm always hopping over to Wicker Park, you know? He's going to get suspicious. When I'm with Ansel, I just kind of lose it. I can't imagine being able to enjoy the portrait in the presence of the man...the artist...who made it. I feel like he owns a part of me, now."

Her narcissism made me want to laugh. I imagined her masturbating to her portrait, putting candles before it, making it a shrine. I could just see her with a silver ankh around her neck, high priestess of the Cult of Polly.

"Yeah, tough call," I said, pacing on the platform, which was wet, of course, because it had been raining. Little pools of chilly, toxic water everywhere, and me waiting for my train to come. "At least at my place, there'd be no way Tristan would find out. It's not the kind of thing you'd want him to know about, you know? I mean, if it was at Clay's, there'd always be the chance of Tristan coming down there when you did a reading or something, and that would be hugely awkward."

"Yes," Polly said.

"Plus," I said, and could taste Sääm on my tongue. "I'm the only one who knows about you and Ansel, right? I mean, like for real?"

"Well, you know the most," Polly said.

"So, I'm saying that your secret's safe with me," I said. "I'm like a Swiss bank account."

My El train rolled in at some distance, slow and steady. It stopped when it got to a red light, waiting for the color to switch. The trains looked like inscrutable mechanical snakes, blank-faced and unreflective, without reason or remorse.

"I don't know," Polly said. "I don't want to impose on you. I should just leave it at Ansel's, but he's almost too tempting, you know? Christ, you know what he's like."

I laughed huskily into my phone, watched the train decide at last to approach, to rumble-glide into the station. I walked on board, sat by the window.

"Oh, yeah," I said. "I know how he is, alright."

Part of me wanted to warn Polly about Ansel, like this little sheeple part of me, Little Bo Peep. I imagined myself telling Polly about Ansel, and Polly forever cutting me off, our friendship immediately terminated.

No, I wasn't about to do that.

"How'd the other night go?" she asked.

"Great," I said. "Kind of wild."

She was quiet on the line a second, assessing that. She was like a pretty little bird. I remembered Lee teasing her about her name and that Nirvana song, and Polly expressing dismissive disdain for him and it. But like a bird, one didn't want to make sudden movements, didn't want to startle her.

"But, you know, I'm not his type," I said. "He's definitely way into you, though."

It was worth letting my pride take a hit if it meant winning somewhere else. I mean, Ansel and I definitely had animal attraction (haha), but we got on each others' nerves more than anything else. Like when we weren't fucking, there was something else going on there, just disdain or displeasure, or something. He looked down on me, I could feel it, and it pissed me off. I mean, if the choice was gaining Polly's trust or leaving Ansel twisting in the wind, it was a no-brainer for me. And if gaining her trust meant I got that painting in my living room, how great would that be, if it meant getting Polly in my living room, admiring herself, in the bargain, too?

See what a no-brainer that was? And if it meant sticking it to Ansel a little, like while he was busy sticking it to Polly, so much the better!

I liked the way Sääm thought. Polly didn't know all of that, though; she just knew that I was basically conceding that Ansel found her more attractive than me, which was really just me admitting the facts, as far as she knew them. I mean, what Ansel did to me, well, that was between Ansel, me, and everybody on YouTube.

Polly was gracious in victory. "Ansel has nothing but nice things to say about you, Sam. You should know that."

"Oh, I'm sure," I said. "But I'm not you, Polly."

She could have eaten that with a spoon and asked for seconds. My train car rocked soothingly as it made its way north and west.

"We're just different, that's all," Polly said. "Ansel and I click. My God, do we ever click. It's kind of frightening, in a way. For a second, I think about Tristan while we're having sex, and am wondering if he's doing the same thing, if he's thinking about me. Tristan, not Ansel. I don't know what is in Ansel's head. And when he's there with me, I don't even care."

I wanted to laugh, looked out the rain-flecked window, watched the city pass by underneath, instead, tried to change the subject.

"Hey, did you see that I posted a new performance piece online?" I said. "I called it 'Transformation.'"

"No, I hadn't seen it," Polly said. "When did you do it?"

I opened my calendar, began circling the full moon of every month, so I knew what went where. I wondered how that would go down, exactly.

"Last night," I said. "On a whim. It's already gotten a lot of attention, from what I've heard. I'm going to check it out when I get home, see what kinds of comments people left. My boss saw it, though—it was really embarrassing."

"Why, was he mad?"

"Horny, more like," I said. "I think he wanted me to be his new workplace girlfriend. It was really awkward. I should let him put the moves on me and then sue him for sexual harassment."

Polly laughed, high, lilting, fake. Thanks to her law office play money, she was always so well-dressed. They paid her well, and it made her feel like she was doing something useful when Tristan was out making the real money.

"I'll take a look at it, let you know what I think," she said.

"Great," I said. "Let me know about the painting, too. I've got a perfect spot in my living room for it."

"Will do," Polly said, hanging up. I hung up, pocketed my phone.

My stop was coming up, so I got up and walked to the doors, waited. It was about 6:30, so there was the usual mix of wageslaves and students and crazies on the train, everybody either iPodding it or cell phoning it or Blackberrying it or Bluetoothing it, or just staring out the window, one or two doing Sudoku or crossword puzzles, one or two reading.

Looking at them, I wondered which ones were the weaklings and neurotics. I could almost see it, like the way they held themselves, the turn of a foot, the heave of a sigh. Their weakness was clear to me, or to Säämäänthää, anyway. She could tell which ones were the fighters, the talkers, the runners, the fainters, the squealers. She could tell, and I could tell. It made my stomach growl, made me sweat to look at them, all breathing, a tight little flock on my train. Did they even realize there was a wolf in the fold? Could they even tell?

Prey for them, Säämäänthää thought.

I think it's 'pray,' I thought back.

Not to me, it isn't. There is no 'pray,' only 'prey.'

A few of them glanced at me, but it was just a commuter glance, probably looking at my mismatched eye. I took out my shades and put them on, dragged my gaze out the window as my stop slipped into view.

I couldn't wait for the doors to open, to step out into the dirty rain and the cold air, to lean against a lamppost, watch the commuters walk around and past me, watch the train go its less-than-merry way. Watching the faces go by like some demented filmstrip, everybody looked like walking corpses to me. It was misting, not even bothering with proper rain, and I wiped my face, walked home, passed that car with the busted hood, saw that my window had been replaced with a wooden board by the landlord, after I'd reported it. I hated when they crept around my apartment when I was out, I always liked to be in there, keeping an eye on them, and was grateful as fuck that I'd cleaned the hell out of the rug after I'd been done showering last night. I'd taken Scotchguard and sprayed that foam all over the rug, scrubbed it up. It wasn't entirely clean, but it didn't look like the bloody mess it had been when I'd come back in.

There was a note from the landlord complaining about the broken window, how I'd have it come out of my security deposit, but I didn't care. That's what security deposits were for. They said the replacement window would come in next week. Until then, I had to be content with the board in the window.

The landlord, Mr. Ludovico, had grilled me on how it had happened, since he'd found the screen for it on the ground below. I told him I had slipped and fallen against the window, which had shattered against my back. I think I was convincing enough, because he was asking me if I was okay, and had I seen a doctor, and I'd told him that I had seen a doctor, that I was on some antibiotics, and was feeling a little light-headed, and that this was probably part of the problem, because I wasn't supposed to take them with food, and I guessed that I had fainted or something. Ludovico sternly told me that I needed to eat, and I agreed with him, told him how sorry I was about the damage. And I was superficially sincere—I meant what I said, even though I was just saying it to keep him from being too nosy.

I could still smell Old Spice, could smell where he'd been in my apartment. I actually paced around the place, tracked the ghost of his scent. A hint of cigarette, and a lot of aftershave. He'd walked throughout my place.

Creep. I hated landlords, felt my stomach growl, went into my freezer for some soy patties and broccoli, which I nuked, while I turned on my computer, checked out my video.

20,000 hits since I'd posted it. That was fucking sweet. I'd posted it this morning, so that was like 10 hours ago. Awesome. It got four stars. I scrolled down onto the comments. There were a lot of idiots and near-illiterates on YouTube, but sometimes there were good commentators.

*Gorehound: SHEEZ FAWKINSWEET!*
*Whimsicle: Aw, cmon! Totally fake. UCAN see the glue & CUTZ!*
*PrinceNasty169: I liked it.*
*Kingfisher: I'd like to give THAT dog a bone.*
*Fangloria: Wicked. Awesome. You GO, GRRL!*
*Wolfmotherlode: Don't FUCK with the FUR, Babeez!*
*Cyberclown: OMG! What movie is this from?*
*Whimsicle: Am I th eonly one who getz it? Fake! This is so CHEESY!*
*Slackie Onassis: I think it's a comment on femininity in the postmodern era, like you can hear her gobbling food off-camera, and then she returns to the frame with food all over her muzzle. She starts as a woman, ends as one, and has basically this orgy of eating in between, but out of sight—like she's ashamed of eating, even though she's not ashamed of being a monster. Reminds me of classmates, really.*
*Antichristo1848: You're crazy. She's just an attention whore.*
*Viscountess: S'okay. It totally reminds me of that movie with the wolves in it.*
*Stickler: You mean Jaws, right?*

*PrinceNasty169: I really liked it.*
*Flipperz: I swear I see a zipper like at 5:28. Right at the neck.*
*GRRL: Sucks. There's no drama in it. Like in The Howling, where there's somebody else watching the transformation, to provide, I dunno, tension, but here, it's just her. No drama, just spectacle.*
*Wolfmotherlode: We're the ones watching, GRRL. Cha!*

And on and on. About 78 comments so far. I put a comment on there, as Jasmint.

*Jasmint178: I like her work. Did you see her other clips? She's got real talent, a singular vision.*

It never hurt. Then I saw that Polly had left a comment.

*Polytician: Wow, that's pretty impressive. I didn't know you were working on another project.*

That was it. But she'd looked at it, at least. Odds were the others would, too. It's hard to know which of the Boyhemians was the first to come sniffing around my door after they got wind of my video. I mean, there was a Facebook e-mail from Lee, a MySpace message from Reagan, a Twitter from Polly, and a phone call from Gabe. But I suppose I'd start first with Clay, since he actually came into Nonpareil for a face-to-face. Of course nothing from Sheldon, since he was dead.

He had turned up at my work in a grey track jacket with white racing stripes, and black jeans, wiping his hands on his pants, his hair metrosexually tousled, just hints of grey at the sides, Clay crinkling his eyes in a way that he probably thought made him look like Steve McQueen, but really just highlighted his crows' feet.

"Cold outside," he said.

"Yeah," I said. "You should dress for the weather, Bro."

He forced laughter up from his chest like he was stomping on a bellows, fanning frivolity with puffs of air between his teeth.

"You need supplies?" I asked.

"No," he said, staring intensely around the store, before zeroing back in on me. I could never get how Clay got so much play, because he was just like this coiled bundle of frayed wires, current running through him. He didn't come off as charming, just insanely high-strung. I think he must have been handsome once, but dissolution had poked him with her thumbs a few too many times, left marks in his once-tender flesh that had long been overdone, like from prime rib to beef jerky in his 34 years.

"You came to see me, Clay?" I asked, smirking.

"I want you to do that 'Transformation' piece at BacchUS," he said.

"It was a film, Clay," I said.

"Right," he said. "We can run it on screens. Can you hash out another performance piece? Something you could do in-house?"

"What do you have in mind?" I asked. "Are you hiring me, Clay?"

He smiled, showed off his veneers. I don't know which girlfriend had paid for those choppers of his. They were really very white against his tanned skin.

"Not exactly," he said. "But I want to feature you. Give you exposure."

"Pay me $500 in cash," I said. "And I'll come up with something, Clay."

I wanted a new pair of Dolces, after all. And I wanted to see if I could actually wring the money out of Clay, see how horny he was.

"Give me a break," he said. "Me pay you? What planet are we on, here?"

"I'm just saying, Clay," I said. "My Net exposure is already way, way more than anything BacchUS could offer. So, it's not like you'd be doing me a favor; if anything, I'd be doing you a favor, see?"

That took him aback, like he hadn't even thought of that. He probably though I'd gush at the prospect of being featured in his rinky-dink gallery, like the mascot being thrilled to occupy center stage.

"I mean, you'd pimp my appearance by referencing my online video, right?" I asked. "So, you'd be banking on my momentary notoriety. Maybe I should ask for a percentage of whatever you're charging at the door, right?"

He grinned brightly at me. "Mercenary. I like that. Brutal. Ruthless. Hand over fist."

"You can fuck me, Clay," I said. "But, you know, don't fuck me."

"Killer," he said. "Alright, look, yeah, right?"

Clay spoke in clipped sentences, guttural half-utterances, when he wasn't busy riffing on some subject near and dear to him.

"Right, what?"

"I am hoping to, you know, get some attention for BacchUS. Marketing, right? Viral. Word-of-mouth. Buzz."

"Okay," I said. "I know you're being floated by your girlfriend. Everybody knows that's what you do, Clay. So, you have money to burn.

Her money, but money, just the same. So, you give me a percentage at the door, and I'll do something, you know, memorable. How many people can safely fit in BacchUS?"

"Maybe 60, if we pack them in tight," Clay said. "Fire codes, right? Safety fucking first."

"What were you planning to charge?" I asked.

"$10 a person," Clay said, wiping his hands on his pants.

"Larcenous," I said. "Give me half of that."

"If anybody fucking comes," Clay said. "Maybe nobody will come."

I figured I could get people to come, maybe. If I wanted anybody to come. If I was even planning on going.

"I have an idea for a piece," I said. "'Little Blow Peep' is what I'm calling it."

Clay nodded, forehead sagely crinkling. "Yeah, that'll do."

"So, half the take at the door?" I asked.

"Come on, Sam," he said. "Now you're fucking me."

"We can pack the place," I said. "Horrorshow, you know? Go out with a bang."

"Out?" Clay asked.

"You know," I said. "Seems like we're kind of, I dunno, cliquey these days, with the whole Lee/Ansel rift."

Clay laughed, checked out Simone as she walked by. He was always on the make. It didn't matter how many girlfriends he had at any moment.

"Fuck that," he said. "I don't care about Lee's hang-ups. Horrorshow's bigger than that, is bigger than any of us. Everybody should be there. I'll call everybody."

That made me want to laugh. Horrorshow was nothing. We were nothing. Less than nothing. Everything was bigger than we were. Of course, Lee saw our lack of numbers as integral to our vitality, something about us being the bullion cubes in society's soup—too much water thins the broth.

"How about $100?" Clay said.

"My materials will cost more than that," I said. "$500 up front, or else half of the take. Seems easy enough. If I bring in the people, then you've got a chance to make a sale, right?"

It was like a poker game between us, hustler versus hustler, art-whore versus gallery gangster gigolo. He ogled Simone, who manager-walked again across the floor, keeping an eye on us as she made her way to the office. Clay looked like he was in pain at the prospect, grimaced at the prospect of actually paying me money to perform at BacchUS.

"Alright," he said. "Half the take, but you have to promise to do a piece there, and to promote it."

"Promotion costs money," I said. "I'm the one doing you the favor here, Clay. And when were you thinking?"

"This weekend?" he ventured.

"Way too soon," I said. "Unless you don't want anybody there, just Horrorshow."

"We could flash-mob it," Clay said. "You know, something off the cuff, subversive. That way, we get around the promotion costs."

A flash mob. Yeah, why not? That could totally work. A happening.

"Alright," I said. "That could rock. Tell everybody to dress as sheep."

"Sheep?" Clay asked.

"Yeah," I said. "Everybody. They can use their imaginations."

"Lee won't dress like a sheep," Clay said.

"Maybe not," I said. "Still, that's what it'll be—be at BacchUS this Saturday at 9:11 p.m., dressed as a sheep, and to bring camcorders, for a performance of 'Little Blow Peep.'"

Clay smiled into his Blackberry, jotting that down. "I like it. A fucking scene."

"Yeah," I said. "That's what it'll be. People have to show up on time."

"You never know," Clay said. He looked into it, and into Simone, who turned up yet again. Clay excused himself, sauntered over her way, started chatting her up, which was fine by me, because it kept her off my back for talking too long about nonwork stuff.

I doubted any of the others would dress as sheep, but it would be cool if strangers did—that would make it for me.

The phone message from Gabe was pretty noncommittal. "Hey, Sam. Just wondering what you're up to Friday, thought maybe we could go someplace or something."

His lazy drawl was all that I needed. I couldn't imagine spending an evening in its presence. No way. I deleted the message, figured that would be enough of a bruise to Gabe's ego to have him stewing a little.

The MySpace message from Reagan had been something about how she liked my film, wondered if I was going to do anything else this year.

I was finding myself full of ideas.

# 8. SUNDAY EVENING

Everybody went to Reagan's place for her dinner party, including Ansel, who had managed to get invited as Polly's date. Nobody batted an
eyelash when he showed up, wearing a black ribbed turtleneck sweater
and grey slacks. Polly was fetching as ever in three-inch block heels on
tan knee boots, chocolate-brown hose and turtleneck, denim jumper
dress, silver choker necklace, from which a cat's head amulet hung.

Of course, Sheldon wasn't there, and people called him, tried to
find him. I even called him up, left a message. Didn't want to stand
out.

"Nobody's seen him for days," Reagan said. "I hope he's alright."

"I went by his place," Gabe said. "He didn't answer the door."

"Should we report him missing?" Polly asked. "Is that our job?"

"Maybe he's on a bender," Lee said. "Finding inspiration
through inebriation."

"I'm a little worried," Reagan said. "Nobody's seen him since the 28th."

"Wow," Lee said. "That's what, a week? Yeah, that's weird."

"We should do something," Reagan said. "Call the police, tell
them
  we're concerned."

"Maybe he overdosed," Polly said.

"On what? Cigarettes?" Lee asked. "Sheldon doesn't do anything
stronger than nicotine."

That was for sure. The bitter taste of Sheldon was something I
could readily recall. It made my stomach turn a bit.

A couple of Reagan's friends from college came in: Don Walsh,
who was a skinny, bookish gay guy, Gretta Morris, her roommate
from college, her girlfriend. Gretta had mouse-brown hair in a page-
boy, wore granny glasses and clunky black shoes and black broom

skirts. Christina Sinestro, one of Reagan's other friends, had also turned up. She had a wide mouth and a strong jaw, had curling hair down to her shoulders, broad hips and a nice laugh. She was dressed in nice jeans and a pretty blouse, wore an amber necklace. Clay turned up with a bottle of absinthe in hand, bragged that he'd had to get it from Spain, off the Internet. That prompted Gabe to say that Czech absinthe was superior, and the swords were out.

"Czech absinthe is like mouthwash," Lee said. "It looks like Scope, and tastes like ass. The Spanish absinthe is for a more discriminating palate. The range of absinthes available in Spain is far broader than what you'd find in the Czech Republic."

He plunked the bottle down on one of Reagan's sideboards, along with a box of sugar cubes, and a slotted spoon.

"Besides," Lee said. "It's legal to buy it in the States, now. Fail."

Clay looked mortally wounded. The absinthe wars were over, at least in our group. Lee had failed Clay. There was no coming back from it.

"Now, the party can begin," I said.

"Is he being ironic?" Clay asked. "I mean, we just had absinthe on Halloween."

"If you have to ask, you'll never know," Lee said. "They're a couple of absinthe hipsters. I told them that the other day. Clay's trying to make a point, seems like."

Reagan's apartment was in Lincoln Park, and we'd usually kind of mock that, because that wasn't a place for a proper bohemian, but with Reagan, it somehow worked. She was on Clark Street, close to the park itself, had a great apartment and a wonderful view of the lake.

She was a bit of a trust fund brat, so everything she enjoyed was great, like a three-bedroom apartment in Lincoln Park that had more space than she knew what to do with, with everything tastefully decorated in earth tones—leather sofas and chairs, a wonderful writing desk so dark it could have been black, and one of the bedrooms she'd turned into her art room. In fact, most of the walls were covered in her collages and paintings, to the extent that Lee would quip that her home was really her gallery, the Reagan Museum.

Reagan loved playing the intellectual hostess, had arranged a complicated menu for us, had playing cards on all of our allotted places, with a sea of votive candles offering a warm, soft light.

"Each of you will find an envelope on his or her place setting," Reagan said. "I insist that you take that envelope and place it someplace safe. Do not open it. Each envelope contains a playing card. Do not show this card to anyone, or discuss it. We shall play a game later this evening, one most of you might know as Mafia, but tonight, we shall call it Werewolf."

She gave me a knowing look. I felt pleased, like the guest of honor. Ansel looked at me, his face neutral, but his eyes searching. The others chuckled at the name of the game, murmured to each other, pocketed their envelopes, while Reagan readied the dinner.

"I hope you like lamb," she said. "Carnivores, that is. I made you an avocado salad, Sam."

"Oh, I'll try the lamb," I said, which surprised some of the others. "It smells wonderful."

"Gone to the dark side, have you?" Lee asked, as Reagan dished out this pretty little salad with sliced avocadoes and mandarin oranges and romaine lettuce, with a dash of balsamic vinegar atop it.

"Yeah, that's it," I said. I reached for my fork and hissed when it touched my hand, this scalding feeling, like being touched by boiling water. The heavy fork tumbled into a saltshaker, knocking it over, spilling salt.

"Bad luck," Lee said, "Unless you throw some over your shoulder."

What the fuck had happened? I glanced at my hand, saw a little burn across it, like seared meat, where the silver had touched me. Oh, no way. Ansel looked at me.

"You alright, Sam?" Polly asked.

"Uh, yeah," I said. "Just pinched a nerve. I was doing some of that high-octane yoga the other day, and I think I overdid it."

"Yoga will drive you insane," Lee said. "You'll be swallowing rags in no time. All practitioners of yoga go mad, eventually."

I took advantage of Lee's talking to kind of hide my hurt hand. The silver had stung me. So, it was real? Silver actually did hurt werewolves.

Ansel showed me that he'd taken a napkin and had slyly wrapped his utensil with it, was blithely eating, pretending to pay attention to the conversation. Christ, a fine time to find out that I was allergic to silver—Ansel had said something about it, but I hadn't believed him, didn't think it would affect me. I mean, I was surrounded by the stuff. Reagan had a full silver dinner service. I couldn't swing a dead cat without hitting a piece of silver. I just had assumed it was bullshit, that it was something made up. But then, I didn't believe in werewolves, either.

Gabe was already into his wine, leaned toward me with his elbows on the table, lazily holding the glass of red wine like it was a scepter. "So, how'd you do that Transformation piece, Sam?"

"I'd like to say it was hard work," I said. "But it wasn't so tough."

Ansel sipped at his own wine, Polly by his side at the table. I really hoped that Tristan would get back from Beijing soon. I couldn't believe how recklessly public Polly was being with Ansel.

"The real question," Lee said. "Is what was your inspiration? I mean, is this an homage to lycanthropy, or what? You seemed more *Howling* than *American Werewolf in London* to me, in mean in the presentation, in the look, in the talking."

"Oh, I couldn't disagree more," Clay said. "It was terribly campy."

"Wait, wasn't *The Howling* campy?" Gabe asked.

"It wasn't campy at all," Willa said. "There wasn't a bit of camp in it. It wasn't very good. Technically proficient, I'll give you, but otherwise, almost pointless."

"We're talking about *The Howling*, or Sam's "Transformation?" Lee asked.

I could see the others were wondering what I'd say to that. After Ansel's critical confrontation at BacchUS, no less. And there really wasn't a defense to it, for if I defended it, then it made it seem like the piece needed defending or explanation, which would say that it had failed as a performance piece. The only answerable defense was blowing her off.

"Pointlessness is the new meaningful," I said.

"Welcome to my world," Lee said, and there was laughter around the table. But Gabe was still chewing on his wine, smacking his lips.

"But seriously," he said. "How did you do that? It had to have cost a fortune."

"I'm not telling," I said, glancing at Ansel. "Ancient Chinese Secret."

"More like Hungarian," Clay said.

"I don't like werewolves," Willa said. "They're too common. Overgrown dogs, really. Vampires I can get—suave, immortal, orally fixated. But lupines? Where does that come from? Whatever do they offer?"

"The Beast Within," Lee said. "Man running from his animal roots. A yearning for lost youth, a symbol of repressed rage. A release?"

"Man still is an animal," Ansel said. "He only forgets that from time to time."

"I disagree," Gabe said. "We stopped being animals the minute we made civilization."

Ansel laughed. "You think pottery and writing makes you civilized? Probably the other way around, don't you think? How many wars have been started by civilization? How many have been killed? Man doesn't know the meaning of the word. There is no Mind without Body, and Body is Animal. Bodies makes up Civilization, therefore, Civilization is Animal. Find me a solitary human being, an autonomous one, and you get a hermit. The brutality in Civilization is just a manifestation of our Animal natures."

"Specious," Willa said.

"A materialist, New Guy?" Lee said. "Yes, yes."

Reagan came out with a platter of dolmates, stuffed grape leaves, and set it on one side of the table. They smelled great, and we pounced on them.

Clay joined in, of course, as he always did when philosophy turned up. And as a diehard Nietzschean, we all knew where he'd come in on it.

"Fuck materialism," he said. "I'm a perspectivist."

"Here we go," Lee said, pouring himself some more wine.

"Life is more than living," Clay said. "Life is about power. And knowledge is power. Mind is power. Without Mind, we're dead meat."

Ansel passed on the dolmates.

"You are the life that you lead," Ansel said. "You are what you eat."

"I'm not a lamb," Lee said. "I'm a lion."

"I'm a captain of industry," Gabe said.

"I am queen of all that I survey," Polly said.

"I am hungry," Clay said. "Therefore, I shall eat."

"Has anybody ever eaten dog before?" I asked, which prompted laughter and wrinkled noses. Ansel smiled into his glass of wine, looked at me over the rim of the glass. I knew he'd had a dog or two in his day.

"What kind?" Lee asked. "Are we talking lapdogs or gundogs, or what?"

"Any kind," I said.

"That's disgusting," Willa said. "Who would eat a dog?"

"Savages," Gabe said. "Monsters. Asians."

"Gabe!" Polly said. "Manners?"

"We have no Asians here," Gabe said.

"Well, they're more civilized than you are," Polly said. "More intelligent, too."

"Still," Lee said. "If dogs are man's best friend, then eating your best friend, well, there's probably something to commend it, right?"

"I'd rather eat my worst enemy than my best friend," Willa said.

"That's because you have no best friend," Polly said.

"Because she ate her best friend," Clay said. "With fava beans, I'm sure."

Of course, referencing something as mundane as *Silence of the Lambs* cost Clay a point around the table, but he was willing to take the point for the chance to jab at Willa. I just remembered what Winston tasted like. He'd tasted good. And that memory lingered when Reagan brought out her lovely crown roast of lamb, with the little paper hats on the lamb ribs, and a savory stuffing in the heart of the crown, which Reagan said was porcini mushrooms and sausage. Reagan served it up carefully, and everybody dug in. It was delicious, and I did feel ravenous. Thinking about Winston had whetted my appetite, with some discomfort.

"So, Norm," Lee said, pointing with the lamb's rib he'd already cleaned of meat. For a skinny man, Lee sure could eat. "You do what, exactly?"

"Paint," Ansel said. "I just paint."

"He's rich," I said. "Old money, Lee. He doesn't have to work."

"Ah," Lee said. "How old?"

"Not terribly old," Ansel said. "Three generations."

"New Old Money," Lee said, with a laugh. It was funny to me, because Lee came from a middle class background, though he managed a serviceable jaded aristocrat impersonation.

"Wealth is the death of innovation," Clay said. "The artist is at his most dangerous when he's starving. Show me a fat artist, and I'll show you a failure."

"Show me a skinny chef, and I'll show you a bad cook," Polly said.

"Hunger does clarify things," Ansel said, glancing at me. "Portion control is key."

That earned him a chuckle around the table, and knowing nods from Reagan and Polly, a grumbling assent from Willa. I, however, went for seconds on the crown roast.

"This is delicious, Reagan. Really great," I said.

"I have to say I'm amazed at your transformation," Reagan said. "What happened to your firecracker hair, Sam?"

"I got rid of it," I said. "Red dye has to be kept up constantly."

"Big molecules," Polly said. "Positively huge, they are. Big molecules never last."

"And what's with the eyes?" Gabe asked, pointing his index and middle fingers at his own eyes, before pivoting his wrist and pointing his digits at me. I was waiting for somebody to bring them up, wondered how I should play it. Innocent victim (the truth, in other words), or else some affectation wrought by way of contact lenses? The perversity of the latter might play well with the others, unless they went after me on the grounds of the Marilyn Manson Clause—that anything he did was intrinsically lame. But to claim to be an accident victim gave me no agency, none of Clay's Will to Power.

"I thought it would look cool," I said.

"It's creepy," Willa said. "I don't know which eye to stare at."

"I'm not walleyed, for God's sake," I said.

"It's like there's the Sam we know," Willa said, pointing to my old eye. "And then there's the other one, the one we don't know."

"The Anti-Samantha," Lee intoned ominously. "The meat eater and provocative film maker, wannabe lycanthrope, existential exhibitionist, the toast of YouTube."

"Amazing, isn't it?" Willa said. "Such a simple little video, but people are eating it up. Just shows you what the sheeple are willing to stomach."

"Speaking of stomachs," Clay said. "Yours is ripped, Sam. In the video, I could see."

Ansel set down his wineglass. "I have to say I've never seen anybody do that, Sam. Where would an idea like that come from?"

"You know," I said. "Around."

"Saw you in the news," he said, quietly. "You shouldn't be eating out. Look, if you need a place to crash, you can drop by my place. You're going to need to on the 24th."

"Thanks," I said. "You don't think Polly will mind?"

"Meh," he said, winking at her. "We're not married."

After the meal, Reagan had us take seats in her living room, all of us in a loose circle, surrounded by candlelight. She put on The Kinks "Arthur," not too loud, but enough for some background noise.

I was grateful to be as far from the silverware as I could be. Even the smell of it was hurtful, seemed to sting my nose.

"Alright," Reagan said. "Is everybody ready? The game we're playing is most commonly known as Mafia, but as I said, in honor of dear Samantha, I thought we'd play it as Werewolf tonight. I'm the Narrator. Everyone open your envelopes, but take a care not to show anyone, and certainly not to tell anyone what you have. One or two of you have Jokers. You are the Werewolves. One of you has the Ace of Spades. You are the Seer. The rest of you are Villagers. Seer, you have the power of Second Sight."

I glanced at my card. The Ace of Spades. I was the Seer. I was really hoping for a Joker. Then again, everybody probably thought I was one of the Werewolves, which, of course, I was, but not in the context of the game.

"As Seer, it means you can detect lycanthropy," Reagan said. "Werewolves, your goal is to slaughter the Villagers. Villagers, your goal is to defeat the Werewolves and survive. Werewolves, you win if your numbers are equal to the Villagers. Villagers, you win if you manage to kill both of the Werewolves. Everyone understand?"

Everybody nodded, and the game began.

"It is night," Reagan said. "Close your eyes, everyone. Werewolves, open your eyes."

As Seer, I was dying to peek, wanted to see who was the Werewolf, but I decided to play fair. It was unnerving sitting in the candlelit room with my eyes closed, just breathing.

"Werewolves," Reagan said. "Pick someone to kill."

There was a few moments of silence, then Reagan said. "Werewolves, close your eyes."

My hands were sweating. Who would die first? Would it be me?

"Seer, open your eyes." Reagan said. "Use the Second Sight, pick someone to ask about."

I opened my eyes, and looked at Reagan, who gestured that I should point at one of the other players. I looked at the others, each in turn. On a whim, I pointed at Ansel. Reagan smiled, gave me a thumbs up. Werewolf. Of course.

"Seer, close your eyes," Reagan said. And I closed my eyes. Then Reagan spoke again. "Everybody open your eyes. It's now daytime. And, I'm sorry, Gretta, but you've been slain by Werewolves. Reveal your card."

Gretta sighed, put her black Jack of Clubs on the floor.

"No more words from you, Gretta. Dead men or women tell no tales. Now, it's time for the Villagers to take revenge," Reagan said. "Who is responsible for this gruesome murder?"

I knew that it was Ansel, but if I jumped out and said that, I'd be next. Who was his partner?

"Samantha, you did it!" Willa said. "You know you did."

"I did not!" I said.

"It would be too easy," Lee said. "Too obvious a choice."

"We have to lynch somebody," Willa said.

I so wanted to out Ansel, but doing so would doom me. I looked at the others, and everybody was looking at everybody else.

"Usually the one who's leveling the blame is the Werewolf," Clay said. "I vote for Willa."

"Me? What the hell are you talking about? I'm not a Werewolf!" she said.

"That sounds like Werewolf talk to me," Polly said, laughing.

Lee scratched his nose, looked from person to person. "What about you, New Guy?"

"Me?" Ansel said. "Maybe it's you. Maybe I'm the Seer."

"Are you?" Lee asked. "The Seer?"

I almost piped up that I was the Seer, but that was probably what Ansel wanted, and I kept mum. Wow, my hands were sweating.

"Maybe," Ansel said.

"Seems kind of risky to put that out in the air," Gretta said. "I mean, won't the Werewolves pounce on you next chance they get?"

"All the more reason to go after me," Ansel said. "Or Lee."

"We have to pick somebody," I said. "Daylight's wasting."

"Willa," Clay said.

"Willa," Polly said.

"Wait!" Willa said. "Samantha!"

"Willa," Ansel said.

"Lee," Gabe said, which made Lee jolt.

"Me? The hell you say," Lee said.

"Samantha," Don said.

"Ansel," I said.

It fell to Lee. I couldn't believe I was already on the chopping block.

"Willa," Lee said.

"You idiots!" Willa said.

"The mob has spoken, and you, Willa, are lynched by the angry Villagers, out for revenge for the loss of Gretta," Reagan said. "Show your card, but do not speak, for dead men...or women...tell no tales."

Willa looked hate on us all, put down her card on the floor. Queen of Spades.

"Fuck," Lee said. "Sorry, Willa."

"Idiots," Willa said, before Reagan hushed her up.

"It is night again," Reagan said. "Everybody close your eyes. The Villagers go to sleep, and the Werewolves stalk the night again, thirsting for blood. Werewolves, open your eyes, select your next victim."

I wondered which one was the other Werewolf. Who could it be? Could it have been Lee? Could he have been faking his remorse? Of course. Lee was a consummate actor, an inveterate liar.

A decision was quickly reached, for Reagan spoke up. "Werewolves, close your eyes. Seer, you may open your eyes, use the Sight. Who do you wish to know about?"

I pointed at Lee. Reagan turned her thumb downward. Villager. Lee was human. Good to know. But who was Ansel's confederate? That was the key. But it all depended on lasting long enough.

"Close your eyes, Seer," Reagan said. "And now, everybody open your eyes. It's daytime again, and, I'm afraid to say that another Villager has been slaughtered by the monstrous Werewolves. Christina, you've been clawed and torn to bits by the beasts. Show your card."

Christina revealed a Queen of Clubs, set it on the floor. Everybody hissed. Ansel looked horrified. Not a bad actor, himself. All he knew was that she'd accused him. Lee was safe, so it wasn't him.

"Again, the mob rises up, enraged at the loss of another of their Villagers," Reagan said. "The time for vengeance is at hand. Who will pay for this brutal murder?"

"Some Seer," Lee said to Ansel.

"I only said maybe I was," Ansel said. "Not for sure. Maybe they know who's the Seer already."

"How?" Lee asked.

"Wouldn't you like to know?" Gabe said. "The Seer's going to lay as low as the Werewolves."

"The Seer throws off the game," Don said. "What use is the Seer if they're too afraid to speak up?"

"I have no idea who's who," Polly said. "I don't see how I can nominate anybody, because accusing somebody is very suspicious."

"You need to participate in more witch trials," Lee said. "Ansel's my pick."

"Pick on the new guy," Ansel said. "You're my pick."

Gabe narrowed his eyes, stroked his beard. "Lee, it's so you."

"I agree with Gabe," Polly said. "Sorry, Lee."

"Christ," Lee said. "A little help, anybody?"

"Ansel," I said, not knowing who else to pick.

"What if we end up with a tie?" Don asked. Reagan sighed.

"That's a problem," she said. "There can't be any ties, not with odd numbers."

"Ansel," Clay said.

"Lee," Don said.

"Fuckers," Lee said.

"The mob has spoken, and Lee, you meet a grisly end in the streets of the Village, torn to shreds by your own Villagers," Reagan said. "Show your card."

Lee set down the King of Clubs, and everybody cursed, looked at each other with greater suspicion.

"Night falls again," Reagan said. "Everybody close your eyes, everybody sleeps."

She paused, then spoke again. "Except, of course, for the Werewolves. Werewolves, open your eyes, choose your next victim."

Gretta, Willa, Christina, Lee. Four down. Ansel was a Werewolf. Who was his confederate? My choices were Polly, Don, Gabe, and Clay.

"Werewolves, close your eyes," Reagan said. "Seer, open your eyes, use your Sight."

I pointed to Don. Reagan gave me a thumbs down. Human.

"Seer, close your eyes," Reagan said. "Daylight has returned, and, unfortunately, the Werewolves have claimed another victim. Don, I'm sorry, but you were hunted down in the night and slain. Reveal your card."

Don held up the Jack of Spades, set it down. The Werewolves were basically one person away from winning, if my math was right. The fur flew, the accusations.

"Christ," Gabe said.

"Ansel," I said. "It's Ansel! God, won't you guys listen to me?"

"Sam, you know it's you," Ansel said. "I mean, look at your forearms, for god's sake."

I blushed that he'd mention my forearms, which I'd taken care to conceal, to shave and cover. Everybody laughed.

"It's not Sam," Polly said. "Can't be, right?"

"No," I said. "It's Ansel. Lynch Ansel!"

Gabe stroked his beard. "Ansel, eh? Can you be the Seer, Sam?"

"Lynch Ansel," I said. "You have to."

"Why?" Ansel said. "For each pointing finger, there's four pointing back at you."

"Not if I point at you like this," Clay said, holding out four fingers at Ansel. "I vote Ansel."

"Ansel," I said. He was the easy target.

"Ansel," Polly said.

"Sam," Ansel said.

Christ, my fate was in Gabe's hands. "Takes one to know one. Ansel."

"Damn," Ansel said.

Reagan spoke up. "The mob rises up and chases you down, Ansel, furious at the loss of another Villager. Ansel, you fall to the wrath of the Villagers. Show your card."

Ansel laid down a joker on the floor, and the rest of the players heaved a sigh of relief at rough justice done, a Werewolf slain. I was glad to have beaten him at something. He gave me a wolfish smile and bowed his head, content to be one of the dead. Ansel. Don. Lee. Christina. Willa. Gretta.

The survivors were Polly, Gabe, Clay, and me. The remaining Werewolf would have to kill two more to win, assuming the Villagers couldn't luck out and lynch them. Then again, with one Villager aced by the Werewolf tonight, it would bring it down to three survivors, which meant that the lynching was vital, like the last chance for the Villagers, because if the lynching got another Villager, then the Werewolf would win. The trouble for me was surviving the next night. Stupid Gabe, suggesting that I was the Seer.

"Night descends on the Village once more," Reagan said. "Everybody shut their eyes."

Which one was it? Gabe, Clay, or Polly? It depended on how they'd voted. They'd all voted my way. That could only mean that one of the Werewolves sacrificed Ansel! The remaining Werewolf had voted against Ansel to save themselves, because to do otherwise would have revealed that they were voting with Ansel.

I tried to remember how everybody had voted. It was hard to keep track of the votes. Instead, I sniffed the air. The air would tell me, the scent. It was cheating, but I did it, anyway. I sniffed the air, with my eyes shut, drank in the scent of humanity seated around me. Which one was the Werewolf?

"Werewolves roam the night again," Reagan said. "Werewolf, open your eyes, choose a victim."

The scent of everybody was intoxicating, the smell of candlewax and burning flame, of cologne, perfume, sweat, pheromones, deodorant. I could smell all of it, swimming in my head. There was tension in the room, resentment, lust, yearning, worry, excitement. Yes, excitement. That was it. I stayed on that scent.

"Werewolf, close your eyes," Reagan said. "Seer, open your eyes, use your Sight."

I didn't need my imaginary Sight. I could tell who it was. I knew who it was. I pointed at Polly. Reagan gave me a thumb's up. Werewolf. Of course. She'd sacrificed Ansel for the game, and he'd not batted an eyelash to betray her. They were a wolfpack of two, already. A mated pair. I should have guessed it would have been here. Reagan had picked out the cards. Was she trying to make some Reaganesque point by pairing them? Or was it just that I was a red herring?

"Seer, close your eyes," Reagan said.

Was I dead? Had Polly killed me? Had she guessed? She had to know I was the Seer by now, didn't she? Or was she saving me for last?

"Daylight comes to the Village, and the Beast has struck again. Gabe, you lost your head, and now you're dead. Show your card."

Gabe grumbled, dropped the King of Spades to the ground, which had Clay and Polly gasping in shock, and me sighing with relief. Polly was also quite the little actress when she put her mind to it, but I guess being an adulterer did that to a person.

"The remaining Villagers, desperate to find the Werewolf in their midst, turn on each other. You must lynch another of your members," Reagan said.

Polly, Clay, and me.

"You're the Werewolf," I said to her. "You know you are, Polly. She's the Werewolf, Clay."

"Polly?" Clay said. "I don't know, Sam. She voted Ansel down last time."

"We all did," I said. "So somebody's lying."

"I'm the Seer," Polly said. "Don't let her kill me, Clay."

"You're the Seer?" Clay said.

"I'm the Seer," I said. "She's such a liar."

"You know who's the liar here, Sam," Polly said.

"Yeah, I sure do," I said. "Clay, she's the Werewolf."

"I'm the Seer," Polly said. "It's her, Clay. She sacrificed Ansel as cover."

"I'm the Seer," I said. I've always been the Seer. That's how I knew it was Ansel from the get-go. That's how I know it's Polly, Clay."

All of the dead were watching intently, now, and Polly was conjuring up crocodile tears and flushed cheeks, and I found Säam stirring inside me, each time Polly would call me the Werewolf. My face flushed as well, as I tried to keep her caged inside. Ansel watched me with great amusement.

It all hinged on Clay.

"What would Nietzsche do, Clay?" I asked, which prompted snickers from the dead, and a grimace from Clay. Nobody could look more intense and thoughtful when he wanted to me. Whether or not he was, it hardly mattered; he looked the part of the philosopher.

"Yeah, I'm the Werewolf, Clay," Polly said. "You should vote for me, if you think that's the right move."

"Yeah, see? She's the Werewolf," I said. "See?"

That somehow clinched it for Clay. "Sam."

"Polly," I said. "You blew it, Clay."

"Sam," Polly said, with a grin, crossing her legs toward Ansel.

Reagan nodded. "The Villagers set upon you, Samantha, and have their rough justice with you, leave you hanging in a tree. Show us your card."

I turned over my card. Ace of Spades. Clay cursed, punched the air. I just breathed out, leaned on Säam's cage in my heart. You're not coming out to play. No. Bad girl!

"And with Samantha's passing, only two remain, Clay and Polly. With no more reason to hide, Polly bares her fangs, reveals herself, and eats you up, Clay."

Polly turned over her card, revealing the other Joker, and Clay tossed away his card, while she mimed gobbling him down, hands out, fingers cocked like they were claws. Everybody laughed. Even Ansel.

"Werewolves win," Reagan said. "Polly wins."

"Werewolves always win," Lee said. "Unless Villagers are smart. Unfortunately, our village had Clay."

Clay got up, poured himself more wine, cursing under his breath. He hated losing, while Polly savored her victory, came over to me, put a hand on my arm.

"Nicely played, Sam," she said. "I knew it was you once you fixated on Ansel, but I wanted to make it last, let it come down to us."

"Yeah," I said. "You played it pretty well; I didn't think it was you until it was too late, I guess."

I felt like I'd gotten Sääm under control again, while Reagan was serving a seven-layered chocolate cake iced with pale green mint ganache frosting. Everybody took a slice, except for Willa, who was still pouting.

"People are idiots," she said. "That's the moral of the story. Sheeple waiting for the wolf to come to their door."

Ansel sat next to her, eating the cake. I noticed he'd taken a napkin to wrap the handle of the silver fork. Smooth. It just looked like he was holding the napkin.

"Interesting philosophy," he said. "Are you going to make a poem of it?"

"Of course," she said, glaring at him near-sightedly. It occurred to me, looking at her, that of all of the others, Willa's eyes most resembled Joyce's. It hadn't occurred to me until I saw her glaring at nearby Ansel. Maybe her whole face looked like James Joyce's, if he'd been a girl, or an anorexic tranny.

"There's not much that rhymes with 'werewolf,'" he said.

"Nothing rhymes with it," she snarled. "Nothing at all. It's a worthless word, useless to me. Just like you; you're useless, Ansel."

"Whoops," Ansel said, taking another careful taste of the cake. "This cake is fantastic, Reagan."

"Glad you like it, Ansel," Reagan said, having treated herself to a token sliver. It was good cake. She must have used dark chocolate. I mirrored Ansel's trick with the napkin, and nobody was the wiser, though I had to be careful not to touch the fork to my lips when I took bites. Clay just glared out the window, while Lee looked contemplatively at us all, and Gabe chatted at length on his cell phone, and Polly watched Ansel and me, having perched seductively on the arm of Ansel's chair, sampling the cake, herself.

Gretta, Christina, and Don were in the other room, Don pouring them some absinthe, carefully pouring water over the sugar cube, watching it turn the stuff from green to a pale, ghostly green-white that called to mind plastic glow-in-the-dark toys.

"You know, Willa," Ansel said. "If we are what we eat, then you are nothing. You've barely eaten anything."

"I've eaten," she said.

"New Guy: she's eaten," Lee said.

Ansel finished his cake, set it on Reagan's coffee table, walked over to Lee, sat next to him, didn't say anything. Lee followed him with his eyes as he went, while Polly looked on, sat down in the seat Ansel had left.

"You call me New Guy like it's a bad thing," Ansel said. "Why is that?"

"This remains our group," Lee said. "You're just here because of Polly."

For all of his rhetorical bluster, Lee was easily intimidated, particularly by other guys. Ansel seemed to sense it, and I was sure he could as I watched them. Just watching him stalk around, I could see it in a way I hadn't seen before. He was sniffing out weakness. It was plain as day to me, and I set down my plate, watched him go. The others didn't even realize it.

"And?" he asked Lee.

"You don't get to be more than New Guy until we induct you," Lee said. "How's that for a lynching by the Villagers, Baron von Wolfenstein?"

"Now, Lee," Reagan said. "This is my party. I'm the hostess. Ansel's more than welcome."

"Sure, here," he said. "But I'm tired of him turning up at our things. Who thinks he should join our group? Show of hands?"

I wanted to laugh at Lee's childish bullying, how he just came out with it. It was like a sheep taking a nip at the wolf circling it. Prey had teeth, too, I guess. Polly looked uncomfortable, displeased with Lee, raised her hand. Reagan raised hers. I didn't raise mine. Ansel glanced at me, nodded, smiling.

"Anybody else?" Lee said. "All opposed?"

His own hand went up, Gabe's, Clay's, Willa's. I didn't raise mine. Sitting on the fence, as ever.

"Four to two," Lee said. "Sam?"

I shook my head. Part of me was glad that Lee kind of called out Ansel a little, and glad that it would make Polly squirm, like forced her to choose who her friends were, and weren't. But part of me was still really into Ansel. Polly looked at me like I'd betrayed her, or something. I shrugged, and I'm sure she chalked that up to me being envious of her and Ansel, and maybe she was right. She turned to Lee, nostrils flaring.

"This is pretty dickish, Lee."

Lee just smiled, his face set, staring at Ansel, who looked terribly amused at Lee's anger.

"You're not welcome, New Guy." Lee said. "The Villagers have spoken. Prepare to be lynched."

Reagan walked over, stood in front of Lee.

"You're not welcome here, Lee," she said. "I can't believe you'd be so rude. I'm going to have to ask you to leave."

She turned to Ansel. "Please, please accept my apologies, Ansel. Lee's what we call an angry drunk around here."

"I'm not drunk," Lee said. "If only I *was* drunk."

"And a sore loser," Polly said. "That's really the heart of it. You should be mad at me for winning, Lee. Not at Ansel because he beat you."

"Alright, I'm going," Lee said. "Consider yourself socially lynched, New Guy."

Ansel didn't have to say anything, just smiled to himself. Lee looked like the asshole. If Lee had known what he'd faced down, he'd have shit himself. I couldn't even imagine Lee managing that much bravado if he'd known what was behind Ansel's face, what was curled up in his heart. Reagan showed him to the door, and Lee went out without another look. The mood was then terribly awkward, weird, with everybody in the room who voted against Ansel kind of looking on nervously, as their spokesman left them behind.

"How old are you guys?" Polly asked, her face pruning cutely in anger. "I mean, for real? What kind of schoolyard bullshit was that?"

Ansel leaned back in his chair, without a word, steepled his fingers, looked like a Mafia don. Was this some kind of plan of his, some bizarre ploy? Break up our group? Divide and conquer?

"Sorry about Lee, Ansel," Polly said.

"No worries," Ansel said.

I knew then that our group would be split over this, with Lee's confederates in the majority, with the rest twisting in the wind. Willa and Gabe excused themselves shortly thereafter, while Clay lingered a little longer, before he left, too. Sääm had wanted there to be a fight, had been watching it through my eyes, heart quickening. She'd wanted Ansel to rip Lee apart, wanted to join in.

"Sorry if I messed up your dinner party, Reagan," Ansel said.

"It's not you, believe me," Reagan said. "I don't know what's gotten into Lee lately. He seems terribly threatened by you. They all do."

I could see our group splitting along party lines, like the anti-Ansel group, and the pro-Ansel group. It was so high school, so foolish. I mean, Ansel was a practicing artist, had actually sold some of his work. There was nothing the others could honestly object to, except that Lee probably felt that Ansel would usurp his de facto position as the leader of our group. That's what it was all about, the whole reason for the nonsense. Lee felt challenged, and we were all supposed to take his side in this. But with Ansel, he might have overplayed his hand. Then again, maybe he'd simply brand us as Ansel's groupies and be done with us. He could be childishly authoritarian if he wanted to be. It always bothered me how groups so often bent to the wishes of the least-diplomatic of the bunch. Like because Lee was rude, he would be able to bully the rest of us into going with his agenda, or else he'd sulk and pout and make it crappy for the rest of us.

Not that Ansel was entirely blameless in this; I mean, I knew what he really was, and who knows, maybe Lee could sense an offness about Ansel, something not quite right, and maybe that's what he reacted to. That's why I found myself in such an awkward position in the Ansel v. Lee issue. I could honestly see both sides in it.

At any rate, Reagan's party adjusted to the exodus of others, and it was a quieter affair after that, but was pleasant, despite the discomfort caused. Reagan really was a great hostess, and was able to get people talking again in no time. And Ansel was as charming as ever, telling stories about trips he'd taken, and people he'd met.

Ansel (and Polly) gave me a ride home, in fact, in the back of his Maybach. I took some satisfaction in the ride, that I'd been in that car before Polly had.

"Some party," Ansel said. "That Reagan's something else."

"She's gay, you know," Polly said. "She's very quiet about it, but she is. Gretta's, you know, her friend."

"Ah," Ansel said, smiling to himself. I thought Polly's declaration amusing, myself. She was already defending her stake in her lover, although I couldn't imagine Ansel going for someone like Reagan. I mean, they had class and grace in common, and, of course, money, but I could never see them being anything more than friends. Reagan's family money went way, way back. I didn't even know how far, but she was our blueblood-in-residence. I couldn't imagine a wannabe like Lee alienating her over the Ansel thing, and yet, he had.

"I can't believe you two," I said. "Werewolves, right under my nose."

Polly laughed, her lilt filling the car. "That game was fun. I liked being a werewolf. Your face was so funny, Sam, the whole time. You had this gaping, guileless expression."

She mimed me, made her big eyes go bigger, her mouth agape.

"I did not look like that," I said.

"You so did," Polly said. "Didn't she, Ansel?"

Ansel nodded. He glanced at me in the rearview mirror. I stuck my tongue out at him, and he just smiled with those perfect, white teeth.

"God, that was so much fun," she said. "Despite Lee's dickery."

"Yeah," I said. "You know it'll be cliquesville from now on."

"So what?" Polly said. "We could form our own group—you, me, Ansel, Reagan. Even Don and Gretta, if they were able to contribute. Your friend, Martin. That would leave Lee with Clay, Gabe, and Willa. Hah. What a lackluster group that would be. Even if Sheldon turned up, it would still not be enough."

The prospect of breaking up our group had never really appeared on the radar, before. We were the self-proclaimed cultural elite of Chicago, artists and intellectuals without peer. That's how our group saw itself; I'm not saying that's how we really were. I mean, aside from Lee, I don't think anybody else had ever gotten published. I don't think anybody had ever sold any of their work. Clay's little gallery was where we showed our stuff, but I don't think he'd ever made a sale. Now, the others would scoff at that, like making a sale didn't mean anything, but any of them would've jumped at the opportunity to do so. We all looked down on the commercial act, the business side of art and letters, but in truth, it kind of mattered.

"You should start your own gallery, Ansel," Polly said. "You could open up a space on the ground floor in your building. The location's great, and you'd incur no extra expense. Just start up your own gallery. Oh, man, would that be priceless. Reagan's got so much stuff on her walls, she'd probably love having a place to show it. And I could do poetry readings there, and Sam could do what she does. There'd be space for it."

"Performance art," I said. "Hello?"

"Right," Polly said. "Like Blue Man Group."

"Oh, please," I said. "That hurts, Pol."

"It's not a bad idea," Ansel said. "As you said, Polly, I've got the space for it. I guess I've just never thought about it like that."

"And Sam and I are good at the online stuff," Polly said. "We could come up with a website for it, and it would be grand. Clay's space is so tiny, so, I don't know, pedestrian. Maybe we've outgrown BacchUS."

I could just imagine how that would go over. Clay would have a fit. Sure, his gallery was tiny and without consequence, but if we were to defect to Ansel's hypothetical gallery, it would be war between us.

"Let me think about it," Ansel said. "Where do you live, Sam?"

"Logan Square," I said, sheepishly.

# 9. MONDAY MORNING: 5 NOVEMBER

I woke up at 1:00 a.m. and couldn't go back to sleep. I tossed and turned, rolled around in bed. My stomach was growling, and then I realized it was me who was growling. My mind was racing, my eyelids fluttering. The prospect of Ansel opening a gallery was dazzling, energizing, and also frightening—being that much more dependent on him wasn't exactly what I was looking for in my life.

Jumping out of bed, I went to the fridge and dug out a packet of bacon I'd bought at the store over the weekend, like because I kept craving meat. It was ridiculous, but nobody ever heard of a vegetarian werewolf, right? It didn't happen. I tore open the bacon and began frying it in a pan, wiping drool with the back of my hand, pacing around like an animal in a zoo, waiting to be fed. Didn't sumos eat meals at midnight? I could imagine me eating like that, pigging out in the early morning hours. Back and forth I paced while the links sizzled in the pan, filling my apartment with the delectable scent.

Sääm wanted to eat it raw. I know she did, but I wouldn't let her. I was the boss. She was the infection, I was the host. She was an uninvited guest, had to abide by my rules. To distract myself, I went to check out the helmet stuntcam Martin had loaned me. Fully charged. Martin really was an artist, but he would never join our group, and, in truth, I doubt they'd have him. He was a photographer and videographer, and we worked together on lots of projects, me performing, him filming.

It seemed retarded, this idea of me strapping a helmet on my head and letting Sääm out of her cage, but the piece was in my head, the germ of an idea, and I had to do it.

The bacon was done, and I just sat there in my kitchen, eating it, piece by delicious piece. I devoured a pound of bacon like it wasn't even there. It was heavenly, the fat between my teeth, the tear of the meat, the crackle of it between my teeth, the savory grease on my chin and fingers. Strip after succulent strip, until I had grease running down my chin. I wiped off my face and belched with satisfaction. With a full stomach, I tried to go back to bed, but the meat woke Sääm up in earnest; maybe she'd been stirring in me all along, and I tossed and turned until 2:00.

"Enough," I said.

"Not enough," Sääm said, kicking off the covers.

I went to the closet, pulled on some black running tights, put on a grey hoodie, put on the stuntcam helmet, put the hood over my head.

"Ready, steady, go!" Sääm said, laughing on the inside. She was mocking me. I turned on the nightvision on the camera, something Martin was particularly proud of, and began jogging. I wasn't sure how it would come out, whether I'd be able to do justice to what I had in mind, but that was part of the torment and the thrill of art—you didn't know what would succeed or fail.

I just ran, while Sääm urged me onward. She loved the running. The running, the killing, the eating, the fucking. That was her wolfen world. I never jogged before, never had the urge to do something like that, but Sääm was all over it, and I hoped that by running, maybe I'd keep her at bay.

Running in the dark, particularly in Chicago, is not something one wants to really do, because the sidewalks are tricky, some smooth, some cracked and broken, ready to snag an ankle, a foot, a knee, a leg. I ran a couple of hundred yards and puked up the bacon. It all came right back up, but Sääm didn't mind, just got me running again, until my lungs were on fire, and I was gasping, my chest heaving. In the dark, I found I could see better, Sääm was helping me see, and I found that I could keep a steady pace, despite the dark, savoring the silence of the city, except for the warm noise of the bars, which were still open. I'd shoot past them in a blur, past the patrons.

The Park. That's where I was headed. It was closed after 11:00, but Sääm didn't care about that. Hours were for norms. Laws were for norms. Faster and faster I ran, until Sääm got out of her cage and I felt my running tights stretch against my bulging calves and felt my shoes split around my feet, had to stop, snarling, screaming, stretching, rending. Changing.

I was in a little park next to a Buddhist temple, where a bronze boy and girl played opposite a bowl, a fountain. Nearby, chrome horses played. I hunched in the shadows, caught my breath, felt myself lengthen, strengthen.

Sääm threw the stuntcam from her head, on the mangled remains of the hoodie, mocking me. She thought it was hilarious, a gag, like Michael Landon wearing his letterman jacket in "I Was a Teenaged Werewolf." The Runner from Hell. Then she showed me what running *really* was, dropped on all fours, arms and legs like pistons. We took off for the Park, for the Lake, impossibly fast, claws clicking a beat on the sidewalk, on the cobblestones, on the brick, on the asphalt, the wind in our faces, mouth open, drinking air, tasting scents.

We shot across Clark street and vaulted into the Park, paused in the shadows by some public sculptures. Cars shot by, unseeing. She ran over a bridge, past the Zoo, past a duck pond, in a dark ribbon of park. There was exhilarating randomness in her movement, a sense of drifting purposelessness that was refreshing to me. Säämäänthää was just taking the measure of her world.

We sniffed the air, listened to the chilly night breeze. Then I realized there was purpose in her ramblings: she was hunting. Turning back the way we'd come, she ran hard down the jogging paths, through the shadow of elms and oaks and maples fast losing their leaves to winter, and back into the noisy glow of the city, itself, to the sound of people laughing and staggering, hooting.

Who else was out this late? Couples on dates, and drunks. Crazies, of course, but Sääm didn't seem interested in them. I tried to stop her, but she started running again, having caught a scent she liked. It was not purely instinctual; there was volition in her actions, and malice. She was not simply a wolf hunting; she was a werewolf, and in her monstrosity there was, an inversion of the natural order, a perversion of it. Predatory animals hunted the weak and infirm—that was their prey. In so doing, they ultimately served to strengthen the herds they preyed upon, for they culled the weak from the ranks of the prey species.

But Man invariably hunted the biggest, healthiest, and strongest of prey; this was Man's error. What was left behind, what was acceptable to Man was the weakest, the most infirm, the most tractable, the most docile of animality, relative to the wildness of Nature.

From her own vantage point, Sääm could see both sides of the coin—she could see herself as a predator who could choose her prey to suit her own needs, versus being dependent on the whims of Nature. She was in a unique position, and she savored it. Sääm didn't have to settle for the old, the infirm, or the weak. She could prey upon the strong and the powerful, and she would prevail. As if to confirm this thought in my head, she let out a great howl, a thing that stopped the merrymaking of the pedestrians who were walking to their cars—suburbanites who drove into the city to party, and then drove drunkenly back home. It happened all the time.

"What the fuck was that?" one of them slurred. A young man in a backwards baseball cap.

"Coyote," another young man said. Their girlfriends or hookups looked around uneasily, and Sääm let out another howl, closer this time. She was enjoying this, was drooling in the shadows. This was much better than bacon.

Some distance away, other wolves howled in answer. Coming from the Zoo.

"Fuck," one of the young men said, fishing out his keys. "Let's get the fuck out of here."

He keyed into his big, shiny SUV, and the others clamored into his car. Sääm could have had any of them, all of them. But she didn't want them, just wanted to scare them. Volition, not instinct. She ran up to the SUV as they were trying to pull out of their parallel parking space, snarled at the passengers, who saw her and started shrieking. Their faces, under thin automotive glass, mirrors of each other, terrified.

Sääm raised an arm and clawed the SUV as it made its way out of the space, leaving deep grooves on its glossy, painted surface. Then, for fun, she ran down the street after the fleeing vehicle, which was drunkenly careening as it made its way sloppily up the street. She could see the white flash of their faces as the passengers in back turned and looked, as if they could not believe their own eyes.

Sääm poured on the speed, and the SUV went faster still, and Sääm gave chase to it, catching up to it, running right up to it. Then the SUV whipped left, a sharp turn, and rolled, only to be sideswiped by a van that had tried to burn through a traffic light. The crunch of the cars, the shatter of glass, was symphonic to Sääm, who shot to her right and over the parked cars, back into the nurturing darkness of the park.

The SUV slid and tumbled messily into some more parked cars, setting off their alarms, and the explosion of airbags. She waited in the shadows as the police, fire trucks, and ambulances came onto the scene, watched with glee in the darkness punctuated by staccato stabs of light from the flashers, watched stretchers get taken from the ambulances, marveled at the glinty brightness of the broken bits of windshield glass, catching the glow of the streetlights.

Then she melted back into the shadows, turned her back on the spectacle, began running about. There were gapers watching the scene of the wreck, and I realized that while she had enjoyed the wreck, it wasn't her primary goal for the evening; rather, it was a diversion. She'd wanted attention drawn to the flashing lights and the braying of sirens, the flash of roadside flares. She'd wanted that. Sniffing the air, she caught another scent, a man walking to another car, talking on his cell phone.

"Yeah," he said. "It's fucked up. Some big wreck on LaSalle. Roll-over, yeah. There's cops everywhere. I'm going to go north, I think, try to get around it."

Just like that, she snaked an arm out and grabbed the guy, hurled him into the Park. He dropped his phone, went tumbling. Sääm was on him in a moment, looming over him.

"No," I said.

"Run," she said to the man, with a toothy grin. "Run like your life depended on it."

The man, late 20s, hair shorn close, reeked of cologne. His eyes were as big as goose eggs as he saw Sääm. He choked out a scream of sorts, but was on his elbows, looking up at her, uncomprehending. Sääm reached down and grabbed his windbreaker, pulled him up, brought him in close.

"I'm hungry," she snarled. "Run for your life."

The guy just started bawling, hysterically pleading for his life. Disgusted, she shoved him aside, crouched over him, peed on him, and ran off into the shadows. He wasn't worth killing. Volition versus instinct.

"Christ," I said. I couldn't believe she'd done that, but Sääm was angrier than ever. She wanted prey, but the sheeple weren't out in force tonight. It was a chilly night. Looking skyward, Sääm howled, furious, then ran toward Gold Coast, probably the best neighborhood in the city. She ran down the broad, tree-lined sidewalks, past stone town-homes and brick-walled mansions, raging, furious.

What a coward that man had been, without even the grace to die with dignity, without the will to even try to run for his life. She'd wanted sport, she'd wanted prey. He was carrion. In this area, the mansions and townhomes formed a kind of wall. The buildings were set close, and Sääm felt sort of hemmed in, didn't like the looming presence of the buildings.

So she ran faster, headed downtown, keeping to the shadows, following the noise. Down here, nearing the Viagra Triangle once more, where the party never stopped, and there were people out and about, looking to get laid. Shiny cars aplenty, pretty, long-legged women with long, blonde hair, an army of Rapunzels, and their squires and silver-haired swains. People of consequence. Sääm watched them come and go from restaurants and nightclubs, watched doormen and valets and cabbies tend to them. She nosed the air, took the scent. Slaughter and mayhem were simple; hunting was hard. And still, nobody could see her. She was hiding in some hedges, studying, searching. There was a man in a tuxedo, walking with a cane, but not because he needed it. His walk was a jaunty thing, the man slim, the cane striking out a steady clack-clack beat as he made his way to wherever he was going.

"No," I said.

Sääm bounded across the street, stalked the man. He smelled good, something agreeably musky, an expensive cologne. He was old, but fastidious, trim and fit. Not so old as to be almost dead, but old enough to have appreciated living at all. Snarling, Sääm stalked after the man, who was walking along Washington Square Park, whistling as he went. Sääm worked herself up into a lather and snarled at the man, who turned with a start, said something in a language she didn't understand, gasped, brandished his cane.

"You old bastard," she said, baring her fangs.

"*Wilkołak!*" the man said, with a cry.

Sääm slashed at him with her claws, ripping the man's cummerbund, sending fabric flying. Then the man smashed her with his cane, right across the head. The pain was immediate and intense, reminiscent of the burning of Reagan's flatware in my hands. Silver. The old fucker had a silver-headed cane. He bashed Sääm across the chops with it, and Sääm leaped backward, rubbing her bleeding mouth with her paw. The man was breathing heavily from the exertion, his pale eyes never leaving us. He said something else in his language.

"*Potwor! Wyraza zdziwienie zdenerwowanie irytacje!*" he yelled, taking another step with the cane.

Sääm hated him more than anybody, circling low, tasting her own blood on her lips, her right eye swollen shut. The silver hurt worse than the sting of a wasp, like a hot rivet had been driven into our face.

The old man held his ground, kept circling, like a dancer, holding the cane up. A knot of silver kept him safe from us. Sääm howled in rage and frustration, setting off car alarms all around us. She was livid and bristling, but feared to brave that damned man and his silver cane. The bloody knot that had been the handle was shaped like a fist, now limned in red.

"Old man," Sääm spat, over the din of the car alarms. Then she turned on her haunches and fled into the nurturing dark, leaving him behind in a couple of bounds of arm and leg, her appetite for slaughter dampened by the pain in our face. She ran and ran, from shadow to shadow, cautious now, furtive. Hunting was hard. Sometimes you caught prey, sometimes you didn't. The monster didn't win every time. I was relieved that the man had not died, although some of his blood was on Sääm's claws. I hoped he would not become infected, did not know whether it was only spread through the bite, or if scratches would suffice. I hoped not. I didn't want him to suffer what I was suffering.

I remembered the camera, the helmet, but couldn't remember where I'd lost it, where Sääm had tossed it away. Sääm howled again, loud and long, and we had a little tug of war between us, as I wanted to recover the cam there and then, hoped the thing survived, while she wanted to leave it behind. Back and forth we went.

I have to get the camera, I said.

"Leave it," Sääm snarled. "Fuck it."

It starts right in front of my goddamned apartment, I said.

"Stupid idea, stupid project. Your fucking fault," she roared. She was hurting, she didn't like being in pain. Sääm could dish it out, not take it. She liked hurting, not being hurt.

We have to get the camera, I thought.

"No," Sääm said. And I realized that she was afraid to go back. She'd never admit to it, but she was. Wounded and afraid. Yes. Sensing my thoughts, she snarled and raged and scratched up a bunch of cars with her claws, slashed tires, broke windshields, set off car alarms on our way back. A tantrum, an orgy of destruction.

By the time we got back to my building, she'd largely worn herself out. I mean, werewolves had endless energy, but even their rage had limits. I noticed that the car with the smashed hood was gone, as we made our way back to my building.

The transformation had been less painful this time, though it still hurt, and returning to my little old normal-looking self did nothing to diminish the pain I was feeling in my face, which was bruised and swollen. I looked at myself in the mirror, and it looked like I'd been boxing. My right eye was bruised and mostly swollen, and I had a knot on my cheek. My head was pounding.

I looked like ass. Even one of my big pairs of shades would only make me look like a woman trying to hide a grievous bruise behind a big-ass pair of shades. Too bad I didn't have long hair; I could have worn it brushed to the front, covering half my face. I even thought about wearing a wig. I could just imagine trotting into work that day, bruised and looking like hell. I desperately wanted to call in sick, but couldn't. As it was, I had to snag a few hours of sleep before going to Nonpareil. I was exhausted, defeated, deflated. I couldn't believe I'd lost the camera. Somebody would find that thing, they'd find my building, they'd find me. Fuck.

I wanted to call Ansel, to cry into the phone and tell him what happened. I wanted comfort and understanding, someone who could relate. Did Ansel hunt at all? He had to know how to. Or did he just drug himself up, lock himself away, instead? I imagined us locked in his special cage, fucking away our brutality and savagery, two diseased peas packed tight in a pathological pod.

The image aroused Sääm a little, as it always did, but she was fairly chastened from the beating she'd received. I felt her squirm around in my heart, sniff at my soul, then curl up and lay her head on her paws, going fitfully to sleep. It wasn't over, she seemed to tell me. I hadn't won. There'd be other nights, other prey.

Ansel had done this to me. Why would I go to him for comfort at all? Fuck him. That's what it was about. I got uneasy, wondered if that was simply Sääm's ideas.

"Stop fooling yourself," I said. "You are Sääm, dumbass."

I am Sääm. Sääm I am.

That's what it came down to. I'd taken refuge in a false dichotomy, one of logic's simplest fallacies, created this Other in Sääm, as if she was other than me. I was Sääm, for the rest of my life. Maybe part of the trouble I ran into was denying that she was me, for even thinking ourselves apart. Maybe that's how Ansel did it. Ansel was the monster that he was.

Embracing my monstrosity, however, hardly seemed the high moral path. I wanted to blog about it, share my feelings with somebody. With Zooey, perhaps.

> I've become a monster. There's no other way around it. Whoever I used to be, she's dead. There's only this new self, grafted onto the old, irrevocably changing it.

I looked at the words, hovering patiently, felt retarded, decided to write some more, for lack of anything else to do that early in the morning.

> Grafting isn't the right word, sorry. It's like I'm an alloy, now. This other element was mixed into me, and we've become something else, together, and it's impossible to extract the original me from the new matrix. I don't know where I end and she begins. This is all the fault of Adonis, of course. He changed me forever. One careless night on my part, and that's that.

*Zipstrip: Yikes!*

Zipstrip was online! I was amazed the Zooey was on that early.

*Zipstrip: Gawd, you're not pregnant, are you?*
*Säämäänthää: Nah. Hahah! Hey, Z! I'm glad you're on. What are you doing up?*
*Z: I always wake up early. Glad you changed your alias.*
*S: ☺*
*Z: It becomes you.*
*S: If you only knew. I'm becoming her.*
*Z: What does that mean, anyway?*
*S: Terribly complicated. You wouldn't even believe me if I told you.*
*Z: Wow, that sounds awesomely enigmatic.*
*S: Where are you?*
*Z: Milwaukee.*
*S: I'm in Chicago.*
*Z: I know.*
*S: We should hang out.*
*Z: I know!*
*S: Why don't we?*
*Z: Let's! ☺*
*S: Okay.*

I went back to my blogging, left the dialogue box open, hanging there. Despite being broken, in pain, crestfallen, I was happy Zoë was up there in Milwaukee. Just a stone's throw away.

I'm just really messed up, basically. Adonis ruined me. Or maybe he saved me. That's the part I'm
wrestling with, where I'm confused. Like either the
ME before SHE came along wasn't worth saving, or,
I don't know. Christ, I'm so inarticulate tonight…
uhhh…this morning. I hurt. I literally hurt. And it's
my own fucking fault.

There's no way I can make things right, except if I
just throw myself off the Sears Tower or something.
That would make things right. A swandive off it, and
splat, and then everything's fine, unless I fell on somebody, I suppose. Then it would be bad.

*Z: Jeez, Säämäänthää. What happened?*
*S: Something bad. I got hurt. I screwed up.*
*Z: Did Adonis hurt you?*
*S: No. Self-inflicted.*
*Z: Cutting?*
*S: No. I'm not a cutter.*
*Z: I am.*
*S: Really?*
*Z: Yeah.*
*S: Why?*
*Z: Why not?*

It was as good an answer as any. I never got cutters, why they did it.
I'm sure Zooey would explain it all to me. Everything paled in comparison to what I'd become. The ice in my icepack shifted and popped
a little. I held it against my face by tucking my chin into my chest, so I
could type with both hands.

*S: Yeah. Why not? Fuck it, yeah!*
*Z: That's the spirit!* ☺
*S: I'm toast; I have to work today. I was up all night. I'm wiped.*
*Z: Poor Sääm. I'll catch a bus to Chicago.*
*S: For real?*
*Z: Totally! I'm very impulsive.*
*S: LOL. How would I recognize you? That Greyhound terminal is a den*
*of scum and villainy.*
*Z: I have lavender hair. Really pretty color. I'm the emo suicide girl, tall*

*and willow-thin, baby-faced, black-eyed. I'll wear a red and black*
*striped t-shirt. You'll be able to spot me a mile away.*
*S: RU serious? You'd just pop on down to Chicagoland?*
*Z: Hells yeah. Seriously. Milwaukee makes me tired. I'll come by this*
*weekend, like Friday. Would that work? You can meet me at the station,*
*we can just hang out somewhere, get coffee. You like coffee?*
*S: I like tea.*
*Z: That works. It'll be kewl.*

The prospect of actually meeting Zooey was exciting, despite how
rotten I felt. She seemed so alive and interesting, she always paid attention to my blog, asked good things of it, and of me.

*A friend is coming to see me this weekend. I'm excited about that. She's*
*great. I can't wait to see her!*
*Z:* ☺
*S:* ☺
*Z: Gotta get ready for work.* ☹
*S:* ☹ *What's work?*
*Z: Print shop. Suckage.* ☹
*S:* ☹
*Z:* 😐
*S:* ☺
*Z:* ☺
*S: Okay! See you soon. Give me details!*
*Z: Will do!*

I was happy to have heard from her. I admired her willingness to
just do something, well, crazy. That took guts. Me, I was feeling more
unsure, more tentative than ever. There was no prize for being tentative. I couldn't go around pretending that I was a norm, being simply
human, or being a half-assed monstrosity. I could be a good person, or
a good monster, or a middling person, or a middling monster. Seemed
like those were the moral choices available to me.

I made a fresh icepack, wrapped it in a fresh wash towel, put it on
my face, whimpered at the pain. Shame was the price of being half-
assed. I bet Ansel would've made a punchbowl out of that old man's
head. Or maybe he was in control enough of his shit to leave the dapper old gentleman alone. My head throbbed, my face ached. I started
crying, not so much from the pain (although it hurt plenty), but be-

cause I felt so trapped. I didn't know enough, and Ansel wouldn't tell me, and I didn't want to beg.

Middling monsters died at the point of pitchforks, burned with torches, or at the butt of silver-capped canes wielded by angry, geriatric Poles. Middling people were dime-a-dozen, emptied souls, shorn sheeple, human husks. A good monster didn't worry about what it was doing; it just did it. A true predator didn't worry about guilt, or being popular, or anything. It just cruised along, living for the kill, surviving. A good person, well, she'd put a bullet in her head or weigh her feet down and throw herself into the Chicago River, holding her breath until she went to the sludgy, filthy bottom, and had to open wide and breathe water until she died.

Fuck. I so wasn't ready to die. I was too young to die. And that image of me in a lab somewhere, behind thick slabs of bulletproof glass, getting blood drawn by faceless scientists in HazMat suits frightened me. I wasn't going to turn myself in. It wasn't fucking going to happen.

Somebody would find that camera, they'd find it, and they'd see what was on it, they'd watch the news, they'd be amazed, they'd sell the footage, they'd find me. They'd hunt me down with pitchforks and torches.

I wept in the dark for what was left of me.

# PART 3

"IT IS IN MOMENTS OF ILLNESS
THAT WE ARE COMPELLED
TO RECOGNIZE THAT WE LIVE NOT
ALONE BUT CHAINED TO A CREATURE
OF A DIFFERENT KINGDOM,
WHOLE WORLDS APART, WHO HAS
NO KNOWLEDGE OF US AND
BY WHOM IT IS IMPOSSIBLE TO
MAKE OURSELVES UNDERSTOOD:
OUR BODY."

– MARCEL PROUST

# 1. MONDAY: 5 NOVEMBER

I cruised into work at ten, wearing my biggest pair of shades, decided I'd keep them on all day. Lance wouldn't mind. Dean and Darryl were in today, looked me over when I clocked in, Dean slouching at his station, Darryl drinking a coffee.

"What happened to you, little tyke?" Darryl asked.

"Fight Club," I said.

"You're not s'posed to talk about that," Dean said, in a conspiratorial whisper. I'd put on a white Izod shirt beneath my Nonpareil uniform, had both collars up, which felt protective, like preppy body armor. I leaned into my station, turned away from the boys. There were a number of customers milling through the store. I'd see them rounding corners in their carts. Johnny Dubrovnik, a couple of hippie-dippy Baby Boomer women with batik dresses and overlong hair, a skinny kid with hair colored art-school blue. He had a silver nose ring pierced between his nostrils. I stared at that silver gewgaw with hate, could smell the galvanic tingle of it from where I stood.

Darryl perched himself outside my station. "Seriously, what happened? You want me to kick his ass? Her ass?"

He was fit and strong, a fine slab of man, and I genuinely liked him as a coworker and a friend. Sääm helpfully envisioned—no, it was me—well, maybe she helped. Whatever. She envisioned me taking Darryl in the back room and fucking him, biting him all over. What a magnificent monster he'd make. He'd slip into monstrosity like a hand into a fine leather glove. Not because Darryl was a bad person, but because he was so comfortable in who he was, so easy in his own skin—for him, skinchanging would be like donning a sport coat.

Dean, on the other hand, would make a middling monster. He'd blunder his way onto the El tracks and get electrocuted or hit by a train in an uncomprehending splatter. Not because Dean was a good person, but more like because he was just a goofy one, not prone to taking much of anything seriously. Lycanthropy was so beyond him. It was more of a commitment than he was prepared to make. Even alcoholism was too much to ask of Dean.

"Thanks, Darryl," I said. "Totally self-inflicted."

He laughed, his face parted into a terribly white grin. "Yeah, right. You get into one of those girlie boxing things or something?"

"No," I said. "Just stupid, is all. I clocked myself on a parking sign while rollerblading over the weekend."

"Gotta watch it, Roller Queen," Darryl said.

Good enough. Darryl appeared to buy it, left me alone. I did my Monstrosity Barometer on everybody who came in that day, wondered who would make good monsters, who would make bad ones, who would make good prey, and why. It didn't matter what the person looked like; it was all inside. Some just seemed to have it, others, not so much. Like there was this old lady who was meaner than spit, who would come in for her mosaic materials, her tiles, and she was just so mean. She'd probably embrace monstrosity, if it gave her new vitality, if only it would let her cut in line more forcefully.

Simone was probably the type to think she'd be a bitchin' monster, but totally wouldn't be able to hack it. Not because she was a good person, but because she was a bad person—and by bad, I don't even mean "evil" so much as not good at being a person. She'd end up going insane, and would, like, devolve into just an animal monster, would get herself caught or killed in no time flat, and if they were able to cure her, she'd not even remember who she was, would think she was still a wolf or something. I could totally see that.

Whereas Reagan, who came in to get some charcoals, would make a terrible monster. Because she was a good person, like genuinely good. Maybe pretentious and affected, but good in her heart. You could tell in the way she reacted to things, like straight from her heart. When she saw my face, she gaped, rushed over, her eyes big and full of real shock.

"My God, Samantha," she said. "What on earth happened?"

"Art project," I said. The lie came out nice and easy, since I'd had that warm-up with Darryl. "I was rollerblading, filming, using a stuntcam, and I wiped out."

"Wow," she said. "Can I snap a picture of it? With and without the glasses? I mean, it's marvelously terrible. When did it happen?"

"Last night," I said. I smiled at her. "What, are you going to paint me?"

"No," she said. "The photos speak for themselves. I was thinking we could do a series, like each day, as you healed, then put them in a ring, facing inward, something a person could stand in the midst of, and it could be spun, so it would appear to be animated, and you'd alternately heal and get re-injured."

"Nice," I said. "I like that idea, actually."

"Maybe a vintage camera," Reagan said. "A Pentax, or something."

"My friend Martin has stuff like that," I said. I was amazed at how readily she took inspiration from my injury. Why couldn't I do that? Maybe because I was too close to it. But the artist took inspiration from everything around them. There I was moping about my botched murder of the night before, and along came Reagan with a great conceptual art idea.

"What would you call it?" I asked her.

"'Personal Injury,'" she said. "Let's do it. I'll give you equal credit on it, since your face inspired it—it's part performance, in a way. Just slow-motion."

I laughed. "Alright. I'll call Martin, see what he can do."

"I'd rather shoot it myself, it's all the same to you," Reagan said.

"You'll want the pictures to be the same quality, right? Same lighting, all of that? Martin is a photographer," I said. "He's good at it, trust me."

Reagan smiled, pleased with me and with herself. "We need to capture it each day. Let's just do it, any which way."

"That rhymed," I said. "You're in the zone, Reagan."

She laughed, covering her teeth with a slender hand, peeping at me over her palm, her eyes uncommonly large and cornflower blue.

"I'm sorry you got hurt, Samantha," she said. "But we'll make art from your injury, and it'll be a good thing, you'll see."

I was impressed that she'd even thought of it, hadn't skipped a beat. But she'd gone to Mount Holyoke, was sharper than a fistful of tacks. She'd never be a monster; there was too much kindness in her. I wanted to hug her in gratitude, for helping me out of my funk. For being human, and creative, and special. For being my friend. I gladly rang up the charcoals and Bristol board she needed, carefully bagged it. She looked angelic with a frilly white scarf around her neck and her camel overcoat.

212 | D.T. NEAL

"Tristan's back in town," Reagan said, while I was finishing up her order. I deliberately took my time, so we could talk. Other customers glumly queued in line with Darryl and Dean, once they realized I was moving terribly slowly.

"I'm sure Polly's delighted," I said. We both exchanged awkward glances.

"I can't believe she's doing it," Reagan said. "With Ansel, I mean."

"Yes, I think we have those in the back, Miss," I said, louder than I needed to. "I'll show you where they're at."

I walked Reagan away from the register, away from Dean and Darryl, into the depths of Aisle 9, where we could have a little privacy.

"I don't know what she's got in mind, exactly," I said, tugging out some matting knives. "Has she told you anything?"

Reagan sighed, bit her lip. "She says she doesn't know if she can stay away from him; she's afraid she'll slip up. Tristan was gone for two weeks."

I shook my head. Only Polly would have a crisis of fidelity after two weeks. That was so her. Maybe with her busy entertaining Tristan, I could book some quality time with Ansel, myself, although what I had in mind was more question-and-fucking-answer, than just fucking. Although who knew what could happen.

"Poor Tristan," I said. "He has no idea."

"I feel like a bad person for even knowing," Reagan said. "Everybody knows. It's embarrassing. Can you imagine the next dinner party I throw, say when Tristan's in town, and everybody will be in there, and him not knowing he's a cuckold? It's horrible. I'm afraid to do it; and yet, if I don't, it's like I'm giving Polly sanction for it."

"It's not our job to cover up for Polly," I said. "She's a big girl. It's her mess."

If only all messes were so easy to clean up. I felt like my own personal mess was only spreading, getting worse. I caught a glimpse of something on the ground, behind Reagan, peeking out from under the shelving. Something shiny.

"Yes," Reagan said. "But we're her friends, too. I feel like we're all implicit in it, her secret."

A bit of plastic. I realized what it was. The earpiece of Sheldon's spectacles. Thankfully, wearing my shades, Reagan couldn't see that I was looking past her.

I thought about it, could only wonder what Reagan would say if she knew my secret. A mere infidelity was cake by comparison. The minute Reagan knew I'd killed Sheldon, that I'd eaten a fucking dog, that would be it for us, and I didn't want that. Nice people didn't eat people's pets. Nice people didn't slaughter their friends. Good people weren't werewolves. Werewolves weren't Good People.

"Everybody has secrets," I said. "Everybody deals with them their own way. This is on Polly. I mean, she's married to Tristan, not Ansel. It's as simple as that."

I'd have to pick up those glasses. It was weird, like how long ago that felt to me, how distant. A relic. Sheldon's glasses. We were standing where his last moments were. We were standing where he died.

Reagan nodded. "You poor thing. Your face looks ghastly. I know that's terrible to say, but it really does. I'll want to use film that'll pick up all of those colors."

Even now, gossiping about Polly's indiscretions, Reagan was sizing me up, studying me. I was impressed by it, by her. It was like I saw her in a new light, caught a glimpse of the artist in motion, instead of just looking at her paintings, her finished products.

"We can shoot it at my apartment," I said. "Or yours. Like something basic, Spartan, against a white wall. Like a mug shot."

"Yes," she said. "My walls are cream-colored, but they're covered in my paintings, unfortunately. I just don't have the wall space."

"We can use my place," I said. "We can have Martin check the lighting levels, set up marks, shoot it the same time every day, same distance, same camera, same film. It should look cool."

"Too fancy—and it's our project, not his," Reagan said, fishing out her PDA. "Let's just do this. When? What time?"

"We can do it during my lunchbreak," I said. "Say, noon at my place."

"Can you get there and back in time?" Reagan asked.

I shook my head. "I was hoping you'd drive me," I said. Reagan drove a Range Rover, forest green, with beige seats.

"Oh, of course," Reagan said. "I'll pick you up at 11:45 sharp, we can drive to your place, take the shots, and then I'll drop you off. It'll be great!"

It was exciting, our own little project. I hoped it would go well. Reagan said she'd shoot it with a Pentax camera first, and also maybe shoot with a digital camera as a precaution, in case there were problems with the film, and see which looked better.

"I don't want to lose any of it," she said, penciling me into her PDA.

"Great," I said. "It's a date!"

We laughed, and I realized I had to slip back to my station before I was missed. I didn't want Lance lecturing me on personal conversations while on the job, any of that crap. Even though he was playing "Team Fortress 2" behind closed doors every day he was in. Loser.

Lance would have made a great monster—so self-satisfied, so lazy, so smug. He'd be a great one, although not in the same way that Darryl would. Lance's slovenly monstrosity would be something else, entirely. He'd be the kind of monster to sit on a park bench, let the prey come to him, indolently picking his teeth from his last meal.

I walked Reagan out of Aisle 9, feeling like a conspirator, with a delightful secret mission, a project. It was great. I couldn't imagine pairing up on such a project with Polly. But then, Polly was a poet, and poets worked alone.

"I'm sorry," Reagan said, playing the role of the customer. "I think I shall have to come back another time, what-is-your-name? Samantha. Yes, another time."

"I'll let you know when we get them back in stock, Miss Whitehouse," I said.

"See that you do," Regan said, primly picking up her bag from my counter. I watched her leave, felt warm and sunny for the first time in days. It banished the gloom that fell with my failed "Finnish Line" project. Christ, what had I been thinking?

*It wasn't a failed project; you just gave up on it,* Sääm thought, petulance rolling off her tongue like drool. She'd been watching Reagan, sizing her up, and that frightened me. I couldn't stop thinking of Sääm as an alien presence within me, this other set of eyes behind my face, watching everything I did. Maybe I wasn't a good person, but I wasn't a bad one, either, was it? Sääm made no bones about her badness. She wasn't just bad; she was evil.

What was I supposed to do? Kill that man?

Well, duh. Christ, what do you think we're doing, here? You think this is just an inconvenience? Supernatural syphilis? It's a curse, as far as you're concerned. I'm not going anywhere—I'm only going to get stronger. And you're not strong enough and not good enough, to keep me locked up, Princess. If I wanted to, I could transform right here. Right now.

I felt a flush, a hint of the limbic tickle that heralded her arrival. Gasping, I clutched the counter, my breaths coming fast. Like I was coming.

"No," I said.

Just making a point. The only reason I've not cut loose is because it would make things harder for me, not because I'm wanting to make it easier for you, or your pathetic little life. You think I like staying indoors all day? I want to play.

No. You're the infection. You're not the real me.

I'm as real as you are, you phony. Your whole so-called life is carmalized pretense goofy-dusted with hypocrisy. That's the real you? Hah.

She was trying to upset me, trying to unhinge me. I had to talk to Ansel, had to know what it was like, what he went through, what he felt. He was on drugs. I had to score some of his drugs.

Oh, Ansel, save me, Sääm said, mewling, whining imitating me. Ansel knew just what he was doing when he bit you. You think that was an accident? Hah. Sucker. He wanted to make you, Puddin.

I brought a hand to my head, hated having her snarling between my ears, pushing outward against my ribcage, straining to get out. The other hand held the counter, steadied me. Everything felt tight. The air itself felt tight, the lights overhead. Confining.

I'm the host. You're the infection.

Boo hoo hoo. Maybe you need some new friends. Reagan? Polly? Grrlfriends, you know? It's easy. Just one bite, a taste. Swapping spit, you know? A little saliva, a little blood. Viral shedding.

She made me drool at the prospect, imagined running down Polly and Reagan, infecting them, and the three of us in a pack, black, white, and red. Three bitch queens.

"Christ," I said.

It's what you really want, Princess. You're barking up the wrong tree with Ansel, I think. You need sisterhood. You need understanding. Ticklefights. Group hugs. Licking each others'…wounds.

She hung there in my head, tongue out, lapping the air, grinning wolfishly.

Reagan needs to eat. Put some meat on her bones. And Polly, why, she's halfway there, already. It's really just a question of whether you beat Ansel to the bite. He'll do her, for sure.

I was sweating, glanced at Darryl and Dean, to see if they noticed, praying I was keeping this all inside. My teeth felt sharp under my tongue.

"You alright, Sam?" Darryl asked.

"Great," I said, through gritted teeth.

You know, Ansel's only going to put up with you for so long. You're on his turf, Princess. Which means, so long as you're here, you're his bitch. Otherwise, out you go.

That wounded me. I mean, I liked Ansel, but couldn't imagine him doing that, being like that. It was a big city; we could share it. I didn't belong to him.

Hah. You know fuck-all about werewolves, Puddin. You're on his turf. Now, you might be his bitch, but if you made Polly, well, then she'd be yours. It's sexual, but it's more intimate than sex. You feel it, you know it, the glandular dance. You could have your own little harem.

She licked her lips, made me lick mine. The door swung both ways; I could hold her back, and she could push me forward. The tug-of-war continued, repulsion versus compulsion. To try to make myself feel better, I imagined her holding her end of the rope in her teeth, a pink bow around her neck.

Funny. You know I'm right. Hell, I am you, right? You were onto something with that half-assed versus whole-hog thing, Princess. Why take babysteps into the Abyss? You should be leaping into it.

Her contempt for me was tangible, had its own flavor, like burnt toast.

"Miss?" a customer, the skinny kid with the silver nose ring, holding out some bottles of India ink, some pens. He looked at my nametag: "Samantha? Hello?"

"Sorry," I said. "Did you find everything you needed?"

He shrugged. "Mostly. Nice shades."

"Thanks," I said.

"I think these belong in Lost and Found," he said, holding up Sheldon's glasses. "Found'em on the floor."

"Thanks," I said, taking them. Evidence. They were evidence, now.

I rang him up, gave him his change, bagged his crap, sent him on his way, tucked Sheldon's frames into my apron. I could hear Lance swearing in his office; he'd probably lost another mission. It amazed me that he got paid to do what he did, which was kissing cousin to next to nothing.

Säämäänthää tormented me with visions of Polly and Reagan running around in my head, this image of us as a pack. And Zooey. Although I'd never seen Zooey, Sääm put her in there, too, made her a dusty grey wolf, youngest of the four of us, the most eager to learn.

You could have your own pack. Even Ansel couldn't stand up to four of you at once. Or any lone wolf. Guys get all weird about it, afraid of losing their niche, but grrls run with scissors just fine, they play nice, or at least in a way that's not quite as chest-thumpy as the boys.

Like you'd know, noob. You're as new to this as I am.

She was quiet, sly, pressing hard on my ribs. I know enough. I know what I am, which is more than you can say.

My phone buzzed in my apron, and I fished it out. It was Reagan. "Hey," I said. "Sup?"

"I couldn't wait, I got a camera and some film," she said. "I'll pick you up at lunch. I want Day One of this photographed."

"Okay," I said. "Great. Uh, my place is kind of a mess."

I tried to remember if I'd left blood on the floor, or anything out of place or weird, anything disturbing. I think it wasn't too bad, given everything I'd been up to.

"It's okay," Reagan said. "We just need a clean, white wall and some natural light."

Then I remembered the boarded window. That would spoil the shot, maybe. I could just imagine Reagan seeing that window, pitying me. Poor Samantha, living in her pathetic little hovel in Logan Square.

"Okay," I said. "11:45, then. I'll hop out front."

I glanced at the clock on my phone. It was 11:00. That worked.

"See you soon," Reagan said. "Bye."

Hanging up, I pocketed my phone, rang up another couple of customers, bided my time until 11:45 rolled around, Sheldon's glasses pressing against my flat tummy.

# 2. MONDAY AFTERNOON

Reagan picked me up and we cruised back to my place. I envied Reagan's freedom, how she could be anywhere she wanted to be, at any time, because she didn't have to go anywhere. No wonder she and Ansel produced so much; having the time to indulge their muse, and the means to get good materials, made all the difference.

As we reached my neighborhood, Reagan reflected on Logan Square.

"It's really come around," she said. "In the 90s, it was really the armpit of North Side, but these days, it's almost presentable. No offense, Samantha."

"None taken," I said. "It's still affordable, which is what matters. This city's getting too expensive."

"You think?" Reagan said. "I don't know. New York's a nightmare. I can't imagine how anybody actually lives there."

We all had a love/hate relationship with New York City. We envied its status as cultural capital of the world, but we hated it for that, too, like how something could signify simply because it came from New York, regardless of actual artistic merit. Lee had a whole canned tirade about the New York City Hardcore punk scene, how rotten it was relative to the rest of the country's, how boring and unimaginative, but how because it existed in New York at all, it somehow signified. But Lee hadn't even been a punk, we were all quick to point out.

I keyed us into my place, and ran a hand through my hair, to tousle it, pointed to one of my white walls.

"There?" I said.

"My," Reagan said, looking around. "What happened to your window?"

"Broke it," I said. "My landlord is taking fucking forever to fix it. I put in a request, but you know how slow that goes."

"Sure," Reagan said. I doubted she'd ever faced a broken window in her life, or a slovenly landlord. Reagan was the kind of person who got things done, and wouldn't settle for anything less than exactly what she wanted. It was an admirable quality. I thought perhaps she'd make a good monster, after all. Monsters were relentless, like children. It was their way, or no way at all.

"What should I wear? I should wear the same thing each time, right?"

"Sure," Reagan said. "How about just keep on your Nonpareil shirt and smock? I like the black and white contrast. Just take off your sunglasses, let's have a look."

I tucked my shades into my apron, heard them click against Sheldon's frames, slipped the shoulder straps off my shoulders, so just the black shirt showed.

"No, keep those," Reagan said. "It could be high fashion, up close."

That made me smile, since I knew far more about high fashion than Reagan did; she was a prep school girl, not a fashionista. I slipped the shoulder straps back on.

"Yes," Reagan said. "In a tight shot, it looks like perhaps you're wearing a jumper dress. This will work."

"What should I do?" I asked, glancing at my wall clock. High noon.

"Be yourself," she said. "Just let me just snap pictures, and we'll see what comes of it."

The shutter clicked, and clicked again. I smiled. Another click. I pouted. It clicked. I frowned. It clicked. I sulked. The shutter clicked. I grinned, and it clicked. I made a wistful expression. Reagan laughed, clicked. I blew a kiss to her. It clicked.

"Oh, you're too good at this, Samantha," she said. "I think we found another talent for you."

"Modeling is performance art," I said. "Not that I could be a model. Too short, too cute."

"I don't know," Reagan said. "You could be my model. I love the looks you give."

I feigned surprise, and she snapped another shot.

"You're just so chimerical," Reagan said. "You're like quicksilver, flowing right before my eyes."

Who even said "quicksilver" anymore? Of course, it would be Reagan. I feigned confusion, and she clicked another shot. I made a neutral, appraising expression, and she snapped that one, too.

"I love it," Reagan said. "Too perfect."

"No such thing," I said. "Nothing can ever be too perfect."

She smiled, almost shyly, and I realized that she had a wonderful smile. I guess I hadn't noticed it before because she was usually talking, and I hadn't been able to appreciate it. Because we're never really been alone, at least not like this. The intimacy of it was stirring.

"God, I look like ass," I said.

"No, you don't," Reagan said. "You look perfect."

I gave her a longing look, a lustful one. Reagan clicked the shot, glanced at me over her camera viewfinder. I held the look, held her with my one good eye, leaned forward, on tiptoe, and kissed her. Reagan put her free arm around me and returned the kiss, and I put my arms around her, and we snogged right there against my apartment wall. And Sääm pounced—I grabbed at Reagan, yanked her close to me, while we continued to kiss. Then we parted, but only barely.

"Samantha," Reagan said. "Wow. I always suspected, but I never knew."

"Yeah," I said. "I'm full of surprises."

She smiled again. "You certainly are. Gretta won't be too happy about this."

"It's just a kiss," I said. "Not a love affair."

Reagan seemed almost disappointed, nodded. "But what a kiss. Your poor face. I wish I could heal it with a kiss."

I kissed her again, bit her lip, drew blood. Just a taste.

"Yipe," she said, wiping her lip with her hand. "You bit me."

"A love bite," I said. "A nibble. God, I'm so sorry."

She fetched a tissue from her purse and daubed it. It was just a little bite. Fuck, what was I talking about? Christ. A lycanthropic prank.

Reagan laughed. "You're so wild, Samantha. You're the wildest girl in our little coven."

"I know," I said. "God help us all."

The mention of Gretta, the pinprick of jealousy, the desire to possess Reagan, to claim her for my own. It's like she'd used my envy to slip her chain, come right out. Sääm was snickering in my head. She'd surprised me. How much did it take? How infective was I? Surely something as inconsequential as that couldn't infect her, could it?

You know why werewolves always go after loved ones? Saam asked in my head. Because they're around, because they're available. They're the ones who you have the least trouble getting to.

You didn't infect her. You couldn't have. Not that little fucking bite.

She just laughed. *Time will tell. You were drooling when you were kissing her, and it's like rabies, baby. Love bites.*

"I should get you back to work," Reagan said, daubing her lip.

"Yeah, I guess so," I said. "I'd much rather skip and play with you all afternoon."

"Yes," Reagan said. "But we can't."

I should warn her. I should tell her that I'm infectious. I should say something. *Tell her. Tell her. Tell her!*

*Tell her what? That you're a fucking werewolf? Hahah. Yeah, go ahead, Puddin. Tell her your dirty secret. And that'll be that. Bye bye, Reagan.*

"Thanks for the pictures," I said, biting my own lip in shame. "I hope they turn out."

"I'll let you know," she said. "We'll do this tomorrow, same time, same place."

"Reagan," I said.

"Yes?"

"Sorry I bit you," I said. "I'm really, really, really sorry."

I wanted to cry, but she just smiled, nodded. "You're passionate, Samantha. I get that, and I love that, and I forgive that."

On impulse, I hugged her, and she hugged back, and for a moment, everything was right; there wasn't any Sääm, no worries. Everything was good and right in my world in Reagan's slender, loving arms.

"We'd better get back to your work, before you get reprimanded," she said, and it broke the moment, and I was thinking about Nonpareil, was envious of Gretta, covetous of Reagan. I wanted her badly.

*And now you've got her. Well, not yet, but soon.*

*Fuck you.*

*No, fuck you, Puddin'. Fuck you very much.*

"Right," I said, popping on my sunglasses again. It was already habitual. I'd been doing it, anyway, to help my sensitive eyes deal with the bright light of day, but my bruised face gave me that much more excuse.

We drove back in relative silence, with Miles Davis's "Kind of Blue" purring from her Range Rover's speakers. I know because I asked, and she told me. She said that Gretta liked jazz.

"'Gretta Likes Jazz' would be a good band name," I said.

"I suppose it would," Reagan said. "You and the boys are the die-hard music heads. God, that situation with Ansel was so awkward."

That reminded me. "Oh, hey, did Polly tell you about her idea? She thought Ansel should start his own gallery, and we could use it."

"Really?" she said. "Where is he?"

"Wicker Park," I said. "He owns this great old building. It's apartments, lofts, mostly, but the ground floor would totally lend itself to a gallery, with all the foot traffic. He said he'd consider it."

"Capital," Reagan said. "You have to love it. Clay's BacchUS is so intimate."

Reagan was, of course, being charitable, probably because Clay had showed her paintings there enough times, although no sales. Never any sales. Not like Reagan needed sales. Calling BacchUS "intimate" was like calling a closet "cozy."

"Was he really interested in it, or just being polite?" Reagan said.

"I think he was into it," I said. "I honestly think it hadn't occurred to him before. That's very Ansel, really. He kind of walks around in a daze."

She nodded, smiled through her windshield at the traffic passing us by. "That Polly, ever the sparkplug. She really is quite industrious, for a poet, I mean."

We laughed, often made sport of the poets in our ranks, who held themselves in highest regard, like literary samurai warriors. They looked down on prose as unworthy of their talent and commitment to perfect words, their elegant dances around syllables and breaks, fricatives and gerunds, assonance and consonance. Never to their faces, of course, for nobody took themselves quite so seriously as poets. As the court jester-in-residence of our cultured cabal, being the performance artist, I relished mocking them.

Nonpareil slid into view, and my comfortable warmth in Reagan's Rover fled me at the sight of it. I wanted to stay with her all day, see where she went, what she did, how she spent one of her wonderful days. Gretta was an assistant professor of history at University of Chicago. They were a very professional couple, except that Reagan had no profession, beyond studying Art History in college.

"Thanks so much, Reagan," I said.

"Thank you," she said, emphasizing the "you." "I can't wait to shoot the next two weeks, see how it progresses."

"I'm a quick healer," I said, wondering just how quickly I'd heal the wounds on my face.

"Well, don't heal too quickly," she said. "I'll send you some thumbnails when I get them developed."

"Great," I said, hopping out of the car, my stomach rumbling. Crap, I'd forgotten to eat lunch. I watched Reagan's car slide away, then went back inside.

"About time," Lance said, waiting by timeclock. "Did you shoot up over lunch? Darryl said you got beat up by your pimp."

I walked past Lance and clocked in, went behind my register, stuffed my coat under my counter. Lance followed on my heels, watched me.

"You know, I could probably sue you so many times for the way you talk to me," I said. "How about a raise?"

"Sure," he said. "Why not? So, what happened?"

"I fell," I said. "Didn't he tell you that?"

I glared over at Darryl, who was busy trying to look innocent, failing miserably. Lance followed my gaze, scoffed.

"Oh, sure," he said. "He told me, but I figured I should get the story from you."

"Rollerblading," I said.

"You should sue the city," Lance said. "What stretch of sidewalk?"

"It doesn't matter," I said. "It was my fault."

More customers were trickling in, and Lance took that as his cue to hide in his office, let the boys and me handle it. Dean was stocking shelves, with Darryl and me at the registers. As I rang people up, I kept playing it back in my head, like whether I should tell Reagan or not. It was the right thing to do, strictly speaking. She had a right to know, she really did.

Sigh. I thought about what Ansel did. He didn't tell me, and I was pissed at him. But then, I knew it was him who had infected me. Whereas the little nibble I did on Reagan, well, that might take months to infect her, and by then, she might not even make the connection.

I clocked out and got out of there.

# 3. MONDAY EVENING

Right after work, I made my way to Washington Square Park, hunted around for the stuntcam, on the off chance that I'd actually find it, like wedged between a car tire and the curb or something.

There were kids playing in the park, and crazies feeding pigeons, and commuters fast-walking this way and that, but I didn't see the helmet, and I looked for a whole hour, until daylight ran away and became night came slouching along.

It was freaking me out. Where was the camera? How could I have been so stupid? Somebody even moderately tech-savvy could play that camera and it would lead them right to my street. I tried to remember when I'd run the thing. It had been at the curb, in front of my building. What if whoever found it went to the police? Fuck. The light faded, the tangerine-hued sodium streetlights came up, and I took my shades off, feeling like I had no choice but to reveal my bruised face, being out at night and all. I walked all the way home, lost in thought, fretting. And there was the old man and his Polish pimp cane. Then again, what did he know? He was old. Still, the absence of the camera gnawed at me, and only a call from Reagan startled me out of my brooding.

"Hello, Samantha," she said. "Just had to tell you, the pictures came out great! You're such a great subject, I can't believe I hadn't thought of it sooner."

She sent me some of them, and I looked at them, marveled at my bruised face. Wow, talk about a roadmap of ruin.

"I look terrible," I said.

"You look gorgeous," she said. "Striking. People will think it was makeup, that nobody could possibly look that way for real."

I smiled, thought about my "Transformation" video, how people reacted to that. Seeing *wasn't* believing, not anymore. Something had happened in people's heads, like postmodernity had leached into their brains, and the senses could no longer be trusted. Truth was so retro. And with technology getting to be what it was, even the voyeuristic veracity of video was suspect. People marveled at that Baby Boomer masturbation movie, *Forrest Gump*, when it first came out, like how they put him into historical events, totally copying the approach of *Zelig*, but really it was kind of a worrisome thing, what it represented.

Like video and film used to be a repository of reality. Like despite all of the Hollywood wizardry and special effects, if somebody filmed something real, it was taken to be real. But now, the effects were so good, people just assumed they were being spoofed. Maybe once seeing was believing, but now seeing was simply seeing; believing was believing, and I think the two ships had passed in the night, and would never meet again.

"It looks wild," I said. "Nicely done, Reagan."

I felt so guilty about Reagan, what I'd done to her, or thought I'd done, and how I couldn't tell her. Sääm licked her chops in my head, coiled around my heart, like the Serpent at the base of a tree in Eden.

She tasted sweet. Like apples.

"Have you heard from Lee?" Reagan asked.

"No," I said. "Why, is something going on?"

"Oh," Reagan said. "There was an outing planned for Wednesday. I'm not going. Café Amaranth is the place."

I checked my messages, but didn't see anything about it. Great. I wondered if Polly had heard. Lee probably felt like he owed Reagan, after being such an asshole, but then again, that was probably more integrity than Lee actually possessed. In Lee's world, guilt was for norms.

"Hadn't heard," I said. "I'm probably in the doghouse because I sat the fence."

"He's such a child," she said. "It's tiresome, really."

"Sure is," I said, wondering if I should call him, talk to him. But I could just imagine how that would go.

"Anyway," she said. "Our first shoot went really well, don't you think? I can't wait for tomorrow."

"Yeah," I said. "Me, neither."

"Hey, I have another call," Reagan said. "I'll see you tomorrow, Sam. Same time."

"Check," I said, hung up.

I got on my El train home, a nearly abandoned car, just a couple of punks making out at the far side of it. In the fluorescent light of the car, their skin looked almost whitish-green. I leaned against the window, saw a circle in the glass, a depression.

Touching it with my finger, I saw that it was a little circular depression, with a tiny hole. A bullet hole? Too small. Probably some wannabe gangbanger with a pellet gun. The hole was near my face. A good shot, assuming they fired at a moving train. It made me uneasy, looking out at the dark city, in my overlit train car, with a bullet hole near my head. The train reached my stop, and I hopped out, made my way home, hands in my pockets.

I decided to blog a little, let off some steam. First, thought, I checked my "Transformation" video, which had gotten over 400,000 hits, and had tons of comments, most of them favorable. That made me happy. At least that was something that was going well. I just wished I'd been able to follow up on it.

Sighing, I logged onto my blog, and then, on a whim, checked Polly's first.

> T's been back for days, and I'm dying. I want A. I hate to think that we're not going to be able to see each other. I've called him, but he's just shunting me to voicemail. I bet S's busy over there, and why shouldn't she be? She's single, for god's sake. What am I doing? I'm a wreck.
>
> I don't think T suspects anything. Why should he? We're a great couple. Still, I've been terrible, just terrible.

I smiled at this. Glad she was feeling some guilt, although she had nothing on me in the guilt department.

> T wants me to go to Europe with him on his next trip, although I told him I couldn't get the days at work, which is about three-quarters true. I mean, Berlin would be fantastic, but I can't possibly bear to be away from A for that long. It's obscene how fascinated I am with him, after so short a time, but I am.
>
> The painting he did of me was transcendent, wonderful. Painting's such a dead art form, but his attention to it is charming, ennobling. I want to have it in my bedroom, or in my walk-in closet. I want it somewhere, someplace I can see it every day. I hate that I

can't, that I'd have to explain it and lie to T, and that lie would hang like an albatross around my neck.

Blah blah blah. Polly needed Prozac. Something to kill her libido, increase her appetite. Something to occupy her time. I went onto my blog, instead. My problems interested me more.

I did something terrible to a friend.

Then I deleted that line. There was such thing as saying too much, even for a blogger. I didn't want Reagan finding out that way, if she even read my blog.

You always hurt the ones you love. That's such a cliché. What's the cure for it? Not hurting anybody, or not loving anyone?

I left it at that. A short entry, for once. That didn't stop some of my readers from commenting. I had made yet another alias, Säämurai.

*DinkaDoo: Are you in love?*
*Taliesinner: Of course she is. With Adonis AND Polygon. You slag.*
*Säämurai: Try not to be a dick tonight, Tally. Not in the mood.*
*Taliesinner: I'm a wise man.*
*DinkaDoo: A wise guy, more like. Stoogian.*

Sigh. I don't know what to do. My instincts tell me to keep quiet, but I no longer trust my instincts; they've become alien to me.

*Taliesinner: I love that. Instincts are overrated. So's intellect, for that matter.*
*DinkaDoo: Words he lives by, Säämurai. I like the new alias.*
*Säämurai: Thanks. Glad my suffering could entertain you, Tally.*
*Taliesinner: What can I say? It's boring where I live.*
*Säämurai: Where do you live? Can I find some way of remedying that?*
*Taliesinner: Isle of Man.*
*Säämurai: No way, really?*
*Taliesinner: Truly*
*Säämurai: Where is that?*
*Taliesinner: Between Ireland, England, and Scotland.*

*DinkaDoo: So, you're Manx? No tail?*
*Taliesinner: I am, yes, tailless. And American. I yearn for American problems.*

Weird to think that he was so far away. No wonder he kept odd hours. I googled "Isle of Man" just to check it out. What a tiny place. On a whim, I ran with it.

*Säämurai: Got any cures for lycanthropy?*
*Taliesinner: Why, you know a werewolf?*
*Säämurai: I am one.*

I sent him and DinkaDoo my "Transformation clip," which they hadn't seen, because I hadn't affiliated it with my blog. They were quiet awhile, watching it.

*DinkaDoo: Awesome! Wicked! Killer! I saw this elsewhere, didn't realize it was YOU!*
*Taliesinner: Great gag! Is that really you?*
*Säämurai: Yup.*
*Taliesinner: You were naked!*
*DinkaDoo: Yeah, she was. (pant pant pant)*
*Säämurai: Is it possible I've offended your transplanted Manxish sensibilities, Tally?*
*Taliesinner: No, but that was pretty vivid.*
*Säämurai: So, how about my cure?*
*DinkaDoo: Silver bullet to the head.*
*Taliesinner: Wolfsbane, of course. It's poisonous, though. Best not partake. Some cure, maybe worse than the disease. Socrates had his hemlock, Lycaon had his wolfsbane.*
*Säämurai: Oh, you're no fun at all.*

It was worth a shot, anyway. I couldn't believe I'd lost the camera. Martin would be so pissed at me. I googled "Lycaon" and didn't see anything about wolfsbane. That was pure Taliesinner, to know who Lycaon was, but to get it wrong. Or maybe he was being witty.

I've become a werewolf, and I know the moral thing I guess for me to do is kill myself, but I don't want to do that. I'm a threat to everybody I know and love, to myself, to everything.

I posted it, figured, what the fuck? Nobody would believe it, anyway. That was the best defense a werewolf had. I kind of hoped Zipstrip would see it, would say something kind, something understanding.

*Taliesinner: There's no morality in suicide; merely resignation.*
*DinkaDoo: So deep, Tal.*
*Säämurai: I should do it.*
*Taliesinner: You should not. You should get a therapist.*
*Säämurai: I can't afford one.*
*DinkaDoo: Maybe Tal will spot you.*
*Taliesinner: I'm an expatriate; not a tycoon.*
*Säämurai: A therapist, eh? That's a thought.*

Taliesinner was mostly full of shit, most of the time, but even a stopped watch is right twice a day, and it wasn't a bad idea. There was a kind of vogue to seeing a therapist, too, like somehow my problems were big enough that they merited actual therapy. I mean, they were big enough, for god's sake. A therapist might actually be able to help me, somehow. Or else get me institutionalized or something. It wasn't a bad idea, which, of course, was why Sääm hated it.

*My fucking god, she said, in my head. That's your answer? Get yourself some drugs, like Ansel? Nice. I wonder if he sees a shrink, too. What is wrong with people?*

Since I was alone, since it was just me, I just talked to her out loud; it made it easier for me to think.

"Why not? I'm in need of some comfort, some help, thanks to you."

*It'll only get in the way. It'll dull your instincts. You need to be sharp, not sedated.*

"But if I'm sedated, if I'm able to put you to sleep, then maybe it'll be okay."

*I won't let you. I'll eat your therapist. Try me.*

"I'm the host; you're the infection."

*Not that again. I won't fucking let you do it. I'll kill the therapist, eat her heart, or his dick. You don't want their deaths on your hands, do you?*

"You wouldn't dare," I said. "The police would find you."

*Don't be stupid. I'm going to have to be proactive, I see, in managing you.*

I doubled over in pain, as Sääm snapped her chain, let herself loose inside me, clawed and bit her way free of me.

*Taliesinner: I'm brimming with wisdom, if only people would listen.*

*DinkaDoo: Brimming with something.*

She was making me transform, right then and there. I struggled against it, but my own agitation was fuel for her.

"Not my Dolces," I slurred, through teeth that lengthened, strengthened into fangs. I fell on the ground, struggled to tug off my jeans before she destroyed them, but my fingernails had stretched into claws, and I couldn't get a grip on the jeans. Instead, my claws slashed right through my jeans, my legs split them open. A $650 pair of jeans, destroyed in seconds, my legs bristling with fur and muscle. I howled in rage as she shredded my whole outfit into bits. I was on all fours, snarling as she took me from Alpha to Omega again, from woman to beast, until I stood there, monstrous, horrible.

*Taliesinner: Säämurai? You there?*

She looked at the computer and cackled. She grabbed the monitor and yanked it from the wall, then threw it against my wall. The thing popped, sparked, exploded, cracked into bits, fell in a smoldering pile.

Not my computer, too! Please! I can't afford that!

Then she went to the computer tower, where my everything was, and she tore the thing open, the metal parting like butter in her talons. She pulled that from the wall and then tore the tower to bits, flinging green chunks of circuitboard everywhere.

"I'm just getting started," she snarled.

Then she went to the wooden board that blocked the window and pried it loose with a tug of her arms. And she leaped from it, landing on the ground. One more leap and we were on the street, sniffing the air. She howled, and then we ran down the street, and my world became a bloody blur.

We ran feral-fast and deadly-dazzling, nose sampling the air as we made our way past startled, terrified pedestrians and hysterical pets. What was she looking for? From the prison I occupied in her mind, it was remote and dreamlike, and she was willing me to sleep, to keep me from thinking us to death. This was another time, this was instinct time. She caught a scent and chased after it, ducking down alleys, carving her way through the neighborhood with ballistic grace.

Then we were at the river, the stinking moat that slid snakelike to the east of me. She went down the hill, past the ribbon of weedy green, past the gnarled trees that clung to the litter-lined shore, and took me

232 | D.T. NEAL

to the river, the stinking liquid monstrosity. Just seeing it made me sick. It wasn't a river; it was a travesty akin to the LA River, an engineering affront to nature. She took me to the river, and then she bent down to drink from it.

No.

Her tongue lolled out and she lapped up the fetid water, drank long and deep. I could feel the icy chill of the stuff going down my throat, into my stomach. Chicago River water. Christ, I was fucking going to die.

She could sense my alarm, and kept at it, until she had drunk her fill. Mocking me. I wanted to vomit. There were things you did and didn't do in Chicago. Drinking from the Chicago River was definitely something you didn't do. They'd reversed the flow of the thing to keep it from polluting Lake Michigan anymore. Before they'd done that, people had died from waterborne illnesses by the thousands in Chicago.

*It doesn't matter. This won't kill you, Princess.*

Then she decided to travel down the ribbon of weedy trees, beneath the rusting bridges. It would have been a daunting hike, but for her, it was easy. Her limbs lent themselves to jumping, running climbing. We passed through the litter of cans and plastic, the broken spars of concrete, beneath the sight of the norms, driving overhead.

At night, this polluted greenway was as black as sin. Even in my dreamlike stupor, I could see Sääm plotting, seeing it as an easy way into the heart of the city, unseen. Maybe not as fast as bolting from alley to alley, down sidewalks, but it was sneakier, and she liked that. In such a place, she could simply vanish, if she had to. My stomach roiled, as I thought of that damned river water festering in there, but it seemed to be doing me no harm.

*If I drank bleach, would it kill me?*

It was nice to torment her mind, for a change.

*I'd rescue you. I love you, Stupid.*

She took me I don't know how far, and how long, but when we emerged, crawled back up the embankment, at a point where the ribbon of weeds butted up against a concrete bridge pylon, we were near a mill of some sort. We were on the wrong side of the river, so she climbed up and over the fence blocking off access to the greenway, and then made her way to the rusting cast-iron drawbridge. Cars scooted by, not seeing us as we made our way across the pedestrian walk, screened as we were by the lattices of the bridge. We crossed the bridge in a half-dozen steps, her loping stride eating effortless distance, and found nurturing shadow behind the mill. We could see men walking about in the dark, to and from the buildings, we took in their sweaty scent. Then we ran alongside the building, until we came to another street. I glanced at it, saw that it was Clybourn, and looked south, where the lights were brighter, where there was people going to restaurants and shopping. Looking up the street, I could see other lights, smell other scents. More to the south, fewer to the north. And across the street, the dark of residential. We ran across the street and into the dark, taking scents, feeling them. The feast of smells was delirium-inducing, psychedelic, a sensory pastiche that overwhelmed my already-taxed brain. She did my thinking for me, caught scents, prowled. She caught the scent of a man running, a jogger, and gave chase before I could stop her.

No.

The man was young, fit, maybe in his early 30s, well-dressed in a stylish track suit, keeping a steady pace, wearing an iPod. I could hear his music, even from where we were. I knew the song. It was "Guilt" by the Long Blondes. I knew the song, and Sääm ran hard for the man. But the running wasn't enough, the hunt, the takedown. No, not nearly enough. Sääm let out a snarl as she ran, loud enough that the jogger heard us over the sound of his iPod, glanced over his shoulder. He saw us, saw the wide set of the jaws, opening for him, the glint of mismatched eyes, the flutter of fur and clacking of claws.

"Fuck ME!" the man said, his face comically open, his mouth a grimace. The fear-stink flew off him in an intoxicating wave, as he turned from us and went from a jog to a sprint, which was, of course, just what Sääm wanted. She wanted the chase.

"Run!" she snarled, full of glee. "Run!"

The guy ran around a corner, with Sääm right on his heels. It was too easy, and this man was a good enough runner, but she was faster. St. Michael's Cathedral loomed in the distance, a towering monolith. The man ran for it, zigzagging across the street while we gave chase.

"Help!" he shouted. "HELP ME!!"

She snapped at his heels, while the man dodged between cars, and we overshot, smashing into somebody's parked BMW, which sounded a car alarm. The man kept running for the cathedral, while Sääm crunched her way over the car, onto the sidewalk.

"HELP ME! CALL THE POLICE!" the guy was shrieking.

She let him get as far as the steps to the cathedral, let him think he would be safe, before she tackled him, a quick dive and he tumbled to the bricks, his iPod sliding across the ground. Then she grappled with him, his arms up to defend his face, his pretty face, eyebrows more plucked than a girl's, smelling of moisturizing hand lotion.

"HELP!" he screamed, swinging at her. She caught his fist in her mouth, bit down, gave him a shake, sliced flesh and tendon, drew blood, tasted meat. He wailed, and she went at his thigh, taking a bite, another taste, while I fought to hold her back, to keep her from killing him, from devouring him. Snarling, she yielded, gave him a bloody lick of the face, ran across the lot of the cathedral, then up one of the streets, while the guy screamed. He would live, thanks to me. He would become infected, thanks to her.

Maybe it's what she wanted all along.

The noise the man had made had people at their windows, looking, but in the dark, it was hard to see anything, and Sääm could blend in so well in the dark. Somewhere a police siren sounded, and she ran up a street lined with townhouses, saw a waifish young woman with long, limp hair walking a tiny little dog, which was barking furiously at us.

Without waiting, Sääm pounced on her, biting her on the arm, taking a chunk from her, snapping the leash that held her little dog, plucking up the little snarling ball of fur before the woman could even scream. As she did scream, Sääm ran away and looked at the little dog, a pug, and she tossed the whimpering thing away, hardly a mouthful. Racing up the street, she came to Armitage, where the noise of sports bars could be heard. And more sirens.

Another infected. Christ.

*Yes. See? You can't stop me.*

*Ansel's going to be pissed if you keep making lupines.*

*Let him be pissed. Let him come for us.*

Then she ran west, along Armitage, past startled commuters on a bus that went by, their faces ghost-pale, their eyes wide and un-comprehending, like they didn't believe what they'd seen. She saw a bicycle cop turn down one of the streets that fed off of Armitage, and she gave chase.

"Officer," she snarled, and the cop glanced over his shoulder. "Help me."

"Holy Christ!" he said, and began pedaling furiously. She ran after him, howling as she went.

No.

The cop drew his pistol and fired over his shoulder at us, the bullet spanging off the asphalt, the report deafening, the flash of it blinding in the dark, tree-lined street.

"I'd like to report an animal menace," she barked at him, cackling. Then she swiped at him with her paws, popping the rear tire, sending him crashing to the ground, dropping his gun, which slid underneath a car. The cop tumbled on the roadway, while Sääm kept at him, landing on him, claws sinking into his protective vest. His walkie talkie crackled, while the police sirens neared, and then went off. Sääm scratched the officer in the face, bit him on his upper arm, just beyond his body armor, took a chunk out of him, gulped it down.

The man swore, tried to jab us in the eye with his thumb, but he couldn't quite get it. She passed over him and ran off into the darkness before he could recover his pistol from beneath the parked car.

*Enough,* I thought.

"Not nearly," she said, spitting him out, and howled, head pointed to the sky, and then we ran back the way we'd come, glancing at the cathedral, where lights flashed. Two police cruisers, one ambulance. Yeah, maybe Ansel would be pissed, but that's what he got for not talking to us, for sharing. It didn't matter. She'd gotten her taste of meat, and I hadn't allowed her to kill anybody, so maybe it was progress, right?

*Hadn't allowed me?* Sääm thought, laughing. *I'm the infection; you're the host. You're not getting better; you're getting sicker.*

We ran back to the river, watching an Animal Control truck shoot by, and a Tactical Operations van cruise by as well, but they didn't see us. Then we crossed Clybourn and passed the mill and got to the river, where she sprang right into the water, a diving splash, and swam to the other side. It was a disgusting, terrible swim. I never liked night swimming, in general, and swimming in one of the branches of the Chicago River made it that much worse. The water was terribly cold, but we hadn't wanted to risk the bridge crossing with the police driving around.

The sirens were still wailing, but were further, now. Nobody was onto us. We swam the river, then crawled out the other side, where she shook herself off. In the chilly autumn air, it made us colder, still, but her vitality was unaffected. It seemed like nothing could slow her down.

*Aren't you glad I didn't kill anyone?*

She mocked me.

*If I'd eaten them, there'd be no problem.*

She had deliberately infected them, as she had with Reagan. But these were strangers. Ansel would be upset to find them in his territory. I would be in trouble.

*If I'd slain them, no problem still.*

*Why won't you let me kill? Wasn't Sheldon fun?*

*I don't remember.*

Again, it was mockery. She could have killed them, and I wouldn't have been able to stop her. No, she'd let them live, had chosen to simply infect them.

*I want your first proper kill to be special; something memorable. Sheldon was just an accident.*

*I'm not going to kill anybody else.*

*Yes, you will.*

It frightened me, stuck deep inside her, in a glass cage of my own, where I could see everything, contemplating homicide, suicide, and everything in between. She left me to my thoughts, though I could feel her laughing at my mangled morality. She ran for home, moving like an arrow shot from a bow, a faultless tracker, her nose a marvel, her sense of place, astounding. We got back to my street, where she paused, sniffed the air. Something caught her attention, gave her pause. She waited a moment, listening, but the street was quiet. We could still hear sirens, far away. They'd probably found the other victims. Satisfied, she crept to my apartment, and leaped into the place. There, on the floor of my place, she let me go, let me return to who I was, traded our skins and left me cold and shivering, naked, alone.

Point made, point taken.

She could take me wherever she wanted, whenever, make me do what she liked. I was her bitch. I looked around the place, felt sorrow grip me tight.

My apartment was a wreck. I couldn't believe that bitch had destroyed my computer. There were pieces of it everywhere, like the thing had blown up. It was a total loss. She'd snapped the boards into jagged bits. Every last one. And the apartment was freezing because she'd pried loose the board over the window. I went to the window and tried to put the board back up. It had been drilled in place or something, and she'd just pried it loose, no problem. I had to take a sponge mop and wedge it on the ground, pressing the dry sponge against the wooden board.

Then I looked at the mess of clothes and computer, and, weirdly, found inspiration in it. Reagan would be so proud of me. I went into one of my closets and fished out some poster board, decided it was too flimsy, and then found my old art class art board, which was made of particle board, dark as buckwheat, firm but flexible. That was just right.

I laid that out on my coffee table, and got out some industrial glue, and went about creating a landscape out of the debris. I turned my destroyed designer jeans into churning waves, and created a beach out of broken glass, made a grassy knoll out of my ruined sweater. Built a city out of circuit boards and broken tower casing. I spent hours working on it. Then, after putting something over the ocean of jeans, I took some spray primer and sprayed the city part a uniform gray. I stepped back from it, a little high on the spray paint, set the can down, looked at my handiwork. It looked pretty good to me. And I liked taking her destruction and turning it into something else.

What to call it? "Remains of the Day?" No, although I was tempted. "Happy Hunting Ground." Yeah. I liked that, jotted it down on an index card, laid it at the shore of the little landscape.

"Ha," I said, snatching triumph from the jaws of defeat. She'd wanted to ruin my so-called life, wanted to smash and destroy it, but I'd taken her destruction and had made something nice out of it.

"Ha!"

I swept up the floor where the debris had been too small to use, and cleaned up the remainder of the mess, admiring my little sculpture. I mean, it wasn't entirely inspired, but given what it had been before, it was better than it had been. The meaning of it was personal. I picked it up and set it on my empty computer table. The absence of the computer haunted me. I missed its phosphorescent companionship, its unblinking blue-white eye. I could access the Net from my phone, of course, but my PC was more companionable, less rushed-seeming.

Putting away my broom and dustpan, I went to the bathroom to clean up. I felt gritty, city-filthy, couldn't believe I'd just been sitting there on my floor, sculpting naked for a few hours, after having attacked—and bitten—three people, after drinking river water. Sääm did that to me, left me dazed, spent.

I went into the bathroom to get cleaned up, looked at myself in the mirror. My bruise was almost entirely healed. Wow. Turning my head this way and that, I couldn't believe it. Somehow, the transformation healed me. It was only taking this long because that Polish pecker had used a silver cane on me.

Wonders never ceased. Putting my finger into my mouth, as far back as it would go, I made myself gag, made myself puke. Blood and meat and river water came right out of me, splashed into the toilet. I flushed it again and again, to make it go away, throwing toilet paper down with it, to help it on its way. I wondered if the sewer department would even notice something like that, prayed that everything would go down, that I wouldn't get a clog, or else I'd be screwed.

I puked until I felt like I was empty, sweating, shaking.

I wondered how Reagan would react, how it would play with her "Personal Injury" piece. She would be amazed at my recovery. Maybe she would be upset. I hoped not. It felt good to be nearly whole again. Turning on the water, I had a hot, soapy shower, cleaned the city from my skin, watched it wash down the drain, around my toes in scuds of soap and water. I stayed in there, in the steam and water, like a baptism, running the water through my hair, head bent, until I felt clean again. Too bad the water couldn't clean my insides—there wasn't enough soap in the world for that.

I toweled off and put on some pajamas, cranked up my steam heat to make up for the chill inflicted on the apartment by the open window all night, and mourned the loss of my computer. I was awake. It was a perfect time to blog, but she'd taken that from me.

So, I took some LPs, laid them out, decided how I felt, what I wanted to play, decided Alice Cooper Group's "Love It To Death" fit where I was at, put it on, laid on my sofa and just zoned out to it.

Eventually, I got up and cooked myself some macaroni and cheese and wolfed it down, not caring that I was eating in the wee hours of the morning, grateful I wasn't eating squirrel, or rat, or some barhound's entrails. Mac and cheese was good enough for me. I ate the whole bowl while Alice Cooper Group offered me dark comfort—mac and cheese with a side of "Black Juju," contemplating my fate in the lonely shadows of my apartment.

The good thing about the moments after Sääm let me go was that I had a few moments to myself. She would be sated for a bit. But I didn't know how long I could hold the reins, or even if I still was holding them, anymore. That she boiled out of me tonight frightened me. She'd wanted to teach me a lesson, that she could come out any time she wanted, and there was nothing I could do about it. She would fight hard for the territory of my soul.

I wasn't sure if I had that kind of fight in me. Fighting was what she lived for—the endless war of tooth and claw. That wasn't what I wanted. But she welcomed the struggle, craved it. What was I to do, except surrender? I mean, victory for me was a bullet to the brain, by my own hand. If suicide was victory, then I'd already lost. If I couldn't keep her tied up inside me, if she gnawed her way out of the bars I'd placed around her, what defense did I have? Did the door swing both ways? Like if she could compel me to transform, could I compel her to return me to normal? It was more than I wanted to deal with. I finished my food, put my stuff in the dishwasher, let the album play out, ran the dishwasher, went to bed with the thrum of the thing in my head.

I felt like I was on the butt end of an abusive relationship, which was absurd, because Sääm was me, but at the same time, that assessment felt right. I was at war with myself, and she was winning, gaining inches of ground, claiming ever-larger slices of my soul, leaving me with pyrrhic victories, at best—infected people instead of dead people, instead of eating them. At some point, I would be gone, and only she would remain, this new me, this other, this triumphant monstrosity.

There seemed no way out of it that didn't require my death. I needed insight, I needed mentoring. I needed answers. I needed Ansel.

Fucking Ansel is what I needed.

# 4. TUESDAY MORNING: 6 NOVEMBER

I got into work a little late, and Simone gave me the stinkeye, but after my exhausting night out, I wasn't in any mood for her bullshit. I wore my shades by choice, since I'd healed up nicely after last night. Simone didn't like that I was wearing shades, thought it made me look like I was on heroin, and asked me to not wear them while I was working. I told her Lance let me wear them, and she said that was fine, but Lance wasn't here today, so could I please just not wear them?

Not wanting to put up with her bullshit all morning, and being a bit late, as I said, and wanting to enjoy the photo shoot with Reagan later, I ceded to Simone, perched the shades up on my forehead, and went about my morning. Since I'd come in late, I got stuck with re-stocking shelves, versus lounging at the registers like Dean was. Darryl had today off. So, I grabbed the inventory cart and went about restocking shelves, which wasn't bad, because it kept me out of the way, out from under Simone's managerial gaze.

"Lance said you were really beaten up, but it doesn't look so bad to me," Simone said.

"Yeah, well I'm a quick healer," I said, carefully stacking boxes of oil-based pastels on their shelf, one package at a time, milking the work.

"You should be more careful," she said. I pointed to her, nodding.

"Words of wisdom, Simone," I said, wondering if she caught the sarcasm, could sniff out the irony. I doubted it. She left me alone, and my morning passed pretty quickly. It was Reagan-time before I knew it.

Reagan couldn't believe how my face had healed. She marveled at it when she picked me up, looking sharp as ever in her Range Rover. She had class to her, for sure. I hated that word, it felt so lower class to invoke class—it seemed like middle class people would refer to "grace" instead, like it was a nobler sentiment than "class," but Reagan had both grace *and* class, and they didn't feel like the same thing. I hopped into her car with a smile.

"Oh, my lord, Samantha," she said. "Look at your face! It's nearly healed. What did you put on it?"

"Nothing," I said. "I told you I'm a quick healer."

"Yes, you did," she said. "But, wow."

She was wearing a red turtleneck and a gray skirt with tan heels, and looked as elegant and graceful as ever. She had a ballerina's neck, carried herself that way. She'd confessed a time or two to doing ballet as a girl in the past.

"Hope it doesn't spoil the project," I said.

"No, no," she said. "We can adapt. It might be a bit of a jump; I really wanted to get a month's worth of shots out of it, but we can always do some Photoshop tweaking of the images, smooth out the transition before we print. I had no idea you'd heal so fast."

Her blonde eyebrows looked a little wilder than I remembered. I noticed it, because she was always very put together, carefully elegant, usually had her hair back with a hairband, away from her forehead.

"How's your lip?" I asked, curious.

"Completely better," she said. "Gretta didn't even notice."

"That's good," I said.

"Although she's terribly jealous of the photographs," Reagan said, turning up my street. "She wants to know why I'm not taking pictures like that of her. I told her if she has a bashed-up face, I'd be happy to oblige her—I said you and I were on a special project, borne of artistry and circumstance. What could she do but accept that?"

She smiled, scanned for parking. Since it was during the day, there were spots to be had, and she managed to get one up the street. As she drove, I found myself looking her up and down, her robust frame, so Midwestern zaftig yet New York chic, she cut a honed, broadsword-like silhouette. I wondered what the infection would do to her, to that. How it would affect her, whether it would. She glanced at me out of the corner of her eye, smiling. Red lipstick, matching her turtleneck, I thought. Pretty.

"You're eyeing me, Samantha," she said. "I have to confess, I haven't forgotten about the other day. In fact, it's kind of kept me, well, distracted."

Reagan eased us into the parking spot, hopped out, and I followed.

"I'm sorry about it," I said.

"No apologies are necessary, Samantha," she said, taking my arm, briskly walking across the street, to my place. "There was something savory in that moment. I didn't notice it at the time, distracted as I was, but I found your pert savagery simply delicious."

Up the street, about a half-block away, was the Dog-Walking Man with his bulldog. He was kind of an institution on my street, this middle-aged, unassuming man who was always out walking his dog. He looked at me curiously from a distance, and I nodded his way, while his bulldog sniffed uncertainly at me, kept his baggy eyes on me. I showed my teeth to the dog, and it whimpered. The Dog-Walking Man glanced at his dog, then at me, his expression unreadable. I turned to look at my building.

I was chagrined to see that Mr. Ludovico still hadn't replaced the window. Christ, how long would that man take with it? It was infuriating, embarrassing. Reagan pretended not to notice, walked upstairs with me after I'd keyed in, kept a hand on my arm. The feeling of her so close to me was intense and erotic. It was something to me, how I'd always had a crush on Polly, but now, with Reagan close to me, I felt something stronger. There was a power to her that I didn't find in Polly, and I found this desirable.

"Savagery, eh?" I said.

"Yes," she said. "You're really quite charming, you know. The others don't appreciate it, but I do. They look down on you, but I realize now that you're a true artist, just like me. The others are poseurs and dilettantes, but you, Samantha, are, like me, a seeker."

She was almost breathless, flushed. It took an effort to key into my apartment, because I wanted to have her in the hallway, right there. It was strong, nearly overpowering. I wanted to devour her. We went in, and she saw my diorama, my sculpture, and cooed at the sight of it. "My God, Samantha, you've been busy. What is this?"

I went over to my albums, took out Roxy Music's first album, put it on my turntable, and Bryan Ferry's voice and Brian Eno's sonic wizardry danced in our ears. She picked up the card, read it, turned it over, replaced it. She set down her camera on one of my chairs, slipped off her butterscotch gloves and held them in one hand, tucked that hand under her elbow, chewed a painted fingernail as she studied my piece, cocked her hip to one side, pulling the skirt tight to her skinny hips. It was like a marionette's impression of Polly.

"What happened to your computer?" she asked.

"That's it," I said.

"You smashed your computer?" she asked, incredulous. I nodded. She was awestruck. "Beautiful, Samantha. Amazing. I can't believe you did it. You destroyed it and made it into a landscape? Whatever for?"

Truth was, I didn't know why Sääm had destroyed my computer. I think she'd just lashed out at something handy, something I valued. It was a case of displaced aggression, perhaps. Lycanthropes were probably prone to things like that.

"For Art. I just acted on instinct," I said, and she smiled, nodding, understanding.

"Glorious," she said. "You are our enfant terrible, Samantha. There can be no doubt about it. How lucky I am to have discovered it."

I looked from the sculpture to her, and back again. "It's not much of a piece."

"Nonsense," she said. "It's wonderful; savage! There's a brutality in it, the juxtaposition of the fleeting of materiality with the desire for a sense of order and purpose. It's like one of those models for a grand architectural project you see, under plexiglass, except this is for a kind of nightmare terrain, jagged lines laid out in a ruthless grid. It's like a construction project for Hell. What's the water made out of?"

"Blue jeans," I said. "My Dolce & Gabbanas."

Her eyes went that much wider. "You slashed them up for this? Fantastic! But it's like I've always known, Samantha: you make art out of what you have, and out of what you are. We should encase this in plexiglass, or Lucite, better still! Can you imagine it in a block of Lucite? How grand would that be?"

I admitted that I hadn't thought that far ahead, but I liked the idea of it. "Just so long as it wouldn't destroy it."

"On the contrary," she said. "It would preserve it, this moment. You should sign it, and we can take it and get that done, after we're done with pictures."

"Really? Another project?" I asked.

"Yes," she said. "Oh, yes."

We stared at each other a moment, smiling, and then were on each other in a flash, making out to "Ladytron," just standing there, snogging, snarling, tasting each other, smelling each other. She smelled of Chanel No. 5 and a shampoo or lotion that smelled of coconuts. Already taller than me, in her heels, she was a glamazon, and yet I negotiated her to my sofa, while the music pulsed and throbbed.

Reagan and I writhed on my sofa, while Bryan Ferry warbled passionately about growing potatoes. She clawed at me as much as I at her, her immaculately manicured fingernails dancing on my skin, my own hands entwined in her hair, while we kept tasting each other, kept kissing.

"Gretta will kill me," Reagan whispered, bit my ear.

"Not if you kill her first," I said, against her cheek.

She laughed, we laughed, and I hiked her skirt up around her hips, dipped down on her, taking her white cotton panties in my teeth and snapping them off, saw her ginger-colored fur down there and went to work on her, lapping her up thirstily until she came, thin legs quaking against my neck, almost to snap off my head, like a dandelion in between the careless fingers of a child. Her long fingers massaged my hair as I worked on her, to electric throb and saxophone caterwauling, while she howled and moaned beneath and above me. I could feel her fingernails claw at my scalp as her body clenched again, as she climaxed again, and saw a flash of teeth, felt her nails grow longer, her blue eyes flash feral in my own, just a whisper, but I knew the tune, and all of the steps of the dance. Perhaps she didn't even feel it, didn't realize it. She was babbling, talking, growling, and I only had the rush of blood in my ears. Then she pounced on me, sitting up, abruptly, pushing against me, teeth bared, sharp little teeth, delicate, really, and sank them into my trapezius, bit down, hard, and pushed me onto my back. I let her claim me, my legs tucked under themselves, thrusting my hips toward her, looking up at her. She was altogether blonde and wild, looking at me down the end of her patrician nose, eyelids half-open, eyes monstrous. How could she not feel it? Not know?

She had to have known. Her hands went to my breasts and slid against them, and she knelt down, taking my nipple in her teeth, her newfound fangs, tugged on it, then tongued it, and the other, and then ran her tongue down my tight little tummy I was so proud of, her tongue wrapping around my belly button ring, holding, releasing, then down, down, down and she was onto me, into me. Now it was my turn to snarl, for Sääm was awake and alert, watching this young pup have at her. But there was not her usual malice; not tenderness, exactly—because she was endlessly brutal, but there was a sense of entitlement and possession about her, a new sensation, a new emotion. Reagan was one of her own, and Sääm would nurture and protect her, would kill and die for her. There was a communion between us that I had felt with nobody, ever, and it had us both shuddering and weak, left us spent and heaving on my sofa, finding ourselves again, the record needle skipping, waiting for further orders. I walked over on weak knees, flipped the side, while Reagan smoothed her hair, watched me with eyes alight with fire, like she was a jack o'lantern.

"My god, Samantha," she said. "What have you done to me?"

"I'm sorry," I said. I knew what I had done to her, and could only wonder if she truly knew what I had done. I got the album playing again, and we listened to the music a moment, and to our own breathing.

"Apologize? No," she said, stilling me with an outstretched finger. "You are my salvation. My god, Samantha."

I went to the sofa, sat close to her, could smell her on me.

"I wish you didn't have to go back to work," she said.

"Me, neither," I said. "Maybe I shouldn't."

She put her hand on my arm. "No, you should."

"I'm off tomorrow," I said, and she brightened.

"Really? Wonderful. I can just come right over, then," she said. "We can snap a few more shots."

"We haven't snapped any this time," I said, laughing, and Reagan laughed, self-consciously hiding her teeth with her hand. She got up and straightened herself out, wiped her lipstick from my face, got her camera.

"Yes, we should definitely take some pictures," she said. "We still have time."

I wanted to have at her again, and again, and again, but time was a-wasting, so I straightened myself out, too, and went to the white wall, actually in front of the dent and scuff in it, where Sääm had thrown the monitor the night before, and let Reagan shoot me, again and again.

"I'd like to have days and days with you, Samantha," Reagan said, while the shutter clicked, while I posed. "A visit to the Art Institute, a whole fun day together. Gretta has class tomorrow, so we could do it. She'll be hunkered down in Hyde Park. We could have the whole day together, just the two of us."

"That would be great," I thought, wondering if this was how it went with Ansel and Polly, the casual intimacy, the effortlessness of it. Was it that easy? If I claimed Polly for myself, would it be the same between us? I could only wonder.

She finished up with me in 15 minutes, and we left my place, me toting my cityscape, at Reagan's insistence. I had demurred, but she'd insisted, and since the piece was really just my own junk reconfigured, I figured why not? We put it in the back of her vehicle, and I looked up and down the street, which was quiet as ever. It was amazing during the day, how different things looked. I wondered what had caught Sääm's attention. Looking this way and that, I couldn't see it.

Reagan started up her Rover, and I got in next to her, and she had her gloves back on, was putting her lipstick back on in the rearview mirror, while the automobile was heating up.

"Tell me," she said, while she was doing her lipstick. "Was that mop against the board on your window a conceptual art piece? Keeping something out, perhaps?"

"Just the cold," I said. "My landlord is being terribly slow about fixing that window, and it was really cold last night."

"Too bad," she said. "I have this image of you turning your whole apartment into art. What could it be next? I try to do that with my own place. I know it's louche of me to put my own art up on the walls, but until I get a proper space, what else am I to do? It's not like I want to store them. I want to see them, to see what works, what doesn't, the lighting, the composition, how they fill a room."

She drove me back to work, and she touched my leg before I left.

"Thanks, Reagan," I said. "I feel like you heal me."

"You, too, Samantha," she said. "I'll stop by around 10:00 tomorrow, if that's alright."

"Fine," I said, leaning into her, giving her another kiss. No teeth this time; just lips, long and loving, soft, sensuous. She brought a gloved hand to my face, gentle, tender.

We parted, and, breathless, I hopped to the curb, gave her a wave, and she waved back, put her Rover in gear and drove off. I put on some mahogany lipstick and went back to work. Simone couldn't touch me. I told her I was feeling sick.

"What?" she said. "You come in late, you take off for lunch, you tell me you're sick?"

"Something I ate didn't agree with me," I said. "Seriously, I feel like I'm gonna hurl."

I went to her trash can, bent over it, and puked. It wasn't so hard. I just thought of the Chicago River, of drinking it, of the night before. The rest was easy. Breakfast came right up, and Simone freaked out.

"Jesus, Sam," she said. "Take that out of here. Get out of here."

I bagged my barf, clocked out, and walked out of there a free woman. It was amazing what you could get your body to do, if you really put your mind to it.

# 4. TUESDAY AFTERNOON

Once I got home, I dialed up Ansel, managed to actually catch him, for once. "Ansel, you owe me a talk, man. Twenty questions."

"What the hell's going on, Sam?" he asked. "I saw the news, some bit about a wild dog or stray coyote going crazy in the city, attacking people."

"Yeah?" I said.

"You need to get your shit together," he said. "I told you, if you're having problems, don't hesitate to drop by. But you can't go apeshit. Didn't I say that?"

"Look, I need answers, information," I said. "I'm new to this."

"Just keep it under control, would you?" he said. "You don't want people getting panicky. You'd be surprised how small a city can get if the locals get hysterical, how quickly you run out of places to hide."

"Can I just come over?" I said. "I feel weird talking about it over the phone."

"Well, you called me, right?" he said. Then he paused. "Sure, come on over."

I didn't waste any time, having gotten a green light from Ansel. It's not like it was a date, but I wasn't about to let it slide. I snagged my darkest, tightest blue jeans and a bright green ribbed turtleneck, some orange track shoes, and slipped on my blue down vest and my worn leather jacket, popped on my big, white-rimmed shades.

Going outside, I sampled the cold air. It would snow soon; I could taste it. Then I went down to the sidewalk, tucked my hands in my pockets, scuffed my way to the Blue Line, thoughts on myself, on Ansel, on everything. I'd have to call Martin, tell him I lost his stuntcam, assuming I couldn't find it. I'd backtrack again my route I took that night, see if I could find it. I wasn't optimistic, and I sure as hell wasn't going to mention that to Ansel, lest he bitch about that, too. I was kind of surprised my attack on that Polish guy didn't turn up in the paper, adding to my secret infamy. But maybe the *Tribune* didn't care, or the guy never reported it, for fear of looking crazy. That probably was the best werewolf insurance there was, like people being afraid of looking crazy.

That's how I ended up being a guy in a wolf suit, or a fucking coyote or a wild dog. People would see anything but what was actually there. Then again, the people I'd bitten, well, their doctors would diagnose them as being victims of animal bites. Rabies shots all around. Poor bastards. I was sorry about it, but at least they were alive. Being alive was everything.

I hopped on my train, took it downtown, toward Ansel's. During the day, the El traffic was different from rush hour traffic. Not packed, though, like it was during rushes. At one end, some people were doing a three card monte, while the robot voice in the train authoritatively told me that gambling and soliciting was illegal.

I got off the train and walked to Ansel's. It was funny heading there in daylight. The whole area had a different, kind of lackluster vibe by day. Dingy buildings right next to anonymous condominiums in putty-colored rows of concrete and stone. His building blended in wonderfully, and I found myself eyeing the ground floor, envisioning it as a gallery. It had the window space, if he opted for it. It had to be cool, having a capital asset like a building. Man, it was easy to be free if you could pay for the luxury of liberty.

I buzzed him, and he buzzed me in. It had felt like forever since I'd last visited him. And, I guess, it had been. Like two weeks, which was, what, 3 months in dog years? The elevator was waiting for me, and up I went, leaning against the side of it, lost in thought, waiting for the thing to get to his floor. He answered the door, smiling, wearing a dove-gray sweater and a midnight blue collared shirt, dark blue jeans, black dress shoes.

"Hey, Sam," he said, ushering me in. His placed was warm and pleasant in daylight. It had good exposure, caught the light and played with it awhile.

"Wow, it's pretty in here," I said. "Daylight works well in here."

"Yeah," he said. "It's a bitch to preserve my paintings, but I put them in special frames with glass that protects them. You want some wine? Beer? Coffee? Tea?"

"Beer would be fine," I said. Sure, why not? He went to his stainless steel fridge that was easily wider than my apartment door, and got me out a bottle of Fat Tire. "Thanks."

Leaning on his wall was his portrait of Polly. I walked over to it, looked it over. She looked sumptuous, iconic, like she'd been plucked from 1928 and plopped on canvas, pertly pretty, her head tilted downward, eyes looking up, mouth open, a hint of a smile, or a coyly lustful leer. He'd painted the smooth lines of her long legs with great skill, giving her a coltishness she kind of lacked in motion. She'd taken her hands and done a variant on the lean n' squeeze, like hands on the stool, which squeezed her breasts together, the folds of the red cloth draped over one leg and blending with the backdrop. Her black bangs shined at the stroke of Ansel's brush, curled around her face. She looked gorgeous, immortal. I envied Tristan, envied Ansel. I wanted Polly in my bed.

"Wow, you did that fast," I said.

"I was inspired," he said, hands in his pockets. "Her skin is so pale, it's nearly luminescent. Photos don't do her justice; she has to be painted."

"Of course," I said, already sick of hearing about Polly, almost regretting that I'd commented on her painting at all. "What about me? Am I worth a painting?"

"You're a photographic subject," Ansel said. "Fast, fleeting. You catch moments and fling them away like trash. A painting would kill you—or you'd kill the painter trying to capture you."

I took a pull on the beer, nodded, walked around, checked out the place. It all looked the same, just different in the daylight.

"Can't have that," I said, taking off my shades so he could see me. "Somebody killing me, I mean."

"Yeah," he said. "Hey, what happened to your face?"

"Got hit," I said. "Some old dude with a silver-capped fucking cane. It was way worse the other day; you should have seen it."

Ansel whistled. "Yeah, that's a bitch. Gotta watch the codgers sometimes. Young people think they'll live forever, but oldsters have one foot in the grave, and damned if they're not going to try to take you with them."

"Sure," I said. "He gave me a shock, yeah."

"Look, Sam, you need to be prudent as fuck," Ansel said, which almost made me laugh at him. "You have a condition, and the norms... the Villagers, right? They're more numerous. They're the herd, but

252 | D.T. NEAL

herds can stampede, they can trample. Don't underestimate them. I wish I could help you."

"But you won't help me," I said. "You won't teach me."

"It's not rocket science," he said. "It's common sense. Don't be stupid. Don't be greedy. Always, always clean up your messes. Never underestimate the norms. If you waste anybody, don't leave a body."

I wanted answers. I asked questions.

"How long does it take to infect somebody?" I asked, thinking of poor, unsuspecting Reagan.

"Depends on how much harm you do them," Ansel said. "A little nip'll probably take awhile, although look at yourself—I didn't take much out of you, and look what happened. The bigger the bite, the more contact with the blood, the faster the infection."

"Is there a cure?" I asked. Ansel actually laughed.

"What, you want me to say wolfsbane is the way out?" he asked. "Yeah, eat a bunch of that, watch what happens. That shit's poison. Sure, that's the cure—the cure for living. Some norm probably came up with that one in the Middle Ages, like payback for lost relatives. Get real. It's a virus, Sam. There is no cure for it. No vaccine. You want to hang yourself? That won't even cure it—your other half will come right out and stop that one."

"What about silver?" I asked. He looked at my face again, winced.

"Yeah, it'll fuck you up," he said. "I don't know why. I'm not a biochemist, but it somehow causes harm. Stuff that you'd shrug off, you get the same thing by way of silver, and it hurts you. Stay away from it. Let's just call it a severe allergic reaction, and leave it at that."

"How fast will I heal?" I asked.

"Usually, you can heal overnight from anything," he said. "We metabolize stuff real fast, hence the appetite. I don't know how it works, but I've been fucking shot, and the next day, I'm fine. Silver, though, takes longer. You're probably going to have that shiner for a bit longer than you'd like. But there's something in skin-changing that heals. I don't pretend to get it."

"So, if some yokel with a shotgun blazes away at me, I won't die?"

Ansel shook his head. "Unless he's using silver slugs, it's just going to piss you off. Sure, it'll hurt, but it's more like getting stung by rock salt than by a bullet. Even head wounds. I don't know how it works, but it's not going to stop you. Not even close. All it's going to do is make you angrier and deadlier. The worse the pain gets, the wilder you'll get. You'll lose it, if you get hurt bad enough, run on pure instinct, all adrenaline. That's a bad spot to be in."

"So, if I jumped off a building, I wouldn't die?" I asked.

Ansel looked at me with bemusement. "You planning to jump off a building, Sam?"

"I'm just asking," I said.

"I don't know," he said. "I doubt it would kill you, frankly. It might hurt you, might even knock you flat out, but I don't think it would kill you. I haven't known any lupines who've done it. I mean, who really wants to test that? Then again, any fool lupines who did it are dead, and when we're dead, we look like anybody else."

"What about the moon?"

Ansel sighed. "It happens. I don't get that, either. Like I said before, you can change any time you like, any time you get wound up, so try not to. Anything—sex, violence, fear, anger—anything can trigger it. But come that full moon, there's something else—that's all-nighter time, like you just will go and go until it's done, and there's next to nothing you can do about it. Me, I lock myself up. That's also when you're least in control of who you are, or were."

"Am I, you know, bound to you?" I asked. I hated even asking that, but I had to know.

"There's always a bond with the sire," he said. "The source of your infection. Yeah, it's there. I know you feel it with me. We'll always have that. I don't know why it is, but it's there."

"Nobody bit you," I said. "You were born this way, right?"

"Yeah," he said. "I'm all-natural. You're infected. Natives are rare, infectives are more common, even though infectives are usually fucking stupid and get themselves killed more often, because they can't handle it."

"So-REE," I said, rolling my eyes. Or my eye, since my other one was still a mess. "What about the drugs you take?"

"Tranqs, mostly," he said. "I've built up wicked tolerance over the years, trying to keep it under. It doesn't stop it, but keeps me on an even keel more often than not, less likely to lose my shit and kill people."

"Have you killed people?" I asked.

"Of course," he said. "Who hasn't? It's not easy, but it happens. People die all the time. People are killed all the time."

"Doesn't it bother you?" I asked.

"Sure," he said. "Of course. Yeah. But I'm not going to give up my life and liberty because of somebody else. And nobody can prove anything. That's the truth of it. Because I'm careful. People just disappear. Hell, more people disappear than are killed. They just vanish."

"Christ," I said. "Do you eat them?"

"Yeah," he said, leaning against his kitchen countertop, arms folded, looking world-wearier than usual. "Of course. Kill and eat. Kill and eat. Load, wash, rinse, repeat."

"Fuck," I said. "Cannibal."

Ansel laughed, held up a finger. "Cannibals eat their own. I'm not human, Sam. Not anymore. I look like a person, but I'm not. Neither are you. You'll get that more and more with time. I mean, we're people, but we're not human—we're wearing camouflage."

Thirteen questions. I'd kept track in my head, wondered if he had been, too.

"When's the last time you killed somebody?" I asked.

"Last week," he said.

That made me freeze, made my heart go cold. I could smell him, smell his cologne, and knew he wasn't lying.

"Last week?" I asked. "Who the hell did you kill?"

"Your doctor," he said. "Resnick."

"What? Christ, Ansel, why in the hell did you do that? What the fuck were you doing?"

"Self-defense," he said. "You didn't see it in the news?"

"I don't watch much television," I said, feeling sick. Poor Dr. Resnick.

"Resnick died in a fire," Ansel said. "Authorities suspect arson. But it was me. I paid him a visit. I couldn't have him taking that blood sample to a lab for analysis. I couldn't have him bringing you in, and then it getting back to me. It wasn't going to happen. I went in there and I cleaned house. Had to be done. It's my own fault, but it had to be done."

He was completely at ease with it, maybe a little apologetic about it, but also dreadfully matter-of-fact about it. I was terrified, couldn't believe it. Didn't want to. He read my expression, shrugged.

"Sam, we're past all of that," he said. "Slave morality, right? What your little peanut friends talk about; I'm living it. We're living it. But not the slave morality; the master morality. That's what we're living. I try, I really try to not hurt people. You don't even know how hard I try. But it happens, and am I going to cry over it? Ruin my life? Lose sleep? Nope. They're prey to me; meat."

"What about Polly? Is she prey?" I asked.

"Your twenty questions are up, Sam," he said. "No, she's not prey. She's special to me, sure. I agree with you, there. You are, too, believe it or not. You both are. I don't even know why, but I get you both. It's funny, because I accidentally made you into a werewolf, and there you are still trying to be all human; and there's Polly, who I've held back on, and she's more wolfen than maybe you'll ever be. Ironic, eh?"

"Yeah," I said. "People aren't meat, Ansel."

"We're all meat," he said. "Meat is all we are, all we will ever be. You'll get that, sooner or later. The first time the hunger overtakes you for real, the first time you slip up. The hunger is closer to you than anything you're going to experience, closer to you than anybody. The Beast is hunger. It's like pressure building; it will build until it overtakes you, if you don't let off steam, somehow. It's not food it's looking for—it's slaughter. It's death and mayhem. Every dog has its day. It will sneak out at night, it'll do whatever it takes to get that fix. The ones who try to hold out longest are the ones who get it the worst, the ones who go craziest."

He let that hang there, looked at me, those seemingly guileless eyes, flat, like a doll's. What had he done to me? What had I done to Reagan? I couldn't even explain it to her, and even if I did, she'd never forgive me. It was worse than careless; it was criminal. My heart might as well have been pinned to my jacket. Ansel could read me.

"You bit somebody?" he asked, then laughed, shaking his head. "Nice one, Sam. So you know just how I feel, then."

I folded my hands under my arms, because they were sweating. Ansel stepped forward, put a hand on my shoulder. A strong hand.

"Everybody wants to live," he said. "Everybody. Whoever you infected, they'll get it, and they'll get over it. This isn't a death sentence, Sam. Or it doesn't have to be. You'll never get sick again, and you won't have to worry about nearly anything killing you. You might not be able to ever be who you were, but is that so bad? You're better, now."

I wanted to cry, but wouldn't do it in front of him. I was so pissed at him, so embarrassed, so angry at myself.

"The important thing is to be there for them," he said. "To support them. The ones you infected."

"Liar," I said. "You don't even care. You fucking blew me off. You haven't been there for me."

Ansel looked almost hurt, almost.

"I'm here now," he said, softly.

I'm sure he'd endured worse. I hated to think of Reagan going through what I was going through, but who knew? Maybe she'd be alright. Maybe she would fight it off. Maybe she'd apply her self-discipline and control to her condition, emerge better than before. Maybe she'd kill herself. Christ.

"I can't fix you, Sam," he said. "It's up to you to fix yourself, to make yourself right. What's fucking you up is that you're busy trying to be two people. Look, I know all of this, have seen it. You are only you. That's who you need to be. Maybe it's a new you, maybe it's not the 'you' you were a month ago, but that is your anchor—that is your leash. If you don't find that, you will become a monster, like the very worst sort of thing you imagine. Like that crazy trucker fucker at the border."

He was sincere, which freaked me out, given what he'd said and done. I mean, what was a monster to somebody like Ansel? He managed an almost casual monstrosity, and I could only think of the banality of evil as I looked at him. Evil was this careless, thoughtless, murderous half-man in front of me.

"But you killed Dr. Resnick," I said, pulling away from him.

"Self preservation," Ansel said. "You think I want NIH kicking down my door? Homeland-fucking-Security? Resnick runs his samples, asks around, publishes a paper, you get a knock on your door, they torture you or pump you full of drugs, and the trail leads straight to me. End of the line. End of *our* lives, Sam. And you think NIH doesn't already have samples? I'm sure they do. They have to have caught lupines in the past, run them through their centrifuges. Dissected them, vivisected them. Autopsies, necropsies, slides, cells. Maybe they want to make super-soldiers someday. Maybe that's what my grandfather was working on during World War II. So, what's the point in them nabbing us? Nothing, just the end of our lives. Maybe they suspended habeas corpus for that kind of thing—snatch and grab, dead of night. Nazi shit, you know? I know Nazi shit. Night and fog, Sam. Night and fog. Secrets are made to be kept. I burned his lab to destroy his files, to cover up, yeah, his murder. I don't know if he got that sample out, or not. I acted on it the day you told me about it."

I hated to think of poor Dr. Resnick, whose only sin was trying to help me. "Christ, Ansel."

Ansel just looked at me, those blue eyes as inscrutable as a couple of buttons. There was just no way of getting past them, of reading them, of understanding them. His eyes were an abyss looking into me.

"Look, I should have just told you flat out about what I'd done to you, so you'd know. But you'd have thought I was nuts. Hell, if I'd been really right about saving my own ass, I'd have killed you once I realized I'd lost it and bit you. I didn't want to, though. I like you, Sam."

I didn't know what to think. Would I end up like him, quietly ruthless, laconically brutal? Was I getting there already? Reagan swam into my head, I imagined her looking in the mirror, checking her lip where I'd nipped her. It was barely a bite, hardly qualified. I imagined her sprouting fur and fangs, bashing mirrors in her palatial home, breaking plates, stabbing herself in the eyes with silver flatware.

"Christ, Ansel," I said. "I come here for comfort, and you end up just freaking me out more. We're still human."

He shook his head. "No, we're not. We only look the part to do what we have to do. People don't do what we do. They can't do what we do. We're special. It's a gift, more than it's a curse, really. You have to think about it that way, or you *will* go nuts. Seriously, listen to me when I say you have to manage it, or the first thing it'll eat up is you. The harder you fight it, the harder it bites back. I've seen it, and it's especially bad with infectives, because there's that shock, you know? The adjustment to the new lifestyle."

"Lifestyle," I said, scoffing. I set down the beer, didn't want another drink of it. He was supposed to be my mentor, but he just made me frightened and confused.

"Yeah," Ansel said. "You can manage it, but you just have to be smart about it, to know what you're doing, where you are, to keep a cool head. It's like playing poker, in a way, all the time. You just keep your head about you, don't let anybody see your hand."

"I'm terrible at poker," I said, sighing. "My face is a billboard."

He laughed. "Yeah, it is. That's what's great about you, Sam. You're so open. That's why you get so easily bruised. You just lay yourself out to the world, and get amazed when the world hurts you."

I managed a smile, and Ansel came over and hugged me, and I buried my unwounded half of my face in his chest. I could feel his chin lightly resting on top of my head. I love him, and I hated him.

"I'm going to need more than 20 questions," I said.

"I know," he said.

"Do werewolves kill other werewolves?" I asked, wondering if Ansel would kill me as casually as he'd killed Dr. Resnick.

"All the time," he said. "But usually it's when they're not from the same pack. Packs share bloodlines. Not just siblings and cousins, but the chain of infection. Like me and you, we're part of the same pack. And the person you bit; they'll be part of our pack, too. Now, if some other lupine comes into my territory, then there's a situation."

The talk of territory galled me, it made Ansel sound like a gangster. That's what he was, really, in that moment I was sure, against his chest. I was in his mafia. I'd been made. There was some warped semblance of honor in him, and that was that. It helped me understand him, to get his casual, affable amorality.

"What do you do when they show up?" I asked.

"Drive them out," he said. "I can't have somebody else hunting in my area. But luckily, there aren't enough of us around for that to come up too often."

I wondered what would happen if there were a whole bunch of werewolves out there. Would it be a bloody Hobbesian war of all against all, waged in tooth and claw? Or would an order arise? What if everybody were part of the same pack? Then what would happen?

*Peace on earth,* Sääm whispered in between my ears. *Détente ala loup-garou.*

Her amusement was palpable, made me squirm. Ansel let me go.

"We good, Sam?"

"We evil, Ansel," I said. "We bad."

"Yeah, pretty much."

My phone rang, and I picked it up. It was Martin. I glanced at Ansel, held up a finger, and answered my phone.

"Hey, Martin, sup?"

"Nothing," he said. "Hey, how'd the camera work out?"

"Great," I said. "Except for one thing: I lost it."

"What? What happened?"

Ansel watched me, which made me self-conscious. I turned my back to him. "I, uh, had an accident while rollerblading, and the helmet came off. I've been looking for it, but couldn't find it."

"Damn," he said. "That sucks. Well, you owe me $130, if you can't find it."

"Okay," I said. "I'll get that to you. So sorry, Martin."

"No problem," he said. "Must've been a helluva wipeout."

"Yeah," I said. "You should see my face."

"Did you lose a lot of footage?" he asked. He was always obsessed with footage, with getting the shot.

"Yeah," I said. "Like an hour's worth, I think."

"Ouch," he said. "That sucks even worse."

"I'll survive," I said. "Alright, I'll get that $130 to you later this week, okay?"

He agreed, and I hung up, turned back around. Ansel had gone into the kitchen, sat on a barstool, drank the rest of the beer he'd given me.

"That footage is a problem," he said. "You really couldn't find that camera?"

"Nope," I said. "I looked everywhere for it, retraced my steps, but it wasn't there. Some bum probably picked it up."

He shook his head, laughing. "I can't believe you went out like that. A werewolf in a stunt helmet? Oh, man. They probably thought you were Skates, the mascot for the Chicago Wolves, run amok. That'd be great."

The AHL team in Chicago was the Wolves. That caught me offguard, made me laugh, and he laughed, too. I flushed, got a little defensive.

"What, only ripped blue jeans is acceptable werewolf clothes? I wanted to do a project, but it got messed up. That's all."

"I wouldn't do that kind of thing again," he said. "I mean, your YouTube video was cute as a one-off, but that's not the kind of thing you make a habit of. It's like those dumbass kids who commit crimes and camcord themselves, and then they get busted, and there it all is, on tape. Word-of-mouth is our best defense, because nobody believes we exist. You keep taping yourself, it'll raise your profile too much, and make things bad for you."

He dug out a money clip from his jeans, took out a hundred, a twenty, a ten.

"No, no," I said. "I've got it."

"Take it, Sam," he said. "It's the least I can do."

I took the money. Why not? He was loaded, I was poor. It made him seem more of a gangster to me, fit with my new conception of him. A gangster, or my dad.

"Hey, did you ever get the prints of us dancing?" I asked, glancing around his place.

"Yeah," he said. "Want to see them?"

I nodded, and he walked me to the far side of his place. He'd gotten four plates printed, on aluminum, as he'd intended. They were stylized, colorized, but it was us dancing, Polly and me. It looked cool. We looked awesome.

"Wow," I said. "I like how you brought up the color and emphasized the geometry of our shapes."

"Yeah," he said. "I photoshopped the hell out of the images, to get them where I thought they should be. Polly in red, you in white, the background in black. It came out better than I'd hoped. I'm thinking of hanging them in the windows downstairs. I decided the gallery idea's not a bad one, I'm totally going to do it. Sure beats that armpit of a place you guys have been using to date."

"What are you going to call it?"

He shrugged. "I don't know, yet. Not Ansel Rupino Gallery."

"How about Polychroma?"

"Sure, why not?" he said. "Polly would love that."

"Yeah," I said. "She loves everything that plays off her name. She used to say if she had been in a new wave band, she'd have named herself Polly Gone."

"That's a good punk name," Ansel said.

"Yeah, it is. Polly's always full of great ideas," I said. "You're not really going to make her, are you?"

"Did I say I was?" he asked. "It's tempting, but you're causing me enough trouble right now; I hardly need the trouble she'd bring to the table."

"Sorry," I said, hated myself for actually being sorry. Like I owed him or something. I mean, he spotted me $130, yeah, but he owed me for turning me into a monster, and I hated that I felt somehow indebted to him, despite it.

"Speaking of trouble: the full moon's on the 24th," he said, glancing at his watch. "You should come here. It'll be like we're camping."

"Won't we tear ourselves apart in your little cage?" I asked. I could imagine a righteous cage match.

"Oh, no," Ansel said. "We won't be doing that."

I remembered the last time we transformed together, how that went.

"Oh," I said. "Yeah, well, tempting, but I don't know, Ansel."

He nodded, accepted that.

"I mean, Polly," I said.

"Polly's not going to be anywhere near here on the 24th," Ansel said. "No way. The alternative is, what? You rampaging all over town? You think you can control yourself? Because I don't think you can. I think if you're out and about, you're going to kill somebody, and you're going to eat them, and I don't know if you can handle that at this point."

What a choice.

Dogfucked by Ansel all night or going on a cannibalistic murder spree.

Welcome to my world.

# 4. TUESDAY EVENING

I left Ansel feeling more concerned and confused than ever, took my train home. Another day wasted, never to return again. I made my way to the El, my head in the clouds. The platform was dry for once tonight, winter-crispness in the air, a bit of a breeze. The steps were old, the barrier fencing painted dirty white, rust pooling at the bottoms. It spoke of age and neglect. I went along it to the steps, and saw a Xerox handout tacked to the wall. It was a snarling wolf. Below it, in big block letters:

*Wilkołak!*

I stared at the thing, took my shades and popped them on my forehead, to get a better look at it. The wolf gaped at me with wild, savage eyes, the mouth was opened wide, revealing fangs. It wasn't possible. That was the word that the old man used when he'd seen me. There wasn't much doubt as to what it meant. I took the handout down and folded it up, put it in my pocket. Then I went down the steps, looking around, feeling more wary than ever. There was another one on a phone pole outside of the El station.

"Christ," I said, looking around. I tucked my shades back down on my face, felt like the whole city was watching me.

*Wilkołak!*

I walked down the street, my eyes out for any more of the handbills. There were a half-dozen more, right next to handbills for the Suck Junkies and the Dung Vultures, who were apparently playing at Salome. When I got to my street, I saw still another of those handbills. By now, I was sweating more than ever, breathing heavily, paranoid. And then down the sidewalk, to my building. The phone pole outside of my apartment building had another of the handbills, only this one had a pair of dimes taped to its eyes with X's of Scotch tape.

264 | D.T. NEAL

I stared at the thing, held up my phone camera, snapped a shot of it, then looked up and down the street. The cars were all dark, lit only by sporadic streetlights. Then I walked down past my building, to see if the handbills continued, and to see if anybody was watching. Christ. The old man had gotten the camera. Probably passed it along to his Polish Mafia friends, cashed in on some favors. I walked down to the end of my block, then turned a corner, went back up the other way, across the street. The poles were bare.

They followed the trail to my doorstep. Every car was a hulking, threatening thing, black, full of menace. No. They should be afraid of me. They're the fucking norms. As I went back up my street, I dared a glance at my building, saw that Mr. Ludovico had finally replaced the fucking window. Thank godless.

Of course, anybody hiding out would have seen me circling the block like an idiot, or like a werewolf on the make. I went a block over, then cut into the service alley, approached my building from behind.

I'm sure the watchers probably covered that way, too, although I didn't see anybody, and I listened in the shadows, waited, sniffing the air, cautious, alert, unseen. My phone rang, making me yelp. I grabbed it, quickly cutting off the chirp. It was Polly. I let the voice-mail get it, stuffed the thing back into my pocket, then crept across the alley, went up the fire escape, got into my building that way.

Then I snuck down my hallway, feeling exposed in the glow of the lights, keyed into my place, careful, quiet. I waited in the dark, listened. No hulking Pole behind my door, silver garrote in his meaty hands. Nobody in my place.

Fuck.

If they knew where I was, why did they bother with the handbills? What possible purpose did it serve? I had to call Ansel. I rang him up, but he didn't answer, I went to voicemail.

"Ansel," I said, in a whisper. "It's Sam. I think somebody's, I dunno, onto me. Somebody posted handbills in my neighborhood, right outside my fucking building."

I thumbed a send of the picture, so he could see it. Grainy, but the grimacing wolf with coins for eyes showed up.

"What the fuck am I supposed to do? Why would they do that? Please, help me out."

Then I hung up, crawled over to my window, peeked out. My street was empty, just parked cars. I couldn't see anybody. Why would they post that? Was it a warning to other Poles, like "Beware of the werewolf?"

I took out the handbill and unfolded it, spread it out, stared at the wolf looking back at me. If they suspected something, why not call the police? Or maybe that wasn't how it was done. Christ. A van cruised down my street, slowly, looking for parking. It paused in front of my building, then slid up the street.

In Poland, werewolf hunters bite YOU.

I turned on my lights, took off my jacket and gloves and hat, then I went online, using my phone. I didn't even know what to look for—didn't even know who was after me. I googled *"Wilkołak"* just to see what turned up. There were over 100,000 hits, people with that as a last name, some death metal band, a wikipedia entry, and so on. Nothing that jumped out at me.

Not like whoever was harassing me was going to be so easy to find. Not like I'd be easy to find, either. They didn't know I came from this building, only that the video started on this street. The only way they'd be able to track me down would be if they conducted surveillance of the neighborhood, like constantly, monitored the coming and going of everybody. I couldn't imagine even somebody able to do that who wasn't the government. Maybe they were the government.

Zooey would be here soon. I hated that I had something else to worry about, when I only wanted to have a little fun. Of course, meeting Zooey would be weird; she'd be the first online person I'd ever met. I wondered how she'd take the whole "Hey, Sam, you're a goddamned werewolf" thing. I heard another car cruise up my street, listened to it cruise by. Everything was suddenly pregnant with menace. My nerves were flayed.

*What's wrong with you? You're the goddamned werewolf. You should sneak out there and ambush those bastards, if they're even out there. Climb a tree, wait them out. They turn up, you get out there and fucking kill them.*

*A little sloppy, yes?*

*Let me handle the killing; you handle clean-up.*

*That sucks.*

*Beats being fucking dead. Or do you want to die? Maybe you could just sit on your front steps, transform, and howl at the moon until they come and blow you away.*

*No.*

Then bear with me, Princess. No defense like a good offense, right? We wait, we watch, they show up, we kill them. You drive their sedan to, I dunno, Calumet City. Leave the keys. Nobody's the wiser.

That image horrified me, me in this blood-soaked car, full of corpses. How casually she contemplated it. How casually I considered it.

How about this image?

Sääm conjured me hanging from a tree, with the *"Wilkołak!"* handbill pinned through my nose with a silver safety pin.

*At least then I'd be a victim, and not a perpetrator.*

That pissed her off. She actually bristled.

*A victim. Christ, what bad luck I have, to be stuck in somebody like you. You think Polly would settle for that? Reagan? Zooey? No. Christ, you're pathetic. Norms are victims. You want to be a victim all your life?*

*I don't want to kill anybody.*

*Ansel had it right: self-fucking-preservation. Self-defense. Whoever's out there wants to kill you. They will kill you.*

*I can call the cops, say guys are stalking me.*

*For all we know, those Polskis have friends on the force. You might as well telegraph who you are, then. Here I am, come kill me, pretty please?*

*What if I find they're just, I dunno, sitting in their car for some reason? What if I get the wrong people?*

It was so much work being a werewolf. Fuck, I didn't know how people could stand it. You had to think about everything, couldn't just, you know, space out. Couldn't do normal things. Couldn't really, truly blend in. Not here, not anywhere.

*Poor baby. Let me worry about the Polskis. You worry about, I dunno, getting Ansel to bone you, or winning the girls over. Or some crap-ass piece of performance art. Like, how about "Apocalypse Know"—where you make an evening dress out of Webster's dictionary pages, and then promenade onstage reading "Heart of Darkness" and then have sex with one of your audience members?*

*Thanks for the suggestion. I have to live with what you do, Sääm.*

*Well and good, but I won't die for what you won't do.*

It was impossible to argue with her, because, of course, she was me. I was the one being unreasonable, being insane, wimpy, craven.

*If I'm attacked, I'll defend myself, I thought. At least then, I'm giving them the benefit of a doubt.*

Sääm laughed harshly in my head.

*By then, it might be too late. These goons know what you are; they don't (yet) know who you are, because if they did, you'd probably already be dead.*

*That's an advantage that could mean life or death for you, Puddin. You think they haven't come prepared? They probably have bandoliers of silver bullets. They're coming for you, Princess. Though you won't accept this, I'm on your fucking team. Who are those people to me? Nothing. Who are you to me? Everything. I can't exist without you.*

It was an almost touching admission on her part. I got that. But what she insisted upon was more than I was prepared to give.

*Then you're already dead. You'd have made a bitchin' zombie. Walking fucking dead.*

*There's more to life than surviving.*

*No, there isn't. Walk into a morgue, find meaning in there. All you'll feel is "Wow, glad I'm not dead, yet. Sucks to be them."*

*How you live matters as much as living, itself. That's why I'm an artist.*

*Uh, yeah. You want art? I'll give you art. The whole world's my canvas. Let me paint on it—people are my canvas, my claws are my brushes, their blood is my paint, death is my subject.*

*That's not art; it's profanity, it's bloodshed, it's slaughter.*

*Art is all of those things. Art is more than your ego, more than your flake friends, more than the materials you use. Art is what you create. So I create mayhem; it's still something. I guarantee people will feel more alive, more grateful for being alive, once they realize I'm out there. I'll shock them out of their stupor, out of their zombified existence. You think those Polish pricks are unhappy right now? They're fucking thrilled. They have something to push against, something to give them nightmares, something to remind them why they're alive. They are living for the first time in years. That's because of me.*

She imagined these beefy fellows in a black van, buzzed hair, a few with mustaches, checking revolvers filled with silver bullets, fucking magnums, big guns, neckties almost as wide as their necks, watching passerby, muttering to each other in Polish, a few with silver daggers. A secret society, medieval in origin, dedicated to the end of lycanthropes.

*I've made more than their day; I've made their lives. You think that's not art? You take those Judeo-Christian values, that moral frosting you like rotting your teeth with, and junk it. Jesus, who needs it? The prey need predators; it makes them stronger. Your pal Clay's boyfriend, Nietzsche, right? "That which does not kill you makes you stronger." The old boy had it right. The downside of it: "That which spares you makes you weaker." Get it? You think you're doing the right thing by wussing out on this whole thing, but you're not. You're not doing yourself any favors, and you're not doing the world any favors. Get out there, make a fucking killing.*

She fell silent in my head. Whatever her nature, her will to live was undeniable, her passion was unmistakable. I wanted that passion. Why did it have to be tied to something horrible, what she wanted?

*Boo hoo hoo, what would Jesus do?*

I didn't need it, not right now. I went back to the window, looked out, didn't see anybody out of place. My phone rang. It was Polly. This time, I picked up.

"Hey," I said.

"Hi, Sam," she said. "Tristan's at the gym, so I thought I'd call you. Have you seen Ansel?"

"I was over there, yeah," I said. "I saw his painting of you."

That seemed to please her. "Isn't it amazing? Isn't he incredible?"

"He's something else," I said. "You figure out what you're going to do with that painting, yet?"

"I want it so bad," she said. "But it does give me an excuse to go over there."

I wanted to laugh at that, like imagining her coming up with some pretext for her pretext, like not telling Ansel she wanted to stare at his painting of her. I wonder if she thought of herself while she was doing him.

"Did he show you the aluminum prints he made of us?" I asked.

"No," she said. "They hadn't arrived the last time I was there."

"Yeah, well they look great," I said. "He's going to put them in the windows of his gallery. I think he's going to do it."

"Cool," she said. "Wow, it sounds like you guys talked about a lot."

"Oh, we did," I said, smiling to myself; if only she knew. "He's going to name it 'Polychroma.'"

She actually squealed. "That's awesome! Oh, I love it."

"I thought you might," I said. "I came up with it."

"Really? It's awesome, Sam," she said. "You're the best. I love that name."

"Yeah," I said. "Hey, are you going to Amaranth?"

"Why, is something happening?"

"Oh, Reagan said Lee said people were going," I said. "Actually, Reagan's not going; she's pissed at Lee."

She paused. I could almost hear her being perturbed, the inrush of air between parted teeth, the click of her tongue.

"Really? I hadn't heard. Gee, are we exiled, or what? The Wrath of Lee?"

"Seems that way," I said. I paced to my window, peeking out. I saw a white van gliding up the street, slowly, watched the thing make its way. "I didn't get called either. I think we're in the doghouse."

"Fuck Lee," Polly said. "Seriously. It's a no-brainer for me: Lee or Ansel? Hah!"

I laughed, kept my eye on the van, watched it slowly round the corner. Were they out there? Were they watching me? Did they even know it was me? If they saw my bruised face, they'd know, sure enough. That was part of it, I bet: flushing me out, trying to spook me, so I'd do something dumb (or dumber) and they'd ambush me.

"Yeah, I'm the same way," I said. "I haven't talked to Lee about it, but yeah. They're probably auditioning replacements for us."

"Fuck them," Polly said. "If you, Reagan, and I left them, they'd be nothing. Can you imagine? Lee, Clay, Gabe, Willa, and Sheldon? Lame."

"I don't know about that," I said. Sure, Polly and I handled most of the Web stuff for Horrorshow, but I don't know. Lee was tech-savvy, just not terribly imaginative. He managed wit and cleverness without imagination. It was an odd matching.

"Oh, please," Polly said. "He's lucky we stayed around as long as we did."

I liked how Polly included me in those ranks, since I always thought myself as more of mascot for the group than a founding member. The founding members were Lee, Gabe, Willa, and Polly. Then Reagan, Sheldon, Clay, and me. They had originally been all poets and writers, before they allowed the rest of us in.

"If Ansel goes forward with Polychroma," I said. "We can have our own group."

"That would rock," Polly said. "I could get some poems printed up, matted and framed."

"Uh, yeah," I said. "Anyway, I'm tempted to give Lee some crap about not getting the invite."

The white van came back down my street, slow, steady. There still wasn't any more parking, guys. I couldn't see the driver, it was too dark. The van cruised back down the street, went around the corner.

In Poland, van drives YOU!

I stepped away from the window, felt exposed, wanted to turn off the lights, hide on the floor. I wanted to be someplace else. Were they out there? Were they waiting?

"Go ahead," Polly said. "Tristan's taking me out tomorrow, anyway. We're going to the Signature Room. He loves that place."

"Should be fun," I said. Ah, yes. Tristan.

My text messaging pinged on my phone. It was Zipstrip.

*Zipstrip: Hi! I got my bus ticket! I'm siked!*

*Säämurai: Hey, you!* ☺

*Zipstrip:* ☺

*Säämurai: What time are you reaching Chicago?*

*Zipstrip: About 3:30 on Friday. Is that a problem? I didn't want to get in too late.*

*Säämurai: No problem. I'll skip out early from work.*

*Zipstrip: Kewl!*

"Yeah, but it's such a boring place," Polly said. "So, I don't know, mun-danely wonderful."

"You were hoping for what, Alinea?" I asked.

"Yes," she said. "Something extraordinary. But Tristan loves the Signature Room. Ansel would take me to Alinea."

"Ansel would take you to Valhalla's," I said, referring to another place in the City, one specializing in Scandinavian fine dining.

*Säämurai: I'm looking forward to seeing you.*

*Zipstrip: Me, too. What do you want to do?*

*Säämurai: Once we meet, I dunno; we could go clubbing.*

*Zipstrip: Fun!*

*Säämurai: And then, you know, eating somewhere.*

*Zipstrip: Also good!*

*Säämurai: After that, we can crash at my place.*

*Zipstrip: Better still! I'm siked!*

*Säämurai: Okay, well I'll be in the station, looking for you. Let me send you a picture, so you recognize me.*

I snapped a phonecam picture of myself, turning my head so my bruised face wasn't as evident. I checked it, then shot another one, until I had it right. Once I determined that picture was alright, I sent it to Zooey.

"I'd even like Valhalla," Polly said. She was one of those people who was a bit of a grammar nazi; she hated the Chicagoan tendency to add the "s" at the end of things that didn't have them. She'd not come out and say "It's not that," but instead would lead by example, using it correctly in a follow up statement.

"When's Tristan out of town next?" I asked.

"After Thanksgiving," Polly said. "He's going to Seoul for a week-and-a-half."

"Poor guy goes around the world for you," I said. I imagined Polly would actually have Ansel over, would fuck him in her own bed. I could just see that. Poor Tristan. Thanksgiving was coming up fast.

I realized that I didn't have any plans. My folks lived in Boston. I wasn't planning to get out there to see them this year. I'd have to sniff around, see what was going on. Reagan would surely have something going on, although she usually got invitations out early, if she was doing something. Maybe she was going out of town with Gretta.

"Yeah, poor Tristan," Polly said, a trifle sarcastically. "I'm such a bitch."

*Zipstrip: Great picture! UR so cute!*

*Säämurai: Thx.*

I could never, ever escape "cute," see? I'd posted one of my fiery red-haired pictures on Hot or Not? and scored an 8.8 on their 10-point hotness scale. 8.8 must equal cute, because that's what I was. I could just imagine what Zooey would think when she saw my bruised-up face. Bruises were never cute; bruises demanded explanation, and explanation killed "cute" dead.

"I'm just saying, Tristan works hard for you," I said.

"Yeah, and I'm there for him when he's around," Polly said. "What else can I do?"

I wanted to tell her "be faithful," but it sounded so prudish, so schoolmarm of me. So I didn't say anything. All too often, I held my tongue, and I think the others did, too, because we were supposed to be these great libertines, and nothing was supposed to offend the sensibilities of a true libertine.

*Zipstrip: Cute is good, right?*

*Säämurai: Everybody calls me it, that's all. I'm used to it.*

*Zipstrip: Well, you are!*

I wasn't a libertine; I was a glibertine. Why should it matter to me if Polly cheated on Tristan? It was their thing, their business, not mine.

"Do you love him?" I asked, thinking of Tristan. I remember Lee referring to him as "Dristan" when Polly wasn't around, called him a drip.

"Ansel? I don't know," she said. "I lust for him, I'll say that much."

"I mean Tristan," I said.

"Well, of course," she said. "Silly Sam."

*Zipstrip: Cute is great!*

*Säämurai: If you say so. I wiped out rollerblading the other day, bruised up my face.*

*Zipstrip: I couldn't tell from the photo.*

*Säämurai: Yeah, the right side got hit.*

*Zipstrip: I'll kiss it, make it better.*

I had little doubt that she would, judging from the pix Zooey sent me. Pertly pretty, prettier than me, long face, crazy lavender bangs, dark eyes, a nose ring, a curious, open expression. Young, perfect. She was curled up in the picture she sent me, peeking at me over her knees, wearing white tube sox with blue and yellow strips at the top, and high-top Chuck Taylors, colored acid green.

If I wasn't so greedy and lonely, I'd have told her to stay the hell away from me. But she was a friend, even if just a ghost. She needed to be far away from me, not up close. Up close she could be hurt. By me. By Ansel. By the *Wilkołak* Brothers. By Polly. By anybody. Looking into her black eyes, I wanted to shelter her. Sääm just wanted to fuck her. I mean, she'd coined her name, and what better way to show her appreciation. And to bite her. What?

*Yeah. She's perfect. Like a wounded angel. I can heal her, make her whole.* No.

"Yeah, that's me," I said, to Polly. "Silly fucking Sam."

Sääm made my fingers do the walking on the keypad, and I let her. I didn't want my wounded angel to fly away on her broken wings.

*Säämurai: I'd love that.*

*Zipstrip:* ☺

*Säämurai:* ☺

"They're special in different ways," Polly said. "Tristan's, you know, bedrock. Whereas Ansel, well, he's magma."

"Volcanic," I said. "Can I be pumice?"

"Yes," she said, brightly. "You exfoliate me."

"And leave you with smooth, shiny skin," I said.

"Lee's sulfur," she said. "Yellow and malodorous."

We laughed, and some semblance of balance was restored.

*Säämurai: I'll see you Friday.*

*Zipstrip: Can't wait.*

*Säämurai: Bye.*

*Zipstrip: Bye.*

I wouldn't be able to control myself. I was nearly sure of that. Sääm wouldn't let me. She wanted her. She wanted Polly, too. She was endlessly voracious.

"Yeah, Lee stinks, alright," I said.

"And he's done nothing to deserve the limitless self-regard he has," she said. "I mean, yeah, he's been published, but that was several years ago. What's he done recently? He acts like he's above it, now, after having gotten his gold star like five years ago."

The poets were always at each others' throats that way, and as a multimedia artist, I was fortunately free of that—they all held me in such glorious contempt. Polly self-published, created chapbooks that she hawked on the Net, on her blog. She had a dozen of them out there in the ether. The chapbook was the bastard stepchild of the zine, or that was how Lee put it, even though chapbooks went back centuries (Polly and Sheldon were quick to remind him), and that neither of them embraced them today to be trendy, of course, but rather, as an authentic mode of expression. From my perspective, it was a cheap way of getting out there, but I kind of agreed (quietly) with Lee that self-publishing felt a little like masturbation, amounted to a vanity press, but I'd never say that to Polly, because she'd have flown into a button-nosed little rage over it, and it would have made things socially difficult for me.

"He's not you, that's for sure," I said.

On reflection, I was in a curious position in Anselgate—I felt like I was not fully committed to either side. I might be able to keep the peace between the factions, to play the diplomat. I wondered what Lee would say if I showed up at his door. I thought it might be worth an exploration.

"Alright, Sam," Polly said. "I'll let you go. Looks like Tristan's done with his treadmill."

"Alright, Pol," I said. "Let me know what you plan to do about that portrait."

"I will," she said.

My stomach was growling. I was hungry, wanted to get something to eat, didn't like my options at home, didn't want to stay cooped up in my apartment, like some kind of prisoner. I put on some dark blue jeans with gilt ballet flats, and a blousy grey sweater with an orange scarf, wrapped myself in a white furry-collared fishtail parka, put a cute little pair of pink earmuffs on, and went out. I wrapped a muffler around my face, put on my shades, thought I looked anonymous enough to pass on the street without the *Wilkołak* Brothers coming for me. I tried to breezily pass down the street, noting that handbill flapping in the wind on the phone pole outside of my building, but not pausing. I just walked city-confidently, steadily, eyes forward, face blank. I wished I'd brought my headphones, for some music, but didn't want to distract myself, wanted to attentive to what was around me.

The Dog-Walking Man was across the street, and his fucking dog was barking at me. Real brave from across the street, you fucking dog. I wondered if the *Wilkołak* Brothers saw that, were noting it. The Dog-Walking Man just looked at his dog, trying to quiet him, and then he looked up at me quizzically, like I'd done something wrong. I mean, I had, but he didn't know about it. Fucking dog.

I glanced at empty cars and empty parking spaces, gauged threats and opportunities, wondered where the *Wilkołak* Brothers would stake the place out, and what would they do, how it would happen. Maybe they'd just capture me, torture me, find out who I'd infected, who'd infected me. Then they'd kill me. End of story. Christ.

I rounded the corner, worked my way to the train, in search of something good to eat, trying not to keep looking over my shoulder, keeping my ears out for anything unusual, anything out of place.

The creak of a door, the scent of pirogis and cigarettes, the click of a pistol.

Anything.

# 7. WEDNESDAY: 7 NOVEMBER

It was great, taking that half-day and then having the whole day off the next day. I took an extra-long shower, got myself all scrubbed, shaved, and clean, then gelled up my hair, giving it a playfully hip, tousled look. I painted my nails, choosing a muted tone, something classy, something I thought Reagan would like. I matched my lipstick to it. Now, this was a date. I was excited.

What to wear on a day at the Art Institute? I was tempted to call Reagan, find out what she was wearing, but I didn't want to be so high school. Unlike Polly, who nearly always wore dresses, Reagan could turn up in a crisp pair of slacks as readily as in a skirt. Since the Art Institute was an all-day endeavor, I figured she'd opt for comfort over style, a choice Polly would never have made.

With my own tomboyish tendencies, I had it easier. I put on an indigo fitted t-shirt, over which I put a white button-down blouse, put on a dark blue necktie, striped with light blue and beige, had it fashionably loose. Then I put on a camel-colored v-neck cashmere sweater over top, and a pair of grey Cheap Monday jeans, sensuously snug, and then decided on the footwear. I decided the stovepipe jeans lent themselves to some dark brown, round-toed equestrian boots, which would work well with the jeans, and would be comfortable, too. I slipped my feet into them, and looked myself over.

"Nice," I said.

Then I put on a dark tweed jacket, checked it out. Yes. I looked like a country squire. It was perfect. Reagan would love it. Then I wondered about continuity with our photographs. I'd be happy to change.

Reagan came over, was wearing an olive turtleneck sweater and a pair of charcoal cuffed slacks and some black buckle shoes, toting her camera. She had her hair back with a white hairband, and I could see that she'd plucked her eyebrows, some. Upon seeing me, her hand self-consciously went to her face, almost shyly.

"Hi, Samantha," she said. "Oh, you look smashing."

"Thanks," I said. "I can put on my work shirt, if you want, for the picture."

She considered it, then shook her head. "It should be fine. My, your bruise is nearly gone. Absolutely amazing."

I wanted to comment about her eyebrows; I had liked them fuller, didn't want to think of her spending time plucking them in the mirror. If they had come from the infection, she was in for a rude shock. She was a little distracted during the shoot, which made me a little self-conscious, too, kind of broke the vibe we'd been building the past few days. My looks went from forlorn to concerned, to nonplussed, to dismayed. I couldn't manage an honest smile, and Reagan seemed eager to simply snap the pictures as quickly as she could, and be done with it. None of the playful banter of the past few days, just matter-of-fact workmanship.

"There," she said, putting away her camera. "I think that should do it."

"Okay," I said. "So, uh, are you okay?"

She looked up at me, like her head snapped up, and she narrowed her eyes a moment, appraising me for a second, and then she went back to Classic Reagan.

"Oh, I'm grand," she said. "Why do you ask?"

"You seem a little, I don't know," I said. "Stressed."

"I'm fine," she said. "Just a little under the weather. It's been distracting me."

I could guess her symptoms. I knew them, myself. I wondered if the Beast had come out in earnest for her, yet. Part of me ached to tell her, to pat her on the back, to reassure her. But the last thing I'd want to do is tell her that I was the source of her sickness. That was something I would never do.

"If you don't want to do the museum, that's fine," I said.

"Nonsense," she said. "We'll go. It'll be fun."

There was politeness in her tone. I wondered if she and Gretta had had it out. Maybe they had troubles. Reagan was the type of woman you couldn't simply make inquiries of. She was a Leo. There had to be a process of discovery, like in court cases. We went outside, and I pointed to the Polish handbill, and Reagan exclaimed, walked up to it.

"Why, that's great," she said. "Did you do that?"

"No," I said, looking up and down the street. The Dog-Walking Guy was across the way, walking his tiger-striped bulldog. He glanced at us with concern, then went on his way, while his dog strained at his leash, trying to get at me. That little fucker.

Reagan took out her digital camera, snapped a few shots of the handbill. "So marvelously macabre. What does that word mean?"

"It means 'werewolf,'" I said.

Reagan's smile froze on her face.

"Why, of course it does. Smashing. I parked down the street."

I nodded, walked beside her.

"Why should somebody put a sign like that on a phone pole?" she asked. "The coins on the eyes are clear enough: that's an old burial custom, money for the Boatman. But why out here?"

"Somebody thinks there are werewolves in my neighborhood," I said, scanning the cars. There was a white van down the street, un-marked. The Dog-Walking Man disappeared behind it. I watched as Reagan got her keys. The Dog-Walking Man reappeared behind the van, kept walking. Was somebody in that van? I stared hard at it, but couldn't see. Why should a white van mean anything, precisely? It didn't. Reagan undid the power locks and I got in, while she opened the back and put her camera bag in there, then came back around. I could see the white van from where I was sitting, wanted to shrink in my seat, wanted to be invisible. Then she got in, and started up her Range Rover. Music played, pianos.

"Chopin," she said. "I find him so soothing. I hope you don't mind."

"Not at all," I said. "Your car, your music."

She put on apricot-colored leather gloves, soft and supple, and slipped us from the parking spot. In the car, I felt safer. It was fun-ny—it didn't feel right calling a Range Rover a truck or a jeep; those words weren't elegant enough for it. It was an SUV, but I hated the idea that Reagan drove something as lame as an SUV, so I just called it a "car." It was a stick shift, and I admired her adroit handling of it, glancing over my shoulder as we left behind my street. The white van didn't pursue, just stayed where I was.

"Are you okay?" Reagan asked. "You seem a little nervous, yourself."

"Oh, that white van back there," I said. "Gives me the creeps."

She accepted that without comment, turned, worked us east, nos-ing us toward Lake Shore Drive, so we could head southbound, get downtown, to the Art Institute.

"How's Gretta?" I asked.

"Great," Reagan said, a little too quickly, I thought. "We're fine."

"Good," I said. "You two are a great couple."

She laughed, more to herself than anything I'd said. "Yeah, thanks. I'm sorry I'm so out of sorts today. I've been sleeping terribly. I keep having these god-awful dreams."

"Really?" I asked, feeling like a complete shit.

"Yes," she said. "They're horrible. I had one dream where I was eating Gretta. Like I'd had this banquet table set out, and I was playing hostess, like I always do. And you were there, and Ansel and Polly, like four sides of the table, and out comes this giant gurney, and on it is Gretta, cooked to perfection, golden brown, an apple in her mouth. She's all trussed up, like a turkey. My Lord, it was horrible."

I could see her eyes tearing up at the memory of it, and her pain upset me. I touched her arm, the only human thing I could do.

"And we ate her," she said. "I served her up with pureed potatoes and savory gravy, and we ate her. It was ghastly."

It gave me chills.

"I keep having that one," she said. "Variations of it. Always eating, always feasting on poor Gretta. And she wakes me up, tells me I'm having a nightmare, and asks me what it's about, and I don't want to tell her what it is, obviously, so I just tell her it was a falling dream, because how can you tell someone you love that you'd been dreaming about eating them? And I have dreams about you, Samantha, too."

"Eating me?" I asked.

"No," Reagan said. "Other dreams. Rather sexual ones. Like the other day, only much more, much wilder. We're rolling around in fields of heather, naked, of course, and pawing at each other. Very sensuous, intense. The smells are wonderful, heady—earth, moss, lavender, heather, clover, you, me, the air—gorgeous, erotic, sensuous. And Gretta will wake me up from those, too, tell me I'm calling to you."

"To me?" I asked.

"Yes," she said. "It's terribly embarrassing. And she asks me what it's about, and I say it's another nightmare, and I make something up, but she says it didn't sound like I was having a nightmare. And then it's awkward."

"How long have you had the nightmares?" I asked.

"About a week," she said. "They're getting worse."

"Anything else?"

She glanced at me, wary.

"No, nothing. Well, I think I've picked up some allergies. Maybe I'm getting lupus or something."

"Lupus?"

"Yes," Reagan said. "I was putting away some flatware, and burned my hand on it. Some kind of autoimmune reaction. It was bizarre. I had to put on a glove to handle the piece."

"What kind of flatware?" I asked.

"Silver," she said.

We reached the Art Institute, and overshot it, went to one of the underground parking decks, so we wouldn't have to walk far. Going from the busy streetside to the dark of the tunnels was comforting, in a way. I put my shades up on my head.

"Have you gone to a doctor?" I asked.

"What, like a therapist?" she asked. "I already see one."

"Really?" I was surprised, in a way. Reagan seemed so grounded. What would she have to see a therapist for? Maybe it was part of her lifestyle, like something she was expected to do. But I was surprised. "Does it help?"

"She prescribed me some tranquilizers," Reagan said. "Says stress is probably getting to me, or something."

I wondered what could possibly stress out Reagan; I mean, I knew what was afflicting her, but in her real life, everything seemed so idyllic.

"I'm sorry," I said. "I wish I could help."

"You are helping," she said, with a smile. "By being my friend, you're helping."

That made me feel guilty, made me want to tell her that I was the source of her woes of late, but I didn't want her to hate me. I'd do anything to keep Reagan from hating me. Lie. Cheat. Steal. Kill. Kill? Christ, I needed therapy, myself. We got out of her Rover, crossed through the parking deck, toward one of the elevators, looking overlit and cadaverous in the fluorescent lighting.

"Hey, did anything happen with the Lucite?" I asked.

"I sent it away," she said. "I should hear something in a week. I hope it turns out well."

"Me, too," I said. "Thanks for doing that. I owe you."

The elevator door opened, we went in, Reagan pushing the button, waving off my thanks. "Please, it was nothing."

"It was everything," I said. "I'm just so glad you liked it."

She nodded, rubbing her forehead. "Yes, it was fun. The real challenge shall be displaying it—sometimes presentation's as challenging as the piece, itself."

"Hopefully Ansel's space will work for it," I said. "I can't see showing it at BacchUS."

She scoffed, nodded, and the elevator doors opened, took us to another hallway, which led us to stairs outside, away from monoxide fumes and fluorescent lights, into city streets and urban canyons and parks and a pair of great lions, watching over us as we made our way into the Art Institute.

The Art Institute was a welcome distraction for us both, and we took solace within its walls, moving from epoch to epoch, medium to medium. Reagan liked more classical works, was less than fond of modern stuff—she didn't like the Museum of Contemporary Art, for example, although I didn't like it for different reasons (hers was that she didn't like the art they had there; mine was that they didn't make good use of the space, didn't have enough art in there).

So much of the modern art on display at the Art Institute was kind of dated, in my eyes—like a norm's interpretation of what modern art should be, or an archivist's idea of it. Not like I'd question the judgment of the curators; they had a job to do, were no doubt eminently qualified to do it, but Modern and Postmodern were showing their wear. Reagan was a diehard Modernist, while many of the others were rabid Postmodernists—I was something else, I thought. Like Post-Postmodern, whatever that exactly was.

"There is reassurance in Classicism," Reagan said, as we walked among the Roman statues. "Western virtues. Timeless, immaculate, like finely-hewn marble."

I could see she took comfort in the bedrock sensibility of such things, nestled cozily in the arms of Apollo. I felt more comfortable making out with Dionysius.

"I just like how they make hard stuff like stone look soft," I said. "They look like flesh."

"Yes," Reagan said, hugging herself. "Would that we could all age so gracefully."

Reagan was 33, the oldest of the women in our group, and was quite aware of it, though it didn't matter to any of us. But then again, we were all on the other side of her. Even sourpuss Willa was only 31. Reagan had joked that 30 hadn't been so bad, that being equidistant between 20 and 40 offered her a unique perspective on life, but year after year, she'd slipped away from the fulcrum, toward a tipping point. And her woes of late surely weighed heavily on her.

"You are the most gracious of all of us, Reagan," I said, giving her a hug. She hugged me back, ardently, beneath the marbled eyes of Roman revenants. "Let's go look at other pretty things."

We made our way through the arms and armor exhibit, marveling at how little knights must have been, in their tiny suits of beautiful armor, and how calfless they were.

"They rode everywhere," Reagan said. "I imagine walking was gauche to them."

"I suppose," I said. "I think I could fit those suits of armor."

"Oh, you could," Reagan said, brightening at the prospect. "We should make a postmodern suit of armor for you. Artful armor."

Reagan and her projects. It made me smile.

"Maybe you could have me encased in Lucite," I said.

"No," she said. "Something altogether grander. I'll have to think about it."

She was such a wonderful woman. I had to tell her what I'd done to her. Not that she could do anything about it, but she had a right to know. Maybe there was a chance to help her, if it could be stopped early enough. I didn't know the biomechanics of it all.

"I'm glad you're thinking up projects," I said. "Art keeps you alive."

She nodded, smiling. "Art is life; kitsch is death. The day I become a kitsch-woman, that shall be the day I die."

"Yikes," I said. "You shouldn't talk that way."

Reagan turned on me, challenging. "There are fates worse than death, Samantha. Kitsch is one of them. The Spanish Anarchists had a saying during their civil war against the fascists—'Better to die on your feet than to live on your knees.'—I respect that sentiment. Fascism is political kitsch; I think the Spanish Republicans understood that, even into their graves. The Falange had a saying, too: 'Long Live Death!' Fitting, really."

I didn't know what she was talking about, though I wondered about living on one's knees. Wasn't it better to live, period? If the choice was life or death—well, death was a choice already made, an inevitability; it was life that was uncertain and fleeting, so I think to die prematurely was a surrender to the inevitable, which didn't feel like courage. Being alive was bucking the trend, since everything died.

"I'd get some knee pads," I said. "Living on your knees would give you terrible calluses."

Reagan laughed, a trifle mocking, derisive to my ears. "Please, Samantha. If the choice is honesty and truth, or trite sentimentality and lies, there's really no choice at all, there is only one way to go."

"I miss your eyebrows," I said, on a whim, hoping to derail Reagan's train of thought, her morbid musings.

"They were getting a little unruly," she said, her hand coming up, defensively, protectively. "I swear my hormones have been going haywire lately. My brows just started turning into hedgerows."

"I think you should be gentle with them," I said. "You don't want to look like Marlene Dietrich."

She gave me a patronizing smile. "I'd rather be Greta Garbo, if I had to choose."

I was amused that her girlfriend was named Gretta, and I almost wanted to ask her if she chose Gretta because of her name, but it felt too cruel.

Reagan glanced at her watch. "I suppose we should be going. We've spent hours in here, yes?"

"What about lunch or something? Are you hungry?"

"Ravenous," Reagan said. "You have no idea."

"I understand hunger," I said.

"Of course you do," Reagan said. "Where should we go? Someplace good, someplace nearby."

"Why not the Garden Restaurant?" I suggested. "Make a day of it here?"

"Fine," she said, and we trotted off to the restaurant within the museum, since the outdoor part was closed after Labor Day. It was busy inside, with tourist families and local lunchers aplenty around us, waiters moving like fired bullets, tablecloths immaculate, the rumble of conversation, the clatter of flatware making me thank godless I didn't work in a restaurant. We got ourselves a table and Reagan got herself some rabbit, I got braised duck and pasta, we shared a salad between us, and split a crab cake appetizer and a bottle of wine. It was like a date, although Gretta's long shadow hung over us, and there were more hulking, haunting shadows looming over us, as well. I tried to banish the shadows with wine, and Reagan seemed game for it, too. We played dueling wineglasses, trading sips and guzzles, alternately pouring for each other.

"Thanks for the nice day," Reagan said, between forkfuls of crab and salad. "And for everything you've given me over the past weeks, Samantha."

"I haven't given you anything," I said, thinking of exactly what I gave her.

"Of course you have," she said. "You've given me hope and inspiration."

I've given you lycanthropy, I thought, a speared walnut on the end of my fork. Christ, I wanted to tell her that, to fess up, to come clean. Guilt made my stomach ache. I would handle it, would manage it.

What about Gretta? Would you handle her, too?

"I don't see how," I said. "There's nothing inspiring about me, Reagan. I'm not a good artist, I'm not hip or cool, and I'm not an intellectual. I fail across the board. I can't even form any steady relationships."

"Nonsense," Reagan said. "You have youthful spark and a winning way about you. You remind me of absolutely nobody I have ever known, and that's a good thing; it means you're unique, Samantha."

"Nobody's unique, Reagan," I said. "Least of all, me. We are like our parents, we pick up everything from our culture, like what we know, what we value. Our genes, they come from a given line—I mean, that whole six degrees of separation thing, it's like we're all ultimately related. Sameness flows through our veins."

Reagan drank deep of her glass of wine, poured herself and me more, shook her head. "No, Samantha. We're not factory-assembled products. We're works of art, each one of us. Well, some of us are kitsch, others are camp, I suppose, but we're all performance artists, really. We're all sculpture, paintings, poems, and novels. Whether we're horror stories, or romances, or westerns, tragedies, comedies, or works of literary genius—that's up to us, opportunity, and circumstance."

I loved when Reagan got buzzed. Her cheeks would flush, and she'd wax philosophically in ways that would have left Lee stammering.

"Human nature hasn't changed," I said. "We're still wolves wearing wool. We dress ourselves up in civilization, in manners, but we're beasts at heart. Even our civilization is brutal. You see bums on the street, and hungry children, and what can you conclude except that we're uncivilized."

"I'll grant you that the unfortunates of the world can surely test one's mettle," Reagan said. "But they are not representative of civilization as a whole—they are dissonant notes. Poverty is, of course, entirely uncivilized."

It was easy for Reagan to say that, coming from money, having known only opportunity and privilege, favorable circumstance. To

284 | D.T. NEAL

somebody in her position, civilization was a warm blanket, beautifully embroidered.

"I don't know, Reagan," I said. "Everybody wants to be loved. Everybody wants success and health and wealth. Those are reflective of our commonality, don't you think?"

"We're all grounded in the physical," Reagan said, as our entrees arrived. "But from that common starting point, we go into disparate realms. Artists do, anyway. We can, and do, think about anything. That is our saving grace, as a species. Biology is a bludgeon; artists rise above it, at least for awhile."

She finished her glass of wine, poured herself another, then went after her rabbit, gnocchi and mushrooms, hacking at it with knife and fork. It almost seemed like Reagan wanted to convince herself of that more than me. I didn't have the stomach to have an extended discussion with her, and Reagan was as politely formidable as a debater could be, so I let her have the last word, and contented myself to eating the duck from my plate.

"So strange to see you eating meat," she said.

"Yes," I said. "I got a taste for it."

"I'm amazed at my appetite of late," Reagan said. "I've been eating everything at our place. Just another worry among many."

Her phone rang while we were finishing up lunch, and she talked to Gretta a bit, and I watched her, wanting that easy familiarity, that love she obviously had for Gretta, wondered how the other day would fit into her world, like was she regretting it, trying to find a way to let me down easily? Because, in truth, I kind of wanted that. I didn't want to mess up her thing with Gretta, and have that added to everything else I'd done to Reagan. Not wanting to me left sitting there while she was on the phone, I dug out my phone and texted Polly.

*wot R U doin? Im w Reagan.*

I was pleased that she replied.

*Slacker! Im @ wrk, of corS. wot R U & Reagan doin?*

*EtN lch @ d art institute.*

*Lucky.*

*wotz ^ w d p8ntN?*

I really wanted that painting in my apartment, or at least for Polly to resolve whatever she was going to do with it.

*Im goin 2 brng it 2 yor plAc; Ansel wntz 2 trash it, I tink.*

*Hes crAZ, U knO.*

*rly? I tink hes gr8.*

Okay. I saw that Reagan was finishing up her phone call, so I thought I should wind my texting up, too.

*Ill TLK 2 U l8r, k?*

*K.*

I pocketed my phone, and Reagan had put hers in her purse.

"Sorry about that," she said. "Gretta gets paranoid when I'm out with you."

"Oh, so she knows?"

Reagan nodded. "Yes."

"Did you tell her about...you know?" I asked.

"Heavens, no," Reagan said. "That was a reckless moment, Samantha. I don't know what came over me."

There it was.

"Maybe you should go to the doctor," I said. "Get some tests."

"I feel fine," she said. "It's just the dreams and the restlessness."

"No, it's not," I said. "It's an infection. I have it, too. I gave it to you."

"Yes, yes," Reagan said. "Creative angst."

"Lycanthropy," I said.

Reagan paused in her meal, laughed at me, fork perched midway to her mouth. "Are you secretly recording this, Samantha? Is this part of a performance?"

"No," I said. "It's not. I infected you when I bit your lip."

"Please, Samantha," Reagan said. "You're being ridiculous."

I looked around, all the norms pushing food into their mouths, and felt more alienated and isolated than ever. But I thought that Ansel had been a creep not to tell me, so I figured doing the opposite of what he did had to be somewhere near the right thing.

"There's no such thing as lycanthropy," she said. "At least beyond the psychological delusion that one is becoming a wolf. I'm not that crazy."

"That video I shot," I said. "I didn't fake that. I actually did that."

She set down her fork, folded her hands in front of her. "Stop it, Samantha. Please, quit toying with me like that, with your bogus gravitas and faux earnestness. I'm not going to play."

"I knew you wouldn't believe me," I said. "But you will."

"Please," Reagan said. "I'm not a believer; I'm a skeptic. How could I possibly think anything else?"

It was frustrating, but I understood where she was coming from. There was a way I could show her, could definitely convince her.

"For all I know, we're not even having this conversation, and I'm just losing my mind. You might be just having your lunch and this is all playing in my head," Reagan said.

"I could show you," I said. "I could change."

"Please, Samantha," she said. "It's nonsense."

Reagan signaled for the waiter, who came, and Reagan paid the bill. I didn't even make an attempt at stopping her. It was like the exercise of the mundane kept the uncanny at bay, like doing laundry to banish the ghosts, or washing dishes to keep the demons away. But the monsters in the margins had a way of creeping back in.

"I could change right here," I said, looking around. "Would that convince you?"

"Alright," Reagan said. "So you're a lycanthrope. Why would you infect me?"

"Because, I got excited. You know, I'm fond of you," I said.

"Fond? Fond of me?" Reagan said. "Is that really the word you want to use? Fond? I'm fond of Matisse, Samantha. I'm fond of Earl Grey tea, as well. You're going to tell me that you're fond of me?"

She swirled the remaining wine in her glass, head tilted, looking down the end of her nose at me. Reagan was definitely buzzing.

"No," Reagan said. "I think you're something altogether more than 'fond' of me, Samantha."

The waiter brought back her Gold Card and she signed for it, eyes on me while she settled the accounts.

I didn't know what to say to Reagan, except "Thank you."

We left the restaurant, more awkward than ever, Reagan walking quickly to the parking deck, me dogging her heels, unsure whether to give chase or to let her go. I didn't know what she wanted me to say, or how she could expect me to say it.

When we reached the top of the stairs that led to the underground deck, Reagan turned on her heel and stopped me with an outstretched hand.

"Stay," she said, in a commanding tone that stopped me cold. "Stay. Good girl."

"Reagan," I said. "I'm sorry."

She nodded and went down the steps, and I let her go, waited until I couldn't hear the clack of her heels anymore, waited until I was alone again in a city of teeming millions.

# 8. WEDNESDAY EVENING

Lee lived in a vintage third-floor walkup on the South Side (where he said all true Chicagoans lived), choosing the top floor as an added security measure. It was like his bunker, with him as slacker Howard Hughes. He was surprised to hear me at the intercom, but buzzed me in, anyway. I trotted up the stairs, feeling fit and fine. Most of the others didn't use the stairs, relied on elevators, which was how Lee liked it. It made him feel secure. He'd talked about it before. I remembered sitting in a café, trying to knit a scarf, while they were expounding on it.

"Criminals are lazy," he said. "They don't use the stairs. They are elevator people."

"I'm not so sure," Sheldon had said. "They seem more like escalator people."

Lee broke the world up into ground floor people, stairs people, elevator people, and escalator people. Ground floor people, according to Lee, had given up on life. They accepted their lot and were reasonably content, or at least had given up on anything better.

"All norms are ground floor people," Lee said. "All sheeple flock on the ground."

"Are homeowners ground floor people?" Willa asked, while cutting up a magazine with a giant pair of editing shears, the kind of scissors that could cut across a long page in one cut.

"Absolutely," Lee said. "They are as ground floor as you can get."

"But what about the American Dream?" Sheldon asked. "Home ownership is a sign of upward mobility."

"No," Lee said. "Home ownership is death. It renders one inert, not mobile. You become entrenched. That's why the largest proportion of ground floor people live in the suburbs. The ultimate ground floor archetype is the peasant, bound to land, hidebound in their think-ing, if they can even be said to think about anything. Stairs people were intelligent and industrious, and never settled for anything less than the best that life had to offer. Elevator people were unimaginative and shallow, addicted to convenience and dangerously naïve. Escalator people were the worst of them all; they were the Herd, the slack-jawed, knuckle-dragging Masses, content to be led by the linked metal steps, seeing nothing, thinking about nothing, just going from one place to the next."

Willa objected to his classification system.

"It's bogus," she said. "I've seen you take elevators."

"I'm a shallow bastard," Lee admitted. "But I never take escalators. Escalators offend me, they really do."

"And what about people who live in high-rises," I asked. "They'd be crazy to take the stairs."

"No person of Quality can possibly live in a high-rise," Lee said. "The very act of living in one robs you of Quality. People live in high-rises so they can hold what they think is the high ground, but they're misguided."

Sheldon was concerned. He lived in a ten-story building.

"What do you consider a high-rise?" he asked.

Lee looked him over. "Anything with more than three floors. Any place with an elevator."

"I think the cutoff should be 15 floors. Or 20."

But Lee wouldn't have it. When he got drunk, he got vehement about his classifications. "I suggest you get out of there soon, Shel. Sooner than later. That's what Gabe did, and he's turned out okay."

I reached the top of his stairs, rapped on his door with a mit-tened hand, took off my earmuffs, stuffed them in a parka pocket. Lee opened the door, looked me over, up and down, guarded. For a guy so affectedly blasé, he was also very tightly wound.

"What brings you south to my mean streets, Sam?" he asked.

"Can I come in?" I said. He nodded, let me in.

"Whoa, did you get in a fight?" he asked, glancing at the hint of a bruise on my face, all that was left of the gentleman's cane.

"I fell," I said.

"Yeah," he said. "Like into somebody's iron fist."

Lee's apartment was a cross between a cloister, a library, and a mu-seum. He had wall shelves dedicated to books, comic books, and record albums. His stereo and turntable were enshrined in one corner of his living room, while his computer was opposite. A little hermit's kitchen was adjacent to the living room, and his one bedroom and bathroom were down the hall. The place smelled like album cleaner and wood polish. It occurred to me that I'd never actually been upstairs to Lee's place before; he didn't like having people over, would usually meet people streetside, or at clubs.

"Hope I'm not imposing," I said.

"No worries, you're not," he said, gesturing to his beige sofa. He sat in a chair opposite me, to one side. "What's on your mind, Sam?"

"I was thinking about Anselgate," I said, taking off my jacket, leaning forward, forearms on my knees. "And other stuff."

He smirked at that term. "Yeah, and you're, what, playing Kissinger? You know, he's a war criminal, Sam."

"Oh," I said. "No, I mean I was hoping it wouldn't mess up Horrorshow, you know?"

"There's nothing on this earth that could harm Horrorshow," Lee said. "We're invulnerable, untouchable. Certainly not by Ansel 'Who *Haven't* I Laid?' Rupino. I can't tell you how pathetic Polly's little tryst is, in all of our eyes. I mean, I don't care what she does, but that she'd actually fall for somebody like that, what does it say about her?"

"He's a werewolf," I said.

"Yeah, I'll bet he is," Lee said.

"No, really," I said.

Lee sighed, ran a hand through his blonde hair, looked at me without a word. "What are you on, Sam? Some clubber pimp something special to you? You want an ice lolly?"

He got up and fished out a purple popsicle from his freezer, brandished it. He had a freezerful of them. Double-barreled ones, too, not the singletons one usually found in stores.

"I want a popsicle," I said.

"What flavor?"

"Green."

He dug into the freezer and pulled out one, holding the white-wrapped, quiescently-frozen confection up to the light.

"I think it's green," he said. "It's hard to tell until you unwrap them, unless you've got a flashlight handy, or X-ray vision."

I took it and tore it open. It was green. I was relieved.

"Anyway, I'm not going to defend Polly in absentia," I said. "She's doing her own thing. I just didn't want the group to suffer because of you guys bickering."

"What's to bicker?" Lee said, waving the popsicle like it was a scepter. "Ansel's scum. A no-talent hack. We reserve the right of free association. Now, if Polly wants to bring him like he's some kind of fashion accessory, that's telling. It tells me a lot about her."

"What does it tell you?" I asked, nursing my green popsicle, icy, cold, tangy lemon-lime.

"That she's having a quarter-life crisis," he said. "That she's evading her own poetical mediocrity, trying to find some spark in her humdrum life of bourgeois privilege. That she's abandoned poetry for the transitory narcotic of the flesh, and sacrificing art for sex. That she's sided with a no-good bum she picked up in a bar a few weeks ago against her peers in Horrorshow. That's unforgivable; we're like the mafia that way. You never side against us. She's out."

"What about Reagan?" I asked. "What about me?"

"Reagan was within her feudal rights as a hostess," Lee said. "I'll give her that. And you, well, I don't think Willa likes you very much."

"I don't like Willa, either. Her poetry sucks," I said. "And I'm not even a poet."

The image of her reedy voice, her nearsighted gaze, her funereal lack of presence, and the sheer crappiness of her verse, it just offended me. Her very existence oppressed me.

"It's not my fault her poetry's bad. What do you want me to do about it?"

"I just think it's weird she would do it at all," I said.

"Willa's weird," he replied. "We know this."

"She wants you."

"I know. She's dropping by later."

"She wants you all to herself," I said. "That's what part of this is about; she wants to recast the group, kick out all the people she doesn't like."

"And, you've come to me to intercede on your behalf," he said. "To kiss the ring, as it were."

He shrugged, biting off the top of his Popsicle. Lee's shrugs were monumentally nonchalant, his slumping shoulders weighed down by their world-weary burden, the shrugs shaking off responsibility in an avalanche of elemental ennui.

"How's your work coming?"

"It's possessing me," I said.

Lee's tongue turned purple as he chewed. "Possession might as well be ownership."

"Everybody thinks I'm crazy."

Another shrug.

"Everybody *is* crazy. Who cares WHAT they think?"

"You say that, but don't mean it," I said. "You care."

Lee broke his Popsicle into two pieces, and slowly devoured one side, and then the other. He was so weird, so in your face and evasive at the same time, so benignly creepy.

"I liked your video," he said. "I thought it was good. I don't know how you did it, but it was fun. Was it art? I don't think so. But it was, creative, imaginative, and bold. And you got naked for it. You trumped everybody. Gabe thinks you have a great future in Web pornography. Willa thinks you're a lunatic, thinks you spliced yourself into some movie, thinks you're a fraud."

"I'm not a fraud," I said.

"I don't think you're a fraud," Lee said. "I think you're for real."

"You think I'm a werewolf?" I asked.

"Hell, yeah," Lee said. "Everybody has two faces, Sam, private and public, real and fake; it's all just a question of whether your private face is your real face, or whether your public one is your real face. Few people have the stomach to put their real face out there, but you'd be surprised how many people have their fake face on, even in private."

"What about you, O Wise One?" I asked.

"I'm a total phony," he said. "A near-total fraud. But therein lies the secret to my oily authenticity: I *know* I'm a human fraud. Most don't, or won't fess up to it. What about you, Sam?"

"I'm not human," I said. "Not anymore."

"Intense," Lee said. "Humanity requires choice—free will. No free will, no humanity."

"That's it," I said. "I no longer have free will."

"Because you're really a werewolf, masquerading as a person," Lee said.

"Right," I said.

"Riiiiiiiiiiiiight," Lee said, drawing out the vowel. "Are you coming to Amaranth tonight?"

"Am I invited?" I asked.

"Sure," he said.

"But you didn't invite me," I said.

"Willa."

"She's a fraud. She's just envious that I've gotten some attention with my video."

292 | D.T. NEAL

Man, I wanted to kick her ass. I wanted to do worse. That the be-spectacled, haggard harpy would even insinuate that was too much. Like I'd have needed to do that, even if I hadn't been infected. I fuck-ing hated her. It made the hair on my neck bristle to the extent that I had to get myself under control.

"Nobody said you were lying; everybody thinks you're a little cra-zy, though."

"But crazy is really as bad as lying."

Lee tossed the empty sticks into the garbage, then went back to his freezer and snagged another one. A yellow one. He sat back down, across from me.

"Crazy is *worse* than lying. Cuz at least when you're lying, you know you're lying. But crazies believe their own lies."

"I'm not crazy. I'm a werewolf."

Lee bit off a chunk of his Popsicle, and his tongue went from pur-ple to brown.

"I don't care WHAT you are."

"Oh, really?" I said. His endless uncaring was infuriating, made me bristle. I set the Popsicle down on the white paper. His eyes followed the Popsicle, then drifted back to my face.

I walked over to him and sat down on his lap, straddling him. Lee looked up at me, all at once a bit boyish, uncertain. I guided his Pop-sicle to my mouth, while he watched, holding it. He was enough of a germaphobe that I knew he'd not take another lick from it after I'd deep-throated it.

He squirmed a little beneath me, and I took the Popsicle from his grasp, bit the top off it. Bananas. It was bananas. I put the thing on top of the white wrapper for it, on the little table by his chair. Lee's eye went to it, then back to me.

"No words, Orator?" I asked.

"Not yet," he said. "You're not my type, Sam."

"That's for sure," I said.

Just a taste. I wanted him to feel me, to plumb the depths of his uncaring. I let loose of the reins, let Sääm crawl out of her cage, felt my eyes flash, my face stretch. The pop of my jaw was fierce and audible in his quiet apartment, my teeth stretched in my mouth, became fangs. Lee's perennially half-lidded eyes went wide.

"Oh my fucking god," he said, wiping his face with a shaking hand. I flexed my thighs, stayed on him. He was pinned to the chair.

"I'm sorry you don't care what I am, Lee," I snarled, my voice dripping with aggression and irony. My fingernails lengthened, my fingers stretched, and it hardly hurt; it was a welcome pain. And I pulled her back inside me, forcibly, because she strained at her chain, wanted to continue the conversation with Lee, sawing syllables out of his throat with her teeth, to school him in the poetry of slaughter, the beauty of bloodshed. But I held fast, and she went back inside me, made me grateful I wore stretch denim. Lee gazed up at me, speechless, his face bright red, his forehead sweating. I picked up the yellow Popsicle and finished it in a few frosty bites.

"Fuck," he said. "Jesus fuck, Sam. How?"

"Doesn't matter," I said. "But I'll be damned if Willa's going to shitcan my work."

"F-fuck," Lee said. "It's not a performance. It's for fucking real?"

"See, I'm not a fraud, Lee," I said. "I'm for real."

He tried to get to his feet, shaking his head, like a boxer, trying to clear it after receiving a haymaker.

"Get off me, Sam," he said. "Let me up."

"How do you think Willa would receive that performance? She'd probably chide me for calling it back," I said. "Like that I should go through with it, the full thing, and eat you or something. Or how she likes vampires so much better."

His face was grey. "Don't hurt her. Don't hurt me."

"Mmm," I said. "Write me a poem, Lee. Like your life depended on it."

"I think you should leave, now," he said. "Get the fuck off me."

"Is that how it begins?" I asked, leaning in to give him a kiss. He turned away, and I only got a cheek for my troubles.

"Get out," Lee yelled, his eyes closed, like he couldn't bear to look at me.

"That doesn't rhyme," I said.

"You want me to write you a poem?" he asked. "Are you fucking insane?"

"I want you to perform one for me, Lee," I said. "And whether or not you live or die depends on how well you perform it."

Lee sat ashily beneath me, shaking, blinking fast. I'd never seen him in such a state.

"Sam, I can't do that," he said. "I won't."

"You'd better," I said.

"I don't do slam poetry, Sam," Lee said. "What the fuck do you think I am?"

"You said it yourself," I said. "A human fraud."

"Christ, Sam," he said. He fidgeted beneath me. "Get off me."

"Come on, Poet," I said, not fully me. Not anymore. Sääm was watching him, now. "Entertain me with your words. Right now you're wondering if you can get to that phone over there. But you can't; I'm faster."

Lee was sweating, shaking.

"Consider this a fuse," I said, picking up his Popsicle. "And me a time bomb. The only way to keep me from detonating is to make a poem for me before I'm through. If not, you're fucking dead."

"Sam, this is fucking nuts," he said.

"Time's a'wasting," I said, slurping on the Popsicle.

"If I believe you," I said. "If you move and convince me, then there's hope for you, yet. And best of all, not a fucking soul will believe you. Can you imagine what people would say?"

"I'd just tell them that you threatened me," he said.

"Yeah, me, a wee scrap of a girl," I said. "I don't think they'd believe you. Maybe they would. It doesn't matter to me. What matters is *right now*, Lee. This is the most important moment in your whole life."

"I'm not some trained poetry monkey," Lee said. "It's not like that."

"Didn't Scheherazade do it?"

"Scheherazade was a whore," Lee said.

"You're a whore, too, Lee," I said. The Popsicle was three-quarters done. I held it up for Lee to see. I tasted like fake cherries and FD&C Red.

"Amaranth," Lee said. "My poem is Amaranth."

*Amaranth*

*Am I blind alas,*
*am I blind,*
*I too have followed*
*her path.*
*I too have bent at her feet.*
*I too have wakened to pluck*
*amaranth in the straight shaft,*
*amaranth purple in the cup,*
*scorched at the edge to white.*

*Am I blind?*
*am I the less ready for her sacrifice?*
*am I less eager to give*
*what she asks,*
*she the shameless and radiant?*

*Am I quite lost,*
*I towering above you and her glance,*
*walking with swifter pace,*
*with clearer sight,*

He paused, sweating, seemingly spent, as I finished the Popsicle, slurped the sticks, stuck them into the torn white packet, tossed the packet away.

"Is that it?" I asked. He nodded, chest heaving, shaking. "You came up with that yourself?"

"Yes," Lee said, hesitating, glancing at the Popsicle sticks, at the phone, at me, at the books on his walls, at his feet. He smelled like shame.

"Really?" I asked. "You just whipped that up off the top of your head?"

He nodded slowly.

"I think you're lying, Lee," I said. I knew he was, I could smell the deceit.

"Get out, Sam," he said.

"It's not your poem, is it?" I asked.

"No," he said. "But I can't create with a gun to my head. Nobody can."

"Too bad," I said. "I thought you held yourself in higher regard than that. But a threat's a threat, right? I mean, I told you you were fucking dead."

I let Sääm out of her cage, felt my eyes and teeth change, watched my fingers lengthen, sharpen. Just a taste, Sääm.

Lee pushed away from me, trying to reach his telephone, but I held him fast with my thighs. I leaned into him and gave him a toothy kiss, while he whimpered, recoiled, hammered at me with his fists. I yanked the phone cord from the wall, held the thing up for him to see, grinned toothily at him.

"Fuck," Lee said, his eyes wild, looking for something, anything to save himself with. I saw his eyes go to a letter opener that was shaped like a little saber. His eyes went to the door, but he'd have to go past me to get to it. He'd have to get me off him, but his poet's hands were too dainty for that.

"What's the matter, Lee?" I snarled, through my fangs, drool hitting his lap. "I thought we were friends."

"So did I," Lee said. He tried to push me off him, but I was too strong. His knees were buckling, and I could hear his heart pounding in his chest from where I sat. Sääm sniffed at him, the muzzle against his ear. Poor sport. She wanted him to fight, or at least to flee. But pinned and cornered, he cowered. There was no breathless resistance, no stirring oratory; there was only Lee sitting there, sweating profusely, breathing hard, shaking, ashen. There was just surrender. I balled my claws into fists, felt the claws dig into my palms.

"And this is just a taste, Lee," I said. "I'd show you everything, but I don't want to ruin another outfit. I'm got a party to go to, right? Amaranth?"

"Don't kill me," he said, closing his eyes, turning away.

"Maybe I'll let you live. Somehow, I think that's worse for you than death. Then again, is there anything worse than death? What's that line about the coward's death? 'The coward dies a thousand deaths?'"

"Shakespeare," Lee said, barely above a whisper. "Julius Caesar. 'Cowards die many times before their deaths. The valiant never taste of death but once.'"

"Enjoy your many deaths," I said. I don't know what I expected of Lee, or why I even went after him. Maybe part of me had hoped he would attack me, pull some silver rabbit out of a hat and kill me with it. It was probably asking too much of him. He was a wordsmith, not a warrior.

I pointed a lone finger at him, my index finger, and slashed him across his face, over the bridge of his nose. His flesh parted for my claw like it was tissue paper. He yelped, blood poured from the wound. I tasted his blood, my finger as a Popsicle. Blood dripped down his face, spattered on his thrift store shirt. He was shaking. I stepped off him, surveyed the wreckage.

"Goodbye, Lee," I said.

"Fuck you, Sam," Lee said, shaking, sweating, crying.

Sääm laughed, threw the switches inside me, dropped me to my knees, while Lee backed away, eyes on the door. He looked ready to bolt, but I cut him off, tackled him.

"No, Lee, fuck you," I said, rocking my hairy hips against his pelvis. He tried to scream, but I caught his throat in my jaws. My jeans had split, my whole outfit was a tatters as I had transformed. Lee found himself in his last moments, trying to pry me loose with bloody hands, no words left because I had him by the throat, and bit down hard until he crunched between my teeth.

Lee didn't taste like nicotine. He tasted like carefully-prepared single-serve meals, lonely little bachelor hipster cuisine. He tasted like hypochondria and neurosis, like narcissism and…hmm…Willa. Yes. I could taste Willa on him. It made me more savage, I tore him to bits, right there on his chair, until he was a big mess. I didn't eat him, beyond a few bites.

I got up, hunted around for a mop. He just had a Swiffer. This looked far beyond that. In a corner, a Roomba cowered in the shadows.

"Fuck this," I snarled. I was tired of cleaning up my own messes.

Then there was a knocking at the door. I padded over there, listening.

"Lee?" came a reedy voice. Willa.

I crept behind the door, while she rapped on the door. Then I heard some keys rattle, then one find the lock. She had keys to his apartment? Figures.

I remembered Lee fretting about dying alone in his apartment, during one vulnerable night of hard cider—he worried about choking to death in his apartment and nobody finding him until days later.

The lock clicked and the door knob turned. I was covered in Lee's blood. Some of it was dripping to the floor.

"Lee?" Willa asked, peeking in. From her vantage point, she couldn't see the carnage of the room. I wanted her to get a little more into the room. It was marvelous, this sense of anticipation, the lure of the hunt. I had wanted to kill Willa before I'd become a monster. Now, the excitement was almost too much to take. I could hear her breathing.

She stepped into the room, and without hesitation, I shoved the door shut with a slam. Willa saw me and didn't scream, to her credit. She just jumped, startled, and stared.

"Sam," she said, shaking.

I didn't realize she'd recognize me, stepped toward her. She stepped back.

"Willa," I said. "You knew?"

"The eyes," she said. "The eyes."

Her own eyes were obscured—magnified and flattened—by her thick frames. She stepped away from me again, and I stepped toward her. No blubbering, no screaming, just…silence? She was braver than Lee.

"Lee?" she asked.

I nodded toward the other room. I was between her and the door, now. There was no escaping.

"Want to see?" I asked, my voice throaty, monstrous. Not a snarl, something altogether worse. It didn't seem untoward to grant her a last request.

Willa shook her head, and tears were in her eyes. I could only tell because they ran down her face, past the flat shields of her eyeglass lenses. Her nose ran, and her mouth parted, teeth set. Horse teeth, I thought. She had to hate the betrayal of her body, the emotions that rose up. Despite her admirable level of restraint, I could smell how upset she was as the loss of Lee—I could taste the love she had for him in the air, hear it in the heaving of her chest.

Her matchstick body was in olive drab, while my own was squat and broad, covered in fur, rippling with muscle. If not for the breasts I was sporting, you'd have thought I was a man. Or had been one.

I wanted to make Willa last.

She turned and ran across the room, toward his living room window. I bounded after her and landed just as she got to it, grabbed her hair in my hands and yanked her head back, clamping a paw on her mouth before she could let out a scream.

"Shhhh," I said. "I want to show you my latest body of work."

I walked her into the other room, where Lee sat with his head in his lap. There was blood everywhere. She shut her eyes.

"Look at him," I said. "Lee's dead. I call this one 'Reflective Narcissus.'"

She was so light, like she was made of straw. Some part of me actually felt a measure of compassion for her, of sympathy, even.

I set her back down to the floor.

"If you scream, I'll tear out your throat," I said. And released her.

She wiped her mouth with the back of her hand, glowered at me behind those thick lenses. "Murderer."

"And cannibal," I said, smacking my lips.

"Monster," she said.

"I'm going to make you something, too, Willa," I said, flexing my claws. They clacked against each other with as sound like tumbling dominoes.

"Make me one of you," she said.

I held up a finger, wagged it at her, the claw so beautifully sharp and long. Of course that would be Willa's stance. She held humanity in such withering contempt.

"No," I said.

She took her glasses off, tossed them onto Lee's coffee table. I don't think I'd ever seen her without her glasses. Her eyes looked tired. She looked both sad and old, her mud-colored eyes full of a dopey kind of sorrow that called to mind farmer women on the Great Plains in the Great Depression, captured pining for better times. Something about Willa's scarecrow visage called that to mind. Barren fields and blowing winds.

"Then do it," she said. "I'm not going to beg for my life."

"No?" I asked. She just stood there, staring at me with those big brown eyes. Willa would never be pretty. There was nothing in her that could even remotely pretend to be beautiful, except, perhaps, her way with words. I thought of her library of books, and then I thought of her.

"You're not afraid to die," I said. "Because you know your poems will survive you."

Something in her face moved. I could smell it. I reached out and grabbed her throat. She gasped, grabbed my hand in hers, but she did not scream.

"Of course," I said, hot breath on her face. "A poet's passing makes her words grow louder. Maybe even better than throwing yourself into a lake, yes?"

She didn't speak, just looked hard at me, fearful, tears in her eyes. But no begging, I'll give her that. A scarecrow she may have been, a mere pretender in her humanity, but this scarecrow was stuffed with iron filings, not leaves or batting. No wonder she wanted in; donning a wolf suit would have been the most natural thing in the world for her.

I licked her face, tasted her. She even tasted forlorn. I saw her empty dwelling, her lonely nights, pining in silence for Lee, hating him, loving him. Schedules kept, ascetic evenings with fountain pen in hand, inking words no one would ever see. That was the way to get to Willa. That was the key to her. It made perfect sense. The things that everyday people valued, Willa held in contempt, and she could do so because of her work. Her work gave her life.

I almost wanted to keep her alive, just so she could see me destroy every one of her poems. But she'd try to thwart me, and the moment was so perfect. I had her life in my hands.

"I'm going to kill you, Willa," I whispered. "And then I'm going to your place and I'm going to make a bonfire of your work. I'm going to bring you with me. It will be your funeral pyre. I'll pile up the stacks of books around you, cover you in gasoline, and light you up. What do you think?"

She squirmed in my grasp, could not speak, but I could tell from her evident discomfort that I'd touched a nerve.

Sääm always knew how to find her prey, how to sniff them out of hiding.

"If I were sporting, I'd let you go, and we could race to your place," I said. "But I know you; you'd cheat. You'd call the police. Unless I took your tongue."

She clawed at my hand, kicked at me. Reed-thin, an apparition fighting for its so-called life. A ghost departing her séance.

"I thought of making you eat your own words," I said. "That was the original piece I had in mind, Willa. But burning you like a witch on a pyre of your own poetry? So much better, so much richer, don't you think? Lyrical licks of flame?"

I knew I had the right of it, thanks to Sääm. Cruelty was like breathing to a werewolf. It was instinctual. I wanted to tilt my head back and howl. The last detail, however, was whether to keep her alive or not, to behold the spectacle.

This was part of being an artist, the aesthetics, the choices one had to make, the impact. My original piece was intended to mock Willa's love for narcissistic Lee, to have them dead together. But the funeral pyre was just too perfect.

"Do you want to see it?" I asked, leaning in close. Willa strained against my grasp. "Do you want to see them burn?"

Burn books and people follow. Wasn't that the saying?

I knew it was the right thing to do, so I throttled Willa until she passed out. Just held her and watched her squirm in my arms, watched her face turn white, then red, then blue, as she flailed against my grasp, until she stopped moving, was unconscious. I dropped her to the floor.

Looking over the room, headless Lee sitting there with his head in his lap. Blood everywhere. I should have cleaned it up. But looking at the room, the way everything was, it was perfect as it was.

Almost. I walked over to his record collection, that monster wall of vinyl he'd spent his life collecting, and I nosed through it. I found the record I wanted: "Real Wild Child" by The Victims. Perfect.

But my claws weren't right for the task, so I went back into my old self, stood there naked by his record player. Then I slipped the disc from the album and put it on, careful not to leave any fingerprints on it.

Then I set Lee's record player to repeat. I set the needle to the sixth track, "I Want Head." The room filled with the sound of the music, the throbbing pulse of overdriven electric guitars, and a sleazy harmonica. It was perfect. Doing anything else to it would've spoiled it. It wasn't a still life; it was a still death. I wished I'd had a camera to capture it. I'd have to rely on my memory.

While the music played, I unleashed Säämäänthää again, and it was easier, like it was sex. I dropped to a crouch and let her boil out of me, like I was a kernel of lycanthropic popcorn, the new me bursting out of the shell of the old. Sääm had no complaints; she knew what I was doing, was more than happy with it. The pain wasn't even so bad as it was before. If anything, I craved it, the wash of sensation that flowed into me as I became her, the ultimate rush.

I picked up my clothes, tied Willa up with them, then hefted her to my shoulder. She was comically light, like she was stuffed full of newspaper.

Then I opened one of Lee's windows, sniffed the air. I slipped through the window, perched on the narrow ledge. It was easy. I was born to this kind of thing. Then I closed the window, stood there with slender Willa on my shoulder.

The music still played in the room, and I snickered at my cleverness in picking the album. It worked on so many levels. The Victims. That was Lee, a victim. "Real Wild Child" – that was kind of like me. And "I Want Head" both played on the decapitation of Lee, and his own rather retrograde notions of man-woman relationships. Fucking perfect. I could imagine the police on the scene, analyzing that.

The me that used to be me worried about cleaning up the mess, but the new me didn't care, felt entirely beyond it. What were they going to think? That little old me came in and tore the fuck out of Lee? It looked like he got ravaged by a monster. But the cops would try to fit their crime scene into something they could comprehend. And that made it so much easier for me. Norms would only see what they could stand to see.

I could have jumped to the street, could have horrified the norms. But something told me that stealth, and not outrage, was the thing to do.

So, I reached up above me and caught the edge of the roof and flipped up there with one arm, then sprang from rooftop to rooftop with feral grace, cutting across the neighborhood to where Willa lived. She always kept herself within Lee's general vicinity—not so close to be confining, or with any expectation of reciprocity or relationship, but close enough to credibly feel like she was in his world.

We got to her place, and I pried open the window with a flick of my finger. Willa was coming to, was straining against her bonds.

"Shhhh," I said, slipping into her place. I'd only been to Willa's place once, when she'd had a bunch of us over under the pretext of seeing Lee socially.

Her place was like a cloister, devoid of anything—no paintings, no adornment. Just a plain bed, a plain writing desk, white walls, and black books on the shelves. Everywhere, her black books.

She had made hundreds of these books. They lined shelves along her living room walls, all little black books with something pasted to the spine to identify the volume. Never words—only pictures. Across from me was a series of books with eyeballs on their spines. Nearly 100 of them, all staring at me. They were blue, black, brown, amber, red, purple, green, yellow, orange. Some were animal eyes, though most were people eyes, magazine people eyes, touched up, airbrushed, perfect, and carefully cut to eliminate any white borders. The eyes unnerved me with their disembodied sameness and relentless stares, took me back to the past, to one of the early times she tried to put me in my place, in front of the others.

It was weird remembering it, because, in the moment, the others were like ghosts to me, now, as I'd killed them. It hadn't been like that when we'd all been there, it had been a low-key, druggy kind of party. But in my current state, the memory was skewed and altered. Willa and her books, Lee and Sheldon lurking nearby, voiceless, dead.

In those books she carefully placed her poems, using cut-out ransom-note-style letters. She clipped these letters from things she read, and kept them in a little embroidered green box that must have once held buttons. It contained many small partitions, little hollow squares she had since filled with letters she had accumulated over the years. This letterbox landfill also contained a tiny pair of scissors, a silver-plated pair of tweezers, and a tube of cement.

"You could simply write your poems in the book," I had said, not knowing my place back then.

"That would defeat the whole purpose of cutting out letters, now wouldn't it?"

"I'm saying you don't have to."

"And I'm saying that I do."

She held up her tweezers defiantly, while the others watched. She had an "O," small and white, pinned between the tweezer's talons. She applied the cement and stabbed the "O" into the book.

"I made a poem for you."

"You shouldn't have."

Willa waved me off and dug through her little book, the pages stiff with glue and letters.

"It's called 'Ghost Buffet.'"

"Why?"

"Because that's what I called it. Do you want to hear it or not?"

"Sure."

She cleared her throat and read it to me:

> Samantha's ghost insists
> On being seen
> The rest of us resist
> Whatever can that mean?
>
> I think that she's insane
> Stark, raving nuts
> She's got herself to blame
> Neither if's, and's, or but's
>
> She scolds us, we doubt her
> And her vision
> For all I know, it's whim
> That drives this ghostly frisson

She turned back to the page she was working on.

"That's terrible," I said. "No matter what letters you use."

"Like you're in ANY position to judge me," she said, plucking a baroque red "P" from her letterbox, pasting it in the book, gracing me with a glare. "You know next to nothing about verse."

"Are you saying I'm crazy?"

"I think you're saying that. I'm saying you're tasteless."

She dug out a "U" and jabbed it in her book, after dabbing it with an amber bead of cement. "What does the ghost say?"

Lee's ghost watched her root through her letterbox. Lee, holding his head in his hands, now. Sheldon chain-smoking through a torn throat, smoke curling out through the tears in his neck.

"They don't say anything," I said.

"Maybe you're just not listening. I know how you like to talk. Maybe he's not a ghost at all. Maybe he's simply a vision. Or a haunt. Or a shade. If I were a ghost, I guarantee that I would have something to say."

An idea occurred to her, and she jumped up, nearly knocking over her letterbox. She set it on a nearby table and disappeared without a word.

Willa came out, toting a Ouija Board, atop which were four squat red candles. "Come here," she said. I obliged her, and she led me to the blonde wood floor of her living room. She handed me the candles, and sat down, the board on her lap, her legs crossed.

"Place them in a circle around me. Around us."

I put the candles in place.

"Do you have your lighter? Any matches?"

I nodded. The candles were chubby.

"Light them. Oh, and turn off the light. Then sit across from me."

I sat down, watching the candlelight gyrate off of Willa's glasses as she set up the board, which had only two pieces.

"Our knees must touch. Sit like me."

She set the board between us, putting the pointer on it. It was shaped like a heart, or a spade, the point of it aimed at me.

"Put your hands on the pointer. Like this."

"I know how to use a Ouija Board," I said.

She ignored me. Lee sat nearby, just beyond the candles. He leaned back, stared up at the ceiling. Sheldon nursed his cigarette.

"Who are you?" Willa asked, pushing on the pointer. I could feel her pushing it, so I pushed back.

The pointer slid fitfully across the board, settling on "YES."

"Yes, is Samantha insane?"

The pointer pushed its way to the number "7."

Willa frowned. "'Insane' is only 6 letters, Yes."

"Why are you hunting her, Yes?"

"There is no 'Yes.'"

The pointer glided over to "X."

"X marks the spot," I said. "You pushed it there."

"Maybe 'X' is only a variable," she said. "Like any other reason is as good as any other."

"Yes, is Willa going to sleep with me tonight or what?"

Her eyes flashed, my temerity, and in front of Lee, no less. It was a call to arms.

I pushed the pointer toward YES, while Willa struggled with it, sending us off to the side. Lee stopped looking at the ceiling and watched us, while Sheldon stubbed out his cigarette. Willa and I strained against each other, until the pointer flipped out of our grasp, clattering under her bland futon.

Willa jumped up, knocking over a candle, spilling wax on her wood floor. The wax settled into the gaps between the boards. She brushed her hair out of her eyes.

And I was back in the here and now, with Willa yelping and straining against the bonds with which I'd tied her.

I sniffed the air and knelt on the floor, found the wax exactly where it had fallen, years past. I could smell it, could taste its age.

"I thought about leaving you with Lee," I snarled. "But you'd have wanted that, right, Willa? Dead at his feet?"

She strained against the bonds, cried out behind the gag. I put her in a chair, then began yanking down her books of poems from their orderly shelves, plucked the eyes out, one by one, three by three, four by four, piling them around her.

"This is a more fitting end," I said. "Witches should be burned, right? You were always a witch, Willa."

Her eyes widened as she saw what I had in mind for her, her life's work a mountain of black covers and white pages, carefully clipped letters. Tons of paper, mounds of poetry. Her words. Her verse.

"A poetic end to you," I said, cackling. Sääm was loving this. This was her poetry, this was her art. It came to her naturally, instinctively.

It took several minutes to take all of her books and pile them around her. I'd not stacked them neatly, as I'd wanted the paper to be exposed, the glimpses of verse.

Willa was fighting for her life, now, trying to be free, and a teardrop of compassion splashed in the sea of my cruelty at the sight of her. Willa, my rival and nemesis, completely at my mercy, at a time when mercy was a foreign language to me.

Sääm, the whole motive force behind my monstrosity, was silent. She was watching intently, but would not raise a paw to help me in this. She was watching to see what I would do.

I stood there, hulking shadow that I was, and Willa fought to be free.

"I want you to see this, Willa," I said, realizing that her glasses must have fallen off when I'd carried her across town, as she was gazing at me with wide eyes, unencumbered by her spectacles.

That bothered me. I didn't want her vision blurred as she beheld the architect of her passing. The aesthetics of that were just off to me.

"Do you have another pair of glasses?" I asked. An absurd request, and Sääm cackled inside me. Willa shook her head, but I nosed around her place and found some, by her nightstand, in a case, in a drawer.

Her bed was a queen-sized thing, with a drab grey comforter atop it. There was nothing on the bare white walls. The bed was black metal. The place was dreadful. I saw her cat, James, hissing at me in the corner. Wretched little thing. It was terrified of me. I hissed back at it, thought about snagging the cat and eating the damned thing in front of her. That would really boil her biscuits. But I didn't want to keep her waiting.

I snatched up the spare pair of glasses by the tip of my claws, for my hands were not so suited for fine tasks such as this, and I went back to her, taking great care to not break the frames, to open them, and slip them on her face.

She tried to whip her head away, but I steadied her head with one hand, and shoved the glasses onto her face with the other.

"There," I said, stepping back. "I want you to see this."

Then I pulled Sääm back inside me, although inside and outside were relative terms, now. Quaintly Modernist conceits, these. I had moved beyond them. Willa watched me draw the beast back inside me, and for the moment, stopped struggling. For surely, even in her long-cultivated aura of ennui and cynicism, she had never seen anything so wondrous and horrible as this. I imagined her writing a poem for me.

*Samantha, Samantha*
*Although I can't stand ya*
*Making monstrosity matter*
*And causing such a foul clatter*
*No one will ever doubt you again.*
*Though I am tempted to pray, Sis*
*How could I ever gainsay this*
*Abomination!*

Or something.

I stood naked before her, grinning. Little old me. She cursed behind her gag and struggled, dislodging some of the books I'd piled at her feet.

"I'm going to set you ablaze, Willa," I said, and walked into her kitchen, looked for flammable things. Found bottles of vodka in a cabinet. Three big bottles.

I took them out and poured them, one by one, on Willa and on her books of poetry. Now she was really fighting to be free.

"A Viking funeral, Willa," I said. "For you and James."

At the mention of her cat, I saw her eyes grow wilder. Totally worth it.

And again, that hint of guilt, a whisper, a swatch of gossamer against my cheek. But Sääm was not going to let guilt be a killjoy. Not when killing was itself such a joy. She understood rending, tearing, biting, consuming. This was an entirely human brand of evil, and Sääm watched with fascination. For to be what I was meant walking between two worlds—I was the blurry line, the smudge between civilization and barbarity. She wanted to learn, was eager to see what I could teach her.

I went into the kitchen and fetched some matches, a box of those Diamond everlights, the ones that you could strike anywhere. The room reeked of vodka and fear, as Willa called out from behind her gag, wailing, flailing.

"Your work dies with you, Willa," I said. "But your memory lives on in me."

I struck a match, tossed it onto the soaked pages, and was rewarded by the whoosh and flash of blue flame, as the alcohol ignited.

"Oh, I almost forgot," I said. I grabbed a chair and went to her smoke detector and tried to reach for it. Too high. Damned high ceilings.

Willa was shrieking behind her gag as the books started to burn. Was she mourning her fate, or the fate of her works? I wanted to ask her, but to take off the gag would mean she was screaming, and that might interrupt this piece of performance art I'd crafted for her, my audience, my victim.

I found a broom, her witch's broom, I thought with a laugh, and climbed back atop the chair, popped the smoke detector off, took out the battery, set it on her coffee table, while the fire grew larger.

Then I put the broom into the growing fire. And the fire was massive, having gone from blue flame to bright orange and red as the paper burned. Willa's screams gave way to strangled coughing and gasping, then screams again, as the flames kissed her skin, lit up the wool of her skirt, soaked with vodka.

The roar of the fire was tremendous, as the greedy thing sucked down air. I danced around the fire once, twice, three times, circling, while Willa fought, and as I danced, I let Sääm loose again, admiring how the bonfire cast my shadows on the empty walls of Willa's place, the emptied bookshelves, saw my little woman's body gyrate as the flames danced in time with me, saw that shadow give way to the larger form that was truly me, now, that had claimed me as surely as the flames were claiming Willa.

That teardrop of compassion was diluted in the larger body of water, it stood no chance. Sääm and I ran around the monstrous fire like we were chasing our own tails. Around and around we went, until Willa stopped moving, until the smoky air was filled with the stink of burning flesh, until the sound of firetrucks could be heard over the roar of the flames, until I went to the three windows in her living room and opened each of them, then popped out the screens.

I stood in the middle window frame, looked back at my handiwork, this great blaze, consuming her apartment, and soaked up the aesthetics of it, aware that anybody on the street would see this monstrous thing silhouetted by the fire. Something that walked on two legs, but which was no longer a human being.

I jumped from the window, landing softly on the ground, and let out a howl that set off a score of car alarms, and bounded off into the night.

There was no going back now.

# PART 4

"TO KILL A HUMAN BEING IS,

AFTER ALL,

THE LEAST INJURY

YOU CAN DO HIM."

– HENRY JAMES

# 1. WEDNESDAY NIGHT

Amaranth did not disappoint. It was spectral and sultry, with lurking Mayan masks and Aztec accents on the walls, creating more shadow than they deflected from the track lights that seemed so far away.

Everything seemed that way. After Lee's and Willa's, I was in a kind of delirium, like the walking dead. The dead was Samantha, the original me, the skin shell that I wrapped around myself. The epidermal envelope that encased the fanged, furry, monstrous me. Sääm had turned me inside out, and I felt like I was only going through the motions, was kind of a puppet in my own life. I went home, got cleaned up, took a long, long shower, then got dressed to go out. Slicked my hair back with product, put on some big earrings, slipped on a tight black dress and some knee boots. Put some mahogany lipstick on, and made my mismatched eyes fade to black with eye shadow. I looked feral, menacing. Finished it off with a light quilted jacket, dove grey.

I just showed up at Amaranth like I'd been invited there.

I glided remotely through the café, past potted palms and florid turquoise tiles on restive, load-bearing columns, in search of my so-called friends, sniffing the air, passing patrons who drank bitter liquid chocolate in oversized cups and sampled Aztec cuisine with forks and fingers, laughing, talking, biting, consuming.

It was the perfect place for my rebirth. On one wall was a fresco of an Aztec taking somebody's heart out with a knife, ridiculously bloody. On another was a rack of skulls, carefully rendered in paints, the skulls peering out behind the dark racks that reminded me, absurdly, of licorice, and my mind held those skulls to be candy confections crafted out of compacted sugar.

Sugar skulls and licorice cages.

This was where my head was as I hunted down my remaining friends.

They'd taken the sofa at the far end of Amaranth, past the languid bar that meandered beanlike across the far wall of the place. Beneath larger track lights, a prime position, of course, on a blood-red sofa.

There was Clay, whose hair stood up with the aid of chemical gels. He wore an open-necked shiny shirt, and stylish, slate-blue jeans that made him look like a hipster pimp in training pants. Odd that he had his back to the door, since Clay usually sought out the power seating, was keenly aware of the geometry of influence.

To Clay's left was Gabe, wearing a moss brown corduroy blazer and olive black slacks, and thick black shoes. He was leaning forward, stroking his beard, nursing a glass of wine with his other hand, artfully outstretched, lazily holding the glass.

"I'm saying we are artistocrats," Clay said, waving his own glass of wine like it was a scepter, and he was the Pope, giving some kind of benediction. He was throwing out a lot of bull, that was for sure.

"That's not a word," Gabe said. "Artistocrats?"

"It is, now," Clay said. "Artistocracy demands we point these things out, that we rise above them. I mean, what am I to make of the cultivation of the Hip at Target, for God's sake?"

"You shop at Target?"

"Only ironically," Clay said. "They sell ironic t-shirts, now. And trucker hats. Target. They actually do a crappy job silkscreening them so they look old, well-worn. Instant hip, ready-made for the norms to consume. Mass-market Hip."

"If it's at Target, then it's not hip, now is it?" Gabe said. "It's Hip Lite. All the cred, half the effort."

Gabe saw me before Clay did, eyes well-accustomed to ogling the womenfolk.

"Hey, look who's here," he said, and Clay turned.

"What up, Sammy?" Clay asked. "You look, hmmm, wicked."

"Where's Lee?" Gabe asked.

"How would I know?" I asked. "Am I his secretary?"

"How'd you even know about this gathering?" Clay asked.

"Lee told me," I said, crossing my legs, leaning back against the sofa. It was like I was high. I was in another place entirely, had become my own sock puppet, was just miming the parts, while Sääm was sniffing the air, still jonesing for the narcotic of slaughter, like she hadn't had enough already. She was confident she'd find good sport among these people.

"I called him, but nobody answered," Gabe said. "We were thinking of going to Clay's gallery for some recreation, but we wanted to tell Lee, so he'd know. God knows it's hard enough to get him outside on a good day."

I imagined Lee hiding in his apartment, having shoved his sofa against his door, putting "Don't Fear the Reaper" on his turntable, cowering in the dark, surrounded by computer games and comic books, hoping Batman would come rescue him. Then I patted my stomach. Lee didn't have anything to worry about ever again.

"We *were* going to play 'Consequences,'" Gabe said. "Are you up for it?"

"What about Willa?" Clay asked.

"Can't reach her," Gabe said. "I called. Nobody's around."

"Which one is that?" I asked.

"Exquisite Corpse," Clay said. "More or less. But with words, not pictures."

"Sounds lame," I said. "Are we game? I mean, with only three of us?"

"Nah. Fuck it," Gabe said. I think the fellows were grateful that I'd turned up, because even as blown away as I was in that moment, I was at least a woman willing to sit with these two, making them feel, well, less gay.

"I think there are better things we can do," Clay said, looking me up and down. "Forget Will and Lee. Fuck them."

"Well, this is fucking boring," Gabe said, playing with his pipe. He collected them. "We should just leave."

"Maybe we should just stay here and drink," Clay said, ogling three Latinas who were cruising past our little enclave.

"Maybe we should just trek over to Lee's and see if he's okay," I suggested. Nothing hid guilt better than innocence. Only I didn't feel guilt. Guilt was for norms.

"Maybe we should not talk about Lee for like five minutes," Gabe said. "Sheesh."

Gabe and Clay leaned toward me, like Roman conspirators.

"I say we go to BacchUS," Clay said. "I've got wine."

"Yeah," Gabe said. "Let's ditch the others; leave Willa obsessing over Lee."

"Sure thing," I said, smiling at them both. "Let's just get up and go. Maybe they'll show up later"

We all got to curbside amid plenty of laughter, while Clay hailed a cab. Piling in, Clay gave the cabbie the address for BacchUS, while I sat between them. Now, I didn't feel anything for either of them, but as co-conspirators, it was damned funny. We were all laughing about it, and I became very aware of the guys on my flanks, leaning toward me, Gabe trying his cod liver oil charm on me, smelling of cherry-scented tobacco.

"So, Sam," he said, smacking his lips. "Can we get an in-house performance of 'Transformation' by any chance?"

"Yes," Clay said. "That would be sweet. She's going to do 'Little Blow Peep' at BacchUS on Saturday. Wear wool, my droogie."

"Wool?" Gabe asked.

"You have to dress like sheep," I said.

"Sheep?" Gabe asked. I nodded.

"It's a performance art piece," I said. "I need audience participation."

"It's gonna be a flash mob," Clay said. "We worked out the details already, she and I."

"Nice," Gabe said. "Is a sheep mask enough?"

"It's perfect," I said.

"I'm intrigued," Gabe said.

"You should be," I said, patting his leg, which kept knocking into mine.

"Our little artiste," Gabe said, leaning into me. It was a big cab, but was feeling crowded. Sääm wanted to take these boys tonight, at BacchUS. Such a perfect ambush, such a great surprise.

*We can do Clay's little flash mob idea on our own. We don't need them.*

*But I want them to see the performance.*

*Give them an advanced screening.*

It was nice to hear her talking again. She'd been so busy savoring the evening.

"Yeah," Gabe said, cackling. "How much wine do you have at your place, Clay?"

"Plenty," Clay said.

"Can we really get a sneak preview of your performance?" Gabe asked, taking out some Chap Stick, stroking his fish lips with it in slow, elliptical, effeminate turns.

"Sure," I said, rolling with the moment. That was one of the key ways of surviving lycanthropy—you just had to roll with the moment.

The cab rolled up to BacchUS, and we all got out, Clay paying the cabbie, Gabe and I fishing out cash for Clay. Then we were watching our breath and hopping in the cold, while Clay got his keys and got us into BacchUS.

In the dark, the gallery was less than nothing, but with a few deft snaps of switches, the track lights came on, and BacchUS came back to life.

"Let's have our own bacchanalia," Gabe said. "You get to be the bacchante, Sam."

"Alright," I said, while Clay turned up the heat, told them there was wine in the back. Gabe came out with a box of wine and three big glasses.

"A fucking box?" Gabe said. "Clay, what about bottles?"

"Bottles are for openings," Clay said. "This is just for fun."

"What vintage is this box?" Gabe asked.

"Fuck you," Clay said, opening the thing, pouring out red wine that poured like fresh blood. We all took a glass, and I walked around, looking at Reagan's paintings and Sheldon's sculptures, still unsold, sitting there, mutely.

It was forever and a half a go, it felt like. I looked at this world like a visitor from another planet. I was a tourist in my own life.

Gabe and Clay were bickering over the wine, while Sheldon's ghost was lurking on my heels, hovering just past my shoulder. The pictures called him up in my head, and Willa's, and Lee's. My lord, I had been bad.

"You like my stuff, don't you," Sheldon said. "My art."

"Mmm," I said, not having the heart to tell him the truth. I thought that was funny, like sparing his feelings, given what I had in mind for the others. Me, not Sääm. I accepted full responsibility for it. I didn't have the heart to tell him that I had done what amounted to a mercy-killing: in killing him, I had made him more significant than he'd ever be in life. He had been my first victim.

You always remembered your first time.

I swigged down the wine, felt it settle nicely in my tummy, set the glass on the table near the box.

"Do you have music, Clay?" I asked.

"Sure," he said. "Why?"

"It's showtime," I said.

"Let the boxed wine bacchanalia begin!" Gabe said, ignoring a sidelong glance from Clay, who was muttering as he went to turn on his stereo.

And me, I took off my coat, laid it down on the table, next to the wine. Then I took off my jacket, and then my boots. At this point, I had the full attention of Gabe, who sat down on the dais, his glinty eyes upon me.

"Do you have a bucket and mop, Clay?" I asked. "It could get messy."

"Yeah," he said, from beyond the divider. "A Swiffer, too, if you need it."

That got Gabe snickering. The music came up. It was Daft Punk, and that worked just fine for me. I slid off my boots.

"Get off the dais," I said. "That's for me."

They scootched out of the way, got more wine, drank it down, while I tugged off my socks, went about slipping off my dress. Winter was all about layering. I threw the socks at Gabe, who dodged them, laughing.

Clay grinned intensely at me, got up, fetched himself some more wine. I walked over to the front door, the wood floor cold against my bare feet, and locked it, turned the deadbolt, and then went to the lights, turned them down low, so BacchUS was robed in shadow, the boys now apparitions, their faces almost invisible to me.

There was no shame in surrendering to the inevitable, was there? Like, if a shark bit you, it was just because that's what it did. Sharks bit things. Ate things, too. God, I was hungry. Lee had been just a snack for me, and I hadn't even taken a bite out of Willa. I was ravenous.

I wadded up my dress, threw it at the table. It landed below the table, slid against the wall.

"What is this piece?" Clay asked. "Is this 'Little Blow Peep?'"

"This is called 'Sex & Violence,'" I said, nodding to Gabe, who saluted me with his glass of wine.

On the dais, there was a spotlight overhead, dimmed like the others, but it was my own light, like God's eye upon me. I slipped off my last layer, a thin, mint-green camisole, and threw it at Clay, catching him in the face. He laughed, brushed it aside. It was just me and my bra and my panties. I had their full attention. It was almost too easy.

Then Clay's phone rang, and he took it out, went back behind the divider. I unhooked my bra, wondering who was on the other line, flung it at Gabe.

Now, I was breathing heavily, and the gallery was getting warm, and I went to my knees and rolled onto my back to tug the panties off. There was no elegant way to do it, but Gabe was more than eager to join in, grabbing at my panties with his free hand, yanking them off of me with a snap. It was just a thong as a trophy in Gabe's hand, and Clay behind the divider. Was it Reagan? Polly? Who? Hang up, you fuckers.

"Clay?" I asked. "You're going to miss it."

"Let him," Gabe said, guzzling wine, backing his way to the box, pouring more.

"There in a sec," Clay said. "It's Reagan. She says to turn on the television."

"You don't have a television, Clay," Gabe yelled.

"I know," Clay said.

I dropped to my hands and knees, crawled up to Gabe, pawed at his corduroy trousers, while he cackled. Sääm was coming. Sääm was here.

"Let her be pissed," Gabe said. "Fuck her."

Sääm wouldn't wait, she couldn't. I hunched over, gnashing my teeth, trying to keep the noise down. Thankfully, Clay had the Daft Punk up some, so it might camouflage things a little. Terrible to be thinking that way, but it's where I was. I just had to roll with the moment.

The pain was still there, the stretching of my limbs, my extremities. In the shadows, all I could hear was the popping of the joints, while Gabe looked on, commenting, laughing. Not seeing. He even turned to get more wine. It was dark, but I felt darker still.

I heard the glass fall when I reared my head back and howled, the fur flying out of my skin, the teeth long and large.

"Jesus fuck me," Gabe said.

Clay was still on the phone, goddamn him. Spoiling my performance! I pounced on Gabe before he could say anything else, just took his throat in my jaws, remembering the daydream I'd had in what seemed so long ago, back at Nonpareil. I bit down hard, and Gabe's throat gave way like it was dry spaghetti between my teeth. His blood splashed onto my face, and he went down, hitting the floor with a watermelon thump.

It happened so fast, Gabe had just finished pouring his wine, was tipping his head back for a swill and a snappy retort, when I was on him, taking him to the floor, sending his wineglass flying against the wall. I pinned him to the floor with my claws, and promptly ate his face, just bit into it like he was the crust on a chicken pot pie. That thought bounced absurdly in my head.

Chicken pot pie.

"What the fuck?" Clay said, rounding the corner. He'd hung up, didn't have his phone in hand, and slipped on Gabe's blood as he entered the room. He went right up, spilling wine, landing on his back. I landed on him before he could get up, and bit him on the shoulder. He was tough, sinewy.

Clay screamed and swung at me with his good arm, catching me in the face. He cocked his fist back to hit me again, and as he did, I caught his fist in my teeth, snapped off most of his fingers like they were carrot sticks. It was fucking easy.

Chicken pot pie and carrot sticks.

Then I dropped onto my forearms and took his head off. It was insanely easy, just a closing of my vice-like jaws, and off came his head, bouncing across the floor, while his body jetted blood at me, flailing on the ground.

Then it was just me panting in the dark with them.

"Show's over," I said, and went about cleaning up my mess, one bite at a time.

# 2. THURSDAY MORNING: 8 NOVEMBER

It took me hours to clean up BacchUS, to eat the two of them. I don't know how Sääm did it, where she found the room. But by the time the bacchanalia was done, there was just blood and clothing left on the floor. Sääm was gorged, sated, asleep in my head, content to let me put her back in her cage, leaving me naked there, covered in friend-blood.

I went in the back and found Clay's mop, filled the yellow bucket with water and Mr. Clean, then cleaned up the place. Back and forth I went with the mop and bucket. Wash, rinse, repeat. Over and over, until Mr. Clean and I had BacchUS looking almost normal again. I put their clothes in a Hefty bag. I'd have to find a place for that. This was beginning to become work to me. My arms ached from all the mopping.

And yet, there was something therapeutic in the mundane, in the spicy tang of Mr. Clean, in the slopping of the mop, the rhythm of labor, back and forth, back and forth, across the wooden floor, praying to nameless gods that the blood didn't soak into the grain of the wood, hoping that the varnish and wax kept it at bay.

It was absurd to mourn the murder of my friends, ridiculous to grieve. I'd done it. I'd known what I was doing, and I hadn't been able to stop it, hadn't even wanted to. There was no rationalization big enough for it, no accommodating dodge wide enough to accept it. I'd killed them, I'd eaten them. It was almost too much to bear. Almost.

Still, as I wrung the mop, dumped it, refilled it, used more Mr. Clean, it didn't stop me from trying somehow to explain it away. The mind would tell itself anything to keep going, even when there was no point in it. You couldn't argue against instinct, but it didn't stop me from trying.

"They weren't real friends, anyway," I said in the dark, to the mop. Sääm was snoozing contentedly. She wasn't more than half-listening. It really was me alone in there. Me and Mr. Clean and what was left of my all-dead half-friends.

I'm probably supposed to say I felt bad, but I didn't. I felt good. Tired, but full. It was hard to have a guilty conscience when you had a full stomach. What I wanted to do was sleep, not cry for Gabe and Clay. What I thought about while mopping was how they'd tasted. Sheldon had tasted like the cigarettes he always smoked. Clay tasted best, but had been a little hard to chew. He'd obviously taken care of himself, ate well. Gabe was the right mix of flavor and flab. Okay, so that was gross. It didn't do to think too much about what you ate.

I stuck with mopping, back and forth, until the floor was clean as I could possibly get it. I wouldn't turn up the lights until I'd gotten myself cleaned up. It wouldn't do to have some pedestrian walk by BacchUS and see a naked bloody girl mopping blood from the floor. I turned off the music when I was done.

The only reason I cleaned it was because I still had use for BacchUS as a performance space. That was the only reason.

Then I went to the bathroom in the back, looked at myself in the mirror. In the fluorescent light of the restroom, I looked like a goddamned ghoul. I was covered in blood. It took another hour for me to get cleaned off, scrubbing myself off with paper towels and water and soap, throwing the paper towels in the Hefty bag.

I'd taken the guys' wallets and cell phones and keys and laid them in a row. Opening the wallets, I took the cash they had on them. $50 cash, 15 credit cards between them. I wasn't about to go on some kind of credit card-theft bender. I might have been a lycanthrope, a murderer, and a cannibal, but I wasn't an identity thief.

I took out their licenses and IDs, anything that identified them. It was strange to see how much of one's identity was stuck in a wallet. Student IDs, driver's licenses, state IDs. All of it came out, until the wallets were empty. I figured I'd throw them separately into different trash cans, put the Hefty bag in yet another. I thought about chopping them up into little bits.

As for the cell phones, I popped them open, checked out their e-mail messages. Nothing of consequence jumped out at me. I didn't know what I was going to do with those. Christ, it was so difficult being me. I turned off all of the ringers and stuffed the phones into the pockets of my jacket. I bet vampires didn't have half the trouble I did;

they had it easy; they didn't even have to really pretend to be human. Not the same way, anyway.

I pocketed the cash, the keys, and the cards, figuring I'd do something with the cards, chop them up or something. Maybe make a mosaic out of them. That would be kind of curious, although a little ghoulish. Better to just shred them, dice them up and be done with them.

Then I went around the corner and turned up the lights, surveyed the room, walked back and forth across it, sniffing the air, looking for anything out of place. It looked alright to me. I took the box of wine and drank from it, poured myself a glass.

"To friendship," I said, toasting the empty room, feeling lonely. After finishing the glass of wine, I carried the box back to Clay's fridge, put the wine in there, and then rinsed the glass in the sink, put it back in the cabinet. I wiped down the fridge handle.

Then I tied off the Hefty bag and turned out the lights, went to the front door, unlocked it, then fished my way through the keys to find Clay's, and locked the place up. After that, I felt bereft, this unpleasant sorrow for what I'd done, remorse curdling behind my eyes and in my heart, kindled with shame. It had been a busy, busy night. I'd murdered four of my friends. I was exhausted.

"Sorry, guys," I said. It was entirely inadequate, but it was all I felt, all this human sock puppet could feel, anymore. Instinct was a bitch. You couldn't argue with instinct; it simply was. It was like trying to talk your way out of a pregnancy—you didn't do it. Either you had the baby, or you killed it, but either way, you were forced to answer the call. You couldn't ignore it.

That's how it was with my disease. It wanted slaughter, it wanted murder and meat. And it would do whatever it needed to do to get it. That was my new reality. I had to answer this particular call of the wild, or it would only get worse for me. Part of me wanted to call Ansel, to get some wisdom from him, if any was forthcoming. He'd be proud of me, cleaning up so tidily.

I walked through the neighborhood, until I found a dumpster that looked remote enough from BacchUS to merit a dumping, and carefully threw the bag into it, down deep. Maybe that was stupid, but I didn't know what else to do. I thought having bloody, ripped clothes and shoes on me might be a little obvious.

*Too bad there's all that blood on the shoes.*

Sääm surprised me that she was awake at all, but making me a little less lonely. It was nice to hear another's voice, even if that voice was inside my head.

*You could sell them to a thrift store.*

"Eww," I said, closing the lid on the dumpster and walking through the dark and lifeless neighborhood, working my way toward transit lines, hoping I'd find a bus or something. I had no idea what time it was. Maybe two in the morning? Three? I threw away their wallets in other dumpsters, trying to be random, hoping that they'd be inconspicuous. I didn't know how this stuff was done.

I caught a bus, sat in the back. There were two other people on it, besides the driver. Just ghosts like me, human phantoms. We got back downtown, and I could see that it was 4:43 a.m. Once I was downtown, I walked around awhile, checked out the drunks and the party people driving around under the sodium lights. Some folks honked and screeched tires, and the lights seemed to change really quickly.

I had failed Reagan across the board as a friend, and it gnawed at me, left me numb. And I don't know why I had gone after Lee; it was instinctive, a reaction to his blasé manner, his uncaring and apathy. It had set me off. Willa I'd killed not quite on instinct, but simply taking advantage of the opportunity. And Gabe and Clay—that was something altogether worse. It was greed and monstrous opportunism. They were there, and I took them. There was no poetry of slaughter in it; it was only slaughter. It made me wince. Everything seemed to do that now. My nerves were stripped bare.

Desperately tired, I watched the sun rise as I caught my El train home, watched Chicago go from evening black to morning blue— not the sky, but the buildings, where everything was the same darkling shade of pre-dawn blue, while the sun peeked over and the city opened like a flower, began its day. I could see commuters on the El platforms, ready to go downtown. I put on my shades, covered my eyes, hid inside myself, without precisely knowing what that self was, anymore.

Today was a workday for me, and I'd been up all night, only wanted to sleep. It's all I cared about; I was exhausted. I practically sleptwalked home, passed morning commuters on my way. I'd call in sick. It was the only thing I could do. I had a condition, for god's sake. I'd murdered four of my friends.

And if that wasn't bad enough, the *Wilkołak* Brothers finally found me.

Up my street, a young dude, brutally blonde, straight-nosed, blue-eyed. He looked like Hitler's wet dream, wearing a black, ribbed commando sweater and jeans, combat boots, a grey trenchcoat. He was walking down my sidewalk, eyes intent, looking right at me, hands in his pockets. In the morning light, the shadows cast deeply on his European face.

"Wilkołak," he said, his teeth bared. "It's you, yes?"

His voice was frosty, crisp, matter-of-fact.

"Huh? No, that's not my name," I said.

"No bullshit," he said. "We've been on this street all week. We've been watching."

"Excuse me, I need to get home," I said. He didn't move out of my way. My nose went no higher than his chest.

"Little girl," he said. "You've been very naughty. We know, we know."

Sääm woke right up, spoiling for a fight. I could feel her bristling inside me. Her appetite was insatiable. Three, four, five, six. A thousand. Come one, come all. Step right up.

"Are you out of your mind?" I said, raising my voice, looking around. A truck started up somewhere behind me. Fuck. He pulled out a silver dollar from his pocket, held it out Lady Liberty in profile, on the face of the coin. It said 1921 on it.

"A wager," he said. "If you can hold this in your hand without it burning your skin, you can keep the coin. But if not...."

He just grinned at me, and I could smell that he was afraid. I could hear the vehicle pulling out of its parking space. I couldn't believe this was even happening to me. I glanced over my shoulder.

A white van.

*The* white van.

"What are you talking about?" The puppet knew her lines, could lie like a rug.

"Take off your glove, hold the coin in your palm, grasp it tight," he said. "Catch and release. If you can, you're free to go."

"Get out of my way," I said.

"No," he said. His eyes were like icewater. "I'm sorry."

The van was pulling up alongside us. I could imagine me being nabbed, taken to a warehouse, them with silver shears, taking my fingers off, one at a time.

Sääm wanted to kill this man, and I could feel her trying to come out, and I was thankful that I had put my shades on, that he couldn't see my eyes. He was probably nearly sure I was the lupine they were hunting, but had this final test. Or maybe he was trying to scare me into transforming. The van had two men in it, both in black ski masks, their eyes on me, one with a cigarette dangling from a thick pair of lips. Their eyes were flatly afraid.

Without a word, I turned on my heel and ran from the man with the coin, who gave chase. The van would have to drive around the block to come back; there wasn't room to turn around on my street.

*"Wilkołak!"* the man shouted, running hard after me. He was in shape. Fuck.

Fortunately I knew my neighborhood inside and out. Sääm had seen to that, had shown me the ins and outs of alleys. I could navigate it with my eyes closed. I dug out my rape whistle and popped it into my mouth, blowing on it as I ran, while the blonde man cursed, running hard for me. Sääm wanted to get him, to kiss him with her teeth, but I knew that's what the men wanted, and if I paused to claim this man, his peers in the van would arrive and finish me off. And that assumed that I would be able to transform in time. I didn't know how much of a margin I had.

"Help me!" I screamed, between bleats on the whistle. "Police!"

I was aware of the irony of my situation, given what I'd been up to all night. But I didn't care. I rounded the corner and could see the van at the far side of the opposite block, running a stop sign to get back on track to pursuing me. Cutting the corner sharp, I just evaded the man's outstretched hand. Glancing at him, I saw he had a commando knife in his hand, a dagger, a stiletto, cruel, triangular. Silver.

"Help!" I shrieked. I would not give him the satisfaction of transforming; not here, not now, even though Sääm was howling in my ears, I could feel my fingers stretching, saw tips of claws slicing through the gloves. He snagged my jacket with his hand, as I turned my arms so the thing slipped off me. He threw it down, kept running. The van was hauling ass, heading my way, so I cut a hard left and went up the service alley that led to my building, poured on the speed, glad as hell that I'd worn my running shoes today, because I was able to get some more distance.

*"Wilkołak!"* he yelled. "You can't fucking run forever. Why don't you change your skin?" To his credit, the guy stayed on me, was in serious fucking shape. He was like a Polish commando or something. Probably right over from Danzig, first generation. He had an accent.

We went up my alley, and I could hear the van cruising up behind my own pursuer. I cut a hard right around somebody's garage, then ducked beside a dumpster, panting. As the guy cleared the turn, I threw myself out of my hiding place and against his knees, and he went flying over me, cursing, tumbling to the ground. He dropped his dagger, the thing skittered away.

The van rounded the corner and as I got up, the passenger threw open his door and caught me with it, knocking me off-balance in a glancing blow. I saw a glint of metal and saw he had a gun, and sprang at him fast, faster than he was. This guy was big, but was stout, too. I raked him across the masked face with my claws, right across his fucking face in a vicious slash that had him yelling, blood pouring from the ribbons of red I'd made.

His free hand went to his face, instinctively, while the driver yelled out in Polish, a stream of words and curses. Without hesitation, with Sääm's instincts in play, I pounced on his gun arm, brought my mouth right to his wrist, and bit down hard on him with teeth that were sharper than Grandma's knitting needles. I just sank my teeth into him and severed flesh and tendons, and the man howled as I'd taken a chunk from him, the gun falling from his slack fingers. Then I snatched up the pistol and aimed it at the blonde, who'd recovered his knife and had been sprinting my way.

I'd never fired a pistol before, but assumed it was a point-and-flick affair, like in the movies. I banked on Sääm making me strong enough to handle the kick from the thing, a revolver. I squeezed off two horrible, deafening, blinding shots before I knew what I was doing, and the blonde guy was knocked flat on his back, with half his head gone in a spray of blood and bone. Then I took the pistol and turned it on the driver, fired off another three shots, until he had become a bit of abstract expressionism in the inside of the van.

Six shots, what a revolver had, right? I had one left.

I kicked the surviving guy in the nuts and pushed him to the ground. He looked at me with wild eyes, his face a wreck, his hand ruined. If he survived, he'd be a werewolf with a fucking limp.

There wasn't much time. I dragged the wounded man, leaned him against the wall, put the revolver in his wounded hand, held it there, while he strained against it with his other hand. To a casual observer, it looked like maybe a drug deal gone wrong, at least until the coroner found silver bullets in the guys, forensics guys determined maybe that the ballistics weren't quite right, maybe. Maybe.

"Who sent you? Who are you?"

"Fuck you," the guy said. *"Wilkołak* bitch."

"Yeah, yeah," I said. I could hear a siren. Somebody would be here, soon. Somebody official. "You're part of the club, now, Sport. Welcome to my pack."

His pale eyes widened, the horror of it, the certainty of his fate. I doubted his fellow *Wilkołak* Brothers would be into that.

"That's right," I said, fishing through his pockets, found some more bullets. Silver motherfucking bullets. They burned my fingers, I let them go with a hiss. Found his cell phone, which I pocketed. Another for my collection. I'd have to fetch my jacket.

"Who sent you? Who are you?"

"This won't change anything," he said, gasping. "We're going to get you, *Wilkołak.*"

"Let's hope you Polish commandos do it right next time," I said, glancing around. From where we were, in the alley, there weren't good vantage points. The siren was louder. Somebody had called 911, but nobody could see anything. I leaned hard on his wounded hand, turned the pistol toward him, despite his efforts to point it my way.

"Christmas comes early for you, Lech," I said, and let Sääm run loose again on her leash, forced the gun upward, the long snout of the thing toward his face. He grunted, strained against me, but I crouched against him, my thighs pinning his legs to the ground, denying him leverage. The guy's eyes widened, and he took his good arm and tried to stop me, gasping, straining with all of his might against me—my little clawed hipster girl hands in split-knit gloves on his ruined, hairy, Polish man-wrist, pointing the revolver toward his shaking, sweating, bloody face, and his burly man-hand on mine, trying to stop me. Failing.

I grinned at him, while he jabbered at me in Polish. Christ, Sääm was fucking strong. Even mostly human, even just a whisker fuzzy, I was lots stronger than this guy, especially two arms to one. Up the barrel went, and in, like a falling tree, moving in slow motion, .44 magnum blued steel. I could see the caliber along the barrel, up close and personal. Big game hunter, this guy was. He was in a jam, because I had the pistol stuck in his damaged hand, and the twisting was causing him agony, his eyes were tearing, and he couldn't strike at me with his one good arm, because then I'd get the barrel to his face that much faster, and he'd be dead. I mean, he was dead, anyway, but it would come faster.

His wrist, the flayed one, creaked, leaked blood, and he gritted his teeth, tried to fight me, silver crucifix dancing on his chest as he strained, smoky breath in my face. He shouldn't have been a smoker. No endurance. Up, up, and away went the pistol, and he was shaking, and I felt like a goddess, my shades slipping down my pointy nose, so we were eye-to-eye, and he gazed at my mismatched eyes with terror and mute understanding, his own brown eyes bloodshot, veins bulging at his forehead.

"You're dead," I said.

The siren grew louder, closer, and we strained, he and I, face to face, hunter and hunted, predator and prey. I had to fight back the drool.

"This isn't o—"

I stuffed the gun into his mouth when he'd tried to say "over."

Leaning way from him, my arms tight, I was amazed at the leverage I had on him, could feel his legs trying to get out from under mine.

"Beg to differ," I said, pulling the trigger. The pistol made his head disappear, made me tumble backward into the van, deafened again at the thunderclap of the monstrous thing. He fucking exploded, sprayed the garage behind him with blood, bone, and brains. What was left of him fell over, lifeless, the empty gun smoking in his wounded, twitching hand.

The poetry of slaughter, back in bloody spades.

It was a tableau in my mind, these three would-be avengers, these vigilantes, dead in an alley. I drank it in, the blood draining into the winter-wet bricks, the silver dagger on the ground, a lovely thing, the unused bullets scattered around the headless man like spent confetti, the dead man in the cab of the van, slumped to one side, broken head against broken automobile glass. The moment held me spellbound, my head still ringing from the gun's report, my eyes full of spots of green. I understood why poems were made of wars, long ago, when victors could savor their triumph over the vanquished, before "winning" became a four-letter word.

I was getting better at killing.

Then I ran from the scene, fast as my limber tired little legs would carry me, went to the back of my building, up the stairs, keyed into my unit the back way, just as the police cruiser nosed into the alley, flashing electric blue. Somebody had seen; they'd called. Neighborhood watch.

I slipped off my gloves, pumped soap on my hands, washed them in the sink, over and over, watched my hands go from claws back to nails, watched my fingers return to their normal length. Over and over, like a squirrel worrying a nut, I washed my hands, until they were clean, pristine, human. Looking in my mirror, I saw Sääm looking at me, in all her lupine glory.

*Oh, Princess. I'm so proud of you. I knew you had it in you. You're a fucking killer.*

"I'm not the killer," I said. "You are."

*Beg to differ. I mean, you could have blown your own head off with that last bullet, but it never occurred to you; you want to live. And that means, you know, living with me. We're roomies, Princess. Til' death do us part. Oh, and the way you set up that crime scene, classic! I love it! Me, I just wanted to tear out throats, eat their hearts and cirrhotic livers. You turn it into a bogus crime scene, you turn it into art, my love.*

I cringed at the thought. Yeah, I could have shot myself. I should have.

*No more thumbsucking, Princess. The gloves are off, now, right?*

She raised a clawed finger.

I glanced at the shredded remains of my gloves, the fingers popped like spent firecrackers. I picked them up, threw them in a trash bag, grateful to be away from that ghastly reflection, the mismatched stare of the Beast. Then I paced around, went to the back door of my apartment, peeked out the window. The police were looking around, talking on walkie talkies. Another siren sounded, and an ambulance turned up.

*I didn't even know you supported assisted suicide. Christ, that was beautiful. A masterstroke. I just helped a little with the heavy lifting. That was all you, Princess.*

"They wanted to kill me," I said.

*Yeah, they sure did. Pity you left your coat on the sidewalk. Hope the pigs don't catch that. But pigs usually sniff around the easy pickings. You made it look enough like what it could be that they probably won't suspect much. Russian Mafiya kind of thing. Probably people called when they heard the shots.*

I tried to remember when I heard the sirens. I think they came after the shots. It was hard to know, because the gun had my head ringing. What a horrible thing a gun was.

*I mean, I was thinking of starting you off with one, but you go and bag seven. Grrl power!*

"Self-defense," I said. "They wanted to murder me. And the others, well, that was, I don't know what that was."

*And you've been whining about wanting to die for weeks. Why the change of heart?*

"You made me do it," I said.

*I was an accessory; you were the perpetrator.*

"If not for you, it never would've happened," I said.

*So call the police. Confess to it. Put that gliberal morality to the test, Princess.*

"Jail won't fix me," I said.

*Isn't it funny, like how jail was meant to protect the individual from society? How weird is that? They're like spleens, or livers, accumulating toxins. But tasty, so tasty, remember?*

I saw another police vehicle turn up, an unmarked car, and a meatwagon, or at least that's how Sääm saw it. A place to put the bodies.

*Mmmm, meatwagon.*

She filled my head with images of fresh, bloodied bodies, and my mouth watered. I backed away from the window, went into my apartment, hoped I was safe.

*Living in denial. Such a waste of time and energy. You don't have to be scared, anymore. Nobody can touch you.*

"I'm afraid of what I might do," I said. "What I have done already; what I will do."

*Speaking of that, don't forget to pick up Zooey at the bus station tomorrow. You wouldn't want anybody nasty to scoop her up, wouldja?*

I saw the *Wilkołak* handbill and took it in my hands, turned it over, looked at it.

*You should get that framed. Like a trophy. Like a work of art.*

Samantha 3, *Wilkołak* Brothers 0.

I dug out the dead Pole's phone, turned it over in my hands, wondered what I should do with it. It was evidence, put me at the scene of the crime. The phone belonged to Curtis Lepinski.

*Sorry, Curtis,* I thought. *Bad day, eh? Fuck your luck. You tried to murder me.*

The smart thing to do would be to put it someplace nobody would ever find it. But part of me wanted to see the guy's contacts, see who his associates were, what e-mails he got.

Fabian Kowalczyk; Urban Kowalczyk; Curtis Lepinski; Krystian Kaminsky; Edward Jaworski; Roman Romanowski.

I wondered if these guys were the ones who were in on the attempted hit on me, like did I kill some of these other guys? I had to have. But which ones? I'd have to scope a newspaper, see what I could find, once it finally got around to covering the slaughter. I missed my computer, hated having to depend on my tiny cell phone and the snail's pace of the daily paper. I was living a fast-forward life, couldn't afford to waste time.

I'd become a hustler.

Maybe I could check into a cybercafé, use their computers. I pocketed the names, pocketed the phone, figured I'd drop it in the lake or break it into a bunch of pieces. Something like that. I'd google those names, try to look them up, or, if that failed, find something in the phone book, try to find them. Maybe go from defense to offense. If it was only a half-dozen fuckers after me, I had, perhaps, a chance to shut them down before they killed me.

*Now you're thinking. You find'em, let me handle the wetwork. What a team! Not that you need help, Killer.*

The notion made me queasy, both the concept, and the execution. These guys were vigilantes, sure, but they knew what I was, and at least in their heads, they were doing the right thing. And, given my track record of mayhem to date, they were vindicated. They were doing the right thing, the human thing. They were the Villagers, trying to lynch the Werewolf, only they had the right target. They knew who the bad guy was. The question was whether the others knew.

Then the dead guy's phone rang, playing some anthem I didn't know. I looked at the caller. I jotted down the number. It was Urban Kowalczyk. Then I turned off the phone, afraid that the ring would somehow get the police up here, pocketed it again, looked around. The phone had me at the scene of the crime.

Just like the phones of the others. I was getting quite a collection.

I had to get rid of it, of all of them. But first, I had to get my jacket.

Down I went, hands in my pockets, head down, step-by-step. Fortunately, people worked in my neighborhood, and nobody was usually around during the day, or nobody much. Seemed like nobody, anyway. I looked around, felt a little paranoid, like what was behind those glass windows, who was watching, who had seen? It was better not to look, better to be uninteresting, unremarkable, anonymous.

I went around the corner, where the guy had thrown my coat. A news van rolled by on a cross-street, toward the scene of the crime. My coat wasn't there. I looked around, without wanting to be obvious, but the fucking thing wasn't there. Somebody had grabbed it. The thought made me fearful, edgy. I looked around, half-wild. Had the cops found it, already? Was I caught?

No.

I didn't have to be afraid. Not anymore. Sääm was right about that. Maybe the *Wilkołak* Brothers would be back, but I'd be ready for them. And if they got the drop on me, then they'd put me out of my misery. But I wasn't going to make it easy for them. No way. I was going to make them work for me.

And speaking of work, I called off.

No way in hell was I coming in today.

# 3. FRIDAY: 9 NOVEMBER

Today was the day Zooey was arriving.

I glanced at my watch. There was still a few hours, but I had to get downtown to pick her up. Would the Polish mafia keep coming after me? Would the *Wilkołak* Brothers return? Of course they would, it couldn't have just been those three nutjobs. I put on a green knit Peruvian cap, thinking that would make me look a little different. Cuter.

I went out the front, locked up, glanced at the wolf on the phone pole, snarling blindly behind the dimes, and went down my street, shaken to be traveling down the street again, where I'd had to run for my life the morning before. Now it was just a normal, boring Chicago street.

I got on my train, rode downtown, dialed up Zooey while I rode on the train. To my delight, she picked up.

"Hey, Zooey," I said. "I'm heading downtown. Where are you?"

"Hi, Sam," she said. "We crossed the state line awhile ago. Not sure where I'm at, exactly."

"Well, I'll be there," I said. "In a green cap and a cream-colored, quilted overcoat."

"Kewl," she said. Her voice was husky and sweet. I couldn't wait to meet her face to face, and caught myself—I shouldn't be excited about it, but I was. It was amazing how you could compartmentalize your brain, when you had to, how you could lose yourself in the minutae. Maybe it was an old lycanthrope trick, wrapping yourself up in enough wool, calling yourself a sheep, hoping nobody caught the whiff of corpse on your breath, saw the dried blood under your nails.

Nobody paid me any attention, not the half-dozen students half-way down the train, nor the worried-looking businessman standing by the door with a monogrammed metal attaché and cordovan wing-tips. They were all norms. Nobody was the wiser.

We crossed the river, which bubbled and steamed in the oncoming winter cold. They pumped dye into the thing, to keep it looking somewhat palatable, versus the putrid foulness green that it really was, from all the pollution in it.

I got off at the Clark and Lake stop, since it looked like I had time, and walked into the Thompson Center, that painful architectural bunion in the heart of downtown, what looked like an alien mothership that had landed, Klaatu dead at the helm, Gort with a smoking visor.

Walking through there, stuffing my ripped knit gloves into an innocuous trash bin, I got out streetside, checked my watch, saw that I still had time, and went to the LaSalle Street bridge over the river. I turned the phones on, opened them, and dropped them over the side without any fanfare, just a quick glance to watch them fall, hoping they didn't land on the heads of some tourists on a fucking architecture tour. The phones hit the water with innocent little splashes, vanished from view. I hoped that rotten river water would soak into the circuits, frag the things, turn them to junk in no time. Water always wins.

I felt guilt-free, blameless, cleansed. It was an unfamiliar, yet pleasing feeling. I had been challenged, and I had triumphed. I wanted more, wanted to celebrate with Zooey, with Reagan, even with Polly. Not like I could come out and say why I was celebrating, exactly, but, you know, just to feel good about feeling good.

*Wilkołak* Brothers 0, Säämäänthää 3.

I was looking for the sweep. Just pondering that phone call right after the ambush, could just imagine Urban wanting to ask Curtis if I was fucking dead, or caught, or whatever. I guess Curtis was supposed to call in, maybe he was overdue. They'd find out soon enough on the news.

I was hopeful that Blondie had wanted a final test before he pounced on me, so that made me think that while they suspected I was the lycanthrope, they didn't know for certain. It gave me hope that all of the *Wilkołak* Brothers didn't know I was definitely the target. Then again, maybe they suspected, and wanted the test as a fail-safe. Either way, they could hardly run to the police and complain that I'd bumped off their hit men, that I was a werewolf. Even with the "mad dog" stuff circulating in the news, there was no way they'd be able to say that. What's more, I was so small, there's no way in hell that they'd think I was the guilty party. Little old me, versus three strapping men? Please. Nobody in the City of Big Shoulders would buy it.

But the *Wilkołak* Brothers would. They would know that their strike team had made contact, and they had fucking lost, and that their target was likely onto them. That meant I had to get busy, and fast.

It was kind of exciting, I had to admit, walking south on LaSalle, making my way toward Harrison, where I'd turn to get to the bus station. I felt like a secret agent, and, really, I was. Plotting intrigue and murder.

If this was just a small group of hunters, not some big fucking organization, then I could pounce on them fast, finish them off, and sleep easy. If it was an organization, then I could at least gain intelligence on them, find out what they were about, if they had a name, if Ansel knew fuck-all about them.

But if it was just this group of yahoos, then so much the better. They'd probably continue to spy on my place, but this time, I'd be ready for them, and I'd take out their next strike team without waiting for them to hit me first. That's how you played "Gotcha!" I remembered playing that in college, getting a squirtgun in my face, not lasting a day. But that Sam was a fucking norm, a world away from me, from what I'd become.

Christ, I could hardly wait to have a go at them. That thought kept me warm as I hoofed it, block after block, to the Greyhound station, then found myself a seat among the runaways, derelicts, vagabonds, crazies, students, oldsters, single moms and other unfortunates who had to rely on the bus to get someplace. I remembered taking the bus when I was in college, and hating it.

The terminal had televisions perched around it, showing news about an apparent murder-suicide in Logan Square that claimed the lives of three men: Fabian Kowalczyk, 35; Curtis Lepinski, 33; Krystian Kaminsky, 28, all from Avondale. Authorities said it appeared that Mr. Lepinski shot Mr. Kowalczyk in the chest during some altercation, and then shot Mr. Kaminsky, before turning the gun on himself. There were also preliminary reports of a possible fourth party at the scene, and police were talking with witnesses, and area police encouraged residents to come forward if they had any information. Other details of the investigation were being withheld until forensic results were returned. The murdered men had both been shot three times at close range by Mr. Lepinski.

Some of the people watching expressed dismay, while I took out my list and crossed off names, was left with Urban, Edward, and Roman. I couldn't wait to meet these guys. I'm sure they were shitting themselves, wondering what went wrong. My guess is that Urban was the leader, since he called Curtis, although who knew for sure?

Witnesses? I hadn't seen any witnesses. Maybe it was just the police throwing out some bullshit to try to lure me out. I hadn't seen anybody, not even the Dog-Walking Man.

All the *Wilkołaks* could be sure of was that they didn't catch the werewolf. I loved that, tucked the paper in my pocket. Their guys had blown it. Thinking about it, I wondered if the team that had come for me had been their best guys. Seemed logical, right? Why lead off with your benchwarmers? Although I didn't want to be cocky, that gave me hope. Maybe they had underestimated me because I was a girl. Maybe they weren't entirely sure at first. Maybe I'd just been lucky. No. It hadn't been luck; it had been strength. I'd been stronger, more savage, crueler, more cunning, more ruthless. They had underestimated me. They thought they could cow me. Just some bitch.

"Get in the van, Bitch!"

Hah. I had the last laugh. And speaking of that, I saw that authorities were investigating the murder of Willa Powers, 32, at her apartment building. Somebody had tied her to a chair and burned her to death. They had used dental records to confirm her identity. Police were continuing their investigation.

That filled me with an uneasy satisfaction. I mean, it was kind of great to think that Willa was gone, that her poetry was so much ash beneath her corpse, was the source of her immolation, but that I'd done it myself, it made me feel a little icky. Maybe a lot icky.

"Hey," said Zooey, standing lankily above me. I just knew it was her.

She nudged me with a sneakered toe, had a pink Samsonite suitcase beside her. She was wearing a very long, black-and-white striped scarf, a green Army jacket with a fuzzy pink sweater and a denim skirt with black Capri leggings, striped socks, acid-green sneakers. She smiled shyly at me, had a ring in her nose, between her nostrils, like that kid I'd seen at Nonpareil. She had a half-dozen little rings up both her ears, had a lip ring, had perfectly shaped eyebrows, full and luscious, had gorgeous lavender bangs peeking out from under a red, white, and blue stocking cap—white pom-pom, blue cap, red rim. Her eyes were big and dark and beautiful. She was beautiful, had this long face, high cheekbones.

I jumped up, and we hugged. I barely reached her shoulder.

"Ohmigod," I said. "Zooey, you're so tall!"

"And you, you're like a doll," she said.

"Hey, I'm an action figure! How long have you been here?" I asked. The easy familiarity just came naturally. I'd expected awkwardness, but there had been none. She was as wonderful in-person as she'd been online.

"Just a little while," she said. "I was hanging out, just kind of scoping it out. I was starving, so I ate a soft pretzel at the food court, and I saw you come in. I knew it was you. I was tempted to call you or prank you or something, but you looked totally focused, like in your own world."

"That's me," I said. "Definitely. Oh, come on, we have to go someplace fun, get out of this purgatory."

"Sure," she said, picking up her suitcase. She had chipped nail polish, black, and had sweatbands on her wrists, green and yellow.

"Can I help you?"

"No, I'm fine, really," she said.

"I love your little suitcase," I said.

"My worldly possessions," she said. "Well, stuff that mattered, anyway."

Seeing her just made everything great, her slender stride, her easygoing way. She was adorable, terribly cute, despite being an amazon. Her eyes were pitch black, which contrasted her lavender hair perfectly, drew all the right kind of attention to her face: her slender, long nose, her wide-mouthed smile, the angular planes of her face. She could be an alternamodel.

"Zooey, you're beautiful," I said. It made me almost shy to look at her. She was that lovely.

"Thanks, Samantha," she said. "I can't believe you made a big deal about the bruise on your face; it's nothing."

My hand went to my face unconsciously, and she laughed, took my hand, held it in hers. She was wearing rainbow knit gloves, each finger a different color.

The bruise had healed up, like it was never there. Wonderful!

We made our way to a Starbucks near the El, decided to talk some, get acquainted, first. She ordered a straight black coffee, while I got myself a cappuccino, and we sat across from each other, our knees lightly touching. She leaned close, head hunched forward, savoring her coffee. She had a cute little overbite. I liked how her upper lip massaged the rim of the cup as she drank.

"Samantha, I loved your 'Transformation' video," she said.

"Yeah?" I said. She nodded.

"It's why I wanted to see you," she said, playing with her cup with her long fingers.

"It's been getting a lot of hits," I said. "But I've had a little trouble following it up. Computer troubles."

Zooey nodded, kept turning the cup in her hands. She looked up from her cup, long lashes, the blackest eyes I'd ever seen on anybody.

"I kind of had an ulterior motive in visiting you. I know that clip was for real," she said. "That's what I want you to tell me."

"What, that it was real?" I asked. She nodded.

"I mean, I studied it," she said. "I watched it over and over again, frame by frame, and there aren't any cutaways. No edits, except for that one moment later, when you're coming back. But the transformation is one take. Either you're totally rich, and could afford the special effects that would cost, or else it's for real. And your blog entries, you know?"

I nodded, sipping my drink, touching her knee with mine. Her own foot played with mine a little, and she leaned close on her elbows.

"You really are one, aren't you," she said. It wasn't a question.

What to say to that? I kind of thought there was no point in pretending. Secrets were meant to be shared. Looking around, I nodded. It felt wonderful to be able to come out and say it to someone. Of course it would be Zooey, my sudden suicide girlfriend. When I nodded, her face brightened, her obsidian eyes flashed bright, and she took my hands in hers again, smiling.

"I knew it!" she said. "I fucking knew it! Holy shit, Samantha! I mean, like, fuck!"

She laughed, and I laughed with her. Somebody in on my secret who didn't want to kill me!

"Most people would be freaked out," I said. "I showed a friend of mine, and he kind of flipped out."

Good thing I put Lee out of his misery; it was a mercy killing, truly.

"I'm not freaked," she said. Zooey looked at me, licked her lips, pawed at her cup of coffee. "I think it's cool. All my life, I've looked for different things. I mean, *different,* you know? I got piercings, tattooes, went weird places, did weird things, met weird people. I'm a Suicide Girl, you know what those are, right? Who they are? I mean, I'm not officially, but I'm so going to be."

I nodded. Who didn't? I sometimes thought about posing for them, back when my hair was atomic red. I missed that, I had to admit, although where I was at now made that seem pale by comparison.

"Well," Zooey said. "I like extreme things, but the extreme gets mundane in no time flat. Like ten years ago—"

"You're 19, Zooey," I said. "Ten years ago, you were fucking nine."

"Yeah," she said. "But I'm just saying, yesterday's extremism is today's tameness, and is tomorrow's lameness."

She glanced around the shop. "I mean, if I asked how many people here had tattoos, I bet the majority would raise their hands. And we're in what, a Starbucks? Twenty years ago, maybe one or two, but today? Everywhere. Same thing with piercings—now, it's just a contest to see who can get the most piercings, in the most uncomfortable places, or who can lodge hockey pucks in their earlobes, that kind of thing. It's like the normals are biting back, you know? I hate them. Some day, heroin will be sold at drugstores, like convenient as can be, as easy as aspirin, put in gumwrappers, because it's what the norms will eventually want. Then what will people do for kicks?"

I could feel her pain. When the herd moved, it trampled everything flat.

"Even cutting's fucking mainstream," she said. "Well, it's like mainstream subcultural, now—that bugs me, too, like the layers of subculturality."

Drinking my coffee, I enjoyed listening to Zooey shpieling. It was intoxicating. I felt a kindred consciousness in her. She was like Reagan on fast forward.

"'Subculturality,'" I said. "Great word. Did you just make that one up? It feels so social anthropological."

"It's all splintered, and the real avant-guardians are almost invisible," she said, like I hadn't interrupted her. "The real artists, the innovators; they're almost drowned out by the stampeding of the herd. It's like there's the innovators at the apex, and then the wannabes, and then the poseurs, and then the hipsters and scenesters, and then after that, there's, I dunno, the mundanes, like the ones who are sincere but boring, and the sellouts, who might have talent but who are whores, and then there's the herd, this great, fat mass of nothing that is like ready to consume the next big thing, so long as there's somebody there to cut it into little bite-sized pieces for them. Whether fake vampire books, or some new toy, or doll, or whatever they're told to like."

I had no idea Zooey was so culturally preoccupied. It was fascinating, watching this beautiful girl rant.

"But eventually, the herd just consumes everything," she said. "Art becomes kitsch, served up on coasters, placemats, and t-shirts. The machine gobbles it all up, spits out the bones, until even the extreme is patented—it's like Extreme™ as a trademark. What the fuck, you know? I was seriously contemplating suicide, because it just gnawed at me, left me feeling less than empty inside. But then I saw your video, and it fucking blew my mind, Samantha. I was like 'Jesus fucking Christ, she's a fucking monster.' I knew it in my heart, even before my head could catch up to it. I wanted that. I wanted what you had. You *reached* me."

"You don't want that, Zooey," I said. "It's a big pain in the ass. It's so much work."

"No," she said, putting her hands on mine yet again. I didn't pull away; I liked the feel of her on me. "I want it. I want you to infect me. I want you to teach me. I want to be your disciple."

"Disciple?" I said, laughing. "I'm not a prophet."

"No," Zooey said. "You are. You fucking are, Samantha. Because while I was getting high and watching that clip, over and over again, masturbating to it, I thought you had really done something, there, something real. I mean, we've heard about werewolves our whole lives, right? Who doesn't know about them? But you came right out and ran with it, filmed your fucking transformation. I mean, I thought that was just awesome. That was art. And that it was for real, my god, Samantha. I came to your video, left myself breathless, wanted to run wild with you, wanted to taste the pain, to feel the whole thing, experience it all."

"It's a one-way trip," I said. "You can't go back."

"I don't want to," she said, her teeth set on edge, her black eyes staring hard into my own. "You think I want to go back to this?"

She tossed her lavender head at the coffee shop.

"You think this is living? I mean, I know you know better, because you fucking know, you know?" she said. "But having seen you, known you, I cannot fucking go back to what I was. I would kill myself, first. I already decided that, like if you wouldn't make me one, I'd either kill myself, or find myself another lupine, try to get them to make me.

Maybe Adonis, you know? That's part of the thrill, you know, the danger of it, like not knowing if he'd do it—you, I mean, I don't think you'd kill me. If you did, I'd forgive you, I swear; I'd understand. I mean, what a way to go right? Death by werewolf? Fucking-A. But I feel like there's trust between us, that you wouldn't kill me, and that's why I had to come."

I patted her hands, which held onto me like I was a life preserver. I reached out and petted her, touched her pretty hair. Death-by-were-wolf was just death. I doubted Sheldon, Lee, Willa, Gabe, or Clay would have disagreed. The Poles? Who knew what they thought?

"You'd lose all of this," I said. "The dye, the tattoos—it's a skin change, is what it is. Something happens, and you change. I lost mine the first time."

"Fuck it," she said. "Leave it to the mundanes. I want what you've got."

I thought about what I'd done just that morning, could only imagine how Zooey would've handled it.

"It's a disease," I said. "There is no cure."

"I want it. Give it to me," she said. "Tonight. Please."

I'd be lying if I didn't say I wasn't tempted. To not be alone.

"I mean, I'll do *anything*," Zooey said. "Anything you wanted, whatever you said. Lycanthropy, I mean, like, wow, right?"

I nodded, smiling at her youthful exuberance, her half-considered spiritual insurrection. You didn't bungee jump into the Abyss; there was just that pause before leaping, and then the point of no return. I had blundered blind into it, hadn't known what I was getting into; Zooey just thought she knew what she was getting into.

"Have you wasted anybody?" She asked.

Of course the *Wilkołak* Brothers and the others were in my head. How many had I killed? Seven?

"I've wasted and tasted them," I said.

"Wow," she said. "Awesome."

She was my fallen angel, my tarnished beauty, and I felt my heart swell for her, as we shared our tiny table at one of probably hundreds of Starbucks in Chicago.

"What do people taste like?" she asked.

"Veal," I said. "They're pretty tender."

"How random," she said. "I bet where I come from, people totally tasted like milk-fed veal, because of all the cheeseheads."

"Some taste better than others," I said, not bothering to clarify that. "We really are what we eat. The life we lead shows through in our bodies."

I wondered whether that applied to lycanthropes, too. Would my life catch up to me?

"Oh, I'm sure," she said, finishing her coffee. "Garbage in, garbage out, right?"

"Sure," I said. "One thing I should tell you: there are people who're hip to the whole scene. Hunters. Killers."

That sparked her interest. A hint of danger, like a whiff of cinnamon. "What, a secret society? That kind of thing?"

I nodded, looking around. Streetside, an Animal Control truck tooled by, and for an absurd moment, I thought maybe they were looking for me.

"There are these guys who're hunting me," I said. "At least a half-dozen, though, uh, I killed three of them yesterday morning."

Zooey's jaw dropped, and her heavy-lidded eyes were full of lust and admiration for me, for my transgressive audacity. She was fucking impressed.

"No way," she said. "For real?"

"Yeah," I said, quietly. "We should keep that quiet."

"Yeah, yeah," Zooey said, nodding. "For sure."

I was being reckless, but I could smell Zooey's scent, this mix of girlie-musky cologne and ardent longing, I knew she would never betray me, was confident that she idolized me, thirsted for me.

"But silver will hurt you," I said. "It can kill. And these guys know their stuff."

"Not enough," she said, smiling wickedly at me. "I mean, you got them, Samantha."

"Yeah," I said, praying I'd be as successful next time, but I didn't know who to pray to.

"We have to do it tonight," she said. "We totally have to. We can get a shitload of take-out Thai, just pile it on, pig out, and then we can have sex, and then, like around midnight, you can just do it to me. It'll hurt, right?"

"Well, yeah," I said. "I mean, I'll have to bite you."

A couple of norms were drinking their coffee a table over, a Baby Boomer man and woman, Woodstock-meets-Coldwater Creek. They were eavesdropping, it looked like.

Zooey caught me looking, smiled, played around with it. "Truss me up nice, this time. It chafed the last time we did it, you know? I mean, I like pain, but chafing's just annoying."

"Sure," I said. "Girl Scout's honor."

"I'm so glad they added Bondage and Domination to their merit badge system," Zooey said, glancing at the couple, then back at me. "I mean, I had to learn through trial and error, but it's nice that they've updated it all."

"Well, we should get going," I said. "It'll be dark, soon."

"Yeah, can't have that," she said. We got up and went out holding hands. I liked walking with Zooey. She looked so tall next to me. Anybody casually looking at us would think she was leading me on, instead of the other way around.

"You are one sick puppy, Zooey," I said. "I think I love you already."

"Yeah," she said, giving my hand a squeeze. "I so am not going back to Milwaukee."

She was looking every which way, taking it in, like a tourist. She even brought a digital camera, was snapping off shots of me, of us. She really was a puppy, all waggled tails and playful nips. What would I do to her if I infected her? What would she become? I knew myself before and after, but eventually, the after overshadowed the former. I wasn't sure I'd even recognized myself, anymore. Who knows what Ansel was really like. Probably just the same. The thought of Ansel raised my hackles, like Zooey saying she'd seek out another lupine if I didn't do her. There was no fucking way that was happening. She was mine.

Still, I wondered if the *Wilkołak* Brothers had regrouped, what they had in mind. That would be problematic for me, like what to do, where to go. I had no other place to go, not for what I had in mind. There was no way I'd introduce Zooey to Ansel, at least not before the transformation.

And yet, I was worried about how safe my neighborhood was, anymore. My guess is that the *Wilkołaks* would hang back, wait until the heat had died down, because they'd figure I would let my guard down, that they would get me when I wasn't looking, wasn't thinking.

But I was always looking, always thinking. I was an artist. They were going to be my next piece. Zooey and I windowshopped our way to the El, and then caught a train north and west, to Logan Square, Zooey keeping up a playful, endless patter almost the whole way there. She caught her share of admiring and admonishing glances, like norms wondering why a pretty girl would do that to her face, like the rings through her nose and lip, the wild hair, the loud clothes. But I loved her look—she was like Rainbow Brite on PCP.

We got off at my stop, and I pointed to the *Wilkołak* handbill, flapping in the breeze. Somebody had drawn a little party hat on the werewolf, a cone jauntily turned to one side.

"What's that mean?" she asked.

"Werewolf," I said. "In Polish."

"Intense," she said. "I like the hat."

"They canvassed my 'hood with those," I said, looking around, to see if anybody was paying attention. Zooey took the handbill, folded it up, pocketed it.

We went down the steps, and I pointed them out everywhere I saw them. Some were ripped, some papered-over with other things, many of them drawn on. Like somebody had drawn a shiner on one of the faces, and other had drawn glasses.

One had written "Wendy" on it, with an arrow pointing to the grinning wolf.

We passed locals on the sidewalk, Zooey toting her suitcase contentedly, like there was nothing to worry about. For her, maybe. But I worried for us both, imagined some fat-bodied Pole with an AK-47 loaded with silver bullets, emptying it into my chest.

We got to my building. As I was keying in, I heard a man call out to me.

"Miss?" he said.

I turned. Zooey turned. It was the Dog-Walking Man.

"Yeah?" I said. He was carrying a bag. What, was he part of the Polish Mafia, too? I tensed, and Sääm bristled, and Zooey looked from him to me, searchingly.

He held out the bag. "You dropped this the other day."

My jacket.

"Dropped what?"

"Your coat," he said.

"How do you know it's mine?" I asked, suspicious. I hadn't seen the Dog-Walking Man that day, although I'd had a lot on my mind.

"I saw you lose it," he said. "When those men were chasing you."

Fuck. Zooey broke into a nervous grin. "Whoa."

"Thanks?" I said, taking the bag, looking into it. Sure enough, my jacket was in there. I looked him up and down, tried to get a sense of him, like whether he was a threat, whether he knew or saw anything. He had to have known that the guys chasing me that day were dead.

I stared at him, and he stared at me.

"I was looking for that coat," I said. "That was a pretty crazy day."

"Yeah," he said. "Did you talk to the police?"

"Oooh, I'm not supposed to say anything," I said. "They're still trying to iron out that case."

"Really?" he asked.

"Yeah," I said. "Those guys were Russian Mafiya, like connected to it. Something with running guns or something. I was in the wrong place at the wrong time. They thought I'd seen something, and wanted to throw me in the van, so I just took off. I was terrified."

"We have a neighborhood watch," he said. "Just so you know. On this whole block."

"Yeah? Well, you can't be too careful," I said. "Safety first."

He nodded, looking at me, and at Zooey.

"So, hey, Sis, can we get inside?" she said. "I'm *freezing.*"

She put a lot of emphasis on that, drew out the "eeee." I nodded, smiling.

"Yeah, thanks for the coat, uh," I said, holding out my hand.

"Stan," he said. "Stan Hardy."

"Thanks, Mr. Hardy," I said. "You're the best."

I went back up the steps, with Zooey dogging my heels, smiling blandly at the guy, who watched us go in. I locked the door, checked my mail, glanced back at him.

"Weird fucking guy," Zooey said.

"Yeah," I said. "Shit. He was out the day I got chased by those Polish Mafia guys. I wonder what he saw. Nice one, saying you were my sister, by the way."

She grinned. "What about you? You were smooth. Smooth as glass, cool as ice."

Lying was easy. I did that all the time. My whole so-called life was a lie; what mattered were the details, and the flow. Practice makes perfect.

Keying into my apartment, I held the door open, let Zooey in. She checked it out, went from room to room, while I checked a note from Mr. Ludovico, who wrote that he'd deduct the charge for the window from my safety deposit, and that I'd have to be more careful.

I checked out the window, wondered if the workmen were tied to the *Wilkołak* Brothers, like if my apartment was bugged or something. Paranoia was a real bitch.

Zooey came back out, empty-handed. She'd dropped off her suitcase in my bedroom, had taken off her jacket.

"I'm starved," she said. "Do you have anything good, food wise?"

"I think I have fried chicken in there," I said. "If you can't wait for Thai."

"Kewl," Zooey said, went to the fridge, took out a bucket, snagged a breast, began eating it cold, took a seat on my sofa, looked around. "Hey, where's your computer?"

"I smashed it," I said. "When I was, you know…."

"Whoa," Zooey said, gnawing the fried chicken to the bone. "I was wondering why you hadn't posted; I was worried you'd changed into a wolf, had run away, or maybe that somebody had caught you. Taliesinner's having fits."

I took out a drumstick and dug into it, while Zooey went for another breast, tore into it. It was nice to see that meat-eating would be no trouble for her.

"I brought my laptop," she said. "If you need a fix."

"I'm good, actually," I said. It was weird, but I kind of didn't miss it. What I had on my mind, I could hardly blog about, and so it didn't bug me too much not to be able to. I had so much more to worry about, now. "I don't miss it."

"Yeah," Zooey said. "You're onto bigger things. You know, this place isn't so bad. I mean, it's a little bigger than my place in Milwaukee. I live with my folks."

"Yeah? Wow, I'd hate that," I said.

"It's not so bad, I guess," she said. "They leave me alone, mostly."

I kind of wish she hadn't mentioned her parents, because it gave me pause, made me think that I shouldn't infect her. She didn't know any better. She was a kid. Her parents would worry about her. I didn't want anything bad to happen to her.

"Zooey, we shouldn't do this," I said.

She paused in mid-chew. "Which part?"

"The real part," I said. "The bad part."

Zooey just smiled at me, winningly, fetchingly, waving a chicken breast at me. "That's the *best* part, Samantha. Look, I want you to, alright? I'm giving myself to you of my own free will, right? I'm a sacrifice."

"Eww," I said. "I don't want to think of you like that. What if I eat you?"

"Oh, well," she said. "What a way to go, like I said. But I don't think you will. You need me. You need a friend, somebody on your team. A packmate."

She was kind of right about that, I had to agree. It was lonely being a lupine. I had already murdered and/or eaten most of my friends. Ansel was exactly no comfort at all, all wrapped up in himself. What a dickbag he was. How I hated him. I had to see him again.

"You have such pretty tats," I said, admiring her arms, where an angel fought with thorns and brambles over a setting sun. She had a Pegasus on her other shoulder, and a winding snake that had a ruby in its mouth, and a prism that shot skeletons in each color of the rainbow, and a tramp stamp along her back in the form of an electrical outlet, and a bar code on the back of her neck that she told me valuated her at $6.66, shyly telling me that she wanted her own Mark of the Beast. Her whole body was a tapestry, splendidly, proudly, carefully defiled.

"Yeah, they're great," Zooey said. "But I'd trade them in the wag of a wolf's tail for what you're carrying, Samantha."

We finished eating, licked our fingers clean, and stared at each other awhile.

"I want to see," Zooey said. "I want to know. The video doesn't do you justice."

"Alright," I said.

I don't know why, but I went into the bedroom with her. It seemed the right place for it; the living room felt too exposed.

"What do I do?" she asked.

"Just watch," I said. "Watch and learn."

It was weird, doing it this way. I took my clothes off, not wanting to shred yet another outfit, and crouched in front of her, while Zooey sipped her soda, playfully kicking a foot against my bed as she watched.

Sääm was, as ever, entirely ready to come out to play, had been wanting Zooey since the bus terminal, although she'd held her tongue—or maybe she was just merging more fully with me, and didn't need to talk like she used to. Since I was pretty relaxed, I could pay attention to it, the details, I wasn't distracted. It felt like a flare in my head, like my skull splitting, and this odd sensation in my forehead, and incredible heat all through my veins, from head to toe, doubling me over, because with the fiery flood came pain, as my joints grew limber, began to stretch and strain against the confines of my flesh, to violate the rules of my biology, to challenge the requirements of physics. I changed, and strained against the floor, my nails stretching into claws, my fingers finding easy purchase in the hardwood floor, the slats creaking as my body added mass.

"Holy mother of fuck," Zooey said, staring, the soda held motionless in her hand, straw inches from her mouth, lips parted.

My body lengthened, grew broader, my shoulders knotted with muscle, my stomach, my ribs stretched, the pain was breath-taking, and I took great gulps of air, my face lengthening into a hateful, monstrous snout, full of wicked teeth, my eyes setting back in my head, as red-brown fur sprouted all over me, like a carnal crop on time-lapse photography. My ears lengthened, as did my tongue, while Zooey just watched, a single tear running down her face.

Sääm was here with her, in the close confines of my room, moving up from a crouch into a stand, my head touching the light that hung from the ceiling.

I reached out, took Zooey's soda, brought it to my lips took a long, triumphant pull on it. It was a testament to my level of control that I could even do that. I was getting better.

"Fucking awesome," Zooey said, meekly, her face blanched almond-white.

"Zooey," I said. There wasn't going to be a last chance for her; Zooey had blown it the moment she'd crossed the threshold, the moment she'd agreed to it. She wasn't going to leave the room the same as she entered it. If she had second thoughts, there wasn't anything she could do, as I snagged her in my long arms, her bones like those of a bird, holding her fast, picking her up, right off her feet, like she weighed nothing.

"Sääm," Zooey whispered, her eyes wide, lips apart, close to my face. I slipped off her top with a couple of shakes of my fingers, long nails slicing the fabric like it was gossamer, revealing her exposed flesh, her hard, pierced nipples, her heaving stomach. "Fuck."

I took a bite out of her shoulder, and she cried out, tears running down her face.

"Yes! Christ almighty, don't you dare fucking stop!"

I'd never done this before, licked her wound, this great, gaping chunk I'd taken out of her. She tasted sweet, like marshmallows.

Lapping up the blood on her wound, I fought hard on the urge to take her by the throat, to shake her dead. Instead, I laid her down, while she wept, and ran my tongue down her front, painting her with her own blood, down her breasts, down her stomach, catching on her belly button ring, and then down to her crotch, down her thigh, to the fold of flesh above her slender knees, took a bite out of her there, a little nibble, and she cried out again. I worked my way to her other side, took a bite out of that shoulder, too. Ansel had said the amount of wounds determined how quickly one transformed.

"It burns," she said. "An icewater burn."

How much was enough? How long would it take? How much could she take?

"More," she said. "More more more!"

I nipped at her other thigh, forced myself back. She sat up, pale, gasping, her wounds bleeding, while I concentrated on not tearing her to bits. It was hard to dial back on it, and even Sääm, who liked Zooey just fine, could be tempted to overdo it. The urge to destroy was terribly strong.

*The urge to destroy is also a creative urge.*

Zooey rolled over, bleeding on my bedspread, and I'd cursed myself for not thinking of towels. She was weeping.

"Fuck," she said. "You barely touched me."

I grabbed her, picked her up, carried her to the bathroom. She almost fell over, had to brace herself.

"I'm alright," she said. "Almost fainted."

Then she did faint, knees buckling, grasping at towels, falling. Was she going into shock? I didn't know, didn't know first aid. I remembered something about the feet, like they were supposed to be elevated, right? That was good? And blankets, like keeping her warm?

I took her long legs and propped them up on the lip of the tub, and put bath towels on her. She was breathing shallowly, her eyes open, sightless. I leaned in close, looked into her eyes.

I realized I was useless in this shape, that a werewolf was only good at a few things, and healing wasn't one of the things. So, I forced Sääm back into her pen, let my old skin return, crunched myself up tight like a wad of paper in a fist—it was funny; early on, I saw Sääm as exploding out of me, and now I felt like she was looking at me the other way, like forcing something into a bottle that was too big for it, stuffing her inside me. It got harder every time, going back to the old me.

It felt like forever, me on my hands and knees, becoming human again, while Zooey moaned on the floor. I called her name.

"Zooey? Zooey? Can you hear me?"

Naked, fleshy again, I dug under my sink for a first aid kit, wondered how to handle that, exactly? Like would first aid heal the bite of a werewolf, prevent the infection? Did I let it get infected? I could just imagine asking Ansel that, him laughing at me, calling me an idiot, wondering why I'd even want to do that. I mean, I'd just put some Bactine on mine, that hadn't done anything.

I put a gauze bandage on her shoulder wound, and another on her leg, figured I'd start with that. Then my intercom buzzed, and I jumped up, closed the door, ran to my bedroom, snagged a bathrobe, closed the bedroom door, and went to my living room, looked out the window.

It was Polly. She saw me, waved. She was carrying a big package, something that looked like the painting. I waved back, went to buzz her in. There was nothing else I could do.

Then I tasted blood, realized I had it on my face, ran to the kitchen, wetted a paper towel, rubbed it on my face, scrubbed it as quickly as I could, and grabbed a dark chocolate bar from my cupboard, tore the wrapper from it, took a big bite of it. Something to camouflage my breath a little, and all the blood on my teeth. I threw a record on, something to make some noise. It was Slint's "Spiderland."

There was a knock at the door, a pert little rap-rap-rap of her no-doubt fashionably gloved knuckles. I ran back to the bathroom, turned on the shower, made it warm, stepped over Zooey, shut the door again, ran down my hallway to my door, unlocked it.

"Hey," Polly said. "Sorry to pop in on you like this, Sam."

"No problem," I said, taking another big bite of the candy bar. "Want some?"

"Eh, no," Polly said. "I brought Ansel's portrait of me."

It amused me, Polly falling for this shell of a man. That was so her, like her attention to surfaces, her inability to get at depths. So, of course, Ansel would be perfect for her, this blank slate for her to project herself upon, like a movie screen. Polly was one of those types who would date somebody because they reminded her of themselves, versus finding somebody to complement her.

"Wow," I said. "Come on in."

Polly trotted in, wearing high-heeled shearling boots and black tights, an emerald jumper dress, and a black long-sleeved top beneath her fur-collared overcoat.

"I didn't come at a bad time, did I?" she asked.

"Just about to shower," I said.

"Ah," Polly said, leaning the painting against the wall. "I was really up in arms about where to vault this. Ansel said it wasn't perfect, but he's wrong. And I was afraid he'd get mad and trash it or something, so I figured it would be good to vault it here, at least for now. I really, really want it back at my place, but I have to figure out how to pitch it to Tristan."

"Why don't you say you had it done as a gift for him?" I said, my mouth full of melted, masticated dark chocolate. It was like it had never occurred to Polly. Her eyes brightened at the prospect.

"Yes," she said. "I suppose I could say that. But what if he wanted to see the artist? Can you imagine Tristan and Ansel in a room together? Tristan would be furious at the prospect of me posing naked for him. And Ansel could break Tristan over his knee. No, it's probably safer to have it here, at least for the moment. Nobody would suspect you, Sam. Tristan thinks you're weird, but harmless."

"Hah," I said, covering my mouth with my hand, to keep from spraying Polly with blood and chocolate. "Weird, but harmless, eh? Thanks, Tristan."

Man, that made me want to track Tristan down and bite him. Wouldn't that be a trip? I could just imagine that blowing up, a love trapezoid between Tristan, Ansel, Polly, and me. I threw myself into it because I figured I'd have bitten both Polly and Tristan by then.

Weird, but harmless.

"Oh, don't mind him, Sam," Polly said. She glanced over my shoulder, down my hallway. "Do you have company? I thought I heard a thump."

"Oh, yeah," I said. "Zooey. A friend of mine."

"Zooey who?" Polly asked. "Do I know her?"

"From Milwaukee?" I said.

Polly wrinkled her nose, shook her head.

"So," I said. "I'll hang your painting up on this wall, right here."

I nodded to the blank wall, where there were a couple of track lights that had come with the unit. Polly clomped over to it in her heels, appraised it.

"Yes," she said.

"Great," I said. Zooey moaned from the bathroom.

"Is she okay?" Polly asked. "Wore her out, eh?"

"Something like that," I said.

Polly was the type of person who reveled in how liberal she was by openly embracing my bisexuality. It's like it was scratch-and-win bohemianism, exactly what Polly was all about. She put her hand on my forearm, cocked her head.

"Would you mind if we hung the painting now? I'd really like to see it, how it looks, and snap a picture of it with my digital camera."

"Uh, sure," I said, and she brightened so much she was almost luminous. I went to my foyer closet and dug out a toolbox, got a hammer and a nail. "I don't have any picture nails."

"Not a problem," Polly said, holding up a packet of them. "I came prepared."

I took them and hammered into the wall, once Polly had determined the height she wanted. Then we opened the brown wrapping on the painting, and hung it up, Polly eyeballing it, me with a level, checking it, until we had it right.

Turning on the track lights, there was naked painted Polly, in all her slender, elfin glory. She smiled, nodded. "I feel just like Dorian Gray. My life is over, Sam. Can anyone ever capture me better than this?"

I looked from her to the painting, shrugged, put the tools back in the box. "I don't know. I bet I could do something more evocative, more passionate."

"What, in performance?" she said, scoffing. "I'd like to see that."

"Would you?" I asked. "Would you really?"

Her wide-set eyes leveled on me. A challenge, almost. Sääm understood it, sniffed it out. The key to owning the moment was to take those moments when they came. Opportunity was a whore, she was always knocking, trying to get in.

I reached out and grabbed Polly's hand, bit it, bit down hard, tasting her blood. I licked the wound, as she jerked her hand away with a yelp.

"My God, Sam, what on earth was that?" she asked, rubbing her hand where I'd left my mark.

"My autograph," I said, wiping her blood from my lips. "You wanted a performance. Consider it a self-portrait."

Her ego wouldn't let her admit I'd gotten the drop on her, so she waved it off. "Oh, ha ha, Sam. Nice performance. What do you call it?"

"'Infection,'" I said.

She flexed her hand. "I can't believe you just bit me."

"I can't believe I haven't bitten you before," I said. "Let me get you some Bactine."

I left her in the living room, peeked in on Zooey, who was breathing shallowly in the steamy bathroom. I turned down the hot water a little in the shower, fetched the Bactine and some bandaids, closed the door before Polly could nose in there.

I gave her a couple of squirts of Bactine, and handed her some gauze and some tape, along with the bandaids. She shook her head, cleaned the wound.

"Not your most inspired work, Sam," she said, finishing with her hand. She flexed it, checked it. "If it had been my writing hand, I'd have killed you."

"Sure," I said. "Sorry, Polly. I'm a little high."

"I should have guessed," she said.

I didn't feel a bit sorry. I was entirely glad I'd just infected her. That worked on so many levels. Ansel would shit his pants, knowing that I'd done this. I wonder when and how he'd know. And Polly would be a dreadful werewolf. I couldn't even imagine the lifestyle working for her. Then again, maybe she'd craft a poem about it, win a prize.

While she fussed over her hand, I looked at Ansel's painting. The painting did look good. We paused, admiring it, and Polly took some pictures of it, like ten pictures, different angles, up close, far away, getting it just the way she liked it. And then she snapped a couple of pictures with her cell phone, just to compare. I'd never seen anybody eyefuck themselves more strenuously than Polly.

"I think Ansel's getting sick of me," Polly said.

"Yeah?" I asked, watching her snap a few more pictures of her portrait.

"Yes," Polly said. "I don't know what it is, exactly. But there's something...off. I don't know what I did."

"You were just you," I said. "All you could be. Sometimes that's enough."

Polly bit her lip, pondered that, what she'd say in reply. Then Zooey came out of the bathroom, wrapped in towels and sheathed in steam, her lavender hair frizzed up. She'd covered her wounds, made a beach towel toga of sorts, and looked pale as death.

"Hi," she said. "I'm Zooey."

"Polly," Polly said, snapping her good hand out, which Zooey shook.

"Whoa, nice painting," Zooey said. "Let me guess: it's you, right?"

Polly laughed, chirping, birdlike. I was struck by what a human fraud she was, how she carried herself. Was there anything genuine about Polly Drinkwater? I didn't know. But she was so wonderfully put together. Maybe lycanthropy would fit her like her gloves did.

"Sam and I had an arrangement," Polly said. "I needed this painting put someplace safe, and she volunteered her place."

"Generous," Zooey said, leaning on the hallway wall. I didn't want her fainting again.

"You should go back to bed, Zooey," I said.

"I'm good," she said.

"Well," Polly said. "It looks just perfect, Sam. Now, you take good care of it. It's on loan, you see? Once I have a good exhibit space for it, I'm taking it back."

"Fine," I said. "The curator will bill you by mail."

"Wonderful," Polly said. "Well, I'll leave you two girls alone."

Zooey had blood soaking through the shoulders of her toga towel. I tried to catch her eye, but she woozily ignored me, doe eyes on Polly.

"Yeah, great meeting you, Polly," she said. "I'm from Milwaukee."

"Really?" Polly said. "Do you know Paul Turanian, by any chance?"

"Nope, Zooey said, swaying on her feet. "Can't say I do."

"Do you do art?" Polly asked.

"Only body art," she said. "Tattoos and, you know, piercing."

Polly nodded, putting on her shades, which was her usual "I'm leaving" mannerism. I wondered if she'd seen the stains soaking through the towel.

"But no fine art, eh?"

"I think tattooing is just fine," Zooey slurred.

"Ah, well," Polly said, turning on her heel, facing me. "I'll talk to you later, Sam. Thanks for being such a good sport. Take care of me while I'm gone, will you?"

She bobbed her head in the direction of her portrait, while Zooey clutched at one of my chairs. I went to the door, opened it, to whisk Polly away.

"No problem," I said. "I'll take care of it. Bye."

"Goodbye, Sam. We'll talk later," Polly said, then turned to say goodbye to Zooey. "Bye, Zooey."

Zooey gave her a thumb's up, and Polly smiled phonily and I closed the door, then went to Zooey, helped her sit down, unwrapping the toga, getting a look at her shoulders, which were awash in blood and other stuff I didn't recognize.

"Jesus fuck," I said. "I'm going to bind those right."

I ran into my steamy bathroom, grabbed my first aid kit, then ran back to Zooey. I prayed that I didn't fucking kill her. Werewolves were made for killing; it was what they did best. They were animal machines, killing machines. I walked her to my futon sofa, set her down. Taking the Bactine, I sprayed the wounds, and Zooey cried out.

"Ouchless, my ass!" she said.

Then I tore open packs of gauze and wadding and pressed it onto her wounds, then took the white medical tape and crisscrossed it over them. I repeated this on both shoulders, at her knees and thighs.

"Stop fucking squirming," I said.

"It hurts," she said, sweating. "It fucking hurts."

"What did you expect?" I asked.

Zooey reached out, touched my face with her hand. "I'm not complaining."

"Stop moving," I said. "You'll reopen the wounds."

I should have laid her out on my bed, in my bedroom, but now there wasn't any time.

"I'm thirsty," she said.

"Okay," I said, went to the kitchen, got out a Chinotto, my favorite little Italian soda, and popped a cap, gave it to her. She drank the little genie's bottle of brown liquid.

"What is this?" she said.

"A magic potion," I said. "Just rest."

I watched her for the rest of the night, had the television on to distract her, kept an eye on her, kept her hydrated, prayed that she wouldn't die, but to whom I prayed, even I can't say, because I didn't know, anymore.

# 4. SATURDAY: 10 NOVEMBER

I must have dozed off, because I woke in the morning, with Zooey poking me, grinning at me in her bloody beach towel toga.

"Hey, Sleepyhead," she said.

"Hey, you're alive," I said.

"Yeah," she said. "I have to commend you on your restraint, Samantha."

She pulled aside her towel, surveyed her wounds. "They're already better. I mean, not really better, but better than they were last night. You got me good."

True enough, the wounds didn't look as horrible as they had during the night. They still looked like she'd been savaged by something, but at least she was walking around.

"These'll go away, right?" she asked.

"Yeah," I said. "First time you skin-change. Along with your tats, and your marvy hair."

Zooey pouted at the prospect of losing her lavender locks. "You know, I'm actually a blonde. Like whitish blonde. Generations of Wisconsinites in me, Nordic blood, farmers, that kind of thing. Interbred. I'm almost a who's who of recessivity—blonde, fair, freckled, tall."

"Great," I said. "Well, I'm sure the retrovirus will love you, then,"

I cut her "huh?" off at the pass, explained to her what Dr. Resnick had told me about it, about the nature of the disease.

"That's how it changed your eye," she said.

"Guess so," I said.

"I hope it doesn't change mine," she said. "You know how rare it is, blonde with dark eyes?"

"How rare?" I asked.

"Fucking rare," she said, with a crooked smile. "I must have Carthaginian blood in me, too; they say that's where it first came from. Blonde girls with dark eyes."

"But the Romans pillaged Carthage," I said.

"Yeah, but they enslaved the women," she said. "I mean the ones they didn't kill, or rape to death, or whatever. So, the blood was passed on."

"Lucky you," I said.

"Lucky me," Zooey said. "I ate all the chicken. We need more food."

"I'll see what I can do," I said.

"Cool," she said. "I'd help, but, you know, I'm recovering."

"Gotcha," I said.

My phone rang, and it was Reagan.

"Hi, Samantha. Are you at work today?"

"Uh, no," I said. "I go in later."

"Okay, well, I'll just drop by our place around ten, then," she said.

I wondered how Reagan would react to Zooey being there. I had no idea how she'd take that. Probably with grace and decorum. That was how she was. All her I's dotted, all her T's crossed.

"Polly said she dropped off her painting at your place," Reagan said.

"Yeah."

"She said you bit her hand," Reagan said.

"Uh, yeah," I said. "She was giving me shit, so I bit her."

"Is this a new performance you're working on?" Reagan asked. "Polly's in a lather, said none of the boys are answering their phones. Did you see what happened to Willa?"

"Yes," I said. "Horrible."

"Yes," Reagan said. "Who would do such a thing? And where is everybody?"

"I don't know where anybody is," I said. Zooey was staring at the picture of Polly, her dark eyes almost blank.

"I should like to see Mr. Rupino's work," Reagan said. "He of the rather strenuous artistic opinions."

That made me smile. I could just imagine. Looking over at Polly's painting, I thought Reagan, particularly Reagan, would be impressed by it. It was her kind of work, although bolder in technique. I was just glad Reagan was talking to me again.

"She said you had a friend over," Reagan said. "A charming, willowy girl, I think was how she put it. Zoë?"

"Zooey. Yes," I said, glancing at Zooey, who had gotten up, was busy guzzling down my orange juice.

"What is she to you?"

"A fan," I said. "A friend. A co-conspirator. An accomplice."

Zooey glanced at me, grinning around her orange juice glass, her throat working as she drank it down. For someone so slim, she could certainly eat and drink her share. But I figured it was her body responding to the infection.

"Marvelous," Reagan said. "I just can't wait to meet her."

"Sure," I said. "That'll be great."

"Ten o'clock, then," Reagan said. "I'll be there, camera in hand."

"Alright," I said, and we hung up. Turning to Zooey, I said, "That's my friend, Reagan. She's coming by to take some pictures of me. It's a project of ours."

"Reagan? Hahh, for real?"

"Yeah," I said. "Her dad was a big fan of the Gipper."

"Wow," Zooey said. "I'd kill myself if I had a name like that."

I didn't even want to tell Zooey what Reagan's last name was. In a way, her father had been ahead of his time, naming Reagan that in 1976, before the country had gone insane over the Gipper. But I doubted Zooey cared so much about that.

"Reagan's pretty great," I said. "She's nice, a total blueblood."

"Nice person to know," Zooey said. "Are all of your friends rich?"

"No," I said. "Really just Reagan. The others just pretend they're landless aristocrats."

That made me a little sad, thinking of Sheldon, Lee, Gabe, and Clay; ghosts inside me, now. Only Polly, Reagan, and I remained. And I was the Werewolf. And Reagan. I wondered how she was doing with that. She had to be feeling it in a big way by now.

Zooey considered that on her last swallow of orange juice, then put the glass in the sink. "Sorry, I drank all your juice. I'm wicked thirsty."

"Salright," I said. "We'll take care of groceries, later."

"Mmkay," Zooey said. "I guess I should clean up before your, uh, friend shows up."

"Yeah," I said. "Reagan might have a question or two."

I wondered how the pace of the infection would pass with Zooey, like how quickly would it manifest, given the damage I'd done her. There was no way of knowing; it was all very touch-and-go. Zooey went to the shower and got scrubbed up, crying out when the water hit her wounds, while I looked around the apartment, tried to imagine it in Reagan's eyes, like whether it would pass inspection. I wanted to vacuum, but that would have to wait until later.

I went to the window and saw Stan the Dog-Walking Man on my side of the street, walking Boomer the bulldog. He actually stopped at the phone pole with the *Wilkołak* message on it, looked at it, then around, then turned and looked at me, which startled me a little.

Uncertain, I waved to him, a single shake of my hand. Stan raised his own hand in return, his face unreadable. I didn't have blood on me, did I?

Glancing down at my clothes, I saw that I was okay. Boomer peed on the phone pole, then snuffed around, and Stan went away. I wonder if he was a Vietnam Veteran or something. Like some crazy guy who was on pension of some sort, didn't have to work. That was the life.

I was hungry, too, so I went to the cabinets and hunted around in there. Nothing really caught my eye, struck my fancy. Was I losing my taste for people-food? I hoped not.

Zooey came out of the shower, went into my bedroom, got changed, came out in a pair of blue jeans, a black and white striped long-sleeved t-shirt, and a union jack sweater over that. She was wearing matching Chuck Taylor low-tops. Very colorful, very busy.

"Feeling all Cool Britannia this morning?" I asked.

"Sure," she said. "God Save the Queen."

I got showered, and put on my work uniform, since that's what Reagan was expecting in the photo shoot. Looking in the mirror, I saw that my wounds were completely healed. Amazing how that worked. My face was its pristine, button-cute self again. I smiled, admired my mismatched eyes. I could almost get used to them. My face felt like a mask, anymore. I knew it was fur-lined, but looking at it head-on, you couldn't really tell. Maybe something about the eyes, something feral. Hungry eyes.

When I came out, Zooey laughed at me. "Oh, man, that sucks. Do you have to work today?"

"Yeah," I said. "Suckage."

"Totally," Zooey said. "What should I do, in the meantime?"

"I'm sure you'll find something to amuse yourself," I said. I kind of hoped she'd get a job, like if she was just going to be crashing here. "Will your folks be worried about you?"

"Oh, I think it'll be fine," Zooey said. "I'll call them, tell them I'm going to hang out here for awhile."

"What about the copy shop?" I asked.

"Fuck them," Zooey said. "I can always work at one down here."

I thought that was kind of admirable, like her utter willingness to blow off her job. So juvenile, so amusing. I should give that a shot.

"Your folks, do they know you're here?" I asked.

"I just said I was staying with a friend," she said. "It's no problem."

I was feeling a little like Reagan, like overprotective, worrying. But I felt protective of Zooey, didn't want anything bad to happen to her. Well, anything worse than what I'd done to her, anyway.

We watched daytime television until Reagan turned up. Every now and then, I'd go to my window, peer out, fearful that the *Wilkołak* Brothers were out there, imagined a silver-bullet sniper on a rooftop, waiting for his shot, taking my head from me with a squeeze of a trigger. Not liking that image, I went away from the window, back into the depths of my apartment, although I realized that even though I was on the second floor, somebody in the building across the street could, if they wanted to, look into my apartment. Maybe they already had. I went to the window and lowered the blinds.

"You're fidgety," Zooey said. She was shivering, her cheeks flushed.

"I'm paranoid," I said. "All this time I've been dicking around, you know, and somebody could be watching me."

"You're a fucking werewolf, Samantha," Zooey said. "You have absolutely nothing to be afraid of. You're the goddamned monster!"

She shook her head, looked disgusted with me. And she was right, it was kind of chickenshit of me to worry about it, to still live in fear. Seemed like that was what being American was all about. Fear was the thing that united the United States—fear of terrorists, fear of conservatives, fear of the government, fear of fundamentalists, fear of gays, fear of immigrants, fear of corporations, fear of environmentalists— we had 33 flavors of fear, served up daily, ice-cold. With sprinkles.

And, yeah, what was I afraid of, anyway? I was one of many things that went bump in the night; it was stupid to be afraid. And yet, there it was. The fucking *Wilkołak* Brothers had been a major buzzkill. I should have been enjoying myself, but instead I was afraid they were going to catch me and kill me.

I was afraid of those Animal Control vans I saw tooling around the city, blank and white, dark windows, mysterious. I was convinced those vans weren't being run by the City of Chicago, but were, rather, federal vans, run by agents. Looking for lupines. Then again, those agents were just norms. They were like the worst of the norms, so normal they were abnormal, these men of law and order, themselves operating outside of the law, working to maintain Order, if not uphold the Law. Animal Control. Yeah, I'll bet.

"There's not enough of us," I said to Zooey.

"That can be remedied," Zooey replied. "I already feel contagious. I'm burning up."

"An infectious insurrection?" I said. Zooey nodded.

"Why not? Beats the alternative, you know, cowering, living in fear every day. If even the monsters are running scared, what does that say about society? Know what I mean?"

I nodded, thought Zooey brought an interesting perspective to things. But I was an artist, not a politician. I didn't really think in a political manner. Spectacle, I could understand, outrage, I lived for— but ideology felt too confining. Too *normal.*

"Maybe we're the remedy," Zooey said. "The real fix for the mess we're all in. I mean, if society's the solution, then what's the problem, exactly? You think homeless people living in steam tunnels care who's president? Or that kids who can't get drugs give a fuck about tax cuts? We can make them care. We can force them to care, or at least do a better job pretending that they care."

Zooey sat on my sofa, tucking her legs underneath her, wincing as she did so. She'd begun healing quickly, but not completely. The full healing wouldn't come until her first transformation. Then she'd never be sick again.

"The government talks about solutions," she said. "But really their only concern is ensuring that they're the ones who are making the decisions. It doesn't matter how great an idea is; if it's not coming from the right source—and from the right direction—well, then it's a bad idea, it's a problem. Why do those homeless sleep in steam tunnels?"

"To keep warm," I said. "Because they don't have any place to go."

"Because they're afraid," Zooey said. "Because they are afraid the cops will come and throw them on the street. But what if they were werewolves?"

That grossed me out. "Eew. You'd bite a bum?"

Zooey laughed at me. "I'd bite a bum on the bum. Let them all get infected, watch the fun times commence. Bet they'd eat all the pigeons. Maybe get the Canada Geese, next. The point is, they'd be empowered—Economic Man is ruled by market forces; his wallet is his sword and shield."

I didn't realize she was so political, so radical. It was a curious side of her, but then, she'd been only a cyberfriend over the past few years, and there were, no doubt, many shades of her I had no clue about.

"So, what we're talking about is an end to the dominance of Economic Man, and maybe Man in general. This—" She nodded toward her wounds. "—Is the way out. For you, for me, for everybody. If everybody's a monster, then nobody's a monster. Then there is no monster."

"Okay," I said. "And then what? A new order will still have winners and losers."

"Sure," Zooey said. "But for the right reasons, not because somebody had a trust fund, or bribed the right politician at the right time. The winners will be winners because they deserve to be there. Liberties aren't given, Sam; liberties are taken. You take liberties."

Her black eyes were like smoldering coal, and I wondered if the old cliché about eyes being windows into one's soul, what was lurking inside Zooey, and what I had inadvertently unleashed upon the world. She looked rabid.

"Economic society urges us to consume," Zooey said. "So, the lycanthrope is, like, the ultimate consumer, isn't it?"

"Well, they're not talking about *that* kind of consumption," I said.

"How do you know?" Zooey asked, letting that just hang there.

"Because if you eat all the consumers, pretty soon you're out of business," I said.

"Meh. I'm talking about consumption, here," she said. "Not business. The thing is, society *isn't* taking care of its own. It *isn't* practicing what it preaches. Across the board. Liberals abandon the poor, the weak, the vulnerable—conservatives aren't conserving anything but power. Everything is entirely up for grabs, even as people are busy pretending the system is, like, working. But we change that. Suddenly, those who are busy pretending to stand for what they believe in are going to be forced to actually walk their talk."

"What are you talking about, Zooey? Some kind of werewolf ideology, here?"

"People are going to have to start living like their lives depended on it," Zooey said. "Right now, everybody can coast; they can fake it; they can go through the motions of their day because there are not stakes in capitalist society for most. Sure, there are players out there, people who drive change, but they are a minority, and they aren't even the best-suited for that role; rather, they're just in the right place at the right time, a very capitalist virtue."

"Are you in college, Zooey?"

She nodded. "University of Wisconsin at Madison."

"Shouldn't you be in college right now?" I asked.

"I'm on a little sabbatical," she said. "Don't throw me off the scent, here."

"Alright," I said. "Proceed."

She really sounded so undergraduate, it made me very amused, and perhaps a little sad. Zooey didn't seem to notice that, instead went on with her diatribe.

"But you throw us out there, and the very real possibility that someone, anyone out there might die on any given day," Zooey said. "Suddenly, people are going to be alive again. In a way that they've never lived before. That's the salutary effects of predation on the human species. It forces the prey species to shape up."

I bet she studied sociology, or perhaps social anthropology. I wanted to ask her, but she looked like she was just warming up.

"Yeah, people will die," Zooey said. "Good people, bad people—but the survivors will not be clueless consumers; they'll be people again, with a very keen awareness of their own mortality. Economic society runs away from death, tries to hide it. Death isn't marketable except for anybody selling coffins. Capitalist society is busy trying to sell people endless distractions from their own mortality—you can be young forever, you can be pretty forever, you can be wealthy, thin, strong, sexy, popular, powerful—forever. It's all a lie. Sure, it's a Big Lie, so people swallow it, because the alternative—I will die—is frightening. But the thing is, the embrace of that illusion is what keeps more people from being artists."

"Huh?"

"People are more concerned with their credit ratings than what they're actually doing with their lives. It's easier just to buy something, not to make it yourself. Easier to turn off your senses than to use them, or to shut down your brain and embrace a fad, follow a fashion. To live an empty, unexamined, artless existence. But you know what drove art? Mortality. Those cavemen painted scenes in ochre on their cavern walls because they wanted to gain control of their world, because they knew that their number would come up sooner than later, and because they wanted to leave something of themselves behind before the cave bears or saber-toothed cats ate them. That's the essence of the artistic spirit. And we will give them that motivation, that desire to live and be remembered."

"By hunting and killing them?" I asked.

"Exactly. Liberalism tries to have it both ways, to value the individual and to protect them from their worst instincts. That doesn't do people any good. And Conservatism worships Economic Man; for all of their Bible-thumping, it's Mammon they worship, not God, and surely not Jesus."

"You're talking about, I don't know, fascism," I said.

"Am I?" she said. "I put value on the individual, on the artist. Certainly not on the state. But you infect some homeless, and they won't be homeless for long."

"Yeah, because they'll go attack some people and take over their homes," I said. "How is that just?"

"Oh, it's not," Zooey said. "But it'll at least make sense to me. Those homeless will have a pack to protect them. The alternative is ignoring them."

"They probably have that, already," I said.

"But this pack really could...and would...protect them. Can you imagine some kids trying to set some werebums on fire? It'd be a big mistake, and a fatal one. And best of all, those bums would eat well that night, and the world would be less one more person inclined to set bums on fire."

It sounded like she was endorsing a kind of lycanthropic vigilantism, which sounded like all kinds of bad. It was weird for me to be in the position of the responsible adult, the voice of reason, with what I'd done. This was a place I wasn't used to being, wasn't a role I was comfortable with.

"Criminals are society's predators. We already have the predation you talked about."

"Sure, the criminal is the apex predator of Economic Man, just as the terrorist is the apex predator of Political Man, the censor is, like, the apex predator of Literary Man, and the fascist is the apex predator of Liberal Man," Zooey said. "But Physical Man, the man who matters most, has no apex predators. Not anymore. And as we've moved further from them, we've lost our way. But this lycanthropy scene, it shows a new way."

I wondered who the apex predator of Cultural Man was. The barbarian? Were there still barbarians in this day and age? Who would qualify? The fundamentalists? The hipster wasn't a predator, alas; the hipster was merely a cultural scavenger. It was tricky, these organistic assessments of society, but Zooey took right to it, and I wondered how much of it was her, and how much was perhaps tied to her spreading infection. Just as I had gone from a wannabe performance artist into a fucking serial killer, I could see Zooey perhaps undergoing a similar transformation, from suicide girl to revolutionary.

"Don't get ahead of yourself, noob," I said. "You haven't even undergone the change, yet. You don't know what you're about to get into."

"I'm not worried," Zooey said. "I can handle it. I told you, I like pain. I thrive on suffering. Give me pain, or give me death."

"I think it's liberty or death," I said.

"Death is liberation from life," Zooey said, held me with her black eyes. I wondered as I looked into those twin black marbles, whether I'd made a big mistake in infecting this girl, if I'd made a huge blunder. But I figured it was just bravado, just her trying to establish herself in my eyes, like to have credibility. Like a tough girl, playing at being tough, staking out her turf.

"How many of us are there?" she asked, opening up her laptop with a grunt.

"I don't know," I said. "Ansel said there's maybe five in the city that he knows about."

"Not counting us?" she asked.

"Yeah," I said.

"So, that's 5 out of 2.8 million," Zooey said. "Just counting actual city dwellers. Hey, we should blog about this."

It hadn't occurred to me; I was so busy hustling in the real world, I'd really forgotten about my so-called life online.

"Nah, it's okay," I said. "You can blog about it."

"Oooh," Zooey said. "I totally will."

My doorbell buzzed, and there was Reagan, about to walk into the wolves' den. I hopped up, buzzed her in, and wagged a finger at Zooey. "Be good."

"Why start now?" she said with a sigh, stayed in her spot on the sofa, as I let Reagan in. Reagan's eyebrows were a little wilder. She saw me notice, and her face showed me that she noticed.

Zooey was on her back, turned her head, looked Reagan up and down. "You must be Miss Manners."

"Miss Manners?" Reagan said.

"What Sam calls you on her blog," Zooey said. Reagan smiled, looking at my wryly.

"I didn't know you had a blog; and what's more, that I was in it," she said.

I was embarrassed, but there was nothing to do but cop to it. "Yeah, I've kept a blog for years. There's nothing bad in it."

"Oh, sure," Reagan said. "Miss Manners, eh?"

"Yeah," I said. "Because you're always so polite."

Zooey beamed at me, insolent to a fault, but there was nothing for me to do at the moment. So Reagan knew I had a blog; so what? She didn't know what it was, or where. Although if she mentioned it to the others, word would get out in no time. Not like there were many "others" left in our group, thanks to me. Maybe I'd just delete the whole thing, just to play it safe. I mean, I'd said all kinds of things on there.

"Naturally," Reagan said. "Courtesy is society's salvation."

"Yes," I said, keeping my glare on Zooey. "Being rude is bad."

"Manners are so middle class," Zooey said.

There was no way I could pose for pictures with Zooey lurking in the living room. "Zooey, would you mind going into the other room?"

"The bedroom?" Zooey asked. "Oh, sure. Nice meeting you, Ms. Reagan."

"Whitehouse," Reagan said. "Reagan Whitehouse."

Zooey laughed. "For real?"

Reagan's smile was frosted courtesy. "Yes."

"Wow," Zooey said, sauntering into the other room, closing the door. Reagan looked at me quizzically. Judging, of course.

"What a curious creature," Reagan said. "And speaking of creatures, Samantha, I suppose I owe you an apology for my behavior the other day."

"What? No," I said. "Please."

"Shall we take the pictures? Can I drive you to work once we're done?"

I didn't give a fuck about the pictures; what I wanted was to know Reagan's heart and mind, where she was at.

"My therapist has prescribed me some capital tranquilizers," she said. "Something to help me with the unsettling dreams. I told her everything, all I'd been dreaming and experiencing. She thinks I'm expressing a neurotic reaction to loss of youth. Isn't that ridiculous?"

"I told you what it was," I said. "Did you tell your therapist?"

She snapped pictures of me, and my posing was off. I was busy trying to converse with her, and the concern showed on my face.

"Please," Reagan said, between shots. "I don't want to be institutionalized. Things are already getting a little rocky between Gretta and me."

"Really?" I asked.

Reagan nodded. "It's all my doing."

"That should do it," she said, then looked at Polly's painting. "My, look at the deft hand of Ansel Rupino. He really did do her credit on this. She looks like she belongs on canvas. Shall we take you to work?"

"Alright," I said, hoping we'd talk more in the car. "Zooey, I'm off to work."

"Can I come out, now?" she asked.

"Yeah," I said. And Zooey came out, looking searchingly at both of us. "Alright, Zo: I'm going to work. Try not to wreck the place when I'm gone."

I didn't think Zooey would be going anywhere in her current state. She needed her rest. I hoped the *Wilkołak* Brothers would stay the hell away from her, gave her my cell phone number, just in case.

Following Reagan outside, I wondered what I should do. The street was weekend-busy, or busy as it got in winter. There was Stan the Dog-Walking Man up the street, talking to some old guy I didn't know, and further on, a couple of kids with their mom, I presumed. And a young man working on his car, checking his tires with a tire gauge.

"I'm right here," Reagan said, gesturing to her Rover, wedged in between a Pontiac and a Chevy. I got in, and Reagan smoothed her hair as she keyed the ignition. "I hadn't expected you to find yourself a roommate, Samantha."

"She's a friend," I said.

"Curious creature," Reagan said. "A bit of a pop cultural feral child."

"That's what I like about her," I said.

"I'll bet," Reagan said. "Have you heard anything from the others? Polly's been trying to reach everybody, can't find anyone. Did you see what happened to Willa?"

"Yes," I said. "Horrible."

"They say it's murder," Reagan said. "Whoever did it burned her to death. Who would do such a thing? I mean, Willa?"

Reagan pulled out and went down the street.

"They say sometimes people burn crime scenes to cover up evidence," I said.

"Well, can you imagine? All of her poems. All that paper," Reagan said. "Up in smoke. Gone. I always told her she should get backups for it, but her insistence on writing everything out by hand, oh my. Dreadful. I hope they catch whoever did it. I mean, really. Who burns someone to death? It's so retrograde."

I shrugged, unsure what to say. I just remembered the stink of her as she burned, the roar of the flames, my dancing around the fire, her muffled shrieks as she'd died. It wasn't the happy memory I had thought it would be. I hadn't even known why I had done it, except that she'd walked in on what I'd done with Lee, so she had to die. It was as simple, as horrible, as that. She'd gotten in the way. I wondered if I'd be capable of doing that to anybody who got in my way. Could I kill Reagan like that? Zooey?

"Have you heard anymore from Polly?"

"Polly? Yeah, we were supposed to talk," I said. "I saw her yesterday. That's when she brought the picture. She thought she and Ansel might be on the outs."

"It's about time," Reagan said, but that had me wondering. I dug out my own cell and dialed up Polly, got her voicemail.

"Polly, it's Sam," I said. "Call me when you get a chance."

I hung up.

"People are disappearing left and right," Reagan said. "I talked to your Ansel, and he changed his mind about Polychroma, said he didn't want to go into the gallery business."

"Too bad," I said. What had happened? What had Polly done? What had Ansel done? Or had he done something because of me biting Polly? Ansel, Christ. That fucker had never called me back. I opened my phone, gave him a ring, too, got his voicemail.

"Ansel," I said. "It's Sam. Where the fuck are you? Where's Polly?"

After what I'd done to Sheldon, Lee, Willa, Gabe, and Clay, I had this premonition that something bad had happened to Polly, that Ansel had gotten pissed off or something. Polly had been saying something about that, like things going south between her and Ansel. But he wouldn't just fucking kill her, would he?

*Why not? Isn't that what you did? And she's fat.*

*She's so not fat.*

*Elfin, alright? I bet that's how Ansel likes 'em.*

*Stop it.*

*I bet that's what drew him to her to begin with.*

*Quit.*

*Feeding time. Just like you and the boys. Or maybe he caught your scent on her. Maybe he couldn't stand to think of her being yours.*

"Samantha?" Reagan said. "Are you alright?"

"Just worried about Polly," I said. It was stupid. Nothing happened to her. I mean, I just saw her yesterday, for fuck's sake. Still, she said she was going to call me.

*But you bit her. You stole her from Ansel, right out from under him.*

"I'm sorry about the other day," Reagan said. "I've been terribly moody lately. You should see me with my tranquilizers, my anti-depressants, my sleeping pills. I haven't painted in days and days. Not a single brushstroke. I've tried, but everything's just sort of gray. Except for the dreams. They're vivid, of course. Sometimes waking dreams, like when I'm walking around, thinking about things. But no painting. I really don't know what's wrong with me."

Things were getting out of hand, out of control. Too many plates in the air, me trying to catch them all. Ansel. Polly. Reagan. Zooey. It almost made me grateful that I'd murdered the others, just got them out of my mix.

"I told you," I said. "I'm what's wrong with you. It was my fault."

"Stop it," Reagan said. "You're blameless in all of this."

That made me laugh, bitterly. I was the perpetrator, not the victim. I was the Werewolf, not the Villager. As far from blameless as evil was from good, as light was from darkness.

She dropped me off at Nonpareil, and when we said goodbye, it felt like we meant it.

# 5. SATURDAY AFTERNOON

Ansel finally called me, gave me an earful when I got home.

"Sam, what the fuck are you doing? The news said those guys in that van had a bunch of weapons in their van, said they were arms dealers or silver smugglers, or something. They're all over the whole silver bullet thing. Calling them The Silver Bullet Gang."

"Not my fault," I said. "Self-preservation, Ansel."

"Yeah, and what about, what's her name, Willa? I know you did that."

"Also not my fault," I said, clearing my throat. "She walked in on me and Lee."

"They found him, too," Ansel said. "What the fuck, Sam?"

"I don't know what you're talking about, Ansel," I said, acutely aware of being on a goddamned cell phone while he was saying this.

"You're playing it way too big, Sam," he said. "You need to be on the margins, not on the front fucking page. A footnote, not a headline, not a sidebar. You want agents out there, hunting you down?"

"You should have killed me, I guess," I said. I wouldn't tell him about the others. That would really set him off.

"I still can," he said. "You need to lay the fuck down, roll over, play dead, Sam. Seriously. Those people you bit, what the fuck? Polly?"

Mercy-killing was the watchword, it seemed, in werewolf society. "What, easier to kill and eat than to wound?"

"You fill the city with lupines, and we'll have serious problems," he said. "I feel fucked even talking about it; they're probably listening."

"Let them," I said. "Fuck them. Fuck hiding, Ansel. Fuck your therapeutic regimen, your hiding in the grass, pretending you're people. I can't be that way. I won't. You said I needed to get a handle on it, and I have."

"A rampage isn't getting a handle on it," he said. "More like a binge. And killing some Hunters, that's going to cause you no end of headaches. Those people get serious. I've had that before."

Finally, something I could use. I didn't want to hear Ansel's carping, but if he'd run up against the *Wilkołak* Brothers before, maybe it would help me.

"Where, here?"

"No," he said. "Because I'm not an idiot. But out west. Some ranchers, pissed off that I was culling their stock. See, I was doing them a favor, picking off the weak ones, taking a side of beef here and there. And then they come after me with silver bullets blazing, these motherfucking rancheros. They're all over the place. I bet the government even has guys who deal with it."

"Well, fuck them," I said. "Fuck all of them. I'm not afraid."

"You're not invulnerable, Sam," he said.

"I'm not chickenshit, either," I said.

Ansel laughed into his phone, barking, contemptuous. "Yeah, while you're playing Little Miss Badass, those guys are sharpening their knives. There's always more of them than us."

"Maybe that needs to change," I said.

"It never works that way, Sam," he said, sighing.

It was weird, arguing it with him. Sure, he was trueborn, had the bloodline, was my mentor, the source of my infection, had the experience, but I felt like, I dunno, he was not being true to what he was, was content with his semi-life. For all of his talk about me needing to get myself straight, he was the one who downed fistfuls of tranquilizers, not me. I was fine with me, with who I'd become, and with what I'd become.

Mostly fine.

"You're busy living on tiptoe, Ansel," I said. "I'm a girl; I'm used to that. That's why I want to do something different. I want to live loudly. Don't you feel it? Don't you want to make some noise? I want the norms to hear me. I want them to know why they're afraid to go out at night."

"You're going to end up stuffed and mounted," he said. "Hanging over somebody's mantle, Sam. In a lab somewhere. A prison."

"We'll see," I said. "How's Polly?"

"She's yours, now," Ansel said. "You tell me."

"She brought over her portrait," I said. "Said you guys were on the outs."

"Yeah, I'm going to need you to give me that painting back," Ansel said.

"She left it with me," I said. "Not a chance."

"Yeah, but it's mine," he said. "She wasn't supposed to do that. She'd gotten into my place when I was out, came in on the fire escape. Can you believe it? She got in that way and walked right in, stole my fucking painting."

"You wouldn't give it to her," I said.

"It's my painting," Ansel said.

"Did you kill her?"

"Sam."

"No?"

"No."

"Chicken." I said. "I mean, how's she really going to get to know you, Ansel? How are you going to take it to the next level, if you hold out on her, hold back?"

Ansel breathed a weary sigh on the other end of the line.

"You should do her," I said.

"Why?" he asked.

"Because you want to. Duh."

"But I don't," he said. "Look, I'm calling about you, not me."

"No, you're calling about you," I said. "It's always about you, Ansel. You're worried I'll upend your little arrangement."

"Just don't," he said. "I didn't bring you onto the scene just to have you spoil it."

"Mmm," I said.

He was so full of shit. So full of himself. Same thing. Who made him the King of the City, anyway? Nobody. He was self-appointed Big Dog.

"Seriously, Sam," he said. "You notice I don't run with a pack? You think I need one? You think others haven't tried to make themselves at home here? I mean, I told you there are some around, but I'm saying some have tried to take my place, tried to take me out, and I'm still here, and they're dogshit."

That hadn't occurred to me; I just assumed Ansel was too much of a headcase to be worth anybody else's time. I mean, he was Ansel. He was big, impressive, monstrous. There was no doubt that what he became was incredible, and I doubted I could stand up to him if we went at it. But how could he stand against a whole pack?

"I've lived in Chicago since '93," he said. "There was this group of bikers, a fucking lupine gang, Sam. They called themselves the Lone Wolves, had nice vests, great patches. A pack of a dozen of them, run by this big bald musclefuck who called himself El Lobo Loco, right? They came into town, thought they'd put a dog collar on the collar counties, thought they'd cut into my turf. I mean, there was twelve of them, and one of me, right?"

"Uh, yeah," I said.

"They're all fucking dead," Ansel said. "Every last one of them. And they knew what they were doing. They started in Las Vegas or something, like in the late 70s, would prey on whomever they got. Lobo got it from a prostitute in Reno, gave it to the rest of the gang. Real bloodhounds. But you know what? I fucked them up. And they were fighters."

I did the math in my head. That was 14 years ago. He'd have been in his early 20s, then. But he was old, now. He aged in dog-years, I told myself.

"Why tell me this? Am I in trouble?"

"I'm saying that you're a pup, Sam," he said. "You're playing around in the baby pool, thinking you're making a big splash, but you're not. Don't make me put a leash on you."

"Oooh," I said. "Sounds kinky. Sound like a threat."

"No more infections," he said. "That's got to stop. It's already going to have Animal Control in fits, will probably bring agents into the city, sniffing around. It's not like how it used to be. Times have changed."

"Jeez, Dad," I said, emphasizing that. "Do I have a curfew, too?"

"I'm just saying," he said. "Lay the fuck low. Quiet down. You are playing way too loud."

"Those Poles are going to fucking kill me," I said. "Maybe you want that. I have their names, for god's sake."

Zooey came in with the printed copies of my own *Wilkołak* handbill, my little early Valentine for the fuckers, held them up with a goofy grin. I nodded, pointed to my little work table.

"You go after them, it'll get worse," Ansel said.

"They're after me, Ansel," I said. "Help me out, here."

"No more infections," he said. "No more newsmaking. We have to let this die down a little."

"Uh," I said. "Hmm, that kind of doesn't work for me, Ansel. If another of those Polskis shows up on my doorstep, I'm going to protect myself."

"Fine," he said. "You do that, but for fuck's sake, Sam, clean up your messes. Do not leave them around for norms to find. Accidents happen all the time, right? Keep that in mind. Nothing stupid. No more performance art, please. I'm saying 'please,' you notice, right?"

"Sure," I said. "Thanks, Daddeo."

"Alright," he said, hanging up.

"Who was that?" Zooey asked, setting out the envelopes and handbills, humming.

"Nobody," I said, stuffing the phone into my pocket.

"It was Adonis, wasn't it?" she asked, leaning over, kissing the back of my neck. "Ansel, his name is?"

"Yeah," I said. "He's pissed at the ink I've been getting, had to pee on my leg a little, I guess, show me he was boss."

"That's so guy," she said, nipping at my neck, before hopping into one of the chairs at my table. "So, what's the plan?"

"We send these to the targets," I said, admiring my handiwork. They were pictograms, like the classic stick figure warning signs. This one showed a stick figure getting torn apart by an abstracted were-wolf, with "Beware of Dog." Written in Polish beneath it. I'd made each one a little different, like in one, the figure had a torch; in an-other, a broken pitchfork; another, a broken rifle. But they all came to the same end, killed by the dreaded *Wilkołak*, hovering over them.

*Uwaga zły pies!"* the sign warned, the werewolf looking impres-sive, looming over the cracked and broken stick figures, open jaws, deadly teeth. I loved it, and Zooey did, too. She grinned at me.

"Awesome," she said. "Killer. We should print those on t-shirts."

"Yeah," I said. "I'll mail them to the three guys on my list, see how that goes. I'd like them to be on their toes, afraid. A little payback. Ansel can't deny me that."

"He shouldn't deny you anything," Zooey said. "Where does he get off?"

"Meh," I said, folding up the signs, tucking them into their enve-lopes. "I'm so glad you're here, Zooey."

"I'm so glad I came," she said, tucking lavender hair behind her ears. I would miss her lavender. She'd kept her piercings in. I won-dered how long she would, though; once she transformed, because they got inconvenient when you were a skinchanger. It was like trying to find a ring you'd dropped in the sink. One unplanned transformation and pop went the jewelry. And forget silver. She didn't like that, but had gold, anyway, which went well with her hair. Without the lavender, she'd really look more angelic than ever, which was a deadly secret weapon. I mean, she looked so sweet and delicate. She'd hardly have to hunt; prey would come to her.

It made my own transition seem so bumpy and inelegant. It's because mine was an accident, and hers was deliberate. Ansel didn't help me at all, and I was there for Zooey. It made all the difference. Sisterhood. Mentoring.

We sat around the table, making our little love letters to the *Wilkołak* Brothers. I licked the envelopes shut, hoping one of them might get a papercut, get infected. Why not? For a werewolf, I could be pretty catty at times.

It was only three letters, not a big production. I'd mail them out the next chance I got. Meantime, Zooey and I schemed and plotted. It was so wonderful having a co-conspirator, an eager apprentice.

"We should do something terrible," she said. "Something they'll write about for years."

"Like what?" I said, thinking of Ansel's commandments to me. I'd already broken his "Thou Shalt Not Infect Another" one with Zooey, Reagan, and Polly, for god's sake. I wonder how he'd take that. Not well. But they were all so perfect.

"I'll know it in the moment," she said. "I'm like that, full of ideas that pop into my head, like Jiffy Pop on a hot stove."

"Do they still make that?" I asked.

"Totally," Zooey said. "We should get some. We should go out, hunt somebody down, then go get Jiffy Pop and watch werewolf movies all night, and throw popcorn at the TV."

"Sounds like a plan," I said, although I was already a little tired of the hunting down thing, I hated to say. I mean, it was a rush, but for Zooey, it was all new, but for me, it was like, it had been done. How many times could you do that? My stomach rumbled, though, at the thought. Sääm stirred at the thought of food.

"I think we should go hunt down that werewolf on the South Side," I said. "Ansel said there's this crazy trucker dude down there, like who hunts hitchhikers. We should hunt him down and kill him."

"He's a lupine?" she asked. "Kill another werewolf?"

I nodded. I wondered if I could do it, if I was up for the challenge. Maybe if I had that under my belt, then I could blow Ansel off. Like how could Ansel tolerate a creepazoid like that trucker-killer? Maybe he really didn't care; that was totally Ansel-like. Or maybe it was just outside of his territory. One could only cover so much turf.

"There's also this one in Boystown, like who masquerades as a serial killer," I said. "Ansel told me about him, too. He uses a knife, stabs them to death. He must be pretty sharp, because he never gets caught, and always seems to get his victims back in their apartments."

"Uh, how does he know he's a werewolf?" Zooey asked. "I mean, if he just kills with his knife? Maybe he's just a mundane."

"Could be," I said. "But you can't go around chewing up people, not for long. I've found that out the hard way."

"What a bummer," she said. "It's like using utensils for finger food."

"Yeah," I said, laughing. Zooey had a way of charmingly simplifying even terrible things.

"What about that Polly?" she asked. "We should eat her."

"Ooh," I said. "No, she's my friend. I just infected her."

"Nice," Zooey said. "See, I'm liking all of these ideas. We're brainstorming!"

I nodded, put my hands on hers. She took one of my hands, brought it to her lips, playfully nibbled at it, watched me with those black eyes. She was so lovely, and so wild.

"We should go out clubbing tonight," Zooey said, holding onto my hands.

"I'm not feeling clubbish," I said. She shook her head, smiling to herself like I was her own personal punch line.

"No no no," she said. "I mean 'out' clubbing."

She held her fingers up over her ears, pointing backward, grinned toothily at me. "I mean, I want my first time to be something special, right? Something memorable. So, let's find some cool place, mingle, and find somebody, you know."

"My, you're eager," I said.

"I want it to be special," Zooey said. "Special-special."

Thinking about my first time, I could only agree with her to some degree. I mean, I'd eaten a goddamned dog. I'd eaten my friends. It shamed me.

"What was your first time like?" she asked.

"Special," I said. Sheldon didn't count. Sheldon was an accident. I hadn't known what I was doing, then. I went to the closet and took out the blood-painting of Sheldon, held it up for her to see.

Zooey looked with wide eyes. The red-brown splash of blood across the canvas.

"What is that?"

"My first time," I said. Zooey's mouth hung open, she laughed.

"You painted with the blood of your first victim?" Zooey said. "Sam, that fucking rocks."

I looked at the piece. It hardly qualified. It was an accidental splash of Sheldon's blood. But the way it had sprayed across the canvas, I don't know. It was bold and horrible. I was more than a little embarrassed by it.

"You should hang it up," Zooey said. "Right on your wall."

"Nah," I said, putting it back in the closet. "Doesn't seem right. I mean, it was a special moment."

"There," Zooey said, snapping her fingers at me. "You see? Special. So, let's make it awesome. Let's get dressed up cool, go someplace cooler, hunt out ourselves some fucking loser, hook up with them, and fucking waste them."

It made me wonder if that's how I ran into Ansel, if he'd been hunting like that. He had to have been, given what had happened to me.

"Don't wear anything too nice," I said. "You'll trash whatever you're wearing. I don't want to hear you whining about losing some vintage tracksuit or something."

Zooey pouted at me. "Tracksuit, right. I'll wear something bitchin, you'll see."

"Alright," I said. It wasn't a matter of being an enabler; I was an accomplice. And after what I'd done already, what did it fucking matter? Another victim, another fucking loser. Seemed like if we just hunted down the biggest loser of the night, everything would be alright. The thought of that made me laugh inside, the image of taking out some skeezy guy.

But I was tired of tearing the shit out of my good clothes, so I went for something simple: black yoga pants with pink stripes up the sides, with a cream long-sleeved blouse, over which I wore a v-neck maroon sweater vest. I wore white clogs with it, and some amber-lensed oversized shades. When Zooey saw me, she laughed.

"What the fuck is that?" she asked.

"My outfit," I said. "What's the problem?"

"You look like, I dunno, a cultist," she said, giggling into her hand.

She was wearing bright red Capri tights, a denim miniskirt, a gray turtleneck blouse, and an electric blue scarf that was really long. She wore this with some zebra ballet flats.

"I'm just saying that anything you're wearing is going to get ripped," I said.

"Not if I take it off before go-time," Zooey said.

"I suppose so," I said. "What, are we planning to ambush this sod in an alley or something?"

"I don't even know," Zooey said, her black eyes full of dark amusement. "Isn't that crazy? I mean, I have no fucking idea what I'm going to do, what's going to happen. How awesome is that? I love living in the moment."

"Pretty sweet," I said.

"Fuckin-a," she said. "Tonight is my coming out party, and you're dressed like a cult deprogrammer from 1978."

Now I was self-conscious about my choices. Like had I lost my touch? No. She was fucking with me, and besides, I'd have the last laugh when she tore up her clothes. I'd be like "I told you so, Zo." It was worth it just for the pout that would surely come from it.

"Alright, smartass," I said. "So, how do we figure out who the biggest loser is at the club?"

"Well, what do you do when you're hunting?" she asked, narrowing her eyes, like she was all set to receive the wisdom from her sire. She didn't need to know that I didn't go to the clubs and hunt. I don't know what she thought I did, but it sure wasn't that.

"I just know it when I see it," I said. "But I've never hunted with somebody else, so that's why I'm asking how we should decide. Let's just decide: male or female?"

"Female," Zooey said. "Definitely female."

"Why?" I asked.

"Because it's too easy to find a loser guy at a club," Zooey said. "I want the worst chick we can find."

"Alright," I said. "And how is she a loser?"

"It depends," Zooey said. "Could be she's the bitchiest. Or ugliest. Or loudest. Or fattest. Or craziest. Or most desperate. Or bitchiest. All of the above? I don't know."

She was ready to go, alright. To my eyes, she looked like a wolf already. "What if we went for the chick who thought she was the hottest there, but really wasn't?"

Zooey liked that, her eyes brightened. "We could, yeah. But, like, how do we determine that? Can we even judge that from a casual glance, or can we only do that if we chat them up?"

"You can tell," I said. "You can always tell the one who thinks she's hottest."

"But we're not actually going after THE hottest chick, right?" Zooey asked. I shook my head.

"No, only the one who thinks she's hottest, but really isn't," I said. I could live with that, could only imagine who we'd nab.

"Alright," Zooey said. "So, where are we going?"

"Avalon," I said. "Gotta be Avalon."

Avalon was downtown, just off the Mag Mile, looked kind of like a castle. It was the absolute best place for that kind of person. It was like hairspray central.

"Avalon it is," Zooey said. "Man, I am so psyched."

The only drawback to Avalon was that it didn't really give you a private place to do what we intended to do. Unless we took the victim to the lakeshore. There was the water treatment place, the spur of park near Navy Pier. It would be a hike for a clubber, but we could take her there.

Fuck, I couldn't even believe I was planning it with Zooey, planning the fucking cold-blooded murder of a stranger. I'd turned into a fur-lined leather glove, with Sääm the hand that moved me. There was no room in my hollow self for conscience, for guilt, strangely enough. I was empty, but somehow something as simple as guilt wouldn't fit inside me, anymore.

"This is going to kick ass," Zooey said. "How will we get her to come with us? I mean, if she thinks she's the shit, why would she come with us? Won't she be scoping a guy?"

"Well, you were the one who said you wanted it to be a girl," I said. "You said you wanted the challenge."

Zooey beamed at me. "Yeah, I did. I admit it. I'm such a stinker. We'll wing it, see what happens. What if I transformed right in the middle of the dance floor? How fucking cool would that be?"

"Pretty fucking cool," I said, stifling a yawn. Zooey didn't notice.

"Yeah," Zooey said. "That would be extreme. I bet even you haven't done that."

"Nope," I said. "I sure haven't. But playing it large that way can get you into trouble. Oh, and what about your ID? You'll get carded."

"Not a problem," Zooey said. "I have a fake ID. A good one. But if I get stopped at the door, I'm gonna ace the fucking bouncer, hows-about?"

"Alright," I said, imagining Ansel tsking me over this. What had he said? Play it quiet, play it smart, keep it quiet, clean up my messes. I could just see Zooey transforming on the dance floor at Avalon. It would cause a stampede.

Then again, if something like that happened, maybe she'd get that fix out of her head, like that urge to murder somebody, and maybe we could settle for just mayhem, and maybe biting some norms, rather than taking some poor chickie to the park and slaughtering her.

But I didn't want to say that, because Zooey would have only scorn and contempt for me, then. She'd say I was chicken, just the way I called Ansel that. Funny how it was, like being a parent; I could see how Ansel probably felt when I was causing him all of that trouble. I probably gave him nothing but headaches. This would be a really big headache, if the night went the way Zooey imagined it would, the way she wanted it to go.

"Sweet," Zooey said. "I want the deejay to play Killing Joke."

"How retro," I said. "I doubt they'll have them."

"Losers," she said. "It would be so perfect. I want it to be perfect. I can steal a Killing Joke CD or something. I want it perfect, Sam. Bring your camcorder."

# 6. SATURDAY NIGHT

We went to Avalon in search of perfection. One challenge I realized that we faced, given what Zooey had in mind: we had our IDs on us, which meant that we were going to have to leave them someplace in Avalon, if we were going to transform.

Sure enough, Zooey managed to slip by the bouncer, keeping a poker face as she got carded. The burly black guy checked her out, looked her ID over, looked her over, and then waved her on through. He checked me out, too, but that was just because I was small. I was always getting carded. It was annoying, although it was nicer than him waving me through and saying "Here you go, ma'am."

Ma'am. Hated that.

"Okay, I figured it out," I said, as we mounted the steps, the scent of hairspray and too much perfume already assailing my nose. "Give me your ID. I'm not going to change."

"Huh?" she said.

"Yeah," I said. "This is your first time, right? So, you do it how you like. I'm going to keep tabs on things, make sure you don't get in over your head. I'll record you."

She smiled, pawed my face with her hand. "You're so good to me."

We went in and the club noise picked up. It was dark, but there was rose-colored neon flanking the stairs up into the place, and a rosy glow from the cavernous dancefloor. I hadn't been to Avalon in years; it was not a place where people like me went. It was a stable for norms. All around us were chads and trixies and tourists and whatevers, mingling, on the prowl. Upturned collars and baseball caps far back on their heads, and big, big hair, every which way. I got a glimpse of the ladies' room, which had the largest collection of hairspray I'd ever

384 | D.T. NEAL

seen in one place, on a table as you went in. One lit match and the whole place would go up.

Zooey knifed her way through the crowd. Her height and lankiness let her make her way with ease, while I was busy dodging shoulders and feeling like I was drowning in norms. It sucked being short. Absolutely everything was easier when you were tall.

ABC came onto the speakers, and I had to laugh at that. It was "Be Near Me," and I wondered if this was a request, or some ironic move on the part of the deejay. Whatever the case, the dancers responded to it, some of them singing along, since the chorus was easy enough to remember: "Be near me/Be near."

What next? Yaz? I was sure that would turn up, although with this breeder crowd, who knew what would pass for dance music.

Zooey waved off a few guys who made passes, and found herself a niche by the bar, waited for me to join her. She handed me her ID, which I pocketed.

"It's a good crowd tonight," she said.

"Yeah," I said.

"The dancefloor's crowded," she said.

"Sure is," I said. "You really want to do this, do you?"

She looked at me, nodded with a grin. "Totally."

"What about your outfit?" I asked.

"Fuck it," she said, licking her lips. I could tell she was excited and a little scared. It was a bold and crazy coming out, for sure. Where mine had been furtive, hers was audacious. "Wish me luck."

"Good luck," I said, and we kissed. From where I stood, I'd not be able to get a good shot of her transformation, so I went upstairs to the balcony, took out the camera, and started recording, while Zooey danced in the very center of the dancefloor. I hoped nobody saw me. A beer girl with serious bangs and broom-straight hair looked at me a moment, swaying boozily at her station, but she didn't seem too interested in what I was doing, and it was dark where I was, compared to the light of the dancefloor.

I zoomed in on Zooey, who knew just where I was, glanced up at the camera, her face diabolical in the light. And then she dropped on her hands and knees, disappearing a moment in the press of the people. I couldn't believe she was doing it, to be honest. It was almost insanely exhibitionistic, but then again, it was so bold, it had a rabid grace to it.

Without even seeing her, I knew what was going on, just from the reaction of the sheeple around her, who were dancing one minute, and the next minute were like "What the fuck is that?" in their body language, like looking around.

In their midst rose Zooey, and in the noise of the club, the confusion and the press of the people, the agony of the transformation was lost except for those nearest to her. By the time people realized what was happening near them (and even they didn't necessarily know what was going on, only that something was next to them that wasn't there before), there was a great white beast in their midst, arcing its head up and howling.

She stood easily a head or two taller than the tallest guys there, and when she rose up, the dancefloor erupted into bedlam, and Zooey went after them.

Seeing her change, I felt a sympathetic tug. Sääm wanted to be down there with her, but after what I'd been up to lately, I wasn't about to let her out of her cage.

Instead, I concentrated on the carnage. Zooey snapped at clubbers to the left and right of her, spilling blood amid the screams. People were running all over each other to get away, and the deejay hadn't yet seen what was going on.

Snap-snap-snap went Zooey's teeth, biting and clawing as she went, knocking people over. There went a dimpled chad; there went a pimpled trixie. She knocked a burly jock onto a table, bounded onto him, took a bite out of his forearm. Then she ran into the crowd, savaging people as she went.

It was playtime for her. Her fucking tail was wagging, for god's sake, which I caught with the camera. Then I realized that we hadn't planned on a way out of there, once things got going. Whoops. People were running past me, and the beer girl ran to the railing, muttered a "What the fuck?" and got out her cell phone, began taking pictures.

Zooey ran across the dancefloor, chased down some more clubbers, bloody-muzzled and wild. By now, the music had stopped, and somebody was turning on the house lights. People were cowering behind tables, the the main stairway in was jammed with people.

Zooey stood in the center of the dancefloor, howled up at the big mirror ball that hung overhead, surrounded by bodies of the wounded and the dead. Her eyes were black, and though her fur was white, she was covered in blood. The fire alarm went off, as somebody had gone out the emergency door.

She charged at the press of the crowd, which only made the panic worse, as guys and chicks both kicked at her, while Zooey snapped at them, drawing blood at every turn.

I thought I'd caught enough video, so I worked my way downstairs, pocketing the camera, while Zooey charged around, slipping on the floor where there was too much blood. There was only one thing to do, and that was to get out there.

I hoped Zooey didn't lose her head, didn't get herself caught.

"Zooey," I yelled, and she turned to look at me, ears pricked up. She saw me run out the fire door, and gave chase. This scared the crap out of the clubbers who'd taken my cue, and Zooey went after them, too, biting and clawing as she went.

I realized as she was running after me, that she'd fully become a wolf. A monstrous big one, but a wolf nonetheless. She ran easily on four legs, gracefully outpaced me. As she passed, she licked my face, leaving a bloody smear across it.

How had she done that? She'd become a true wolf. I'd had no idea that was possible. She ran down some wheezing clubbers, catching the boyfriend's forearm in her maw, shaking him, knocking him off his feet. Then she pounced on the girlfriend, biting her on the foot, shaking her, too. The boyfriend tried to punch at Zooey, but she knocked him over and released the girlfriend, before running away.

I ran about a block and a half before I was pretty winded, and I could hear the sound of police sirens and fire trucks behind us, as the authorities converged on Avalon.

Resting my hands on my knees, I hunched over, breathing hard. Zooey crept up to me, having turned into her hybrid form, grinning at me, all bloody teeth.

"Fantastic," she rasped. "My god, Sam."

"We have to get back home," I said. I could only imagine how many people she'd infected in that spree. Dozens.

"Sure," she said. "How could you resist that?"

I held up the camera. "I was occupied."

"Sweet," she said.

"A white wolf," I said. "Just in time for winter."

I felt self-conscious in the dark. At least I could hide. She stood out. We had a long way to go, but heading north through the Gold Coast, it was darker. There were places to hide, because it was largely residential, without the bright lights that endless, mindless commerce demanded.

We made our way from there to Lincoln Park, and then cut through Old Town, keeping to the shadows and the dark, hiding where we could, darting quickly across streets when we had to, in hopes that we would remain unseen.

I'd never made the trek like this in my old form, and I could see Zooey was getting impatient.

"I'll meet you there," she growled, and bounded off into the darkness, leaving me behind. It was so difficult being the responsible one. Sääm just wanted to ditch everything and be done with it, to run and slay at will. But I wasn't going to lose another camera. Martin would kill me.

So, I got to Logan Square eventually, and then, on a whim, as I looked over my silent street, I turned the camera to low-light, and then crept up and down the street, looking with the camera's eyes, in hopes of finding a *Wilkołak* Brother.

And, sure enough, just down the street from my building, was a man in a sedan, dozing. I walked up to him, gazed at him glowing green in my viewfinder. There was a shotgun beside him. He was a middle-aged man, with a mustache and a short haircut.

I glanced up at my apartment building, and could see the lights were on. Lord knows how Zooey had gotten in.

Then I looked back at the *Wilkołak*, and was startled to find him gaping at me through my viewfinder. I actually recoiled, stepping back and bouncing into a chain-link fence that framed the postage-stamp yard of the bungalow across the street from my building.

Meanwhile, the *Wilkołak* Brother was turning on his car and fumbling for his shotgun. I took off, running down the street. He clumsily got his car out of its parking spot, bumping the cars in front and behind him, and then he took off, disappearing around a corner with squealing tires.

Motherfuckers.

# 7. SUNDAY MORNING: 11 NOVEMBER

Leaving Zooey with the camcorder, so she could savor her coming out, I prepared for my own little outing, with blood on my mind. Zooey had come out of the shower, stunned at how her hair had gone whitish blonde, mourning the loss of her tattoos and piercings. I envied her the ease of her passage, the effortlessness of it, how quickly she went from fey to feral, her breezy brutality.

"Look at me," she said, marveling at the video. "What were you looking at, here?"

"I was just trying to get a sense of the room," I said. "You look beautiful."

"But it's all gone," she said. "Just like you said. I haven't had hair this color since I was little."

"I warned you," I said.

"Yeah," she said. "Man, that was a trip. I'm totally on the news. They're saying some crazed animal got into Avalon, although there's also reports of some kind of furry-related terrorist group. They're saying it might be a rogue faction of PETA or something. Fucking Furries, Sam! Can you believe it?"

"Nice," I said.

"Where are you going?" she asked.

"Out," I said. "Be careful. Lock everything up. The *Wilkołak* Brothers are out tonight."

"For real?" she asked.

I nodded. "Be really fucking careful, alright. Don't answer the door for anybody. Not until I get back, alright?"

"Alright," she said. "You want me to come with?"

She was wearing a simple white t-shirt and some pink boxer shorts, the picture of willowy innocence, all freshly-scrubbed. Not a drop of blood on her.

"No," I said. "I've got this."

"Alright," she said. "Because I totally will."

"I know you would," I said. "But I've got it. You need to rest. You had a busy night."

"Yeah," she said. "I'm totally going to blog about this."

"Knock yourself out," I said, leaving her behind with the click of the door and a twist of the lock. I rested my head against the door a moment, hoped she'd be safe. I went out the back, naked as a jaybird, tasted the night air a moment, listened to the sounds of the night a moment.

Zooey had caused a sensation, sure enough. It was startling, made my tentative, frenetic butchering of Sheldon seem quaint by comparison. Timid. Lame.

But then, there was precious little artistry in Zooey's rampage. It was sensational, yes. Outrageous, sure. But it was like throwing a cherry bomb in a crowd. Of course it would prompt a reaction. There was something lacking in it. I knew at once: art. There was no artistry to her rampage. Not like my own slaughter had been particularly artistic, but it had been personal, had been meaningful. Zooey's was like running naked across the field during a football game.

She was young; she'd learn finesse. I would teach her that.

Having transformed in the shadows, I creepy-crawled to Urban Kowalczyk's place, this unassuming little bungalow in Avondale, really carefully, because I was afraid the Polish Mafia would be leaping out of every shadow to blow me away, but there wasn't anything out of the city-ordinary; just traffic, and pedestrian blankets of urban noise.

Heh. Urban would be making lots of noise when I was through with him. I'd found his place using Zooey's computer. Fortunately the bastard had a locksmith business, so he hadn't been so hard to find. Locksmith. A very useful trade for a werewolf hunter.

I broke my way into Urban's basement, sniffed around in the dark, closed the basement door behind me, crept around in the shadows, paused to listen. It sounded like nobody was home, so I forced the door, rooted around in his basement. There were the usual things: laundry and dryer, water heater, furnace, tools.

I could smell It. It being silver. I crept to a worktable, saw silver bullets, empty shells, ingots of the stuff, molds, and other stuff I remember my dad having in his workroom, where he'd make his own bullets with these little machines, measuring powder, that kind of thing. The smell of the gunpowder was tangy, distinctive.

From the look of things, Mr. Kowalczyk had been busy. I sniffed around the room some more, found my way to the steps, then crept up them, paused and listened, my eyes level with the floor. Urban wasn't home. Was probably out hunting for me with his droogies. Maybe out drinking slivovitz with his fellow fearless werewolf killers.

I reached the doorknob and opened it, slipped out onto a linoleum kitchen floor on my hands and tiptoes, in a crouch, turning my head this way and that. Then I rose up onto my haunches, listened again.

The kitchen was institutional green, with white appliances. I nosed around his dining room and living room. There was a bay window in the living room, facing out into the street, overlooking it. I went to the window, peeked out, watched the sheeple make their appointed rounds to unknown places, watched cars cruise by. Then I became conscious of being backlit, dropped down behind a sofa, into the nurturing dark, waited in the shadows, where I belonged. My stomach growled, and the noise made me wince.

I heard the sound of a car going up the driveway, then stopping. I listened for the sound of the car door opening, and it came. One door slam.

I crept through the living room, then went to the dining room, watched as the man keyed into the kitchen, carrying a paper bag. He flicked on the light, and I could see him, now, with white hair and a mustache, with a jowly face and bleached raisin eyes, and a scarf and windbreaker, work pants, work shoes. The same fucker I'd seen earlier in the evening.

I waited for him to close the door, to lock it, watched him take groceries from his bag, put them in his fridge, and take a box of Malt-O-Meal and open a cabinet, to put it in there. His back was turned. There was no better time than the present. I bounded into the room, landing on his back, knocking him against the cabinet, knocking boxes of cereal and cans of beans to the ground.

"Urban," I hissed in his ear, pressing against him, running my claws up and down him. I found a pistol in a shoulder holster, ripped the thing from his side, slid it across the floor. Then I rolled him over with a brutal shove of my paws, so he could look me in the face. Urban gazed at me with eyes full of hatred and comprehension.

"So, it's my turn, is it, Beast?" he said. "You want me to beg? I won't."

He spat at the ground between us.

"That is what I think of you," he said. "Monster."

"Who sent you? Who are you?" I growled.

He reached for his pants cuff, tugged it up, and I saw he had a dagger strapped there. I let him draw it, saw the flash of the silver, a pretty little diamond-shaped triangular wedge, long enough to pierce my chest and tickle my heart.

"This is who I am," he yelled, going for me. He thought he was fast, but I showed him what fast was. My hands shot out and snagged his, my claws circling his wrist like a pair of cuffs, and he struggled to get me with his knife.

"Charming," I said, squeezing his wrist, breaking the man-bones there. They popped like they were stale breadsticks. The snapping of the bones aroused me, as did his grunts of agony.

Urban snarled, pummeled me in the face with his free hand, but I hardly felt it, caught his fist in my teeth, pinned him with a snap of my jaws. Now he yelled, and I turned my head to the right and left, and yanked his hand free of his arm, with a pop of bone and a spray of blood from ruptured vessels. Playfully, I flipped my head up, caught his disembodied fist in my mouth, crunched down on it, swallowed it, spat out his class ring, which clanked bloodily across his floor, while still he strained against me, cursing me roundly in Polish.

"How many of you are there?" I asked, after swallowing his meaty fist. God, he tasted good.

"Go to hell," he said. "You think you're the first lupine I've crossed?"

"Looks like I'll be the last," I said, knocking the dagger free from his ruined wrist, watching the thing clatter, catching the light. Then I watched Urban bleed a moment. He couldn't get to his feet, with one missing hand, one broken wrist. To stand, he'd have to have pitched his head toward me, and I could tell he didn't want to do that. Even in death, he fought for dignity.

"You're a credit to Hunters, everywhere, Urban," I said. "Does it bother you to be beaten by a girl?"

My voice was hoarse, monstrous, alien to my ears, my overlong tongue dancing across fangs. It wasn't me, but, of course, it was. It was the me that I would be for the rest of my days, however many days I had left to me.

He looked about him. "You'll never beat me. Even if you kill me, you haven't beaten me."

"If?" I said, laughing. "If I kill you? I'm not going to beat you, Urban. I'm going to EAT you; what a difference a letter makes, eh? Beat. Eat. It's all the same to me."

I slashed him across the face, first one side, then the other. He was getting pale, losing a lot of blood through the ruined arm. He'd be dead soon.

"Take this to Heaven with you, Urban: I'm going to hunt down the others, and I'm going to kill them, too. And I'm going to fill the world with people like me. I'm fucking Lilith to you; I'm goddamned Eve; I'm one of Lot's slutty little daughters."

"You'll die, like all the others," he said, his chest heaving. "Like every other plague, you, too, shall pass."

I'd had enough of him, took a bite out of his thigh, watched him while I did it, swallowing the meat, his blood all over my muzzle. Oh, he'd been drinking alright. He was practically pickled.

"Don't die on me yet, Urban," I said. "Not before you tell me about your little group."

He began praying, closing his eyes to me. That pissed me off, him trying to take himself away from me. I went at his other leg, taking big hunks of flesh from him, which took the wind out of his prayer-sails pretty quick, as he moaned in agony.

"God isn't going to help you," I said, between bites. "He sent me, don'tcha know? You sheeple always credit Him with the good things, never the bad. But if nothing is beyond Him, then that means the bad is His doing, too. I'm part of the Divine Plan."

I laughed at that, kept at Urban, sprayed blood on his heaving chest as I did so. "You thought I'd go meekly to my grave?"

He fumbled with a crucifix, a silver thread around his neck. Part of me wanted to take his head, like a trophy to drop in the lap of the other guys hunting me, but instead, I went to his stove, opened it, turned on the gas.

Urban was bleeding too badly to do much of anything about it, too weak, too nearly-dead. But not completely.

"Smell that?" I said. Then I went through his house, looking for things. A computer, maybe? Something. He didn't fucking have one. What a throwback. There were pictures of his wife, and him, and his brother, a whole life in that bungalow-style house, a norm life quickly ending. Back downstairs, I saw that he'd made a cell phone call. He was dead, now. Christ, I'd been stupid. Grabbing the phone, I looked to see who he'd called, pressed the redial.

A man's voice answered, identified on the phone as Ed Jaworski.

"I'm coming for you, Ed," I growled.

Then I hung up the phone, went back to Urban.

"You fucking bastard," I said, amid the hissing gas, and went about cleaning up my mess, the way Ansel wanted it done. Real thorough. I ate him down, almost every bite, until he was just a mess on the floor. I don't do entrails.

Then I rooted through his kitchen for flammables, poured stuff on what was left of him, went all through the place, pouring all of his booze and some lighter fluid and whatever else I could find. I took the silver dagger he'd carried, noted the black handle of the thing, took it and the scabbard for it as a souvenir, held the sheathed knife between my teeth, savored the dread of having silver so close to me.

And then I found some of those long fireplace matches and clumsily lit them, watched the flames catch, then I went down into the basement, while the upstairs burned, and I went through his cask of gunpowder, spread that around the place, figured that would do some damage. Then I went out the back door, pulled it shut.

I could hear sirens, and slipped away from there, while the place burned. I watched flames flicker in the windows, hoped the place would light up properly. Now counting the Willa Powers Bonfire, I'd never committed arson before, didn't know how much of that would be half-assed. The flames hit the natural gas, and there was an explosion, and the place went up properly. I couldn't wait for those silver bullets to catch fire, put the fear in the cops and firemen who came.

Without wanting to waste any more time, I got out of there, running through alleys, wanting to keep going forever. Instead, I went to my neighborhood, hoping the other two guys were there. I got to my street, hunkered down, sniffed the wind.

Then I ran up the middle of the street, hoping to flush the hunters out, if they were even there. I looked at every car, but nobody was in them, there was no sign of the Hunters. Perhaps Urban's last call to Mr. Ed Jaworski had persuaded him to leave.

Or get reinforcements. Christ, it never ended.

I went to the back of my building and sniffed around there, didn't find anything, then made my way up the back steps, got into my building, and then crept to my apartment. The door was unlocked, as I'd left it.

Opening the door, I saw Zooey sitting there, covered in blood.

"Jesus Christ," I said.

Zooey looked up, grinning at me. "Sam! You're alive!"

I slipped in, shut the door, saw that there were two dead men on my floor, one toting a shotgun, the other an assault rifle. The latter had no head; the former had a crescent taken out of his neck.

"Fuck," I said.

"Yeah," Zooey said, shrugging. "Fuck."

"What happened?" I asked, letting myself change back to my little old self, as I talked to her. We were both naked, both bloody as hell. It had been such a busy night.

"These guys broke into your place," Zooey said. "I think maybe they were going to ambush you or something. But, you know, I was in here, and I ambushed them, instead. I'd heard them coming, so I'd changed, and just waited behind the door. First guy came in, then the second, and I took the head off the second guy, and then bit down on the first guy, before they even knew what hit them. It was easy. They sure were surprised; I think they didn't realize there were two of us."

"Wow," I said. "You're a killer, Grrl."

"Yeah," she said. "For sure. What do we do, now?"

I was stuffed full of Urban. There was no way I could possibly get down another dead Pole. Poles were filling.

"You need to eat'em," I said.

"Both? Like fuck! I'll get fat," she said.

"Well, I can't do it," I said.

"Why don't we just drop them in the river?" she said.

"We could put them in their car, then drive their car somewhere," I said.

"Good plan," she said. "Did you find your guy?"

"Yeah," I said. "Werewolves 6, *Wilkołak* Brothers 0."

"Nice," Zooey said. "Why don't we drive this down to Calumet City or something? We can put them in the trunk, maybe park them in some lot somewhere. Nobody would find them for awhile."

"Maybe," I said. I wanted to talk to Ansel; I'm sure he had all kinds of helpful tips on it. "We have to find their car, then sneak them out."

I went through the men's pockets, took out their wallets, their keys, their cell phones. Might prove useful. More artifacts, more trophies. I felt like hanging the cell phones on my wall. How many had I bagged, now? I'd lost count. More food for the river, I supposed.

396 | D.T. NEAL

"We need to get cleaned up," I said. "How long have you just been sitting here?"

"Awhile," she said. "Just taking it all in."

"Yeah," I said. "Let's get cleaned up."

We got showered together, rinsed each other off, just the two of us in the steam and flowing water, and Zooey took my loofah and ran it across my chest, washing away the blood. I took my soap in my hand and lathered it up, and gently, almost tenderly, scrubbed her clean. The blood ran off us and pooled at our feet. I saw that her toenails were painted blue. She'd painted them after killing the Poles. Just sitting there, doing her nails. They were beautiful and glossy, scuds of foam, rivulets of water swirling around her pretty toes.

She saw me looking, and smiled, and leaned in to kiss, me, her black eyes locked on me, her mouth a sensuous smirk, that delightful overbite, taking hold of my lips in hers. We kissed, our bodies pressed in close, the heat in the shower so pleasant, that water so delicious. She pushed me against the tiles, and we kissed, our hands traveling up and down each other. Her breasts were beautiful, her ribs so slender. Long-torsoed, I felt squat and proletarian to her elfin loveliness, my own lean body more ruthlessly practical, my curves utilitarian by comparison. She was sculpture; I was a handgun.

I dropped down to my knees and leaned my forehead against her pelvis, the dark color of her hair against my cheek. She looked down at me, hot water raining down, and smiled, her white hair dreadlocked ribbons of wet, and I leaned in and gave her my tongue, while she parted her long legs for me a bit, let me taste her. I lapped her up, and she turned her face up into the shower head and sighed.

Everything was forgotten, the brutality and the recklessness, the bodies in the living room, the deaths of the days, my fucking God, it was gone. There was just Zooey and me, in the shower, me licking her, her body responding, hands on my head, holding me fast, long fingers gripping my wet shock of hair as I stroked her with my tongue, made her legs quiver as I drove her like a sled-dog toward orgasm. She thumped the tiles with her forehead as she came, yelping, whimpering, laughing, crying, her tears blending with the hot water from the shower.

No blood, no sweat, only soap and tears.

"I love you, Sääm," she whispered, biting her lip shyly. I got up, and we kissed again, turning in the shower, baptized by bathwater.

"My turn," I said, and she went to work on me, and fireworks flashed behind my eyes, purples and greens, my eyes closed, a smile on my lips, leaning my head into the shower water and taking delight in her, the way she cradled my ass as she worked on my cunt with that wicked tongue she had, always wagging, always lolling. Putting it to work on me. My Zooey. Mine.

Before long, we were all washed, looked like wholesome all-American bohemian girls. Then we bagged the guys, put them in Hefty bags, and found their car (I walked up and down the street, pushing on the keychain lock button until I found it. A four-door sedan, a big car). I drove the car around back, while Zooey became lupine and carted the two bodies downstairs, one on each shoulder. It was an absurd image, a guaranteed bad trip if anybody was looking, this white wolf-thing carrying bodies to a waiting car, but I hardly cared.

On a whim, I put the shotgun and the assault rifle in my hall closet, figuring they might prove useful at some point in my increasingly complicated life. Then I took the car back around the corner to my street, found a parking spot, and went back upstairs, while Zooey got dressed. The floor was literally a bloody mess, so we cleaned that up with my Swifferjet and a bunch of the Swiffer pads, until the floor didn't look completely like death. Then we bagged that and took that outside.

"Wow, being a werewolf is *such* a pain in the ass," Zooey said. "I thought it would be all mayhem and slaughter, no worries at all, but you really have to worry a lot."

"Yeah," I said. "It's a lot of work. Lots of cleaning."

"Fuck, yeah," Zooey said.

We got in the sedan and drove off, Zooey putting on a CD burn she'd done while I'd been out.

"Something for us," she said, and we enjoyed the music was we drove south and east. I wasn't really sure what the plan was, except to just ditch the car someplace far away.

Getting outside of Ansel's territory, I wondered if maybe we were entering the territory of that psycho trucker he'd mentioned. Zooey had opened her window, was hanging her head out, laughing, though it made the car fucking cold.

"What's that smell?" she asked. I could smell it. It was him.

"That's the crazy lupine Ansel mentioned," I said.

"We should find him," Zooey said.

"For real?" I said.

"Sure, why not? We can give him these guys as a sacrifice," she said. "Bet he's hungry."

"Mmm," I said. Somehow, I doubted they were his type.

We got to East Chicago, unsure how we'd even find this guy, but Zooey thought we could track him, because lupines had a particular scent. We noticed that while we ranged in our neighborhood, how we could scent each other, and could spot Ansel's scent, like an aroma that wafted over the whole North Side, and the strong, deadly scent of the Boystown Butcher.

I actually felt bad about the poor hitchhikers the trucker was nabbing. I mean, yeah, they were prey, but it seemed too easy, like charging down penned sheep, calling it a hunt. It told me that he was lazy. At least Urban had wanted to kill me.

Part of me just thrilled at the notion of entering into this foreign place, because to date, I'd romped around under Ansel's protective scent, safe in the knowledge that, bad I might be, but Ansel would, a

t least in theory, protect one of his own, if push came to shove. I didn't want to gamble on that; maybe he'd sacrifice me, but I hoped maybe he wouldn't. I was an only child, felt entitled.

We parked the car in an abandoned parking lot, and went outside, sniffed the air. He was here. We could smell him, clear as a bell. Healthy, strong, but in a bad way—the whole place stank of chemicals and death.

"Christ," Zooey said, rubbing her nose, sneezing once, then twice, shaking her head.

For a moment, I thought maybe we'd bitten off more than we could chew, wondered if it was always this way for lupines, like whether they always had to watch themselves when they came into new territory, or whether it was okay so long as they minded their own business, didn't abuse their visitation rights.

Having caught his scent, Zooey didn't waste any time getting naked, which made me laugh, imagining some norm driving past the lot, seeing this model-pretty girl naked in the chilly air, nipples erect, eyes glowing, catching the light, teeth too white and long to be human.

She took out her piercings, piled them into her hand, then zipped them into the pocket of her coat, folded everything, left it on the passenger seat, shut the door, ran a hand through her hair. Part of me wondered why she'd even bothered to put the rings back in to begin with. Silly girl.

"Come on, slowpoke," she said, dropping to her hands and knees, groaning, gnashing her teeth, while I stashed my own clothes, and tucked the car key under the left front wheel well.

Around us, everything was industrial-lit, with darkness in the pockets between the factories, the apricot haze of sodium lamps concealing more than it illuminated. It truly was a happy hunting ground.

Zooey was already transformed, beautiful and white, her black eyes on me. She came over and nuzzled me, gave me a lick, as if to goad me further, faster. Even as a beast, she was sumptuous. I ran my hand through her fur, knelt close, laid my head against her, felt the beautiful beats of her powerful heart. I was amazed how quickly she'd been able to transform. It always felt slower to me, more painful, more work. Ah, youth.

We both howled, announced our presence, hoped that he heard, hoped he was in town. Then we jumped from the parking deck, worked our way groundward, began hunting for real, a few dozen yards apart, zeroing in on his scent.

He had chosen well, because the shadows were plentiful and deep, even amid the flames and clanks of power plants and factories, the blisters of oil drums and gravel escarpments, the constant whirring of highway traffic, far above, and the slow, sludgy pace of barges on the waterways, the towering mounds of slag. It looked like hell, but there was wildness and nature even here, oases of furtive foliage, mangled, polluted, poisonous—hunchbacked trees and blistering weeds that cut and clawed at you as you passed them.

There was desolation in the air, hanging heavy, stinking of sulfur. Little tiny homes, row after row, sooty Archie Bunkers, and nearby, a lake. Zooey nodded to it, and I saw the sign.

Wolf Lake.

We both howled, loud and long and proud, watched the water lap the shore, watched the cars race by in the distance. It was too perfect. Of course the bastard would have settled around Wolf Lake. Why not? Fish and game, state lines, tollways, tourist, hitchhikers, runaways, plenty of opportunities.

We heard an answering howl, some distance way, across Wolf Lake, maybe. It was hard to tell. It was loud, deep-throated, horrible, challenging, ugly.

Zooey and I exchanged looks, then went off in search of him, side by side, two fetching little huntresses, chasing down our quarry with loping strides. We didn't even have a plan of attack, just figured we'd go at him from both sides, hoped we could take him down. It was crazy, but we were crazy, so it was perfect. The adrenaline rush alone was intoxicating. Club drugs were candy by comparison.

He howled again, long and loud, in the dark. Closer. A lot closer. A challenge. Zooey and I kept quiet, didn't answer; we were the invaders.

I wondered if we were faster than he was. He sounded bigger. Zooey and I exchanged looks, kept a little ways apart, hoping we could keep him occupied.

"Maybe we should leave," I said.

"We should stay," Zooey said. "We have to see him."

And see him, we did. He rushed out of the weeds and grasses, this grey-black monstrosity, green-eyed, mouth full of beautifully long teeth, claws like daggers, a scar across his muzzle. He burst out of the foliage and sniffed at us. He was huge, a full head taller than Zooey, and as broad as I was tall. Monstrous. Mammoth.

"Two pretty bitches," he said. "In heat?"

"We have a present," Zooey said.

The other sniffed the air, cocked his head. "And what's that, Snow White and Rose Red?"

"A couple of bodies," I said. "Fresh."

"Very fresh," the other said, looking at us both.

"No," Zooey said. "Not us."

"No?" the other said. "Yes."

He let his tongue hang out, sniffed at us again. "I don't want your trunkbait, pretties."

"What's your name?" Zooey asked.

"Ezekiel," he said. "Zeke."

He sniffed at us, nodding his head. "Ansel's little bitches. Who's he think he is, sending you down here? A gift, maybe? A sacrifice?"

Zeke stepped toward us. Zooey jumped at him, claws out, quick as could be. He sidestepped her, and she tumbled past.

I ran at him as he'd dodged, but he caught my face with one of his clawed hands, threw me to the ground with a cackle. Then he put a foot on my back, forced me down into the dirt with the force of a piledriver. Zooey jumped on him from behind, clawing at his face. He howled at her touch, turned to throw an elbow at her, which freed me up to sink my teeth into his haunches.

He howled.

"You bitches trying to eat me?"

Zeke swung at me, but I circled around his legs, went right for a hamstring, took a bite of it, the thing snapping like a steel cable between my teeth. Zooey was circling, her muzzle bloody, while Zeke was howling in rage and pain at what I'd done. He tasted bad; I spat him out.

"You hamstrung me, you cunt," he snarled, limping.

That gave us the advantage; we could dart in and out of his reach, hit-and-run. Zooey was an amazon, going at him until her hands were covered in his blood, until her beautiful white coat was flecked with red.

I went in after him, too, taking bites out of him, trying to evade his own monstrous claws and jaws. Without his mobility, he was, despite his great size, at a disadvantage.

Around and around we went, a dogfight on the ground, him tearing at us with his great claws, snapping at us with his teeth, while we danced out of his reach, darted in to bite at him and away as he turned. I could see the advantage of a pack, then, the opportunity that came with numbers. The lone wolf was a desperate beast, but the wolf pack was something altogether greater. We needed more. Zooey was just the start. I wanted to find Polly, and to bring Reagan into the pack. We could have a little debutante ball for Reagan. She'd like that. Tiaras. And the four of us would rule the city. It would be fantastic.

Zeke caught me daydreaming, cut me across the ribs with his claws, which brought me back in a jiffy, had me tumbling backward, out of his reach. He staggered toward me, arm raised, but Zooey came in behind and took a bite out of him, which had him turning back toward her, and then I snapped at him next. Back and forth we went, a seesaw slaughter. Soon, he was looking pretty ragged, and called out to us. "Enough! Enough!"

He dropped down, chest heaving, blood pouring off him, lost in himself, matted fur and panting. I wondered how many hitchhikers had met their deaths at his furry hands, and thought of them.

"Not enough," I said, moving in for the kill. He watched me with his green eyes, circled as I circled, grinning with bloody teeth. Such perfect teeth.

Zooey hung back, panting, spent. She'd been a warrior princess, deadly, decisive, relentless, ruthless. I liked to think I could be as savage. Who was I kidding? I was as savage, but not half as graceful as she.

The poetry of slaughter was effortless for Zooey; she was more talented than I was at this. I could just see it. I had given birth to a prodigy, a virtuoso.

"Kill him," Zooey snarled. "Fucking waste him."

Zeke kept his jaws to me as I circled. He was calling my bluff, daring me to go at him. If I tried to bypass that maw, he'd be able to whip around and take a bite out of me. I had to go for the throat. There was no other way. But he wasn't going to make it easy for me. When Zooey and I had been dogpiling him, it had been almost easy. Two-on-one wasn't a fair fight; we knew that, but neither of us could have taken him alone.

But now, it was just him and me. Zooey was watching. Zeke was watching. Around us, the ground was wet with blood, and a breeze blew in the grasses. Wolf Lake lapped dirtily nearby, and sodium lights blared hazily, but around us, up close, was only darkness.

Zeke made a move toward me, and I went at him, took a bite out of his throat. His claws came up and raked at me, but I'd pulled away before he could get a firm hold. He pitched forward, blood flowing from his neck, landing face down. Zeke tried to say something, but only blood bubbled out. I spat him out, my face stinging where he'd gashed me. Zooey sneered.

"Beautiful," she said. "Dueling scars."

We sat together, watched him die, watched the inevitable surrender of fur and flesh, watched him change back to a man, beneath the light of the Moon. A ruined man, grievously wounded, but human, once more, the curse left him. What a strange thing, that we should only be known in life; in death, we returned from whence we'd come. Just a man. A monstrous big man, balding, stubbled face. Unremarkable. Broad shoulders. Old. Middle-aged, at the youngest.

"He's old," I said.

"Yeah," Zooey said. "Now, he's dead."

"We should go," I said, wincing. It hurt to talk. Christ, I didn't want to see myself in the morning. We healed fast, but I suspected that these wounds would take awhile.

"K," Zooey said, and we ran back to the car, to get our stuff. "Fuck, we're all bloody again. I already had two showers."

It wasn't something we'd thought about, like cleaning up.

"We should drive back," Zooey said. "I don't want to have to run all this way."

"Doesn't that defeat the whole purpose of driving this car down here?"

"Let's just take out the bodies, leave them with Ol' Zeke, there, and drive the car back. Then we can ditch it someplace."

That actually made sense, and I went along with it. We dragged out the the dead dudes, put them next to Zeke. Zooey took Zeke's hands and put them in the dead men's crotches.

"What the fuck, Zooey?" I said.

"Just something for the police to puzzle over," she said.

"Sicko," I said.

"Animal," she replied.

"Beast," I said.

"Bitch," she said.

She had me there. We crept back to the car, got dressed, then warmed up the car and drove out away from there. It was awkward, because we were bloody and dirty, even though we were dressed. Hopefully nobody would look at us too closely. I peeked at my face in the rearview mirror.

"Fuck," I said, looking at the bloody scars on either side of my face. "You have to drive."

"What a great night," Zooey said, warming her hands by the car's vents. "I mean, totally wicked. Best. Night. Ever."

"We look like refugees from a zombie invasion," I said, wincing at the pain in my face. "I hope no cops see us."

"Oh, you worry so much," she said. "It'll all be fine. We're a team. We're like werewolf Thelma and Louise."

"They died," I said.

"You know what I mean," she said. "Bonnie and Clyde."

"They died, too," I said.

"I don't think so," Zooey said. "I think they went to Bolivia."

"That's Butch Cassidy and the Sundance Kid," I said. "They died, too."

"Sheesh," she said. "So much death."

My face burned, and it hurt to talk, to flex my jaw, so I sat down next to Zooey, let her drive us back to Chicago in silence, let Zooey just talk. In the mirror, I could see these horrible red furrows going down either side of my face, making it look like my face was this mask I could just pull right off. I was wearing a Sam mask.

"You need to go to the doctor," Zooey said. I shook my head. "You need stitches."

"I'll heal," I said.

"You'll scar," she said.

"Nothing I can do about it," I said.

"Except go to the doctor," she said.

"And explain what happened to me, how?"

We got to my neighborhood as the sun rose, and I parked us a couple of blocks over. It was dark, and we fast-walked home. While walking, I saw Stan the Dog-Walking Man, making his fucking rounds. The guy was always out with that fucking bulldog of his, who sniffed at us and barked, then cowered between Stan's legs.

"Easy, Boomer," he said. When he saw my face, his eyes went big. "Wow, are you okay?"

"Fine," I said. "Oh, this? Just part of a performance art piece I'm working on. I call it 'Fleshface.' Like it?"

"Uh, wow," he said. "Really realistic."

"Yeah," I said. "Really?"

"Sure," he said.

"It's part of her 'Flayed Alive' series," Zooey said. "You should come sometime. The Neo-Futurists do it."

"Ah," Stan said, looking worried, not entirely convinced.

Not wanting to stand there and have him gawk at my face, we went home, instead, where I first surveyed the floor, thought it looked passably clean.

My face, on the other hand, looked like somebody had tried to claw it off. I had been lucky—if Zeke had managed to claw a little lower, he'd have severed my neck veins. Maybe that's what he'd been going for.

Turning my head this way and that, I didn't know what to do. Did werewolf injuries heal slower? I didn't know. But I knew that the process of skin-changing did seem to be fairly restorative, so I went into the shower, turned it on, and cycled through three changes into my lupine self, while Zooey looked on, recording it with my camcorder.

"What are you doing?" I said.

"Capturing this," she said. "It's fucking wicked."

"Go away," I said. The agony of the popping joints danced hand-in-glove with the sting of the gashes in my face.

"No way," she said. "This is tops. Werewolf shower transformation porn. This whole tape rocks."

With each painful passage into my lupine form, less blood flowed from my face, until the wounds closed, become angry red scars, instead of open rifts in my face. But they still hurt like hell, and it appeared that they would stay for awhile, regardless of what I did.

I came out of the shower, turned my head this way and that, for posterity, and went back to the mirror, wiped off the steam.

"Better," I said. "Not perfect, though. I can just imagine people at work asking me about this. Quick, give me a good lie."

"Blame it on your boyfriend," Zooey said. "Stan the Dog-Walking Man, your boyfriend."

That made me chuckle. "Yeah, he's a tiger."

Big, long welts. There wasn't enough makeup in the world to cover it up. I could just imagine myself on the train into work, being stared at. I fished out a bomber hat, put that on with the flaps down.

"Perfect," Zooey said. "What a disguise!"

"I should wear this all day at work," I said. "But then I'd get too sweaty."

It seemed obscene to even go to my job, after what I'd been up to. But I had to make a living, right? I needed that sense of balance.

Still, it would work for coming and going. I put the hat back in my closet, ran my hands through my hair, while Zooey took her turn at the shower. She had been barely touched by our scrap with Zeke. She just had it, I guess. Luck or something else. The Devil as her co-pilot. I don't know.

I mean, could somebody actually have talent for lycanthropy? Seemed like she did, like she was good at it. No guilt, no painful transformation (or at least she didn't mind the pain; I guess I was a big sissy about pain, or something), barely got injured, because she was so quick and limber. I'd done her a real favor by infecting her, I guess. Though she'd cried over her lost tattoos, I think she was more than happy with the transformation, with becoming paranormal.

Going into the kitchen, I got some food, didn't even pay attention to what time it was; I was too tired, and the night had been endless. The sun was rising, the day was beginning, even though it had felt like it would never end.

Zooey was right: being a werewolf was a pain in the ass.

# 8. MONDAY: 12 NOVEMBER

Darryl, Dean, and Simone were all suitably blown away by the scars on my face, which had become pink, instead of red, and which curved straight and true, because Zeke's claws had been so sharp, my flesh had been all too willing to part before it, like the Red Sea before Moses. The scars on my ribs were even more impressive, but I wasn't going to show them those.

"What the hell happened to you, Sam?" Dean asked. "You look like you had a date with a band saw."

"Yeah, it didn't work out," I said. "I like jigsaws better, turns out."

"Industrial chic," Darryl said. "Postmodern primitive. Like tiger stripes."

"It's gross," Simone said. "Seriously, what did you get into, Sam?"

"I got attacked," I said.

"By what?" Dean asked.

"Werewolf," I said. "Y'all better watch out."

"I hear that's going around," Darryl said. "They keep saying it's wild dogs or something, but I don't know."

"I heard there's a crazy cult of furries out there—they dress up as wolves and kill people," Simone said. "They went crazy at Avalon, attacked a ton of people."

"Avalon," Darryl said. "No big loss, there."

"Nice," Dean said. "I hate furries. Like that one in 'The Shining' that's blowing that guy. Fuck. Kubrick, man."

Simone's mention of furries inspired me, made me think of a performance art piece I could do, figuring that a showing at Ansel's would be out, assuming he ever got his ass in gear and worked on it at all.

"I think they just blew up some stories about coyotes," Darryl said.

"Coyotes don't hunt people," Dean said.

"It's furries," Simone said. "Motherfucking furries."

Hearing my coworkers talk, I felt more apart from them than ever, that the Sam I was now was just a mask, and that Sääm was all that I was, now.

I am Sääm. Sääm I am.

My cell phone rang, and I turned my back on my coworkers, checked it. It was Reagan.

"Reagan, what's up?" I asked.

"I need to see you," she said, her voice quaking. "Now. Something happened last night."

"Alright," I said. "I'll be right over."

I snapped shut the phone and looked at Simone, who was giving me her patented stinkeye. "Family emergency."

"What? You've been keeping pretty spotty hours lately, Sam," Simone said. I took off my smock and punched out, went to my locker in the back, got my coat and came back to see Simone blocking my way out.

"What?" I asked.

"If you walk out, I'm going to have to write you up," she said.

"Fine," I said. "Write me up."

I walked around her, and she called after me that I'd better bring a doctor's slip, and that she was going to tell Lance, blah blah blah. Outside, the chill air woke me up, and I wondered what had happened, what was wrong with Reagan. I mean, I knew what was wrong, but not what was *wrong*.

"Sam," said a voice outside my store. It was Ansel. He'd been waiting for me. He didn't look happy. He was wearing black driving moccasins and a dove-grey cashmere v-neck sweater and ivory pants and a black windbreaker. He looked like a hitman.

"Sam," he said. "What the fuck are you doing?"

"I have something to do," I said, wary, defensive. What was he talking about now?

He held up a *Chicago Tribune*, which had an article about the "furries" attacking people in Avalon. Why wouldn't they just say what was actually happening? It was frustrating.

"Yeah?"

"Yeah?" he said, mocking me. "Infection, Sam. You have to clean this up. It said something like 120 people were treated for animal bites. They're saying it was eco-terrorists."

Eco-terrorism? What a joke. Explain to me how nobody ever gets killed from eco-terrorism, and it gets called "terrorism," while, I dunno, neo-nazi hate groups drag gays from chains behind them in trucks, or militia guys actually blow up federal buildings and kill hundreds, and that's not terrorism? Seems to me like hate groups qualify as terrorist groups more than a bunch of granola-munchers spraypainting SUVs. I don't get that one bit. I mean, Group A, the eco-terrorists, haven't killed or bombed anybody, but they're terrorists; meantime, Group B, the hate groups, have killed people, bombed people, their whole ideology is about murder and terrorizing groups of people, and they have declared war on the "Zionist-Occupied Government"—but they're NOT terrorists? What a crock.

"Clean it up?" I said, looking around, seeing if anybody was paying attention. Nobody appeared to be. "What can I do?"

"Can I give you a ride home?" he said.

"I'm not going home," I said. He gestured to his Maybach. "I'm going to Reagan's."

"I won't bite, Sam," he said.

"You already did, Ants," I said. He smiled.

"Get in the car; I'll give you a ride there," he said, holding the door for me, like he was a gentleman. I knew better, but anybody streetside would think I was lucky to get into the car with this handsome man. I halfway hoped Simone was looking, terminal snoop that she was. I hopped in, and he closed the door, walked around the back of the car.

I felt nervous, wondering how the hell he'd expect me to fix the problem with the infectives. What could I do? It started raining, one of those textbook desultory Chicago winter rains that probably really wanted to be snow, but global warming or whatever wouldn't let it be snow, so we ended up with chilly, dirty rain.

Polly had been in the car; I could smell her perfume. Maybe a day ago. I smirked at that as he got in, started up the powerful engine, slid us from the parking space.

"I don't know what you expect me to do," I said.

"Clean it up," he said. "Fix it. You can't have all of those fresh infectives out there. I fucking told you, Sam."

I thought about Reagan and Zooey; he didn't appear to know about them, and I wasn't about to tell him. He knew about Polly.

"You can't expect me to kill them," I said. "Is that what you fucking want?"

He didn't say anything, just drove us downtown.

"You know where Reagan lives, right?" I said.

"We'll take the scenic route," he said. "Look, Sam, I can't be plainer about this: kill them, or else I'll do it, and I'll do you, too."

"What?"

"You heard me," he said. "We can't have a bunch of noobs running around, going crazy. You're on fucking probation. If you can't handle it, I'm going to have to put you down."

"Put me down? I'm not a goddamned pet," I said. "Fuck you, let me out."

But he'd taken us northbound on Lake Shore Drive, and we were cruising. Jumping out of the car would have been messy.

"Them or you, Sam," he said. "You made the mess; you clean it the fuck up."

"Christ," I said.

"I said it before: you make too big a mess, the Feds come in," he said. "They investigate, they find us. We disappear. It's us or them. You bit all those fucking people; I didn't ask you to do that—hell, I told you to do the fucking opposite. And instead, you just go out wilding, you know? Stupid."

"I'm not stupid," I said. "I'm just, you know, passionate. I've been wrestling with things."

"And what's this bullshit about a white wolf, huh?" Ansel asked. "Which one is it? Is it Reagan? I told you, no more infections."

"Reagan was an accident," I said. "That's all. I'm going to her place; she needs help."

We cruised out of downtown, the lake churned like coffee with cream to my right, while Ansel stewed to my left. Traffic was moderately light.

"You don't have to explain that to me," he said. "I know. But you have to cull, okay? Think of it that way. You don't run around nipping at people—you pick somebody out, and you cull them. That's what you do."

"Don't you mean 'kill,' Ansel?" His euphemisms were irritating, his candy-coated carnage that let him get through his day.

"I mean 'cull,' Sam," he said. "Anybody can kill; it takes a hunter to cull. That's what you do. You cull, and you finish them off, and you clean them the hell up."

"You mean you eat them," I said. "That's what you're trying to say. Been there, done that. Christ."

"That's exactly what I am saying," he said. "You don't leave a mess behind. There are thousands of missing people every year—no body, no problem."

"It's not that easy," I said. "It's messy."

Ansel sighed. "You have to cull; you don't do it, you'll go nuts, and make a big fucking mess. Those are your choices; either you get it under control, or I will. That Avalon bullshit was really fucking stupid."

"I can't kill all those people," I said.

"They're your responsibility," he said. "They'll seek you out. It just happens."

He gripped the wheel, took us further north, past rows of brownstones, the park to our right, the lakeshore looming. Ansel looked a little sad.

"What if I didn't kill them?" I said. "What if we formed a pack?"

"Hah," he said. "This isn't the country. And that's way, way too many infectives for a pack."

"They have 100,000 gang members in the city," I said. "Why not a pack?"

He laughed. "That would get messy, Sam. Real fast."

I saw a white Animal Control van go shooting southbound past us, wondered if they were looking for me. I wanted my own pack. It was the way around the whole problem; like a nurturing environment, some measure of self-protection. If my whole block were lycanthropes, I'd be safe as could be. No *Wilkołak* Brothers could get me. It's how mafia dons worked. You stayed in your neighborhood, had your protection all around you. Your kin.

"What if we were smart about it?" I said. "Picked the right neighborhoods. Urban renewal? What's the opposite of gentrification?"

"Neglect," he said. "Dissolution. Destruction."

"No," I said. "I wouldn't have it be like that."

"Sam," he said. "The learning curve is too steep. You get too many people infected too quickly, it gets out of hand, and the norms go berserk and you get mass killings, you get hysteria. You're not the first to think of it. Maybe on an island, someplace remote. But not here, not in the middle of the country, in the Mid-fucking-west. I could see it in Manhattan easier than here."

"You have no imagination," I said. "That's the problem."

"You have too much," he said. "That's your problem. You want a happy little canine commune? A collective? A sorority?"

"Yes," I said. "Why not? You already said that bottling things up causes us to go crazy; so, why not create a space where we can express ourselves?"

"This isn't an artists' cooperative you're talking about, Sam," he said, turning off Lake Shore Drive, heading toward Reagan's place.

"But it could be," I said. "Your way, there's nothing coming from it. Just death and more death, and you doping yourself into oblivion, because you're too chicken to off yourself, or else go out with a glorious bang."

"Those are the choices, eh?" he said, laughing, wringing the steering wheel in his painter's hands. He found a spot in front of Reagan's building, parked his car, turned off the engine.

"You can live, you can die," I said. "But living death? That's for norms. We don't have to make that choice. We have an answer to the call of the wild."

He just laughed, a shrugging of his shoulders. "You're a trip, Sam. You really are. Death doesn't even touch you, does it?"

"It's upsetting," I said. "But needless death is more upsetting. Killing some noobs because they'd inconvenience you, that seems fucking wrong. Nobody can enjoy killing puppies, Ansel. That's what you'd have me do."

He leaned against his steering wheel, turned and looked at me with one opened eye, bluer than porcelain. "It's too messy. It will get out of hand, and we'll all end up paying because you're so fucking stubborn. They'll send in agents to nab lupines, taking them someplace, sequencing them."

"They probably already are," I said. "You said that enough times. So, what if we beat them to the punch? The problem is that there's not enough of us."

"So, now it's revolution? Emma Goldman called, she wants her insurrection back," Ansel said.

"Look around us," I said. "Is this paradise? The best of possible worlds? It's a mess. Even drugged up, you have to sense it. The air is dirty, the water's dirty. The food is bland and lifeless. Each step takes us away from our animal natures, leaves us more lost than before. The disease is our world. We're the cure, Ansel."

"Please," he said. "Don't go all green swastika on me, Sam."

"Just saying," I said. "Everybody bitches about overpopulation. So, here's a fix for it."

"Fuck," he said. "Explain how that fits into your new morality, exactly?"

Ansel seemed able to handle culling well enough. This was only different in scale. But he was used to a world bordered by canvas and wood. He couldn't see beyond the frame.

"It all fits," I said, believing it. "Let the people who want to live fight for it; let the ones who can't hack it, well, you know."

There were people walking back and forth on the sidewalk, oblivious. Norms.

"And once everybody's infected, then what?" Ansel said. "May the best wolf win? The problem with that is everybody always thinks they should be top dog, and get put out once they're put in their place. The war of all against all doesn't make for peace, Sam. I mean, look at your fucking face. Who did that to you?"

"Zeke," I said. "He's dead, now."

"For real?" he asked.

"Yeah," I said, not wanting him to know about Zooey. "I fucking killed him."

"No way," he said.

"Oh, he's dead, alright," I said, touching the scars on my face. "I paid for it, but he's dead. He was old. Older than you, even."

Ansel sighed, shaking his head. "You are one crazy little bitch, Sam."

"I have to check in on my friend," I said.

"I'm coming with you," he said. "You're going to make this all right."

We got out, and I rounded the front of his car, while Ansel went to shut his door. That's when I saw them. *Wilkołak* Brothers. Four of them, in black, brandishing weapons. Looking at me.

"Ansel!" I yelled, and he looked at me, not where I was looking.

"What the fuck, Sam?" Ansel asked, giving me an irritated look. Like I was the problem.

The men were burly and big, broad-shouldered with blond hair and brown hair, sunglasses, mustaches on a couple of them. Black jackets, black guns.

"*Wilkołak!*" One of them yelled, as they fired at me. Ansel turned in time to take a shotgun blast to the chest that threw him against his car door. It knocked the wind out of him, pitched him forward. His blood went everywhere.

Bullets sprayed against the hood of his car, and I spun around and ducked down, even as Ansel fell back into the car, while one of the

*Wilkołak* Brothers pumped round after round into him at point-blank range, splashing the interior of his car with blood.

Four! Four of them. One of them came around the back, leveling some kind of automatic rifle at me.

I glanced at Ansel, who looked up at me through the ruined glass of his car window, dying, dying, dead. I wanted to howl, to mourn. I can't explain it. For all the trouble he'd caused me, for what a creepy pain in the ass he was, I still felt sorrow. They'd followed me. They knew where I worked. They knew who I was. Ansel had paid for it.

Sorry, Dude.

The man who had the rifle pointed at me fired, bullets flitting past my ears like angry wasps, even as I ran at him, more dove for him than anything, drawing Urban's silver dagger, which I had carried with me since I'd killed him. I stabbed him in the thigh with it, and the man let out a cry.

The irony of stabbing a werewolf-hunter with a silver dagger was not lost on me, even as I ran down the street, using cars as shields, while the *Wilkołak* Brothers fired at me, desperate to slay the Beast.

I did a slide between two parked cars as the bullets flew, then ran across the boulevard, using trees as shields. I could see Ansel's feet protruding from his car.

Three of the men advanced on me, one firing while the other two advanced. I remembered Lee rambling one night about how if some-body were shooting at you, you should run away in a zig-zag, not a straight line, so they couldn't draw a bead on you. So I zig-zagged, running for the gap between two buildings.

I ran and could hear the men behind me, yelling to one another. I risked a glance, saw the two men side-by-side, taking aim.

I dove to the ground as they fired, the bullets whizzing overhead. That would hold for a moment, I thought. Then I reached the end of the alley, rounded a dumpster just as bullets struck it. The sound of them was like a kind of drumming, the bullets denting the dumpster, leaving craters that took the paint right off. I could see the rounds, too, mashed in the dumpster. Silver.

A police siren sounded, and for once, I wanted that more than anything. I wanted the cops to show up and rescue me.

*Stop it*, Sääm said in my head, as I hid in a doorway.

Behind the building was a service road for the trashmen, and more brownstones. A chain-link fence topped with rusty barbed wire. I didn't want to risk climbing that fence, with the men running down the alley. I could hear them.

Then I just took my clothes off, piled them neatly in the doorway. With the buildings up around us, there was just a sliver of sky. Plenty of shadows.

"*Wilkołak*," One of the men said, unseen, from down the alley. "We know where you live, honey. Why don't you come out, we make this easier for you."

I bit my hand, making the change in as much silence as I could muster, because I knew to speak would be the death of me, would mark my position. So, I bit my hand. You always bite the hand that feeds you, right? So, I did, and, as ever, I exploded from the inside, my bones stretching, the fur flying from me, the teeth in my hand lengthening to fangs, punching right through the flesh. Some women gave birth to babies in alleys. I could handle this, surely. The throb was dreadful, the urge to howl, undeniable.

"We can put an end to your pain," he said, in a high-toned, nasally voice. "An end to your suffering."

My own blood dripped on the ground below me as I turned, could smell the men despite the stink of the alley, the stench of wet stone and old garbage. They smelled like aftershave. It amused me, the guys having a shave before they went to slay the Beast. Maybe kissed their wives and daughters goodbye.

"We'll get you, and your whelp, *Wilkołak*," he said.

There was no artistry in this. There was only fear. The aesthetics of it were lost to me. Then I looked skyward, at the buildings that split the sky into a sliver, and saw some clouds far overhead, wispy-white against the brazen blue. A plane flew overhead, I just glimpsed it in passing, imagined the passengers aboard, not a care in the world, lost in their little places, and me, just a speck on the ground, invisible, the city a labyrinth.

My cell phone rang, from the confines of my clothes, bringing me back to Earth. The perky chirp of the thing, and in a flash, I sprang from my hiding place as the *Wilkołak* Brothers spun in the direction of the sound and blazed away, their rifles echoing horribly in the alley, the muzzle flash of the weapons blinding and bright.

Again, there is no hesitation, no second-guessing. There was only life, and death. Which do you choose, when push becomes shove? You choose life, right? That's the right choice. Do you second-guess yourself when you're about to eat a salad? Before you bite into a piece of meat? Before you vote for some guy who promises peace and gives you war?

One of the *Wilkołak* Brothers clicked on an empty clip, his finger working CLICK CLICK CLICK and I'm on him in a heartbeat, took his neck in my mouth and bit down hard, and off popped his head, clattering down the alley. While I'm doing this, I'm grabbing onto him, using him for leverage, and I kicked hard against his buddy, catching him right in the chest, sending him flying into the dumpster with a grunt.

Then I'm on the second man, and I know he's the talker, can just tell, as I bite him right in the crook of his elbow, severing tendons, watching his arm go puppet-slack as his strings are cut. The automatic rifle tumbles from his grasp, and I see him drawing a dagger with his other arm, and I stop him, grabbing him.

I want to keep him alive, want to interrogate him, find out how many more of these bastards there are. But there isn't time. I can hear the police sirens. I don't know if they're looking for me or for the Poles. I don't care.

I finished the man's arm off, just snapped the thing clear of the rest of him, and he howled in agony, strained to get that arm up. I forced his dagger into his belly, and I yanked it out, so he can bleed a little more.

This isn't hunger. Not for food. Only for slaughter. For revenge.

The man screamed out for help, the last of his lungs, before I took his face in my teeth and crunched down on it like it was an eggshell. I just crushed his skull in my jaws, left him twitching on the sidewalk. I didn't care about clean-up, about covering up forensically. Let them guess what it was that did this. I couldn't let the man live, not if he knew where I lived.

Instead, I just hopped to the alley and tucked my tail between my legs, got small, got dressed. The man's legs were still twitching while I got dressed.

Glancing up, I saw a little girl looking down at me from one of the apartment buildings. She was looking right at me. I looked up at her and smiled, wiped the blood from my mouth with the back of my hand. She waved back, face like stone. I was terrible at guessing kids' ages. She looked young. I could just imagine her telling her parents what she saw in the alley. They'd put her on Xanax and send her to a special camp. Sorry, Baby. Come see me when you're a little older, and we'll talk.

Okay, so I was the monster. Fine. I was okay with it. Life's a bitch, and so was I.

I ran down the alley, not even sure why I was running, where I should go. Running made it all better. Just putting some space between myself and the men I'd just murdered. I could hardly breathe, not because it was getting harder, but because it was getting easier.

I dug out my phone. Reagan had called again. I played the message, while the man's foot stopped twitching. On impulse, I patted him down for a phone, for an ID, for anything. He didn't have anything on him. Nothing. Maybe my phone call to Jaworski had alerted them to the need to be careful. Maybe this was Jaworski. Who knows. His face was a ragged abscess, now, cracked bone, miles of blood, ruined flesh.

"Samantha!" she rasped. "Where in the fuck are you? Sam. Where are you? Please."

It was from twenty minutes ago. I had to get to her place. Slipping back around the corner, down the street, past sleeping trees and wrought-iron grates and Lexus cars and Benzes, I got to the corner, saw flashing lights and police cars at the scene, although I didn't see Ansel's Maybach. It wasn't there. But there were cops there, for sure, a half-dozen of them talking to people, witnesses, pointing, looking around, gesturing.

This, right in front of Reagan's building. I was afraid to go over there, afraid that somebody would see me, recognize me. I didn't want to go anywhere near there, even though Reagan needed me.

I was afraid to even call her back, afraid they might be listening, and more afraid still that if I called Reagan back, then I'd feel even more obligated to turn up at her door.

But I couldn't abandon her, either. I knew that her condition, her plight, her misery, well, it was my fault, my responsibility. To abandon her in her literal hour of need was to pull an Ansel on her, and I couldn't do that, wouldn't do that.

So, I decided I'd take my chances, walk right past the crime scene, and see what happened. I should have gone to the cops and complained about the men trying to murder me, that's what I should have done, but why they would be after me, and what happened to the men who had shot me, well, that would raise suspicion about me, right?

I took out some gum and chewed it, minty-fresh, just to get the blood out of my breath. I still had that smear on the back of my hand, wondered what I looked like. I took out a compact and popped it open, peeked at myself.

Sääm was right in there, smiling at me. I swear, I couldn't see my own reflection, anymore. Only hers.

*You look beautiful, Darling.*

I snapped shut the compact, tucked it away.

Up ahead were the cops, big guys, fat guys. Mustaches. God, they looked like the *Wilkołak* Brothers. Probably some of them were cops. God, had I killed any cops? That would be precious. Add that to my resumé. Artist. Lycanthrope. Murderer. Cannibal. Cop-Killer. What next?

Terrorist?

Sääm bubbled up inside me as we got nearer to the policemen, her black sense of mischief. She wanted to say something so badly. She wanted to taunt them, toy with them.

I walked on by, wondering if anybody had seen me at the scene. Sure enough, Ansel's car was gone, they'd taken it. There was blood on the ground where he'd been shot. A lot of blood. And bullet holes all over the place, where they'd tried to shoot me.

I was a walking crime scene, if anybody bothered to look. But nobody bothered. I was a short little boho babe. Nobody was going to blink twice at me.

Even I thought I was innocent.

# 9. MONDAY AFTERNOON

I walked into Reagan's building. The doorman looked me over, and I told him I was here to see Ms. Whitehouse, and he called up, and she cleared me. I looked at his middle-aged portly face, could smell the Old Spice on him, and gazed evenly into his eyes with mine, a sense of conquest and power that belied my small frame.

I took the elevator up to Reagan's apartment. It was a clean, pretty elevator, wood-paneled, smelled nice, like they'd rubbed it down with walnut oil or something.

The elevator told me I'd reached Reagan's floor, and I got out, went down the hall. Everything in her building was nice. The floor was this jade carpet with mahogany liners that went perfectly with the cream-colored walls.

I went to her door and I rapped it with my knuckles. Reagan opened it like she'd been waiting on the other side of the door.

Her eyes were wild, and she had blood all over her face. She was wearing a thick, forest green terrycloth robe. She was carrying a big knife, a silver carving knife. It was burning her hand, but she kept holding it.

"It's okay," I said.

"Oh, by all means, then, do come in," she spat, sarcasm like venom on her tongue.

She threw open the door in an exaggerated motion, like a hostess from Hell, and I walked in. The air stank of copper. There was no mistaking the smell. I knew the scent so well. Reagan shut the door and locked it.

Looking down at her nice carpet, I saw bloody footprints. Lupine and human. Reagan's place was a mess; many of her paintings were knocked off the walls, were lying on the floor.

Reagan took me into her living room, which had a stellar view of the park and the lake beyond it. But spoiling the view was Gretta's body, or what was left on it, strewn on the living room floor, surrounded by torn, blood-soaked paintings. Gretta's corpse was artfully rendered, one arm up, the other across her body. She'd been bitten at the neck, and her legs had been savaged, having been turned into bloody strips of flesh. The blood had soaked the carpet in a big splash.

The television was on. The news linked the incident to the whole Wolf Cult story they'd been massaging, about this band of crazy furries attacking people in some kind of ritualistic homicide, as in the El Train Massacre a few days before. They cut to a bloody El train, panicked commuters. Zooey? Oh, my.

In other news, they flashed to three dead men found in East Chicago, identified them as Ezekial Hundkrieger, 58, a trucker from East Chicago, Roman Romanowski, 35, of Avondale, and Ed Jaworski, 38, also of Avondale. They said it looked like the men had been eaten by wild animals by the time they'd been discovered.

The news also mentioned the suspicious death of Urban Kowalczyk, 45, of Avondale, whose house burned down, although police were able to find some of his remains. Kowalczyk had apparently been running guns from his basement, and maybe have been implicated in the silver-and-gun-smuggling operation out of Avondale that led to the deaths of the three men the week before. They cut to footage of the alley. He may be part of the so-called Silver Bullet Gang, believed responsible for some slayings in Logan Square. Authorities were investigating.

"Oh, Reagan," I said.

She looked searchingly at me a moment.

"You look well, Sam," she said.

"Do I?"

Her eyebrows had grown back in, thick and full, and her face had a predatory cast to it, something in the eyes that I recognized, a sharpness in her visage.

"I'm losing my mind," she said. "I can't sleep, the dreams kept coming. Terrible things, Samantha. Killing dreams, and that dreadful banquet dream, me serving Gretta up with apples and onions. I'm going right out of my mind. I'm going to have myself committed. Look what I did, Samantha."

"Committed? You can't, Reagan," I said.

"Yes," she said. "I'm going tonight."

"You can't do that," I said. "They can't help you."

"I can't help myself," she said. "What other choice do I have? Look at this mess, Samantha. I killed her. We had a fight—about you, I might add—and something happened. I lost it. The next thing I knew, I was doubled over in agony, and my flesh was changing, and Gretta, despite our arguing, was asking me what was wrong, and I hated her, every bit of her, and attacked. I latched onto her throat and I killed her."

She started breathing heavy, fast, her eyes wild. Reagan was sheened in sweat.

"What's happening to me?" she wailed. "I feel like a watch that's been wound too tight, like I'm full of lit firecrackers, like I've got hornets under my skin. What did you do to me, Samantha?"

Reagan hunched over, pitched forward.

"I'm sorry," I said. "I told you."

Reagan threw her head back and yowled, and I watched her. I can't believe it was where we'd played Werewolf just the other week. In the waning light of day, with poor Gretta dead there, it was a nightmare. I was exhausted already. How much death in one day? How much could I take?

My own heart was racing, I didn't know what to do.

"Reagan!" I said. "Come on, it's okay."

"Samantha!" she roared, barely lupine, barely human. "What have you done to me?"

"You infected me," she said, her eyes on me. "Your little love bite."

"Not now, Reagan," I said. "We have to make this right."

"I'm a monster," she said. "We're monsters, Samantha. You're a monster."

I held her head in my hands, made her look at me.

"We're not monsters; we're victims."

Then I let her go, got a Wet One from her purse and wiped off her mouth, like she was a baby. All clean, all the blood is gone, Baby. Magic trick. She let me, her eyes bloodshot, uncomprehending. She leaned into me, and I held her.

"All those times you apologized, I didn't know what you were sorry for, Samantha."

"Sorry," I said.

"You're a monster," she said.

"I'm an artist," I said.

"A con artist," she said, her mouth set tight, her chin digging into my shoulder. "Masquerading as human. We both are, now. I feel like quilting a scarlet W for us."

"Another project?" I said. She nodded.

"Something beautiful. Well-made," she said. "You know, I have our projects in the back. I was going to give them to you when I flipped out."

"Gretta—poor thing: she wanted to help me. I should have had her fetch me this silver carving knife when I had the chance."

"No," I said. "If I can handle it, you can, Reagan. Come on."

"But you haven't handled it, Samantha," she said. "What have you done since you've been infected?"

"Nothing," I said. "Self-preservation."

Self-defense took many forms: there were many selves to defend, after all. Reagan shook her head, clutched herself, looked angelic in the daylit glow, her curly blonde hair spilling onto her shoulders.

"I can't believe what I did," she said. "It's like it wasn't even me."

"I've been through all of this, Reagan," I said. "And I had nobody to help me."

I hoped Ansel could hear it, looking up from Hell.

"It was Ansel, wasn't it?" she said, shaking her head, smiling to herself. "He's the Werewolf. He infected you. You infected me."

"Yeah," I said.

"Chain reaction," Reagan said. "Chain of infection. It doesn't end, unless we end it, right?"

"I'm not going to kill myself," I said. I liked being alive. Okay, so maybe the life I had now was keeping me pretty busy, but I preferred that to death.

She looked at me awhile in silence, eyes like searchlights, looking for a soul that wasn't there, if it had ever been. I looked back at her, my mismatched eyes holding hers fast.

"After today, I'm not going to kill anybody else," she said.

"Of course you won't," I said. "It was my fault, Reagan. I can hunt for us both."

"You knew all along, pretended you didn't," she said. "I can't shake that."

"You wouldn't have believed me," I said. "You didn't believe me."

She rolled her eyes, sighed, looked out the window at the silver lake and the park.

"This isn't time for your classicist morality, Reagan," I said.

"There is no morality in lycanthropy," she said. "There's no place for it. It's like wanton addiction, isn't it? It controls you. I remember seeing an electron microscope slide of a flea, and the flea had little mites burrowed under its scales. Isn't that something? A pest as irksome, as odious as a flea itself has parasites sucking life from it. Then I wondered if fleas only bit because the mites drove them to do it. Maybe it's the fault of the mites that fleas bite, and the fleas are just agents of the mites, whose only goal is making more mites—like the fleas are the victims of the mites. So, maybe this infection is really what's responsible, and the virus just alters us in order to make us more effective vectors for it, so it can spread itself indefinitely."

"I'm still me," I said, knowing I was lying when I said it.

"Yes and no," she said. "Yes and no. Do we still have free will, Samantha?"

"Does anybody?" I asked.

Reagan sighed.

"Let's find out," she said. "Together."

"We have to clean this up."

Reagan looked at me with swollen eyes, her face red. "I should have laid out some dropcloths, eh?"

"You didn't know," I said. "We can clean this up."

I didn't see how, couldn't imagine how we could.

"First," I said. "We eat."

"What?" Reagan said. "I'm not hungry."

"We have to," I said. "There's nothing else we can do."

Then Reagan began to change, her face growing savage, stretching, her hair growing long, her limbs strengthening, nails becoming claws, her robe falling away, her flesh covering with golden blonde fur, her teeth bursting through her gums.

"Samantha," she said. "We have to die."

"No," I said. "I'm not going to die."

She stared at me with her animal eyes, blue around the sea of golden fur, her long, proud muzzle. The only sour note was the burned hand, where she still clutched that silver knife.

"Just beautiful," I said. She looked it. I was so proud.

Tears ran from her eyes.

"Beautiful?" she said. "This?"

"Yes," I said.

"Beautiful?" Reagan scoffed. "You've got to be kidding me. No beauty."

I laughed. "You're kidding, right? We're not people, anymore, Reagan. Different rules. A different aesthetic."

I am Sääm. Sääm I am.

*That* was my aesthetic.

"I can't live like this," she said. "I can't live with this. Without Gretta."

She held her hands up, cried into them. Her tears landed on the knife blade, ran down it. She dropped the thing to the floor.

"Reagan, you'll be okay," I said. "You're freaking me out."

"Good," she said. "I killed Gretta. And I enjoyed it. I really did. Now, how can I possibly recover from something like that? How can I live the rest of my days knowing that I might do something that terrible again? Or worse, that I surely would? That I inevitably would?"

"People do terrible things every day," I said. "Companies do terrible things, nations do terrible things, and they keep right on going. Please, just take a shower, you'll feel better."

"The thing inside me wants out," she said. "It's been talking to me ever since, you know, you infected me. Louder and louder. She wants to be free."

A splash of guilt, almost unfamiliar to me, now. Like a phone call from an old, half-forgotten friend, out of the blue: Oh, hey. Yeah, what've you been up to? Yeah? That's great.

"It's been coursing through me," she said. "Driving me like a sled dog. The dreams, day and night, the fantasies. On and on it runs in my head, distracts me from my work—or, worse—offers horrible, carnal projects for me to work on. This thing, this virus, my god, Samantha. I feel sympathy for you, having fought this thing alone. I didn't know. Stupid me, I didn't know."

"We can fight it together," I said. She smiled, like I was an idiot, as she forced herself back to her original self, her beautiful, gracious self. She reclaimed her flesh from the Beast, watching me all the while.

"Either your immune system prevails and slays the Beast, or the Beast triumphs. Clearly, this thing has found some way to evade our immune systems, to slide in undetected. To take over."

"We're still fighting," I said. "I'm still fighting. I'm still me."

They were just words. Words were easy and empty.

"I think you lost the battle…lost the war…some time ago, Samantha," she said. "And I think, given enough time, there'll be an inevitable hollowing out, until you resemble Samantha only in outward appearance—you'll be a passenger in your own body, a ghost of a person, a fading memory. Maybe your optimism is part of your weakness, how the Beast fools you, misleads you, gives you hope that things will be better, if only you wait a little longer. It's the tyranny of false hope, really—it's how countries slide into fascism, how they delude themselves and how their hope becomes a noose that eventually hangs them, as they tell themselves 'it can't possibly get worse'—but it always, always does. The abyss is an abyss for a reason. There is no bottom to it, no end to it, except, of course, oblivion."

"Whoa, Reagan," I said. "Easy, there."

She smiled, her eyes full of tears, put her arms around me, gave me a warm, tender kiss that went on forever. There was no lust in it, only love. I could feel her warm tears on my cheeks. She pushed away from me, wiped her tears with the back of her hands.

"Sorry," she said.

"I'm sorry," I said. "We're not alone, Reagan. Not anymore."

"Zooey," Reagan said. "You infected her, too, didn't you?"

"Yes," I said. "She knew; she wanted it. And Polly."

"Sick. It'll never end, you see? Not unless we end it," she said.

"That won't change anything," I said. "I've infected way too many people. So's Zooey. Zooey's gone after more than I have. She's a natural."

"There's nothing natural about us."

"We're as natural as anything," I said. "Nature, red in tooth and claw, Reagan."

She looked at her burned hand, where the silver had touched her, smiled into it.

"Tennyson? He's no consolation," Reagan said. "Not anymore. I'm not going to become a cannibal. But just because we're beasts doesn't mean we need to behave like them, no?"

"This is the new world, Reagan," I said. "We're the point of the spear, we're creating it, making the rules as we go. The decision's already made for you: you're infected. Do you want to live, or just be meat? What's what it's coming down to. That's what the choices are: predator or prey."

"Producer or consumer," Reagan said. "That is the choice. Creator or destroyer, Samantha. What have you created? What have you made?"

I paused at that.

"Performances," I said. "Happenings."

"Murders," Reagan said. "You killed all of our friends, yes?"

There was no point in lying. She knew. I nodded.

"They weren't worthy of life," I said. "I culled them."

God, Ansel's own words, coming back to me. She couldn't possibly understand. Reagan considered it, the mask of grief cracked a little, a bit of herself still visible to me behind it all.

"We deserve to die," she said. "To be punished."

"Suicide's been done to death," I said. "This is something else. This is new. You're an artist, Reagan. That hasn't changed. It's just a new medium. It's always clumsy at first. But you'll get better. You have to have hope."

"Always the optimist, Samantha," she said. "Your optimism is infectious, too. I might be a monster, but does that mean I must be monstrous?"

"It's a challenge worthy of you," I said. "Another project."

"'The Artful Monstrosity of Reagan Whitehouse,'" she said, as if she were envisioning her own memoir. If it helped her think of it that way, I was fine with it. I didn't want Reagan to die. I certainly didn't want her killing herself.

"Well, we have to do something about this," I said. "I can get Zooey to come over."

"What, we'll dine in tonight?" Reagan asked, bitterly. "Shall I open a bottle of wine?"

"Wine would be nice," I said, because, well, it would.

"What goes best with dead people?" Reagan asked, a certain tartness in her tone.

"Red," I said. I already knew, from BacchUS. Red wine, most definitely.

"What about Polly?"

"I haven't talked to Polly," I said. "I don't know where she is. I'm not entirely sure where she is. Ansel may have killed her, and, well, Ansel is dead."

"What?" she asked.

"Before I came here," I said. "He got shot. It's why I was late."

"What?" she asked. "By the police?"

"By these crazy Poles," I said. "They hunt us."

Reagan winced. "Samantha, I can't deal with this. I murdered Gretta. I can't possibly go on like this."

I put my arm on hers.

"It gets better. The first is the hardest."

She recoiled from my touch, gazed at me with those teacup eyes of hers, her face a mix of revulsion and disdain. It hurt me to see her looking at me like that.

"Samantha," she said. "How can you even say that? How can you be so callous?"

"It was Sheldon," I said. "He was my first. I didn't plan it. It just happened."

"All that time, you were pretending you didn't know where he was. You were lying to us all," she said. "A wolf in sheep's clothing. A wolf in the fold."

What was I supposed to say to that? To her?

"Samantha, I can't live without Gretta. I just can't. Not with what I've done."

Her eyes went to the carving knife, the wicked silver thing, and I kicked it away from her before she could do anything stupid.

"No no no no," I said. "No, Reagan. You're not going there. Please."

Reagan's eyes filled up with tears as she looked at poor, dead Gretta. I felt terrible for even suggesting what I did. What was I thinking? Reagan wept silently, perched on the floor, on her knees, and I held her, or tried to, anyway. She stiffened in my arms, pushed away after indulging me a moment, treating me to a few snuffles on my shoulder.

"I think you'd better go, Samantha," she said, wiping her face with her hand.

"Not without you," I said. "We can clean this mess up."

"No," Reagan said. "It doesn't wash off as easily as that. This isn't one of your performance pieces, Samantha. That isn't red dye; it's blood."

She was really going apeshit. She was like a gasoline fire I was trying to put out with my hands. I didn't know where to touch, or for how long.

"Reagan, please," I said. "Why don't you go in the other room and just rest. I'll clean this up, okay?"

Her eyes narrowed, suspicious. I'd never seen that look on her face. It hurt me more than a little.

"What do you have in mind, Samantha?" she asked.

"You just let me worry about that," I said. "You lie down, try to rest. I will make this right."

I didn't want to. I really, really didn't want to. I didn't even like Gretta very much. But friendship was friendship; you did what you had to do. Reagan needed this. That's what friends were for.

She slipped on her robe, smoothed it with her hands, walked into the other room, and I stripped and piled my clothes on a clean part of the sofa. It was a shame to see her place like this, such a mess. Reagan had always been so tidy, so organized, so neat. I hoped the transformation didn't change that in her.

I looked at dead Gretta, wondered if I could get her all down myself. Sääm was always keen to eat, but in that moment, I wondered if I had the stomach for it. I leaned down to take a sniff of her. She was fresh, looked like she was sleeping, except for the blood. She looked like she could awaken at any moment.

Reagan came back in, looking more composed.

"You should rest, Reagan," I said. "You don't need to see this. Not yet."

She shook her head.

"We should have Polly over," Reagan said. "Have a nice little gathering. Wouldn't that be splendid, Samantha? Call your little pup, bring her over."

I couldn't tell if she was being sarcastic or not, couldn't read those cornflower eyes of hers, wide and wild in a way they'd never been before. Her face was composed, but her eyes were wild.

"For real?" I asked.

"Yes," Reagan said. "I'll call Polly."

I dialed up Zooey, told her where to go, told her not to fill up before she came over. "You bitch. Where are you? I've been biting bums, just like I said I would. Just one bite, though, because they're fucking gross. Still, I'm doing it. I'm infecting them."

That Zooey, always coming up with her wild ideas. It really would make people better, would heal them, make them whole, even as it was splitting them in two. Sometimes you needed a little duality to make yourself feel whole.

"Great, Zooey," I said. "But right now, bring a change of clothes for you and me; it'll probably be a slumber party at Reagan's."

I gave her the address.

"Sweet," Zooey said. "Be there in a jiff."

"Watch out for any *Wilkołak* Brothers," I said. "They'll be the ones with the guns. They, uh, shot Ansel."

"Wow," Zooey said. "Bummer. Are you okay?"

"I'm alive," I said. "Sometimes, that's enough."

"For sure," she said. "I'm on it. See you soon."

She hung up, and I looked over at Reagan, who was watching me the whole time, her eyes not like a dog's at all, but like a cat's. Inscrutable. Had she really accepted it? Or was she just playing me? She got up, fetched her cell phone, and dialed up Polly.

"Polly? Reagan," she said. "Yes, we've been worried sick about you, thought something might've happened to you, dear. No, Samantha's here. Yes."

She looked at me, and I shook my head.

"No, it's just us," she said. "We'd love to have you join us tonight. Yes. Wear red. Yes, red. Something festive and revolutionary. It's going to be a performance art piece Samantha's been working on. A dress rehearsal, if you will. What? But we'd love you to be in it. Oh, Tristan's home? Really? Splendid."

She cupped the phone with her hand. "What's it called?"

"'Pollyanna's Last Supper,'" I said, figuring Polly wouldn't be able to resist something with her name in it. She was just that easy. Reagan repeated it.

"Yes, isn't it? It is so very Samantha," Reagan said. "How about 8:00? A late dinner? No? Oh, that's a shame. Yes? Well, I hope you feel better, Polly. Something's going around. I haven't felt so well, myself. Some other time, perhaps. Goodbye, Polly. Sam says 'Goodbye,' too."

I shook my head, laughing. I didn't say Goodbye; I said Hello. I was all about Hello, hated saying Goodbye. I wondered how Tristan would find Polly, how the infection was taking in her. I couldn't wait to see what happened to Polly, like how she'd react to her new reality, to the paradigm shift I'd thrown her way. I'm sure she'd whip up a poem about it.

*Bitch*

*Samantha's salivation wrought my ruination*
*Dental indentation, mental incantation*
*Now I shave my legs with garden shears*
*And howl about my darkest fears.*
*My poetry comes in snarls and fits*
*The words won't come: you fucking bitch!*

Or something.

Reagan hung up, glanced at her grandfather clock. It was 4:16. I was glad I'd talked Reagan back down. Tick-tock, tick-tock, said the clock. Comforting, really. Peaceful. Stately. Graceful. Very, very Reagan. Probably had been in her family for generations, that clock. It must've been nice, having that kind of continuity with family.

"You clean," she said, glancing at the body. "I'll cook."

"It's fine as it is," I said. "You don't have to do anything. I've got it covered."

She stepped back while I began to change, flesh snapping and bones popping as I underwent my transformation, hunched onto my elbows. Reagan padded over to me barefoot, running her hand through my hair. I was amazed at her fortitude, resisting the urge to change with me right there. Then she put her hand on the back of my head, stroking my auburn locks, watching my hair become fur. I felt longing shoot

430 | D.T. NEAL

through my blood at the sight of her, as her robe fell away, revealing only naked flesh beneath, and the flash of silver.

Silver?

Reagan held a long sterling silver knife, serrated, in her hand, and took the long blade and slid it across my throat, in a savage, decapitating arc that had me sputtering.

"Fuck," I said, my last word, because everything else I said came out as blood spilling on the carpet, splashing on dead Gretta's face.

"Homo homini lupus," Reagan said. I knocked Reagan back with a swipe of my arm. She still held the knife, the long, antique sterling silver blade, covered with my blood, even as the handle burned her, staggering against the wall.

She threw the knife away, shaking out her hand. There was another ugly burn against her flesh. What was she feeling? Thinking? I couldn't know. Reagan sat down, hugging herself, wanting comfort.

I couldn't believe what she'd done to me. I dropped to my elbows, my hands to my throat, blood gushing as my body fought to transform, to heal itself, even as my blood poured from my mouth and throat, soaking into Reagan's thick rug. The gash was wide and ragged, and there was a tug-of-war in my flesh as it fought for supremacy over the wound. It was like I was vomiting blood, black settling around the edges of my vision. Black was death. Death!! I clawed at the carpet, tried to get to her.

"'Man is a wolf to man,'" Reagan said. "Plautus. Latin."

I'd never read Plautus, but she didn't need to know that. I didn't even know who Plautus fucking was. I thought about Zooey, prayed she'd be alright. My last, my greatest creation, my masterpiece. My Zooey.

I stared at Reagan, who was watching while I crawled toward her. I was trying to say something, but only blood came out, and I collapsed at last, a clawed hand just short of Reagan's bare foot. The black turned my vision into a tunnel, and I saw Reagan take out a silver dollar, a Liberty dollar from long, long ago, and flip it in her hand. It burned where it touched.

Then she put the coin on her tongue like it was a Communion wafer, and she swallowed it down with a muttered prayer. My fucking God, Reagan. A prayer? She smiled down at me, even as her eyes boiled red with blood, blood flew from her lips, staining her smile, and she collapsed over me, dropped to her knees and lay across me, while I struggled, couldn't fetch back the life she'd taken from me.

My flesh surrendered to the inevitable, and there was—

PREVIEW:

# THE WOLFSHADOW TRILOGY | BOOK 2

Fourstar Ambulance just wasn't fast enough to deliver a dead man to University Hospital; fortunately, the guy came back to life four blocks from the emergency room. Mark Manning was losing his mind in the back, while Steve Clarke was just trying to drive down Marine, trying to keep from rolling their vehicle in the afternoon traffic.

They'd gotten the call from near the Polish Embassy, a frantic call about a gangland-style assassination that had taken place in front of their building, some talk about paramilitaries with assault rifles killing people in a car, some talk about terrorism.

When they'd gotten to the scene, the car was gone, driven off by whoever had done the shooting. Only the dead man was there, bullet-riddled on the boulevard. They had taken his pulse, and Steve could've sworn there hadn't been one, but the guy had gasped on the bloody curb, had coughed up blood, and the two of them had snapped into action.

There was no way somebody could have taken that many rounds and survived. To Steve's eye, there were a dozen bullet wounds, right across the man's chest. The volume of lost blood alone should have killed him. He was a good-looking guy, too, young. Dark-haired, he looked Greek, maybe Italian. He assumed it was some Mafia thing, though why they'd done the shooting in public was anybody's guess.

Steve was used to seeing strange things. In five years as a paramedic, he'd seen things. But this guy was something else. He was coming back from the fucking dead. And, if Mark was right, the guy was actually getting stronger as they got closer to the hospital. It was hard to tell, because Mark wouldn't stop yelling.

"He's fucking alive, Steve," Mark said. "He's expelling the bullets."

Steve could hear the clatter of things on the floor of the ambulance, what he assumed were the bullets Mark was yelling about. He couldn't look, couldn't see; he had to drive. But each time there was a clatter,

Mark would moan. Manning had only been on the job for two years, so he was still shocked by stuff.

"Just hold on," Steve said. "We're like 5 minutes out."

"He's healing," Mark said. "Steve, he's getting better."

Steve glanced over his shoulder, swerving to dodge a cab that darted in front of them. He couldn't pause to look, he had no idea what Manning was talking about.

"Just calm the fuck down, Markie," Steve said. "Four minutes."

The man had been dead.

He'd been dead.

Steve had seen.

Then he heard something else in the back, heard a growl, heard the ripping of clothes, and he heard Mark screaming, heard bottles breaking and things overturning. Steve felt the ambulance shift, he felt the weight increase, felt the shocks soak up the load, felt something grow in the back, felt the ambulance get out from under him.

Three minutes away, and Mark wouldn't stop screaming.

Steve couldn't do more than glance in the rearview mirror, because the traffic was always tight downtown, even with the sirens blaring, people wouldn't get out of the fucking way. Everybody was so slow.

There was a snap and a gurgle and Mark stopped screaming, and Steve figured that he'd chilled out and gave the victim a sedative to calm him down.

"Markie, talk to me," Steve said. "C'mon back to me, Buddy."

He glanced in the rearview mirror, and he saw a big pair of blue animal eyes looking at him through the pane that separated the cab from the rear of the ambulance. Big blue eyes and a mouthful of teeth, hot breath right on his shoulder.

Now it was Steve's turn to scream. He rolled the ambulance in front of the Hancock Building, went right over the curb, right onto the sidewalk, right over the railing, into the fountain courtyard below. The ambulance went over, and the thing in the back of his ambulance howled and snarled as it tumbled with him. Mark tumbled, too, his lifeless body banging around the back.

They came to a jarring halt, Steve gagging on his seatbelt, which dug into his neck, while the airbag blasted him in the face. The thing in the back howled, a deafening sound in the narrow confines of the ambulance, and then Steve could feel the pressure on the metal, on the frame of the ambulance, as the thing propelled itself out the back, tearing open the doors with a swipe of its arms.

And out it went with a leap and sound of crunching metal. It was gone. Just like that.

# ACKNOWLEDGMENTS

I would like to thank all of my readers, who offered their time, attention, and opinions to the writing and revision of this novella. I would also like to thank Christine Marie Scott of Clever Crow Design Studio in Pittsburgh for her wonderful cover art and her invaluable assistance with the layout of these pages.

# ABOUT THE AUTHOR

D. T. Neal is a fiction writer and editor living in Chicago. He won second place in the Aeon Award in 2008 for his short story, "Aegis," and has been published in *Albedo 1*, Ireland's premier magazine of science fiction, horror, and fantasy. He is the author of *Saamaanthaa*, *The Happening*, and *Norm*, known collectively as the *Wolfshadow Trilogy*. He's also written the vampire novel, *Suckage*, as well as the Lovecraftian cosmic horror-thriller, *Chosen*. He has written three creature feature/eco-horror novellas, *Relict*, *Summerville*, and *The Day of the Nightfish*. He continues to work on several science fiction, fantasy, horror, and thriller stories.

DTNEAL.COM

# THE HAPPENING

Zooey's werewolf insurrection has exploded beyond the confines of the city of Chicago, appearing throughout the country, with only the members of a secret government agency to stop it. Meanwhile, Polly seeks to rebuild her life in the wake of her own infection, and Ansel recovers from his near-death at the hands of the werewolf killers who stalked him. While Zooey fights to make her lycanthropic revolution spread, her adversaries work together to try to overcome it, and the monstrous evil that grows inside them. But will they be too late?

# NORM

It's been eight years since Zooey's lycanthropic insurrection—known as the Happening—broke out across the country. Werewolves are everywhere and nowhere at once, ignored and disregarded by the media and officially denied by the government. Norm Stockwell, an elite, paranormal counterinsurgency agent, is desperate to reclaim his former life in the face of the ongoing lycanthropic epidemic. Working with members of the secret society of the Synowie Srebra, Norm hunts down the ever-elusive Ansel Rupino in an effort to put an end to the Happening once and for all. All that stands in his way are highly organized pack-gangs of Lupines who prowl the bloody streets of Chicago by the light of the moon, in their relentless, instinctive search for prey.

NOSETOUCH PRESS™

Nosetouch Press is an independent book publisher
tandemly-based in Chicago and Pittsburgh.
We are dedicated to bringing some of today's most
energizing fiction to readers around the world.

Our commitment to classic book design in a digital
environment brings an innovative and authentic
approach to the traditions of literary excellence.

*The Nose Knows™

NOSETOUCHPRESS.COM
Horror | Science Fiction | Fantasy | Mystery
Supernatural | Gothic | Weird